Vivaldi's Muse

A Novel

Sarah Bruce Kelly

Sarah Bruce Kelly

Bel Canto Press

www.belcantopress.com

ISBN 978-0-9836304-0-1

Cover Art: "Young Woman With Morning Glories in Her Hair" (detail)

-Jules Joseph Lefebvre

For my family and friends, without whose patient support and encouragement my over ten-year quest to research and write this novel could not have been accomplished.

Author's Note

Vivaldi's Muse is an expanded version of my young adult novel, *The Red Priest's Annina*, and some scenes have been repeated to serve the story's integrity. *The Red Priest's Annina* encapsulated about eight years of events into a single year, and much had to be left out. In *Vivaldi's Muse* the chronology of events follows the actual calendar and incorporates every significant occurrence in Vivaldi's and Girò's twenty-plus-year relationship.

Although the reading level is more advanced and the subject matter more mature than that of *The Red Priest's Annina*, *Vivaldi's Muse* contains no material that would be inappropriate for young readers.

Inter poenas et tormenta,

Vivit anima contenta,

Casti amoris, sola spe.

Amid anguish and torment,

Lives the contented soul,

Chaste love, its only hope.

from Vivaldi's sacred motet,
Nulla in mundo pax sincera, RV 630

Prologue

Saturday, 29 July 1741
St. Stephen's Cathedral, Vienna

The priest looked at Annina helplessly, his eyes filled with pity. She shivered. Despite the glint of first light through lofty windows, the cathedral's chilling grandeur made her blood run cold.

In the eerie glow of foredawn the dragon-like gargoyles, whose sinister glares had greeted her on her arrival, seemed to embody the demons that had tormented her through the night. Now daybreak suffused the vast sanctuary with an awesome luminance and cast a chiaroscuro of light and shadow over the nave's ghostly plethora of statuary, pillared arches, altars, and sepulchers.

She gazed past the priest at the panel that loomed over the high altar, depicting the stoning of St. Stephen, the cathedral's patron. Her heart smarted and sagged at the horrendous spectacle—then lurched, as a thrilling sound flooded her ears. Some unseen violinist was playing a melody she knew well, music that spoke directly to her heart.

Her eyes met the priest's. He smiled and glanced toward a nearby vestibule. As if a magnetic force were drawing her she walked toward the vestibule, trembling with anticipation. She peered around the entrance and was astonished to see a dark-haired boy, bowing away so earnestly she almost could have believed it was the composer himself playing. She stepped quietly through the archway and listened, mesmerized, until the music of the boy's violin slowly diminished with an exquisitely tender trill. When he finished he lingered silently for a moment with closed eyes, then lowered his instrument and gazed at her, his eyes wide with apprehension.

"*Es tut mir leid*," he said in a bright, high-pitched voice. The child was apologizing to her, and her heart went out to him. His hangdog expression was punctuated by his pathetic homeliness. He was sallow-complected with a long, bulbous nose too large for his gaunt face, and his lower lip drooped unattractively. Thick black eyebrows nearly obscured his dark eyes—yet in those eyes she detected fiery determination.

She struggled to think how to respond. "*Das macht nichts*," she said finally, then thought she'd better add, "*Das—war—sehr gut.*" She realized her faltering German was barely adequate to reassure the boy and tell him how impressed she was by his playing.

"*Danke*," he replied softly.

"I—um—*ich spreche wenig Deutsch*," she murmured regretfully.

He eyed her curiously. "*Parla italiano?*" he asked, quite comprehensibly, though in a heavy German accent.

"Ah, *sì*, it's my native language. So you speak Italian?"

"*Sì*, signora, rather well, I think."

What a relief to have at last encountered someone she could communicate with, even if it was only a young child.

"The Pater doesn't mind that I'm here," he said, his eyes shifting toward the high altar. Then he looked at her anxiously. "You won't tell Herr Maestro Reutter, will you?"

She assured him she would not, though she hadn't a clue who

Herr Maestro Reutter was.

"I know I shouldn't be here," he continued, with touching sheepishness. Then his dusky eyes brightened and darted upwards, as if to visually embrace the Cathedral's boundless magnificence. "I just can't stay away, though. It feels so safe and comforting here, so filled with the mysteries of life."

And of death, she thought, dabbing her eyes with the handkerchief she clutched in her hand.

The boy's beatific expression faded, and his eyes shone with concern. "Are you all right, signora?" he asked.

"Oh, yes, I'm all right. It's just that I was so moved by your playing. It reminded me of someone very dear."

He took a few steps toward her and seemed to flinch with pain as he moved.

"Are you hurt?" she asked, reaching to aid him.

He declined her offer of help and lifted his chin, almost defensively it seemed. "Nothing to make a fuss about. It's only that at the *Cantorei*, the choir school next-door where I live, the maestro gives us more beatings than food," he said, his ugly, drooping lip trembling slightly.

"Ah, *poveretto!* " She looked at his emaciated body and nearly forgot her own troubles. She wanted to take the pitiful little fellow into her arms and comfort him, but something about his proud bearing prevented her.

"Well, that's just how it is, I suppose. But a pretty lady like you needn't worry about such things," he said, drawing himself up with manly dignity.

He almost seemed to be flirting with her. She studied his face for a moment as he looked up at her with eyes that exuded a strange combination of innocence, wisdom, and mischievous charm. Finally, to soften the subject, she said, "I don't suppose you know who wrote that piece you were playing, do you?"

The boy's face lit up, and his homeliness dissipated in the brilliance of his smile. "Oh yes I do! The composer himself taught it to me."

She was speechless for a moment. "Do you mean to say Antonio Vivaldi taught you that piece?"

"*Sì*, signora," he said, beaming proudly.

The tension in her mouth melted into a smile. "And did he teach you to speak Italian as well?"

"*Sì*, signora."

His grin was endearing, and she began to feel genuine fondness for him.

"You couldn't have studied with him very long," she said.

"No, signora, only a few months," he said, as his euphoric look dimmed to sadness.

She put an encouraging hand on his shoulder. "You must be a very intelligent boy to have learned so quickly."

"*Sì*, signora," he said with a weak smile. "That's what Herr Maestro Vivaldi told me. He said it was because of my ear for music."

"Then you must have an exceptional ear indeed." She squeezed his shoulder, then withdrew her hand. "You know, you're about the age I was when I first met him."

The boy gazed at her. "Are you a friend of Herr Maestro Vivaldi's, from Venice?"

"I was born in Mantua, and many years ago he was court composer there," she said quietly.

"Is that where you met him?" he persisted.

The weight of memories made her knees droop. She sank onto a marble bench, and the cold stone walls surrounding her became a hazy blur.

Chapter One

Mantua, Northern Italy, 1719

Annina feared what might happen if she were caught. The virile outline of the palace wall with its pointed, darkly red arcades looked forbidding, but she was determined to enter. She gathered her skirts, and with all the vigor her wiry nine-year-old body could muster she bolted across the Piazza Sordello. As she darted through one of the wall's many vaulted archways she slipped on a mossy cobblestone. Her knee smacked the slimy pavement. Tears sprang to her eyes, and she tightened her mouth to muffle her cry of pain. She scurried behind a hedgerow to shield herself from the palace guard's vigilant eye while she examined her knee. The gush of blood from beneath her torn stocking told her this was more than a mere scrape. With stinging fingers she tore a strip of cloth from the hem of her petticoat and bandaged the hideous gash. Her legs wobbled as she stood. She smoothed her skirt and looked around to make sure she hadn't been detected. Then, flinching with each painful step, she made her way along the stone path that led to the Teatro Arciducale, the royal opera house.

She peered into the theater. Its crescent-shaped auditorium rose in tiers, and its curving walls were bedecked with statues of toga-clad men. "Members of the Gonzaga family, dressed as Greek gods and heroes," her father had told her once with a disdainful chortle. "Mantua's doomed ruling family, overthrown by the Austrian Habsburgs two years before you were born." Despite her aching knee, she giggled at the sight of the ludicrous Gonzaga effigies, realizing they looked neither godly nor heroic. As she crept further into the auditorium the laughable icons ebbed into shadows, and her giggles converged in a strangling gasp. A personage the like of whom she had never seen—with kohl-rimmed eyes, lips thickly rouged, and bosom amply swelling from a boned, lace-frilled bodice—strode toward the proscenium and proceeded to soar through an aria that made Annina quiver with envy and awe. The music of the small orchestra billowed beneath the singer's shimmering voice like a surging tide.

She shifted her gaze to the lead violinist and was seized by a spasm of girlish excitement. He wore a priest's collar, but the rest of his clothing was like any other man's. What most caught her eye was the brightness of his hair. It almost had a glow about it, and everything around him seemed to shimmer in its light. He'd raised his violin to his shoulder and was filling in the pause between the aria's two major sections with a violin solo that sparkled with fire. She watched his fingers fly like lightning over the strings as his swift bow thrusts brought the music to unimaginable melodic heights. The astonishing golden hair swung forward with every thrust of his bow. With mercurial ease he lowered his violin and raised his bow to signal the continuation of the aria. She'd never seen him before, but she knew without doubt this was the great Venetian maestro, Don Antonio Vivaldi.

She inched her way closer to the stage until she was almost

alongside the orchestra area, where she had a clear view of his face—the strong curve of his nose, the stray lock of red-gold hair that dangled over his forehead and mingled with tiny droplets of perspiration, the crinkles at the corners of his deep blue eyes. His alluring vitality made her insides tingle. She couldn't get her fill of gazing at him.

He lifted his instrument to his shoulder again, and the other players followed suit. Her rapture grew as the music of the violins blended with the singer's voice and flooded the theater with exhilarating sound. There was an intense, anxious quality to this music that grasped her and held her in its energy. All the while, the maestro led with his violin and sustained the music's dizzying motion while bringing out every tantalizing nuance. She yearned to stand before the footlights, to sing her heart out and exult in the eloquence of that music. But all too soon the aria drew to a close, and he gestured the orchestra to silence.

The singer glowered at him. "*Maestro!* I cannot possibly sing that aria in tonight's performance. I've decided it doesn't suit me." Her voice was shrill and grating, and suddenly she seemed much less attractive.

Annina was piqued. *What a witch!*

The maestro echoed her thought. "*Strega,*" she heard him mutter. His voice tense with impatience, he said aloud, "That's the fourth rewrite of that aria I've done for you, Signora Gualandi. If this one doesn't please you I'm afraid you'll have to make do with it. There's no time to write you another one."

She propped a plump fist on her sturdy hip. "Well I won't sing it. So you're just going to have to find the time to rewrite it."

He ran a hand through his fiery locks and gave an exasperated sigh as she flounced from the stage. The other musicians and singers gawked in silence. Then the maestro glanced in Annina's direction, and his look of vexation changed to one of curious surprise. Her instincts told her to duck out of sight. But she felt frozen, conscious of nothing but his blue eyes gazing into her dark ones.

At once she realized how untidy she must look. She raised her fingers to her silky chestnut hair, which had fallen around her face in a wild, unruly way, then glanced down at her torn, bloody stocking and moss-stained dress. At that same instant her father appeared from backstage, carrying a large box that bore his wig shop's emblem. Her heart floundered.

The maestro turned to him. "Signor Girò—"

"Ah, *monsieur* maestro . . ." he gushed in his thick French accent. "Here are the hairpieces ordered for tonight's—" Before she could slip from his view he spotted her, and his ingratiating look was darkened by a disapproving frown. The wig-box fell from his shaking hands, and he bustled down the stage steps and took hold of her arm. "Annina, *ma petite!* " he said, much too loudly. The corners of his lips dipped all the more, causing his jowls to sag and quiver. "How many times have I told you that you are not even to come near the theater? Yet you have deliberately disobeyed me and demonstrated to all my associates what a willful and undisciplined child you are. And just look at you. You are an unbecoming sight and have been up to much mischief, sure*ly*." His voice shook with anxiety, and his hand tightened around her arm.

She was certain everyone present was staring at her, though her eyes were glued to the floor. Her face aflame with embarrassment, she struggled to free herself from her father's grip.

"You must excuse my naughty Annina's outrageous conduct, monsieur Vivaldi," she heard her father say. "It is my fault, *of course*. I have spoiled her to the point where she has no regard for propriety. I beg you to accept my deepest apologies on behalf of my wayward daughter, monsieur maestro, for disrupting your rehearsal and causing such a disturbance."

"It's quite all right, Signor Girò," came a voice from the direction of the stage. She looked up and saw the maestro smiling at her. "Your daughter hasn't disturbed us in the least. Signorina Annina, I'm delighted to meet you and hope you'll be my guest for the rest of the rehearsal."

Her ears drank in his graceful Venetian accent, gentle and fluid now that his anger had evaporated. She felt a little flood of warmth inside and smiled back at him.

"This is most gracious of you, kind sir," her father interposed, with a forced, fawning smile. "But I am afraid my wife is expecting her at home."

He loosened his hold on her arm and lowered his voice to a stern whisper. *"Go home immediately to your mother."*

COULD HE POSSIBLY have made her humiliation more complete? She felt mortified. Her father had caused Don Antonio and his entire opera company to see her as nothing more than a troublesome imp. She plodded across the Piazza Sordello, seething with fury and wounded pride while icy winds snatched at her aching legs. She'd often begged her father to let her go with him to the Teatro Arciducale when he delivered the singers' hairpieces just before the dress rehearsals. He'd only grumble about "bad influences" and "dangerous elements" that weren't safe for a young girl to be around.

But she could no longer resist. The Carnival season was at its height, and the town was aflutter with preparations for Prince Phillip's forthcoming marriage to the Mantuan heiress, Eleonora of Guastalla. Everyone—from housewives at Market Square to old men playing cards and drinking wine outside taverns—was talking about the operas, serenatas, and cantatas *il prete rosso* was composing and presenting as part of the celebrations.

People often called Don Antonio *il prete rosso*, the red-haired priest, and that intriguing nickname had only heightened her desire to get a glimpse of him. Yet for the entire year since he had been Prince Phillip's court composer she'd had no opportunity to do so. If not for a lucky meeting the day before she might have missed her chance. It happened that her father was so busy with wig orders for the ongoing festivities that he didn't have time to come home for the noonday meal. So she was sent to deliver his dinner in a basket. When she arrived at the nearby shop a striking young woman was perched on a stool, waiting to be fitted for a hairpiece. She told Annina that she had a small part in Don Antonio's new opera, which was to premier the following night. Their conversation ended when her father appeared from the back room to tell the lady he'd have her order ready by the next day's rehearsal. That brief encounter with a real live opera singer had fired her determination to visit the opera house. And while her father scolded her that evening for "consorting with a vulgar actress," she started to plan the next day's adventure, which had now gotten her into so much trouble.

She started to shiver. It was warm for February, so she'd worn no cloak or shawl when she scuttled from the house earlier that afternoon while the sun was still high in the sky. But now that evening was approaching there was a gusty chill in the air. She hugged herself and limped along the narrow cobblestone street that led to her family's home. As she neared the house, the delicious aromas of basil and leeks wafted from the kitchen window and flooded her nostrils. This meant her mother had roused herself from the melancholy state she'd left her in a couple of hours before and was feeling well enough to prepare supper.

Bartolomea was not an affectionate mother. Most of the time she was cold and distant, lost in her own inner world. But when she spoke there was no one so eloquent with words. Sometimes, to Annina's delight, she'd tell stories of long ago, but always in a detached, half-mesmerized way. The only times she came to life were when she sang her beloved opera arias, or when she was angry. She was happiest when she sang, and Annina would joyfully sing along with her. But when her mother was angry, she stayed out of her way.

She entered the fragrant kitchen warily. Bartolomea turned, her face flushed from the steaming soup pot. She scanned her daughter's appearance but made no move to comfort her or tend to her injured knee. "And what deviltry have you been up to?" she said, scowling.

She flew to her mother, threw her arms around her waist and poured out the story of her ordeal. Bartolomea stood stiffly and didn't return her daughter's embrace. When she mentioned Don Antonio, she felt her mother's fingers clutch her tangled locks.

"You saw him?"

"Yes, Mamma. He was conducting the opera rehearsal."

None too gently, her mother pushed her away and searched her face with wide, unblinking eyes. "How did he look?" she asked

The question seemed odd. It was the kind of thing you'd ask about someone you knew but hadn't seen for a long time. "He's the most amazing person I've ever seen," she said, anxious to talk about the maestro.

But Bartolomea's faraway gaze showed her mind had drifted. She sank into a chair by the kitchen table, her eyes aglow and brimming with some wondrous secret.

Annina sat too, her hurt feelings slipping away as her curiosity became aroused. "Mamma," she asked, "do you *know* him?"

Her mother looked at her with glazed eyes and said, "I used to know him. Long ago, before you were born."

Her astonishment knew no bounds. She fidgeted in the big wooden chair. "How did you know him, Mamma? And why haven't you ever told me this before? Was it when you were growing up in Venice?"

"It's not something I like to talk about," she said, her eyes misting.

"*Please*. Mamma. You *must* tell me!"

Bartolomea stared at the table for what seemed like an eternity while her daughter squirmed with impatience. When at last she began to speak her voice was remote.

"When I was twelve years old, my parents and I moved across town to the Campo San Giovanni, in the Bragora section of Venice. The Vivaldis lived on the opposite side of the *campo*. Sometimes when my mother and I were at the cistern in the middle of the square doing our laundry, Signora Vivaldi would be there with an infant at her breast and a tiny, smiling, red-haired girl clinging to her skirts. The little girl's name was Margarita, and her baby sister was called Cecilia. Their mother was friendly and kind. She was always happy to let me hold baby Cecilia or dance around the square with little Margarita."

She paused and stared into the distance, as if she were in another world. Annina caught her breath. It was one of those rare and wonderful moments when her mother was in a story-telling mood, and she braced to savor every word.

Finally she went on. "Early one morning I was fetching a bucket of water for my mother and had a chance to meet the rest of the family. A pleasant looking young man emerged from the Vivaldi home. His blue eyes sparkled and his flaming red hair flowed to his shoulders. He carried a violin case, and clinging to his other hand was a pint-sized version of himself. The little fellow grasped his own tiny violin case. Signor Vivaldi grinned at me in a friendly way, let go of the little boy's hand, and tipped his feathered hat. '*Buon giorno*, signorina! What a beautiful morning!' I returned his greeting and gazed at the boy."

A smile slowly spread across Bartolomea's spellbound face. "He was about five years old and the most adorable child I'd ever seen. His golden hair fell in gentle waves around his sweet little face, and his deep blue eyes shone with an almost mystical aura. He looked like an angel. 'This is my son, Antonio,' Signor Vivaldi said. Little Antonio gave me a smile that was almost melting in its brilliance. But there was an intensity in his eyes that told me there was fire lurking beneath all that angelic sweetness."

She stopped her story as her own eyes seemed to burn with fervor.

Annina tensed with eagerness.

After a bit, Bartolomea continued, her voice more animated. "I soon learned that Signor Vivaldi was a barber by profession. His son went with him to his nearby shop every day and entertained the customers with his brilliant violin playing. Between haircuts and shaves his father gave him lessons.

"One day I was walking by the Vivaldi barber shop with my father and caught sight of the daily spectacle. A group of men sat mesmerized while little Antonio dazzled them with a spectacular violin improvisation. I peered through the shop window and watched his tiny fingers move with unbelievable speed. Signor Vivaldi was tending a customer, but he dropped his scissors, took up his violin, and began to play a melody. Immediately Antonio improvised an elaborate counter melody. The abandoned customer didn't mind a bit and smiled and applauded along with everyone else. I especially remember the glow of love and pride in Signor

Vivaldi's eyes. I'd never seen a father show such adoration for his child."

Annina hung on every word, and her gaze never left her mother's face. Bartolomea paused, and she agitated. "Please go on, Mamma, tell me more."

Her mother's eyes were fixed in a blank stare, as if her daughter wasn't there. "I didn't see much of them after that. My mother heard through the neighborhood gossips that little Antonio never came out to play with the other boys because of an ailment he'd suffered since birth. One lady told us he'd been baptized immediately by the midwife who delivered him, because he wasn't expected to live. Everyone considered it miraculous that he survived. It was whispered that God had sustained his life through the gift of music. That was why he went into the priesthood, they said, because he owed his life to God."

She was so astonished by this story she was at a loss for words. Throughout her mother's narrative she'd sat tensely on the edge of her seat. Now she considered all she'd heard, as endless questions flashed through her mind. But before she had a chance to speak, her mother went on with her story.

"His father never let him out of his sight. They went everywhere together. Before long Signor Vivaldi was able to give up his barber trade and become a fulltime violinist and teacher. When Antonio wasn't out performing with his father, or taking lessons with his father's other students, he was home practicing. Everyone in the neighborhood grew used to the sound of his violin drifting across the Campo San Giovanni and over the gentle waters of the Rio della Pietà that flowed beneath his window. Many of the compositions for which he later became famous had their start in those solitary hours of music making."

"When was the last time you saw him, Mamma?"

"Almost thirty years ago. He was playing in the San Marco orchestra alongside his father."

"Why didn't you ever see him again?"

"My parents both died from the fever that swept through Venice that winter. Then I had to move away." Her voice became flat, and her eyes were fixed in a blank stare.

She didn't know what to say. This wasn't the first time she'd heard the story of her grandparents' untimely deaths. But she'd never fully comprehended the tragedy of it until that moment. To suddenly lose one's parents and be all alone at such a young age was unimaginable. Despite her stinging knee she sprang from her seat, hurried around the table, and wrapped her arms around her mother's neck.

Bartolomea seemed unaware of her daughter's presence and continued to stare into the distance. At last she murmured, "I always knew he'd end up composing operas. His music was made for the theater. From his earliest days the melodies that flowed from his violin were filled with drama and passion. I used to dream I'd one day sing in the operas I knew he'd create. But after my mother and father died I was forced to marry."

Before she could ask another question Bartolomea pulled away from her, rose from her chair, and hurried to the parlor. She followed, her heart flittering happily as her mother took a score from the pile of music papers that covered the little table by the spinet. The score was from Bartolomea's treasured album of Don Antonio's opera arias. She had no idea where or how her mother had acquired the album. She watched her delicate fingers move over the keys and listened to her creamy soprano voice sail through one of her favorite arias.

Suddenly Bartolomea leaped off the bench, whisked her daughter into her arms, and danced about the room with her.

Laughing, she started to banter a silly parody of operatic dialogue. Annina shared her giddiness and felt herself drawn into her mother's fantastical inner world. Just as suddenly Bartolomea rushed back to the spinet and began another aria. Her mother's enchanting delirium enveloped her. She sang along while the music's seductive power moved her emotions at its will. As their voices mingled, she felt exhilaration so intense it seared her insides. Her heart swelled and ached until she thought it would burst with a yearning she couldn't fully grasp.

BARTOLOMEA NEVER PUT supper on the table that evening. Instead, as the afternoon sun melted into a dim twilight she lit a candle by the spinet and poured her evening wine. Her vacant eyes glistened with hidden pain, and her face became mask-like. The mania with which she'd sung just a bit earlier dimmed to a faint echo as she softly intoned a few fragments of her favorite arias. Darkness descended, and the room was bathed in an eerie glow.

Annina's older sister Paolina arrived home, tired and worn, and immediately tended to her little sister's gashed knee and filthy clothes. Then, as usual, she went to the kitchen to finish preparing supper. Annina tagged along to help—until her father walked in the door. She rushed to his side, jumping up and down. Jabs of pain tormented her knee, but she was brimming with too much excitement to care.

"Papà! Don Antonio really seemed to like me. Won't you please, *please* take me to see him? I want to talk to him about singing in the opera."

Pierre sighed. "The maestro is an extremely busy man, my Annina. He has no time to listen to the chatter of a little sprite like you." He patted her head and proceeded into the parlor to greet her mother.

She scampered after him and tugged at his coattails. "But Papà, he seems so nice. I'm sure he'll talk to me if you introduce me to him."

His look became grim. "That will be quite enough, my little one. You are trying your Papà's patience." He bent to kiss his wife. She sat at her spinet, immersed in her aria, her glass of wine and flask near at hand. She didn't acknowledge him.

He shifted his attention to Annina. "Instead of wasting your time on aimless fantasies, you should be learning the arts of housewifery. How will you ever attract a husband and have a decent marriage if you do nothing but indulge in fanciful daydreams?"

"But I don't want to be married and be a housewife, Papà. I want to sing in the opera."

"Enough of this foolish prattle, young lady," he said, as he loosened his collar and headed toward his study. At the archway, he turned and gave her a reproachful look. "We will discuss your unseemly behavior later, little miss."

She shuffled her feet in agitation.

By the time they sat down to supper Bartolomea's mood had darkened. She poured another glass of wine from the diminishing carafe and turned her eyes to Paolina. "And what news of your day?"

Paolina sighed and pressed her lips. "You know what I've been doing, Mamma, assisting Signora Spinella as I do every day."

Her mother downed another gulp of wine and smiled mockingly. "What a pathetic, useless life you have, catering to that doddering relic. Never mind that she has more money than the host of hell. Do you think we'll ever see any of it beyond the few *soldi* she sees fit to throw your way? That pittance doesn't begin to pay your keep. Pierre should have put you in a convent years ago. But no, here you are, nearly thirty years old and snared in the bonds of spinsterhood. Such an embarrassment."

Paolina lowered her eyelashes, and red blotches sprang to her cheeks, as if she'd been slapped. Annina's heart ached for her.

"My dear, please, be kind," Pierre pleaded. "Paolina is engaged in honorable work."

His wife snorted. "Honorable indeed. Groveling to Her Majesty, scraping out her slop pots."

"*Ah, ma chérie, écoute-moi*—"

"Spare me your platitudes, Pierre. You and your foppish French drivel, I've had my fill of it. If Trevisana were alive he'd have long ago found his daughter a husband and I wouldn't be saddled with this aging spinstress. More importantly, I'd still be in Venice and not stuck in this smothering hovel of a house, listening to your nerve-rattling prattle and bearing the burden of your worthless sons."

It pained Annina to see her mother chide Paolina so cruelly and spurn her father's affections. Her heart grieved for them both. And her soul wailed in torment: *If Mamma still laments the death of Signor Trevisana, Paolina's father, and feels such contempt for my father—then how must she feel about me?* She looked into Bartolomea's hard eyes and felt her insides turn over and shrivel as the realization came crashing down on her that her mother was incapable of love. Love is so simple, and so necessary. *Why can't Mamma manage it?* she wondered. She loved her mother, but her mother didn't love her. Not in the way mothers are supposed to love their daughters, by tenderly cleaning and bandaging their gashed knees, holding them in warm embraces, and kissing away their tears.

"*Mon amour*—" Pierre began, then suddenly his sons arrived, noisily and unexpectedly. They were in a rowdy mood, and it was clear they'd been drinking. Annina completely forgot her sore knee. She scrambled from her chair and ran to them.

Laurent scooped her up. "*Anna—nina, Nannina,*" he chanted in his French accent. He tossed his baby sister in the air and slung her over his shoulder as she shrieked with glee.

Paolina groaned. "Laurent, put her down! I've only just gotten her calm and settled, and now you two are stirring her up again."

"In other words, my dearest sister, you've forced the little hellion into an unnatural state," Laurent said, with mock indignation.

"We certainly can't allow that," Marcel added. He reached over, mussed Annina's hair, and pulled her from Laurent's arms. Oblivious to Paolina's objections, he twirled her around and chanted in a sing-songy way, "Come dance with me, Nina, my little Nannina." Distorting her name was one of the ways her half-brothers had always teased her. And she loved it.

"Marcel!" Paolina chided with growing impatience. "Your little sister is not a toy to be tossed about."

"But of course she is," he responded merrily, as he swung her around to his back. "What other possible use could she be?"

She clung to his neck and wrapped her legs around his waist. His chestnut hair tickled her mouth, and she giggled.

Pierre watched his sons' revelry with tolerant amusement. He rose from the table and embraced them both, while Annina hung on Marcel's back. "Ah, my boys," he said, his face glowing with delight. "It does me such good to have you home. If only you would come more often. But of course, I know how busy you must be."

Through all this, Bartolomea glared at her husband in silence. Annina sensed her mother was sinking into an even bleaker mood, but she was too giddy with the pleasure of her brothers' lively company to give her much thought.

"Bartolomea," Laurent said, "why the long face?" He leaned to kiss her cheek.

She pushed him away and continued to glower at Pierre. Annina didn't want her to spoil the festive mood, so she slid off Marcel's back, grasped Laurent's hand, and pulled him to herself. "I saw the opera today! I went to the royal theater all by myself and saw Don Antonio conduct a rehearsal. And someday *I'm* going to sing in the opera."

"Will you indeed?" Laurent said. He grinned down at her, and his hazel eyes, so like his father's, sparkled with amusement.

Pierre frowned. "Yes, she was a very naughty girl today. I forbid her to go near the theater, but she will not listen to me."

"Of course she won't," Laurent said cheerfully. "She has a mind of her own, don't you, little Nina—Nannina?"

Her head bobbed with a vigorous nod.

Marcel chimed in. "Well, if it's opera you want, little Ninanni, why, *I'll* sing you an opera." He cleared his throat with feigned pomposity and broke into a ridiculous imitation of an opera singer, complete with rolling eyes and overly dramatized gestures. She gasped and choked with hilarity.

Pierre smiled meekly and collapsed into his chair. Laurent slid into Annina's empty seat and leaned close to his father. "Papà, dear," he said, with a disarming grin. "Marcel and I are running a bit low on funds. Would you advance us a trifle?"

"Well, I suppose I could spare a few *lire* for my fine sons," Pierre said, with an affable smile.

Paolina sighed, shook her head, and pressed her lips together. Annina looked at her mother and saw her eyes blaze with fury.

Bartolomea sprang to her feet. "Are you blind to how they are using you?" she shouted at her husband. "They only come here when they need money. They're going to ruin us, and you are helping them do it!"

Pierre gazed at her imploringly and started to ring his hands. "My dear, please, you must calm yourself." He turned to his sons with an apologetic simper. "Boys, come into my study and I will see what I have in my cashbox."

The three of them left the room, and Annina watched her mother descend into one of her blackest rages.

AS SOON AS LAURENT and Marcel left, Paolina whisked Annina upstairs to bed. She lay frozen with apprehension, the sheet pulled taut over her chin while Bartolomea raged below.

"They will put us in the poor house!" she heard her mother scream.

"You must not upset yourself so, *ma chérie*," her father said in a pleading voice. "They are only boys, after all."

"They are grown men! Yet they have no sense of responsibility. They spend their days in the gambling houses and their nights in the taverns, cavorting with whores and derelicts, and they do it all at our expense."

"I beg you to collect yourself, my love. With your delicate temperament you will make yourself ill."

"If I become ill it's because you keep me a prisoner in this house. You know how I long to go to Venice, to revisit the pleasures I once knew there. But instead I'm trapped in a life that is suffocating me!" And on and on it went until at last Bartolomea's frantic voice dissolved into loud sobs as her husband struggled to placate her with anxious pleas.

At some point Annina drifted into a troubled sleep.

She woke early the next morning to a chilling silence. She crept to her parents' room and found it empty. The bed looked as if it hadn't been slept in. Fear pricked her insides. Downstairs her father sat alone, his head in his hands. The fire in the hearth was long burnt out, and wind swooped down the chimney and stirred the cold ashes into a frenzy. She felt an icy shiver slither up her spine, her illusion of safety fading like the sun in a skulking dusk.

"Papà," she whispered, almost too frightened to speak, "where's Mamma?"

He looked up, and the flesh of his face sagged heavily. "Your mother has left us."

If the earth had opened below her feet, she couldn't have felt more terrified. Her teeth chattered uncontrollably. She glanced around warily. "Is Paolina here?"

"She has gone to look for your brothers," he said, sounding tired and listless. "They are good boys, are they not? They will help bring your mother back, surely."

She started to feel queasy. She stroked her father's gray hair and tried to smile, but she couldn't control the twitching in the corners of her mouth. Squeezing her arms around herself, she returned to her room. Still in her nightgown, she sat up in bed and felt lost in an abyss of silent panic. Outside her window the day looked bleak. A cold spell had moved in and blotted out the previous day's sunny warmth. She felt an unbearable chill. Yet despite the February winds roaring outside, she knew the icy tremor that had seized her was coming from within. She drew her knees to her chest, hugged her bent legs with all her strength, and pressed her forehead to her kneecaps.

She heard the front door creak open and Paolina's familiar steps tapping across the downstairs floorboards, followed by the sound of muffled voices. But she had no desire to leave her room. To walk through the house would only be a cruel reminder that her mother wasn't there, and she couldn't cope with the pain of her absence. A terrifying thought invaded her mind. If her mother found her so unlovable that she could abandon her without warning, why should anyone else want her? What if her father and siblings rejected her too? What if she were left alone, loved by no one? Try as she might, she couldn't erase the horrifying prospect from her thoughts. Stinging darkness swept over her.

There was a light knock at the door, and she looked up as Paolina entered the room. Without a word she sat on the bed and held Annina close.

"Did you find Marcel and Laurent?" she asked, her words punctuated by strangling sobs.

"No, darling." Paolina smoothed a stray lock from her sister's forehead. "I'm afraid I didn't."

"What will happen to us, Paolina? What will Papà do?"

"It will be all right, I promise," she said as she drew her sister to her again.

FOR THE FIRST few nights after her mother left she lay awake and listened for her footsteps on the stairs. Then a night came when she didn't listen anymore, but buried her face in her pillow to smother her weeping. Daytime was no less painful, when she had to endure the pitying looks of the other mothers on her street as they leaned out doors and windows to call their happy little ones to supper. The sight of those children, with loving mothers and not a care in the world, was more than she could bear. She hung her head and grew more and more despondent.

Then one day she started to notice the depth of her father's sadness. He seemed to have grown older since her mother left and had lost his characteristic nervous energy and bustling fussiness. She decided to put aside her own grief and start a campaign to cheer him.

That evening when he came home she forced herself to radiate merriment. "Papà, shall I sing for you?" she said brightly.

He sighed and didn't respond.

She grasped his hand and pulled him into the parlor. "We'll pretend we're putting on an opera, won't that be fun, Papà? You can play the part of the hero, and I'll be the leading lady."

He smiled wearily and patted her head. "Your Papà has no energy for such frivolity, my little one."

"Then watch me dance, Papà." She leaped and twirled and frisked about him.

He smiled weakly and proceeded to his study.

Her efforts to lift her father's spirits made little progress over the following weeks. So she decided to try a new tack. She gave up pestering him about the opera and sat quietly by the fire with him in the evenings after supper. She would read or sew, activities she'd always found difficult to sit still for. On one such evening she watched her father's sad eyes and tried to *will* him to cheer up, to feel some happiness. "Will you talk to me, Papà?" she asked softly. "What can I do to make you happy?"

He sat in silence and gazed into the crackling flames.

With each passing month he grew more withdrawn. He'd go to his shop every morning, dutifully crafting the vast supply of wigs demanded by opera singers and public alike during the Carnival season. But in the evenings he would simply sit and stare at the fire, as if his mind were far away. If she tried to talk to him, he'd pat her arm or head and turn away. She missed his nagging and scolding. Anything was better than this chilly indifference.

Chapter Two

She was given strict instructions not to leave the house. Since her mother's departure, Paolina and her father had arranged their schedules so one of them could be home with her at all times. On this particular morning, though, they were both called away, and she was entrusted to stay at home, to busy herself with needlework. But it was a misty April morning, and she couldn't endure the loneliness.

She ventured from her house and along the *corso*, the variably hued sequence of arcades leading to the Piazza Mantegna, where she knew she could walk safely and at her leisure since her father and sister would be occupied with their work for many hours. She gazed with comforting awe at the fluted pillars and sheltering arches of the Church of San Andrea. Its ruddy walls seemed to vanish upward toward its elegantly narrow dome. Around the corner was the vegetable market, its profusion of fresh fruits and plants framed by the cheeriness of green, pink, and yellow-painted houses. She continued her venture through arcaded squares toward the Piazza Sordello, over which loomed the Palazzo Ducale. The palace's dark red tint seemed to have faded to a blushing gray, a nostalgic hue. She remembered her brief encounter with the dazzling *prete rosso* a couple of months before and ached to bask again in the brilliance of his music and the warmth of his smile. But the Palazzo Ducale's colonnaded wall remained cold and silent.

Recalling what her mother had told her about Don Antonio, her thoughts became absorbed in the ambiguity of his nature. The co-existence of his exuberantly creative mind and his physical infirmity fired her fascination, yet plagued her with foreboding. How could two such opposite forces struggle within a person without undoing him? The worry of it multiplied her torment. In the blurry mist of her anguish, she watched the Sordello's surrounding arcades fade to a hazy dimness as they appeared to overflow into the neighboring *piazza* and trickle down the stone-paved streets. Gazing ahead at the seemingly endless parade of vaults and stone, she felt the stifling dullness of her own life—its crushing sameness, its static emptiness.

Sadness hung over her like a cloud. She felt doubly abandoned, by her mother physically and by her father emotionally. The fear that had crept into her mind the morning after her mother left gripped her heart anew—a terror of abandonment, of being left alone and having no one at all she could depend on. Her siblings had withdrawn from her too. Her brothers hadn't been seen or heard from since that terrible night, the night her mother left, and Paolina had no time for her anymore. She was too preoccupied with nursing old Widow Spinella and taking charge of the cooking and chores at home. As she plodded home through Mantua's unbroken chain of arcades, loneliness enveloped her like a living death, an entombment.

Then, in mid autumn, her life took an unexpected turn.

SHE JUMPED AND grinned with delight when Prince Phillip's invitation was delivered. She, her father, and Paolina were invited to a private concert at the Palazzo Ducale, to be directed by Don Antonio.

Pierre was less enthusiastic. "It is not a good idea, my Annina. I am afraid I must decline the prince's kind offer."

"But Papà, this isn't a theater performance. You only said I'm not allowed to go to the opera. You never said I couldn't go to a private concert. The prince's note even says he'll send a carriage to fetch us and bring us home."

Her father frowned down at her.

To her surprise, Paolina intervened on her behalf. "Annina's right, Papà. This will be a much more dignified affair than a public opera performance. And I think it would be good for us all to go out and enjoy ourselves. Besides, the prince might be offended if you turn down his invitation."

"Perhaps you are right, my dear," he said,

Her heart leapt for joy.

THE PALAZZO DUCALE'S grand salon buzzed with the kind of festive commotion that pumped Antonio's artistic furor to a fever pitch. He inhaled deeply the bouquet of expensive smelling perfumes that hung in the air like fragrant clouds and almost masked the underlying odor of salty perspiration. His blue eyes scanned the tapestry-like spectacle of sumptuous Venetian silk and powdered wigs. Cumbersome things. He'd endured those inane head coverings for a couple of portrait sittings, but he'd be damned if he'd tolerate the stifling misery of goat hair encircling his head if he didn't have to. And the strawberry-blond locks that fell loosely around his face were part of his professional image. He was proud of his public sobriquet—*il prete rosso*, the red-haired priest.

He greeted the gathering musicians, then opened his portfolio. As he began arranging the concerto score on his music stand, the feeling swept over him that he was the object of someone's attention. He glanced up from the score to find a little girl staring back at him with her artless child's face, her dark eyes wide in the candlelight. He smiled at her and wiggled his eyebrows. She giggled. Then a woman emerged from the lively crowd, grasped the girl's hand, and pulled her back to the seating area. He quickly averted his eyes and went back to his score arranging.

Soon the prince and his consort made their grand entrance along with their entourage, and the white wigs and silk gowns converged into a minuet of stately bows and curtsies. As Prince Phillip and his retinue made their way to their seats, Antonio spotted the girl again. Where had he seen her before? Then he noticed she was standing beside Pierre Girò, the prince's fussy French wigmaker. Suddenly it all came back to him.

The previous winter his opera rehearsal had been disrupted by one of his all too frequent run-ins with that arrogant Gualandi witch. There she'd stood, glaring at him from the stage, preening like a painted peacock and presuming to tell him how to write music. After she'd stormed off the stage he'd felt overcome with anger and weariness. But his fury nearly dissipated when his eyes fell on a wild looking little waif of a girl, standing just beyond the orchestra area and gazing at him in starry-eyed wonderment, as if he were a sort of god. She was a pretty thing, and definitely not the prim and proper type. He liked that.

Prince Phillip motioned everyone to sit, and the room fell silent. Antonio remained standing and played a long note on his violin, which the other string players imitated. Then he gave a quick nod, and the orchestra began a brisk, cheerful melody, to which he responded with his *agitato* solo exhibition.

After the concert he retreated to a settee in a far corner of the room, feeling winded, as he so often did after a vigorous performance. He closed his eyes and tried to breathe deeply, then opened them. There she was again, gazing at him with an anxious look. Her shyness and her wide, trusting eyes were touching. He searched his memory for her name. Anna . . . Nina . . . Annina. That was it.

"Well, hello. So nice to see you again," he said. "Annina, that's your name, isn't it?"

She smiled, suddenly and disarmingly, then bobbed a curtsy. "Yes, maestro, that's what I'm called. But my real name is Anna Maddalena Teseiré, Tessieri in Italian."

"What a lovely name."

She seemed to quiver with pleasure. "Thank you, maestro. But I don't usually go by the name Teseiré. When my father moved here from France he stayed in Venice for awhile, and people called him *il Girò* because he traveled around so much. Now my whole family's called that."

He smiled. "Venetians are like that. They hardly ever call anyone by their proper names. My family's called *Rossi* because of our red hair."

Her smile brightened. Apparently it pleased her that they shared the distinction of family nicknames. He silently marveled at how her former ragamuffin appearance had transformed to one of such sparkling beauty. She now wore an immaculate white dress, and a blue silk sash encircled her wispy little waist. Her cheeks glowed, and the delicate scent of lavender soap floated about her. Yet though her hair was clean and shiny and tied with a blue silk ribbon, a few rebellious strands had slipped free and fallen around her face and down her neck.

"So, Annina, do you like music?" he asked.

Her entire demeanor took on a new brilliance. "Oh yes, maestro. I want to be an opera singer."

"Really? That's wonderful. What are your favorite operas?"

It seemed she could hardly keep from bouncing with excitement. "*Your* operas are my favorites, maestro. I want to sing in all your operas."

The girl became more fascinating all the time. She looked only about nine or ten years old, yet she knew what she wanted and seemed to have no qualms about doing what it takes to get it. He was about to say something encouraging, when the same woman who had dragged the child to her seat earlier came scuffling over.

"I apologize for my sister's boldness, maestro," she said, somewhat nervously and breathlessly.

He rose to his feet and bowed his head politely. "No apologies necessary, signora. Your sister is a delightful conversationalist."

The lady's eyes widened in surprise. "You're much too kind, sir, but I'll take her off your hands now," she said as she clasped her sister's hand.

Annina's pretty little mouth formed into a pout of determination, and her shining dark eyes turned to fire. "No. I want to stay here and talk to Don Antonio."

The older sister's cheeks flushed with anger and embarrassment.

He spoke up quickly. "Your sister is welcome to talk to me as long as she wishes, signora," he said, his smile polite but firm.

"Well . . . I suppose . . . if you're sure you don't mind . . ." she stammered, flustered.

"Certainly I don't mind."

Little Annina smiled up at him, her eyes glistening with adoration.

He wanted to step outside for fresh air, and she joyfully scampered after him. On the veranda the cool October air, the starry sky, and the soft moonlight combined to give a magical feeling. The courtyard that the veranda overlooked was framed by a colonnade of stately pillars, encircled by fragrant clusters of wisteria. He savored the balmy aroma and tranquility of the airy enclosure, but he could see Annina was eager to talk to him. He smiled at her encouragingly.

"Maestro, the violin piece you played tonight is the most thrilling music I've ever heard," she said.

"I'm so glad you liked it."

"What do you call that kind of music, maestro?"

"That was a violin concerto. A concerto is a type of contest between the orchestra and a solo instrument."

"I noticed the orchestra kept coming back with the same music, but your part was always different."

"The orchestra part is called the *ritornello*, because as you heard, it keeps returning and is nearly always the same."

"But your solo parts were wild and *ribelle!*"

He laughed. "Exactly. The solo part is the rebel, the lone voice that's struggling to express itself above the crowd." He looked at her thoughtfully for a moment. Her innocent vivacity and tender zeal were heartwarming. "You have a keen ear for music, Annina," he said finally, "and a remarkable sensitivity to its inner meaning. That's very impressive in someone your age."

She smiled at him ecstatically.

The girl's company was surprisingly engaging. Her intelligence, her instinctive understanding of his music's dramatic structure, and, he had to admit, her unabashed adoration of him, were enchanting. Such a refreshing contrast to the harangues of that insufferable shrew, Margarita Gualandi.

ON THE CARRIAGE ride home, Annina's ecstatic mood was dampened by her father's disapproving glare.

"Your sister has been telling me how naughty you were, Annina. I never would have thought it, after all your promises to behave like a lady."

"But I *did* behave like a lady."

"How many times have I told you, *ma petite*, that little girls should be seen and not heard? But what did you do? You spent the entire evening annoying a very important man and taking up his valuable time with your silly chatter."

"He wasn't annoyed. He liked talking to me. He said so, didn't he, Paolina?"

Paolina frowned and crossed her arms. "Don Antonio is a gentleman, Annina. He was only being polite."

"No, he was really interested in what I was saying. Just because I'm only nine years old doesn't mean I don't have the right to talk to people. *You* were talking to that old man all evening, Papà."

"You must not speak that way to your father," Paolina said sharply. "Of course your Papà can talk to whoever he pleases. But you are only a child and must learn to hold your tongue."

Their relentless scolding was more than she could bear. As soon as they arrived home she ran to her room, burst into tears, and threw herself across the bed. "My family doesn't understand me, and they never will," she whimpered into her pillow, her heart yearning for comfort. Her thoughts turned to Don Antonio. She remembered the honesty in his smile and the kindness in his eyes, and the memory wrapped around her heart like a warm embrace. She thought about his strong profile in the moonlight, and a melting feeling tickled her heart. His music was likewise affecting.

At one moment his playing was tender, almost sad, and in the next brash and agitated. And the contest with the orchestra! The tension of his musical duel with the other string players had built with such excruciating persistence she thought her heart would burst. But the most wonderful moment of all was when he'd acknowledged her empathy with his music. For that exquisite instant she knew what it feels like to be understood. It was a feeling she could never do without again.

SOON AFTER THE New Year, shortly before her tenth birthday, she was sitting on a stool in her father's shop counting coins while he worked on his account books. The task was monotonous but better than the tedious stitchery she'd left behind at their cheerless house, scattered and neglected. Helping her father in his shop was her escape from that wearisome chore. But she still felt fidgety. Her eyes scanned the dozens of goat hair and human hair wigs her father had carefully crafted, perched on wooden blockheads and displayed along shelves that lined the wall behind the counter where she sat. The blockheads' blank faces looked as bored as she felt. She closed her eyes for a moment and breathed in the comforting scents of lavender and orange flower drifting from the cans of hair powder he kept under the counter, aromas that reminded her of her mother.

She placed the last silver ducat in the coin box and recorded the amount. Then she rested her chin in her hand and drummed her fingers to the beat of a tune playing in her head, the melody of an aria she and her mother had sung that last evening they'd been together. She thought about Don Antonio and the magical evening at the Palazzo Ducale a few months before. She hadn't seen him since, yet the memory of his dazzling music and touching smile still burned in her heart. Eager to recapture the joy of that moment, she climbed to her feet atop the stool. "Papà, look at me. Listen to me sing an opera aria."

"Annina, come down from that stool at once," he scolded, "before you fall and break your neck."

She ignored her father's scolding and broke into her favorite opera aria. Losing herself in the dramatic gestures she'd learned from her mother, her heart billowed with the emotion of the music.

Pierre sighed and shook his head in exasperation. "Whatever will I do with you, my little monkey?"

Nothing he said could break the spell she was under. Her outstretched arms trembled with a misty yearning as she sang: *"My heart beats faster when I see your sparkling eyes—"*

The bell above the shop door clanged, and the January wind heralded the entrance of a dapper looking young gentleman. She gasped in surprise and nearly tumbled off the stool. The man darted over, grasped her hand, and helped her regain her balance. Her cheeks flamed with embarrassment.

The man's grin exuded charm. *"Brava*, signorina," he said, clapping his hands, after he'd lifted her down from the stool. "That was splendid. What emotion, what sincerity of feeling. We could use more like you in the opera."

Her heartbeat quickened. She surveyed his finely embroidered waistcoat, satin-lined mantle, and jaunty tri-cornered hat and realized he must be a nobleman.

"I'm sure I've seen you somewhere before, signorina," he said, continuing to gaze at her with his enticing smile. "Ah yes, I remember now. It was at that charming musical soiree I attended last October, at the Palazzo Ducale. You were wearing the most lovely white dress, as I recall."

"Yes sir, I was there," she said demurely, her burning cheeks tinged by excitement at the memory.

"And now I see you possess a theatrical talent matched only by your beauty."

"Thank you, sir," she mumbled, flustered by the unaccustomed flattery.

The man smiled again and winked at her. Turning his attention to her father he removed his hat and held it across his chest. "*Buon giorno*, Signor Girò. My manservant is indisposed, so I have the pleasure of calling on you myself. And may I say," he said, turning to Annina with a smile, "the pleasure is multiplied a hundredfold by the presence of this enchanting young lady."

She dropped a curtsy, grinning and blushing.

"Your Excellency." Pierre bowed fawningly. "What an honor it is that you grace my humble shop with your august presence." Then he glanced at his daughter and frowned. "You must excuse my naughty little Annina's improper behavior, Excellency. I simply do not know what to do with her. She refuses to sit still and attend to her duties like a proper, well-behaved young lady of her station."

The man's smile widened. "There's nothing to excuse, Signor Girò. Your charming daughter should be on the stage. She's quite an actress."

Pierre's expression was a combination of horror and simpering reproach. "You are too kind, Excellency, but naturally, I could never permit my daughter to perform in a theater."

Still smiling, the man turned to her and winked. "Perhaps we can change his mind, Signorina Annina."

She grinned and nodded eagerly.

He turned back to her father. "I regret, signore, that I am here to cancel my wig order and to bring you unpleasant news. The empress in Vienna has died, and a period of mourning has been ordered throughout the Austrian Empire. All the theaters in the monarchy will close immediately. Don Antonio Vivaldi has just resigned his position at the court of Mantua and will return to Venice straightaway, along with his entire entourage."

Her heart leaped with rapture for a fleeting instant at the mention of Don Antonio, then sank with sorrow at the news of his departure.

"He will resume his teaching post at the *conservatorio* of the Pietà," the man continued, "and he already has plans to begin rehearsing his newest opera at the Teatro San Angelo, *La verità in cimento*, in which my protégée, Chiara Orlandi, will sing a starring role. Therefore I must return to my Venetian home. I do so regret to bid farewell to your fair city."

"This is most distressing news," Pierre said.

She knew her father's distress was not due to the opera closing down but to the fact that the enforced period of mourning would also close down his wig shop.

The gentleman gave Pierre a polite nod, replaced his hat, winked at her, and departed.

"Papà, who was that man?" she asked.

"That was the Duke of Massa Carrara, a fine gentleman and a great patron of the opera."

"I don't understand, Papà. Why does our opera theater have to close just because an empress died in Vienna?"

"As I have told you before, *ma petite*, Mantua is a southern province of the Habsburg monarchy. Thus it is part of the Austrian Empire, as is much of Italy. So we must abide by their laws."

"Then why don't the theaters in Venice have to close?"

"Venice is not under Habsburg rule. It is an independent republic. There is no city like it in the world."

Excitement surged in her. "Can't we move there, Papà?"

He looked horrified. "Certainly not. Venice is a city of vice. The people there care for nothing but merriment."

She thought it sounded like a wonderful place.

Back at home, her heart sagged. Not only did she have to face her mother's abandonment and her father's emotional withdrawal, but now Don Antonio and his opera company were going away—to Venice, a city of fun and excitement. And she was stuck in dull Mantua. Her life couldn't sink any lower.

Chapter Three

Nearly three years had passed since Bartolomea's disappearance, and Annina had grown used to her absence. The dullness of her life was alleviated only when her brothers paid their occasional visits to beg for money.

She sat at the little spinet in the parlor. It was a frigid evening early in January, and she was soon to turn twelve. Her icy fingers fumbled to pick out the melody of an aria her mother used to sing with her. As usual her needlework was spread across the nearby worktable, gathering dust. She glanced over at her father as he sat gazing into the hearth, the ashy remnants of the log collapsing in a crimson glow. To her surprise, he motioned her to his side. She scurried over and knelt at his knee.

"What is it, Papà?"

"My dearest Annina, this breaks my heart, but I must send you away." His eyes were moist, and her belly curled into a knot.

"Send me away? What do you mean, Papà?"

"Our noble friend, His Excellency, the Duke of Massa Carrara, has written me, generously offering to sponsor your tuition to study music in Venice. So it seems you will get your wish."

Her eyes widened with disbelief. "But it's been so long since he last saw me. I can't believe he even remembers me."

He smiled at her fondly. "Your talent made quite an impact on the duke, *ma petite*. A man of His Excellency's noble character does not soon forget someone who has impressed him so favorably."

She shivered with mingled excitement and unease. "Will you go with me?"

"No, my little one, I cannot go with you. Paolina will accompany you on the journey and see that you arrive safely."

"You mean—she'll leave me there all alone?"

"Not alone, *ma petite*. His Excellency has arranged for you to lodge at the house of Signora Malvolia Berardi, a former opera singer but a fine lady all the same. I believe His Excellency's protégée, Signorina Chiara, resides there as well. Chiara is from a good family here in Mantua, the Orlandis. So I am confident you will be safe and secure in Venice, among friends, which will be a great comfort to me."

"But I feel safe here with you and Paolina," she said, clutching his knees.

"You must trust me that this is for the best, little one. The duke's offer is a rare opportunity. To turn him down would be an insult."

"No, Papà," she whimpered, laying her head on his knee. "I don't want to go. I don't want to leave you."

"Dear little Annina," he said, stroking her hair and choking with emotion. "You must accept that your mother is gone and I am unable to look after you properly. And your brothers are not dependable. Your poor sister is carrying the burden for all of us, and I worry that it will become too much for her. It will help us to know that you are well cared for. And with the education and refinement you will acquire under Signora Malvolia's guardianship, you will attract a suitable husband."

"But I don't want a husband, Papà. I want to sing in the opera." Her tears splotched the soft wool of his knee breeches.

He sighed wearily. "You must be a good girl and do as I say, my Annina."

She knew there was no point arguing with him. Blinking back her tears, she looked up at him and wiped her nose with the back of her hand. "When will I go?" she asked.

"Next week. Paolina will take you."

She climbed into his lap and clung to him, as he sobbed quietly into her hair.

SHE GAZED ACROSS the blue expanse of water that surrounds Mantua, squinting into the harsh winter sun. The small sailing vessel on which she and Paolina had just embarked was sailing toward *il Fiume Po*, Italy's longest river, on its journey east to the Adriatic Sea. The town's marshy countryside seemed flooded with tears, the mingled water and soil of its landscape steeped in a winsome sadness. Even on this bright day the blueness of the sky and water appeared dulled, as if reflected in a leaden mirror.

The next day, salty sea air and the shrill of gulls flooded her senses as they sailed into the Adriatic and veered north. A bolt of lightning caused a brief stir in the tranquil sea, and she shook with fidgety excitement. Her father had told her the duke would arrange for her to study with Don Antonio, and her eagerness to see him again mercifully overshadowed her anxiety about leaving home.

By the time the little ship made its way into the calm green waters of the Venetian lagoon a pearly haze was spreading across the clear blue sky, signaling the approach of sunset. In the dimming light she smelled the crystal scent of winter in the air and felt its iciness on her tongue. Clenching her cloak about herself she gaped in awe at the towers and domes of Venice, aglow in the pink and orange hues of twilight like an enchanted city that had risen out of the water's murky depths. The lagoon was crowded with sea craft of all kinds, and it seemed their boat would never reach the harbor. In fact, they had come to a standstill. She and Paolina gazed over the rail as an unusual looking rowing vessel glided beneath them. A leather-faced man smiled up at them with a yellowed, gap-toothed grin. He tipped his brimless red cap.

"That's a gondola," Paolina whispered in her sister's ear, "the main form of transportation around Venice's waterways."

"I'll get you fine ladies into Venice much faster than this rickety excuse for a sea vessel ever will," the jovial gondolier called to them, in the colorful language peculiar to Venice.

The city's often cryptic dialect, all but incomprehensible to most *foresti*, outsiders, caused Annina little difficulty thanks to her Venetian mother and sister.

Paolina frowned down at the gondolier. "What is your fee, sir?"

He quoted a rather exorbitant price, but quickly added that for such lovely *donzelle* he was willing to make an exception.

"I've heard about swindlers like you," she scoffed.

"So de chi che te parla," the man replied, with a pained expression and hand on his heart, "I know what you're talking about. But I assure you, signora, my price is the best you'll find."

Paolina reluctantly agreed to the *gondoliere*'s offer. He handed each of them down the ladder that descended into his waiting gondola, along with Annina's small trunk and the rest of their meager baggage. They settled into a cushioned seat, and the gondola smoothly slid away from the boat. Annina's eyes drank in the panorama of enticing sights. Houses and other buildings seemed magically built directly on the water's surface. There were no coaches or horses. Only boats of all shapes and sizes, each with a red-capped rower standing at the stern.

The gondolier studied the sisters curiously. "What brings such fine ladies as you to Venice?"

Paolina gave Annina's wrist a warning squeeze and answered primly. "My sister is here to study music."

"Is that so?" The boatman's rough face brightened with interest. "And what instrument do you play, young miss?"

She was too excited to hold her tongue. "I'm going to study singing, and someday I'll sing in the opera."

Paolina glared at her, and her mouth hardened into a thin line.

The jolly gondolier laughed into the brisk evening air. "Well, you've certainly come to the right place, miss. We Venetians are so taken with the opera our theaters are packed to the rafters every night. I'll be there myself this evening."

"You will?" she said, fascinated that such a coarse character would be so interested in the opera.

"I will indeed. We *gondolieri* are the greatest admirers, and the sharpest critics I daresay, of opera singing. The theater managers prize our support so much they give us free tickets." He drew himself up proudly. "They know we'll tout our favorite singers to the rich foreigners who pack Venice during the opera season. That means more business, and more profit, for the operatic bigwigs." His leathery face stretched into a knowing grin as he swept the heavy oar through glistening water.

Her whole body prickled with excitement. "What opera will you see tonight, sir?"

"Well, miss, there are so many choices. At least six different shows going on this evening, I hear. But I'm itching to go to the Teatro San Angelo. That's where my favorite composer, *il prete rosso*, performs most of his operas."

She nearly sprang from her seat.

"But tonight Maestro Tomaso Albinoni is opening his new opera there. Sad to say, *il prete rosso* isn't putting on an opera here this season. Not sure why. Too busy teaching and composing more operas, I s'pose. Who knows, miss, you may well be studying with him soon. Before we know it, *you'll* be up there onstage singing in one of his operas."

Her heart beat with so much violence she thought it would jump out of her chest. "Paolina, can't we please, *please* go to the opera tonight? I'll be good as gold for the rest of my life and do anything you and Papà ask if you'll take me."

Her sister sighed and looked heavenward.

She turned imploring eyes to their amiable gondolier. "Won't you help me convince her, sir?"

"Hush, Annina," Paolina scolded. "I think you've annoyed this gentleman quite enough with your silly chatter."

"She's not bothering me, ma'am," he said, smiling. "I like to see a girl with a *temperamento brioso*."

At last, someone who appreciated her spirited temperament. Venice's allure was growing by the minute.

The gondola's fender brushed a concrete platform, and she felt a slight jolt. A dock worker secured the boat to a post with heavy rope, and their gallant boatman sprang from his perch and helped the sisters step up to the landing. "Piazza San Marco," he said, with a sweeping gesture. "Welcome to *Carnivale!*"

There could be nothing else in the world so filled with glittering surprise as the scene she beheld. A massive cathedral loomed over the swarms of merrymakers who crammed the square, their faces shrouded in lurid masks. Countless lanterns and torches bathed the sprawling spectacle in brilliant light. Her jaw dropped as an explosion of colors filled the sky.

"*Fuochi d'artificio*," the gondolier said as he lifted her trunk to the *fondamenta*. She turned to him, and an artless grin spread across his face. "I wager you'll be lighting up the stage with your own fireworks before we know it, miss." He lifted his cap and hopped back in the boat.

"Excuse me, sir——" Paolina called after him. But he'd already rowed out of hearing, no doubt anxious to drum up more business before the opera.

"*Santo cielo*, holy heavens. Why did you have to prattle on so, Annina? I was going to ask him for directions to the house where the duke's arranged for us to stay tonight, but he left before I had a chance." she sighed heavily. "Oh, well, maybe someone can direct us."

Baggage in tow, the sisters made their way toward the motley throng that crowded the great Piazza. Soon they were caught in a whirl of masked revelers. Clowns and harlequins capered about, and jugglers and acrobats displayed their marvels. Fiddles sang, guitars murmured, feet pattered, and voices hummed. The pleasant clamor and fragrant sea-scented air were unsullied by the harsh clatter of horse hooves, wheels, and stench of manure that bombard the senses in other cities.

She stared in wonder at faceless figures in ghostly white masks topped with black tri-cornered hats and wrapped in long black cloaks. Others wore sparkly masks, and many were dressed in exotic costumes. Yet no matter how simple or elaborate their attire, an air of mystery and intrigue hung about these masqueraders. She was so caught up in the jumble of images and sensations that she bumped headlong into a dusky-eyed woman dressed in filmy turquoise, as the scent of spicy perfume filled her nostrils. The woman's eyes narrowed and glowered at her over the glimmering veil that hid the lower half of her face.

"*You will suffer much.*" The woman's hissing tone and strange accent sharpened the sting of her sinister words.

Her heart lurched. "*Mi scusi*—" she fumbled to apologize, but the woman cut her off.

"*La moretta.* She will shelter you."

She gawked dumbly at the ghoulish black mask the woman shoved into her hand, unsure how such an evil looking thing could possibly protect her

"*La moretta* was given to me by a countess, as payment for telling her fortune. She has much value. But for you, one *soldo.*"

She scrambled through her satchel for one of the few small coins her father had tearfully pressed into her palm as they said their goodbyes.

Paolina tugged her arm. "*Annina.*"

But she was lost in the mysterious woman's mesmerizing gaze. With shaking fingers she pulled a coin from her satchel and handed it to her.

The woman took it eagerly as her eyes bore into Annina's. "There are no bands or strings. Inside the mask there is *un bottone*, a button you will clutch with your teeth. You will have no voice. The silence of *la moretta* will shield you."

Before she could think what to say, the woman was swept back into the crowd and out of sight.

Paolina's face was pinched with anger. "How could you, Annina? How could you throw away Papà's hard-earned money on that piece of rubbish?"

"Didn't you hear what the lady said, Paolina?" She's a *chiromante*, a fortuneteller. She must be very wise."

"What a pack of nonsense. She's a thieving Gypsy if I ever saw one. I honestly don't know what's to become of you, Annina. You haven't got a grain of common sense in your head."

A shiver of fear swept through her—not at her sister's scolding words, but at what the woman had said: *You will suffer much.*

Groaning, Paolina shook her head and continued pushing her way through the crowd, with Annina close at her heels. They passed through one of the arcades that enclose the Piazza and found themselves surrounded by a baffling complex of narrow canals and *calli*, cramped alleyways. At a dimly lit canal junction they gasped in unison as two passenger-less gondolas collided. The sisters gawked, dumbstruck, at the onslaught of aspersions that followed.

"*Baùko!* " shrieked one gondolier, "you idiot! You've wrecked my boat!"

"*Ti xe goldon!* " rejoined the other, "you ass! It was my right to enter the canal first!"

Fury mounted, and they reviled each other as the offspring of assassins and prostitutes.

"Spawn of a bloody executioner!"

"Bastard of a hideous whore!"

Fists waved and pounded into palms, and faces contorted. With a vehemence that would make the devil blush, they each defamed the other's female relatives down to the remotest cousin. Finally, his passion spent, one of the men calmly gathered his oar and gave the other the right of way.

"What ruffians," Paolina scoffed, after the two gondoliers had peacefully departed. "I would have asked them for directions, but I feared for our lives."

Annina was more fascinated than afraid. "That's the most exciting thing I've ever seen."

"*Santo cielo*, Annina, sometimes I have to wonder about your sense of propriety." Exasperated, she fished through her satchel and drew out a folded leaf of paper. She opened it and squinted in the candlelight that illumined a street-corner shrine to the Blessed Virgin. "Oh, I don't know." She sighed and glanced around. "Let's try this direction."

The streets of Venice, laced with the city's sinuous web of canals, were like catacombs in their dark narrowness and obscurity. The recurrent sound of water slapping the hulls of gondolas echoed from every wall and reverberated eerily through every tunnel and passageway. Annina slung her satchel over her shoulder and clung to Paolina's arm while she gazed about at the bewildering maze of concrete and stucco that entombed the mysterious *calli*.

At last they came upon what seemed to be a theater district. She looked up and a sharp thrill flickered through her. The playbill outside a *teatro* they were passing announced the premier of Tomaso Albinoni's opera, *L'Eccissi della Gelosia*. A man in a red cloak strutted up and down in front of the theater hawking tickets.

She tightened her grip on her sister's arm. "Paolina! Here's the Teatro San Angelo. This is where that nice boatman told us Don Antonio puts on most of his operas. And look, the sign tells about the opera that's opening tonight. I think it's the one the man was telling us about. Look at the opera's name—The Excesses of Jealousy. Doesn't that sound exciting? And we can buy the tickets right here. Oh, please, Paolina, *per piacere.*"

"I can't imagine anything more foolish. Papà would be incensed at the idea. Even if you were allowed to go I'm sure we couldn't afford it, especially after the money you squandered on that worthless Carnival mask. You know perfectly well that with the setbacks he's had to endure his business hasn't been going well. Anyway, this isn't even Don Antonio's opera. Now stop this childish nonsense and do as I say."

Tears stung her eyes, and she clutched her sister's arm more tightly. "But Paolina, you don't know how important this is to me."

"Annina, stop this at once. We're going to find Signora Roselli's guest house. She's expecting us, and it would be rude to keep her waiting. And my back aches from lugging this trunk. I don't intend to do anything tonight other than have a bit of supper and a bath, and go to bed."

Her lip started to tremble.

Paolina's eyes softened, and the hard corners of her mouth relaxed. "Now, now, this is no way to start your new life in Venice," she admonished, but her voice had mellowed. "I don't want you to spend our last evening together upset." She smoothed a strand of wispy chestnut hair from her little sister's forehead and sighed. "All right, then. Let's see how much the tickets are."

Her cheeks expanded into a grin, and she threw her arms around Paolina's neck.

"Are you trying to strangle me?" she said, reaching to disengage herself from her sister's clasping arms.

She hugged her middle and bounced up and down.

"Now listen to me. You must promise not to mention one word about this to your father. He'd never forgive me. And you must promise to stay by my side at all times."

"Yes, yes, yes," she said, bouncing with all the more vigor. "I promise. I'll be so good, you won't even know me." She grasped Paolina's arm and pulled her toward the red-cloaked man.

After several inquiries, they came across a boy bearing a lantern who presented himself as a "city guide." For a small fee he led the sisters through a maze of shadowy pathways to Signora Roselli's house. She greeted them warmly and escorted them to a modest bedchamber. They freshened up and enjoyed a savory supper of pasta, tomatoes, and crispy fried minnows before setting out for the opera.

INSIDE THE *TEATRO*, the riot of vibrant colors and sparkling lights was *una festa*, a feast for her eyes. Elaborate crystal chandeliers hung from the ceiling and held hundreds of twinkling candles. Four tiers of red-painted, gold-gilded opera boxes, filled with chattering, laughing people, lined the walls of the cozy theater and both sides of the curtained stage. She was glad, though, that they'd bought the cheaper tickets and were on the ground level, called the "pit." The sisters found seats on a wooden bench directly behind the orchestra. Hawkers roamed the pit with offerings of candied nuts and fruits for two *soldi*, with the toothpick they were skewered on thrown into the bargain. She glanced around, hoping to catch a glimpse of their friendly gondolier. But the noisy mob that crowded the pit made it impossible to see beyond the second row.

Musicians began to wander in and take their seats. She watched them adjust their music scores and tune up their instruments. A scowling, hump-shouldered man shuffled toward the harpsichord, a thick score under his arm. White bristles protruded from his sagging jowls, and stringy gray hair hung straight and limp from his balding head. He sat at the harpsichord, placed the score on the rack, and adjusted his coattails.

That must be Maestro Tomaso, she thought, with a dim feeling of disgust.

After the opening *sinfonia*, the orchestral introduction, the curtain rose and a man and woman in exotic costumes began a melodic dialogue, called *recitative*. The two characters were engaged in a lovers' quarrel, and the force of their verbal combat made her insides quiver. She fidgeted with excitement when the male character broke into a rousing aria about his jealousy over his lover's infidelity. At one point a torrential fountain of notes spewed from his mouth, and she couldn't contain her exhilaration another minute. She sprang from her seat and rushed to the edge of the orchestra area, grasped the low partition, and jumped up and down to get a closer view of the singer.

"*Annina!*" Paolina's voice was a harsh whisper as she grasped her sister's arm. "Stay in your seat or we are leaving this theater."

She looked about at people eating, drinking, playing cards, and socializing in the dozens of opera boxes that surrounded them. "But other people are moving around and talking."

"That's their business. You said you wanted to see the opera, and I expect you to behave like a lady."

She returned to her seat and tried hard to sit still. Yet as the drama unfolded her excitement grew. Maestro Tomaso's opera didn't have the energy and liveliness of Don Antonio's music, but the singers' expressive performances thrilled her just the same. She stayed transfixed until the opera's finale, when everyone's differences were resolved and a chorus sang of the clear skies that appear after dark clouds and storms have passed. She watched the curtain fall on the final act and knew this was what she wanted to do with her life.

"Don Antonio's going to teach me to sing like that, and I'll sing in his operas one day," she said to her sister as they stepped into the cold night air.

Paolina frowned down at her. "Don't be a goose and start getting yourself worked up for nothing." She brushed a lock of hair from Annina's eye and went on. "Don Antonio is one of the most famous composers in all of Europe and the most sought-after music teacher in Venice. Do you really think he has the time or patience to put up with a silly nymph like you?"

"But Paolina—"

"Seriously, Annina, you'll save yourself a lot of trouble and heartache if you learn to be more practical. I can't bear to think of you bringing senseless misery on yourself chasing some wild fantasy. You are here in Venice to learn the ladylike art of music until the time is right for Papà to find you a proper husband. So you must learn to harness these strong passions of yours and become more realistic. I only say this for your own good, because I want you to be happy."

Her spirits slumped. Paolina had no idea what would make her happy. No one did.

Later that night she lay awake thinking about how glamorous the prima donna had looked onstage. Would she ever look like that? Compared to that dazzling singer she was still, at least on the outside, a little girl. But inside her spirit sizzled with all the ardent longings of a woman. Her heart fluttered as she imagined she *was* that singer, pouring out her impassioned emotions under sparkling stage lights. She could hear the applause and shouts of "*Bravissima!*" from her enraptured audience, and the excitement that fantasy aroused in her sent thrilling shivers up her spine.

DESPITE THE LINGERING afterglow of her excitement about the previous evening's opera performance, her stomach was aflutter with dread. She hugged herself and watched her sister whisk a tear from the corner of her eye, while their gondola glided along Venice's Canale Grande through the frigid morning fog.

Her growing agitation forced her to speak up. "Paolina, why can't you stay with me at Signora Malvolia's?"

Paolina gazed at her with sad eyes. "You know that's not possible. I must get home to Papà. He can't manage alone just now."

She thought about this. "You're more loyal to Papà than any of us. Yet he's not even your real father."

"He's been a father to me for most of my life. Lord only knows what would have become of Mamma and me after my own father died, if it hadn't been for him."

"Did Mamma love Papà then?" she asked in a small voice.

She didn't answer right away. "Marrying him was better than the alternatives," she finally said.

"What do you mean?"

"I mean a woman can't get by without a male protector, unless she wants to end up in a convent—or a brothel."

She shuddered. "Couldn't Mamma have followed her dream of singing in the opera?"

Her sister gave her a stern look. "The theater is no better than a brothel, Annina. It's time you learned that."

She sighed and shifted in her seat.

"I can't abandon Papà now, like Mamma has done," Paolina said softly, with a slight tremor in her voice.

And what about me? Mamma abandoned me too. Yet the thrill that swelled in her blotted out every trace of self-pity. Soon, maybe even today, she would begin her studies with Don Antonio. Her heart sang with happiness.

The gondola entered the broad waters of the Canale di San Marco, and the hazy outlines of the many buildings that line Venice's rippling waterways came to life as slivers of candlelight poured from countless windows, gilding the early morning mist. A gleaming, whitewashed structure on her right towered above its surroundings, a cross rising from its gabled roof.

"Santa Maria della Pietà," the gondolier announced.

The girls' foundling home and conservatory where Don Antonio teaches music, she thought, as she quivered with almost unbearable bliss. A moment later the gondolier docked and lifted her trunk onto the *fondamenta*. The boardinghouse where the duke had arranged for her to stay was across a short footbridge from the Pietà. She found it comforting to know Don Antonio would be so near.

Paolina sounded the bell at the house's main entrance, which overlooked the San Marco Canal. A young girl in a maid's cap and apron ushered the sisters inside, then led the gondolier down a dark hall, Annina's trunk on his shoulder.

An old lady stood in the foyer, dressed entirely in black. Her withering stare made Annina's throat clench. She felt gagged.

"I am Signora Malvolia, proprietress of this boardinghouse," she said. "I understand you are here in Venice to study music, under the patronage of the Duke of Massa Carrara."

"*Sì*," she said, as she sank into a curtsy with legs as wobbly as a newborn colt's.

Signora Malvolia pursed her lips and looked her over. "They call you Annina?"

She nodded warily.

"You may call me Signora," she said, her lips tightening.

"*Sì*, Signora."

"And you are twelve years of age?"

"*Sì*, Signora."

"The other singers in residence here are somewhat older."

Signora's smirking gaze left her speechless. Despair crawled through her like a slithering viper.

"You will begin your lessons this afternoon, with Maestro Tomaso," Signora said.

She remembered the surly looking maestro she'd seen at the opera the night before, and her creeping despair turned to panic. She wanted to scream. All that came out was a strangled whisper. "The duke said I would study with Don Antonio."

"Don Antonio has left Venice," she said, her tone as dry as the clumps of dust that hovered in the foyer's shadowy corners.

Her heart wavered, then plunged with a sickening clunk. "Where is he?" she managed to ask.

"He is in Rome."

"But why did he leave Venice?"

"It is not your place to ask questions."

The old lady's icy glare shriveled her insides. Her eyes darted frantically about the gloomy foyer. January's bleakness seemed to have seeped through its walls along with the dank smell of rotting stone.

"I'd like to speak to the duke about this," she finally said, lifting her chin. She tried to sound bold but couldn't stop her lip from quivering.

The corners of Signora's mouth twisted into a stuffy sort of smile. "His Excellency has left town on business and will be away for some time. He's prepaid your room and board here as well as your tuition with Maestro Tomaso. And now it is time to bid your sister farewell so my maid, Bettina, can show you to your chamber."

Paolina lingered by the front door. Annina ran to her and threw her arms around her neck. The faint scent of lavender, which reminded her so much of her mother, turned her eyes to liquid. Paolina held her close.

"We don't tolerate displays of emotion here," Signora said, gripping her shoulders and pulling her from her sister's arms.

Through clouded eyes she caught a glimpse of Paolina's worried face before she kissed her forehead and said, "Goodbye Annina, write to me," as Bettina ushered her out.

Pain jabbed her belly as she wondered how long it would be before she saw her sister or anyone in her family again.

She followed Bettina down the gloomy hall that led to the stairs. Along the way, the maid pointed out a closet-like room containing a dusty, ancient looking keyboard instrument. "That's where the singers here do their practicing, miss," she said. "Signora will assign you a daily practice time. Yours will probably be early in the morning since all the other times are taken."

Further down the hall, toward the kitchen, they passed another open door. She peered into a cramped room and saw a plump young woman, busy with needlework. The seamstress looked up and smiled, her eyebrows arched with curiosity, then jutted out her lower lip and blew upwards to doff a lock of straw-colored hair from her eye. Her hands never left her sewing.

She felt a brief flicker of warmth. The seamstress's cozy smile was a fleeting comfort.

Bettina led her up a dark, enclosed stairway to a tiny bedchamber. The room's scant furnishings consisted of a cot, a mirror-less washstand, and a flimsy looking wardrobe cabinet. She squinted at the morning sunlight that peeked through a narrow window overlooking the San Marco Canal.

"The necessary's down the hall, miss, last door on the left," Bettina said before disappearing down the stairwell.

She dreaded having to grope her way along that spooky corridor in the dead of night, should she need to relieve herself.

Alone in her room, she opened her trunk and took out the two extra dresses she'd brought, smoothed them and hung them in the wardrobe, then draped her dressing gown on a hook attached to the door. Since there was no chest of drawers, she dragged her trunk to the foot of the cot to store her nightgowns, underclothes, and her few other belongings. She emptied her satchel onto the bed, and her eyes met *la moretta*'s dark stare. Pushing the rest of her odds and ends to the side, she picked up the mask and looked it over carefully in the morning sunlight. "She" was molded from stiff leather and shrouded in black velvet.

Her fingers grazed a spot on the cheek where the velvet was starting to fray. She turned the mask over and saw that a slight crack in the leather was causing the velvet to stretch and unravel a bit. Then she realized the crack led to a small inscription. She ran a finger over the letters *CZL*, which were etched deeply into the leather. She held the mask to her face. Its cold hardness and pungent scent were stifling. Slowly her teeth grasped the little wooden *bottone*, meant to both silence and protect a girl. She quickly pulled *la moretta* from her face and slipped her into the trunk. Then she lay down, wrapped her arms around herself, stared at the ceiling, and tried not to cry. Her heart, which only a few minutes before had bubbled over with such happy anticipation, was now drained of hope. She felt trapped, and utterly alone.

AT THE MID-DAY meal she met three of the other singers who lodged at Signora Malvolia's house. Their ages ranged from about fourteen to seventeen, and she soon learned they were all students of Maestro Tomaso. The youngest of the group was Ernesta, a dark-haired, prim looking girl who spoke little. She seemed to make a point of avoiding Annina's eyes. With raised chin, she set her mouth in a priggish little frown. Then there was Marzia, who looked a year or two older. Her coarse auburn hair was pulled away from her freckled face and fastened into a tight coil atop her head, and her colorless lips were contorted into an ironic looking smile. She continually cut her eyes to Annina and just as quickly looked away, giving her the uneasy feeling she was being watched. The oldest of the trio, and by far the most flamboyant, was Fiametta. She was olive-skinned, and her face was dominated by a hawk-like nose and toothy smile. Half her thick black hair was piled on her head, and the other half hung in shimmering locks down her back. Her voice was loud and strident, and she almost never stopped talking.

She sat in uncomfortable silence and moved her food around with her fork. Bettina had served steaming plates of chicken and vegetables, but she felt like there was a lightning storm in her stomach. She couldn't swallow a bite. The grating sound of Fiametta's incessant chatter only aggravated her inner turmoil. When at last Fiametta paused to take a breath, she turned to Signora and asked if anyone else lived at her house.

Fiametta intercepted with her booming voice. "Well of course there's our resident *celebrity*—our very own singing star."

She glanced around the table and noticed the other two girls respond with smug little smiles. Signora flushed and batted her eyelashes, as if she herself had been paid a compliment.

She looked back at Fiametta. "Who's that?" she asked, her curiosity overriding the sickness in her belly.

"Why Chiara Orlandi, of course. Don't you know her? I felt sure you did. She's from your hometown and until recently was under the patronage of your duke."

She'd almost forgotten. Chiara was the singer from Mantua her father had told her about, and who the duke had mentioned. Her spirits lifted a bit, and she felt anxious to meet her.

Signora gushed with pride. "That dear, angelic girl left Mantua many years ago to study music here in Venice. She has sung in Don Antonio's operas as well as in those of a good many other composers."

Fiametta couldn't restrain herself. "And now she's Maestro Tomaso's star pupil as well as his teaching assistant. She's having her private lesson with him right now. You'll meet her in a bit when we all go to his studio for our group lesson."

"Of course," said Signora, with moist eyes and a simper of fondness, "*I* have taught our darling Chiara almost everything she knows. But she has outstripped me. Yes indeed. She has left me far behind in her meteoric rise to the stars."

A curious thought occurred to her, and she couldn't resist speaking up. "That's strange. My sister and I saw Maestro Tomaso's new opera last night. If Chiara's such a singing celebrity and his star pupil, why didn't she sing in it?"

Signora gave her a hard frown, as if she'd said something impertinent. But before the old lady could respond, Fiametta burst in. "Oh, Chiara's not singing in any operas this season. She's taking a break to rest her voice."

"Rest her voice?"

Ernesta, who hadn't said a word during the entire meal, directed her eyes to Annina and held her in a steady gaze. "Yes, she sang *five* operas in a row last year at the San Angelo and strained her throat." Ernesta's elflike voice contrasted eerily with her dark, serious look.

Signora cleared her own throat and looked down her nose at Annina. "A bit of vocal strain is not unusual for a busy opera singer. Maestro Tomaso has been giving her private instruction to remedy the problem, and our dear Chiara's voice is, thank heaven, nearly restored to its former glory."

Inexplicably, a tremor of uneasiness flitted through her.

Chapter Four

Chiara paced the length of Maestro Tomaso's dismal, crudely furnished studio. *What a blathering fool. As if Signora Malvolia knows anything. Could the dried-up old bat actually believe the Duke of Massa Carrara would drop me for that upstart twit? Never mind that the little tart's also from Mantua, and I'm probably expected to wet-nurse her.* Yet she knew that it was true. Men are so pathetically fickle. Bitter laughter rose in her like a swelling tide, closer to tears than mirth. She clenched her fists and jaw at the injustice.

She thought of Antonio and a wave of erotic excitement swept through her. Things had not gone well between them. It wasn't her fault, though. He had led her on, hadn't he? Making her feel she was the most special person in the world to him. Why in God's name did he have to be a priest and so wed to his priestly vows? It simply wasn't fair. At once she felt such a violent longing that tears came to her eyes. Angry tears.

She had thought she was showing her loyalty by confessing her secret feelings to him, by proposing a radical change of lifestyle. But he'd rebuffed her. Yet she held out hope that in time he would see reason, would have a change of heart. He had not. Still, she'd waited, fuming and expectant. And at last, in her rage and humiliation, she sided with his enemies. His music was, after all, such an iconoclasm of the status quo, a natural target for satire, the weapon of the powerless against the powerful. A merciless exaggeration in its cruelty and unfairness. It hurts people and it's supposed to. It seemed the right thing to do at the time. But perhaps her duplicity had not been wise.

After his departure for Rome things had grown steadily worse. He should have taken her with him, but he hadn't even asked. She felt her blood run cold at the thought. True, she sang in those five operas his rivals put on at the San Angelo. The theater that had so sparkled with the splendor of his music during his time there, but in his absence sank into chaos—the gondoliers standing in the pit, drunk and rowdy, pushing and shoving for a better view. The nerve! What business does that riff-raff have coming to the opera? No wonder she over-strained her voice, trying to belt out the notes over the unruly mayhem. But what else was she to do? He had abandoned her, and now it seemed her voice had abandoned her as well, from the strain. It was all so unfair.

Worst of all, she was stuck with that wretched old has-been, Maestro Tomaso. That aging coot. The tedious technical exercises he made her practice seemed static and pointless. Under his inept tutelage she was spilling herself away, without purpose or reward. *No need to worry about him greeting little miss newcomer with open arms. That repulsive old crank has the warmth and charm of a sea mullet.*

Unlike Antonio. How she longed for him to return so she could work on some real music again. But for now she found herself with too much time and not enough to do. Surely he would return soon. And when he came back he would have seen reason and make everything right again. She was determined that nothing would stand in her way. *All he needs is a little persuasion.*

She had made her plan. Certainly Antonio was on her side after all. He understood how unfairly she'd been treated and how she deserved to be favored. She couldn't wait to see the look on his face when she sang for him again. How perfectly her plan would work. Her cunning in such things amazed even herself.

SOON AFTER DINNER, Annina was told it was time to depart for Maestro Tomaso's studio for singing instruction. Fiametta led the little group a short distance along the Riva degli Schiavoni, past the Piazza San Marco. She gaped about at her first glimpse of Venice in full daylight. The streets were alive with song. A man peddling roast pumpkin hawked his offerings to a melody that pulled her heartstrings. A fruit vendor warbled "Melons with hearts of fire!" and "Juicy pears that'll bathe your chin!" with such gusto her mouth watered. Fishermen and firewood dealers melodiously cried their wares up and down the canals, filling the briny air with cheery music.

They passed a cook shop, and the heavenly smells of roasted chicken and hot cornmeal *polenta* brought rumbles to her belly. Then they turned into a shadowy alley that led to the Campo San Moisè, and the delicious aromas and colorful sounds faded.

"Here's Maestro Tomaso's house," Fiametta told her, pointing to a dingy building that overlooked the small square.

A housekeeper ushered them down the front hall and into a cold, musty smelling room whose sole furnishings consisted of a harpsichord littered with music scores and a couple of armless wooden chairs. The granite floor was bare, and the unpainted plaster walls were crowded with drab looking pictures. Even in its bleakness, the room felt suffocating. The other three girls huddled together, laughing and whispering. She stood alone, unsure what to do.

No NEED TO have worried, Chiara realized. Just look at her, the wretched, panicked little creature. How forlorn and hopeless the girl looked, standing apart from the others. A delightful quiver fluttered through her at the frozen look of terror on the little twit's face. She was surprised at how much she loved that look of fear, how it excited her. How thrilling it would be to see her cower and squirm in fear, to see her surrender in submission. She walked toward her, stopped a couple of feet in front of her, and looked her up and down. "You're the new girl, aren't you?"

The girl looked too intimidated to speak. She merely nodded and attempted an awkward curtsy.

She set her lips in a confident smile, glancing sidelong at the others. Their muffled giggles gave her a cool thrill. "I am Signorina Chiara," she said, returning her eyes to the girl. "I am a professional opera singer and therefore a privileged member of Signora Malvolia's household." She paused, waiting for a response.

The girl said nothing. She merely stared up at Chiara with fearful, awe-struck eyes.

She smiled again at the other three girls, then turned with a swirl of her skirts and walked toward the harpsichord.

Maestro Tomaso plodded into the room, struggling into his musty old coat. He looked tired and stern. He took a seat at the harpsichord and began to sift through a stack of music. She stood nearby with her hands clasped in front of her, determined to exude an air of confidence and control.

The maestro fixed his eyes on the girl. "You there, what is your name?" he said gruffly. He then looked at Chiara.

She stepped toward him, smiling. "Maestro Tomaso," she said, gesturing in the girl's direction. "May I present our new student, Signorina Annina.

He regarded the girl with a studious frown. "We welcome you, Annina." There wasn't a trace of warmth in his stiff greeting. He turned his eyes from her. "Fiametta!" he called in a quavering voice. "Let us hear the cadenza you have been practicing."

Fiametta went to the harpsichord and turned to face the rest of them. Maestro Tomaso played a resounding chord, and she lunged into a rippling cascade of scales and trills. Chiara glanced at the girl and saw her mouth fall open. When Fiametta finished, every eye in the room turned to the maestro.

He stared at a score that lay open on the harpsichord rack. Finally he said, "Your scale passages are sloppy and your trills sound like the bleating of a goat. Return to your place, and don't make me have to listen to you again until you can manage those technical details with absolute precision."

The nostrils on Fiametta's prominent nose flared slightly. She nodded and walked back to where she'd been standing before, exchanging an amused glance with Marzia.

One after the other, Marzia and Ernesta were called forward and subjected to similar scrutiny by the uncompromising maestro. At last he turned to Chiara, and his eyes glistened with fondness. She smiled at him in her practiced way.

"Signorina Chiara will now demonstrate for you floundering songbirds her mastery of technical execution," he said. "What will you sing for us today, my dear girl?"

She exuded cool confidence as she glided over and murmured something to him. He scrambled through his pile of scores and laid open a thick manuscript on his rack, then waited while she arranged her voluminous silk skirts and revealing décolletage into a stiff pose. At a nod from her, the maestro began the introduction to an aria from his opera that had premiered the night before. She soared through every note with stark precision and brilliant accuracy.

When she finished, he beamed with admiration. "How proud I am to have a student as brilliant as you, Signorina Chiara."

She glanced at Annina for an instant. The girl looked utterly defeated. Chiara smiled. Undoubtedly the pathetic little thing had assumed she wouldn't be asked to sing, since this was her first lesson. Indeed, Maestro Tomaso seemed to have forgotten about her in his zeal to shower criticism on the other students and gloat over Chiara. But Chiara hadn't forgotten her. She cast the maestro another charming smile and said, "Shouldn't we allow our new student a chance to be heard?" The look of terror on the girl's face warmed her heart.

The maestro directed his hard gaze at the girl. "Yes, let us hear Signorina Annina," he said. "Annina, come forward."

She could see the girl's cheeks turn crimson with self-consciousness. Her eyes darted to the other girls, who were gazing at Annina with varying degrees of disinterest and disdain.

The maestro's cold lips were pinched. "We are almost out of time, so let us get on with this."

She shoved a score into the girl's trembling hands. "Sing this," she commanded.

The girl looked down at the score. "I don't know this," she said in a shaky whisper.

Chiara raised her carefully groomed eyebrows. "Just sing it," she said. "Surely you can read music can't you?"

To her delight the girl's face blanched and she looked as if she might become ill. Maestro Tomaso began the introduction, and she started to sing in a thin, shaky voice. When she finished there was a long silence. Chiara's eyes scanned the room. She saw expressions of disapproval and bewilderment, mingled with snickering amusement. The maestro frowned and shook his head, and Chiara could not keep her mouth from forming into a smirk.

The quiet control of the maestro's tone as he looked the girl over with critical eyes was almost frightening. "I'm sorry to have to say this, signorina, but I'm afraid your voice has serious limitations." The muffled snickering in the room grew louder, and he gave the girls a weary, ironic look. Turning back to Annina he smiled with pity, then announced the end of the lesson.

Chiara met the girl's pleading, pain-filled gaze with a frosty smile.

ANNINA SPRANG TO her feet in alarm when Chiara abruptly interrupted her early morning practice session. There she stood in the doorway, her shapely body sheathed in an alluring blue silk gown. Every one of her golden curls was perfectly in place, and her eyes gleamed like green glass. She looked down at her with a smile that was as icy as her emerald eyes. "We need to discuss the future of your singing instruction."

"I'd like to study with Don Antonio when he returns to Venice," she said, feeling a little bolder than usual.

Chiara tilted her pretty head back, and her laugh was as coldly charming as her hair and figure. "Have you met him? Have you sung for him?"

"I met him a couple of years ago in Mantua, but I haven't sung for him yet."

"You never will. Don Antonio is on an extended stay in Rome. And so, little miss prima donna, you'll have to take your singing lessons with Maestro Tomaso, like the rest of us. That is, if you're permitted to remain under his tutelage after the pathetic performances you've demonstrated so far. If you think you're going to be coddled here as you no doubt were at home by your doting Papà, you can think again."

Stinging tears came to her eyes at the flippant reminder of her father's tender love. She vainly tried to blink them away and get back to the question that was burning in her mind. "Why *is* Don Antonio in Rome?" she asked, her trembling voice displaying her desperation.

Chiara shrugged. "How should I know? Probably hobnobbing with the Pope and the rest of the Vatican luminaries. He likes to pretend he's so holy."

A surge of indignation rose in her. "Why are you talking about him like that? I thought you liked him."

"Oh? Whatever gave you that idea?"

"Well . . . you've sung in a lot of his operas, I thought."

"Maybe I have. But things can change, can't they?"

Chiara's attitude toward Don Antonio was baffling. But she had little time to dwell on that. She was too preoccupied with wondering why her father and sister hadn't answered her letters. Since the day she arrived she'd been writing to them, and she'd received no response. That was the most painful agony of all, the agony of being cut off from her family and from everyone and everything she'd known before coming to Venice. She was determined not to let anyone know her misery, so she took on an air of defiance. This didn't bode well for her relations with Maestro Tomaso.

One afternoon he called her to the front of the room. "Demonstrate for us the cadenza you have been practicing since our last lesson."

She was really beginning to despise him. As if his acrid personality wasn't bad enough, she was noticing more and more how repulsive he was to look at. His greasy hair and bulging eyes made her cringe. She gazed with disgust at his short, hunched body and weak-looking shoulders. She shuddered at the sight of him.

"Oh, uh," she stammered, struggling to come up with an excuse for why she hadn't practiced the cadenza. The truth was, the high notes he tried to make her sing made her throat feel raw and sore.

The maestro squinted at the score of vocal exercises he held in his shaking hands. The corners of his mouth dipped. "Annina," he said, with a whining edge to his voice. "What are you waiting for? You are trying my patience."

"Yes, maestro." She stared at her shambling feet.

"Return to your place then," he said finally. "You are wasting my time."

She said nothing. If anything, she was learning to conceal her inner feelings and longings. Yet above all she longed to sing in a way that would give form and meaning to her passions and make them real— not only to her, but to the world.

Maestro Tomaso didn't ask her again to sing by herself that day, but instructed her to sing as softly as possible with the group. Then, except for an occasional half annoyed, half pitying look her way, he ignored her for the rest of the lesson.

I don't need pity! she wanted to scream at him. *I need understanding!*

THAT NIGHT SHE lay on her lumpy cot, her mind wide awake. After a while she crept from beneath her quilt, wrapped a shawl around her shoulders, and peered through the window. Biting winter air seeped into the room as pellets of hail started to beat against the glass panes, and the icy waters under her window swirled violently. She shivered and tightened her shawl around herself. She could almost feel what it would be like to be out in that storm, and she ached to sing about that feeling. That's how she yearned to sing—to express how she felt inside about thrilling, even terrifying things.

Tears of frustration filled her eyes as she crawled back in bed. She pressed her wet cheek to the cold, flat pillow and squeezed her eyes shut, desperately trying to stifle her sobs. Again, she wondered why she'd received no responses from Papà or Paolina to her pleading letters. How could they ignore her agony and condemn her to feeling so alone and abandoned? Paolina's parting words had been to write to her. Well she had, almost every day. Why wasn't her sister writing back? She soon learned the reason.

A few days later she was in the practice room going over a set of vocal exercises Maestro Tomaso had assigned. The door swung open, and she looked over to see Chiara holding a small stack of mail. "I suppose you've been wondering about these letters."

"Those are my letters!" she shrieked as she grabbed at them. "How did you get them?"

Chiara smiled and pulled the little bundle out of her reach. "They were never sent. I intercepted them."

"You can't do that!"

"Oh, but I can. Signora has entrusted me with keeping track of all the mail that comes and goes here. So I have access to every letter you try to send, just as I have access to every piece of mail that arrives for you. I've confiscated and read all of them. And I intend to continue doing so. I enjoy reading the interesting things you have to say about me." Her cool smile hardened into a cold, rigid line.

She cringed to think of the things she'd written about Chiara in those letters. She felt ready to collapse in despair.

"Don't even think about reporting this to Signora or anyone else. If you do, I'll destroy the letters and say I did it to protect you—that you were corresponding with a secret lover. Imagine the consequences for you then, when Signora informs the duke. Your ridiculous dreams will come crashing down around you like a hailstorm." Her smirking lips showed how much the prospect pleased her.

If she could have found a way to kill Chiara at that moment, she would have done it. Instead, she fled to her room, threw herself across her bed, and wept. It was clear she had no recourse. Chiara had her completely in her power and would continue to torture her in every way possible.

Still sobbing, she reached for her trunk and pulled out *la moretta*. Her trembling fingers grazed the mysterious *CZL* inscription. "Who are you, *CZL* ?" she gasped between sobs. "Why aren't you protecting me as *la chiromante* promised?" Clasping the mask to her heaving chest, she felt an unbearable longing for home, for everything to be as it was before the night her mother left. Paolina's calm presence, her brothers' teasing and rough-housing, even Mamma's ravings and Papà's fussing—it all seemed like heaven compared to her present torment.

Later that day her spirits lifted a bit. Maestro Tomaso told the girls of a private concert he was planning for the following week, in which they would each sing an aria. She tingled with such excitement at the prospect of singing in a real performance, her feelings of hopelessness scattered like dead leaves in the winter wind. As the big day drew near she practiced what seemed like day and night. She went over and over the exercises the maestro had taught, to try to increase her vocal power and extend her range. Often her throat felt raw and her voice sounded strained and hoarse. But she practiced anyway, bent on conquering her vocal shortcomings. On the morning of the concert she washed, dressed, and rushed downstairs. She and the other singers were to go to Maestro Tomaso's studio for a rehearsal that morning, and then spend the afternoon resting and preparing for the big event. In her haste, she ran nearly headlong into Chiara.

The older girl's icy glare stopped her in her tracks. "I'm afraid you won't be permitted to sing in tonight's performance," she said.

She felt like the wind had been knocked out of her. "But—but *why*?" she croaked, trying hard to fight back the hot tears threatening to flood her eyes.

Chiara sighed, shook her head, and smiled sweetly. "I advised Maestro Tomaso to leave you out because of your pitiful lack of talent. Your vocal performances are awful. So I've decided you shouldn't be included in the concert."

"But my singing has really improved!" She could hear the shrillness of her own voice ring in her ears. "I've been practicing the techniques Maestro Tomaso's been teaching us, and I can sing all the arias he's taught us by heart!"

Her hysterical outburst attracted the attention of the other singers. They clustered about, eyes alert with curiosity, and she felt like the walls were closing in on her. She yearned to escape. But there was no escape from this place. She was a virtual prisoner here. And it was all because of her mother. Her mother, who was singing her heart out one moment, and in the next was gone. *If only she'd come take me away from this cold, ugly place!* She clinched her eyelids and wrapped her arms around her trembling body in an attempt to shield herself from the torment that surrounded her. She longed to be protected, comforted, and told she didn't deserve such vicious treatment. But she was startled back to her senses by Chiara's cynical laugh.

She opened her eyes to see Chiara sneering in wry derision. "Soon she'll be rocking herself the way maniacs do, in madhouses."

Terror spread through her amid the giggles and snickering. Chiara's mocking remark might well be true. What if she'd inherited her mother's unstable nature? What if she was actually going mad? All at once her fear, rage and disappointment fused into a burst of defiance. "My singing isn't awful! I can sing better than anyone! I'll sing my aria for you now!"

Chiara continued to smile and shake her head in mock regret. She looked at the other singers and rolled her eyes, then returned her taunting gaze to Annina.

She braced herself and broke into the aria she'd been practicing with such heartfelt passion. She felt her own stormy emotions course through the music and infuse it with a violent mood. She knew everyone there would see this out of control way of singing as a complete rebellion against conventional performance standards. But at that moment she didn't care.

Chiara interrupted her, her mouth twisted in amusement. "I'm sorry, but I'm afraid we can't allow singing such as yours at our concert. After all, Maestro Tomaso has a reputation to maintain. Your pathetic attempt to impress us with your unfortunate singing just now only proves your ineptitude."

As if Chiara hadn't humiliated her enough by insulting her in front of the others, she turned to them and added, "And to think the silly little creature was stupid enough to believe Don Antonio would want her as a student." Her eyes sparkled with mirth, and the other girls choked with laughter.

It all became too much. Tears streamed down her cheeks and made dark spots on her dress. She felt absolutely wretched. Now everyone would see her as ridiculous—someone to be pitied, perhaps, but not to be taken seriously. She looked about and saw faces contorted in sneers and laughter. Spinning around to run to her room, she felt a bony hand grasp her arm. She turned to find herself face to face with Signora.

"Come with me, Annina," she said, with not a drop of warmth or sympathy in her voice. She virtually dragged her to her private study and ordered her to sit.

"Now," Signora said, after arranging herself behind her desk with much bustling pomp, "what is all this commotion about?"

She was gasping and choking too much to speak. She tried to look at Signora, but the sight of the old lady's cold, lifeless eyes brought a fresh flood of tears. She had to glance down and bite her lip to quell the sobs that bubbled up from her throat.

"I believe I've spoken to you before about the unacceptability of emotional outbursts in my house," Signora went on, with a chilling lack of compassion for her misery. "It is disruptive to our routine and most disquieting for the others who reside here. I must ask you to explain yourself."

What could she say that would melt the ice in Signora's eyes and bring her to some understanding of the injustices she'd been forced to endure? So she said nothing. She merely stared at her clenched hands and quivered with suppressed sobs.

"Very well, Annina," she said at last. "If that is how you choose to behave, there will be serious consequences. I'll consider your punishment and you will be told of my decision shortly."

She raised her eyes and shuddered at the sight of Signora's hard, wizened face.

"And now," she continued, "I'll ask you to take leave of my study and return to your room, where you will stay for the remainder of the day and night, without any dinner or supper. Let your hunger be a reminder of your transgressions." Pursing her lips, she turned her attention to the papers on her desk.

Shaking with humiliation and despair, she walked past the gawking stares of the others who'd been hovering outside the door and returned to her room. Her mind was too gripped by agony to think clearly. She collapsed on her bed and buried her face in the hard pillow. Nothing would ever be right in her life again. The world had turned against her. *I might as well be in hell!* she raged inwardly. Hell could be no worse than this. She sat up and pulled *la moretta* from her trunk and glared into the mask's empty eyes. "You're silencing me, just like *la chiromante* said. But you're not protecting me." Tossing the mask to the floor, she collapsed face-down on her bed again.

By evening her belly squirmed with hunger, and she felt she was being eaten alive by anguish. Why was Chiara so determined to see her fail? Why did she hate her so much? And most puzzling of all, why did everyone worship her so? Her inexplicable power was terrifying.

The next day Chiara pulled her aside and taunted her about the concert she'd been banned from participating in the night before. "You should have heard us. We were superb. Of course, *you* will never experience the kind of ecstasy that comes from being caught in the magic of such glorious music. Your pathetic lack of talent will prevent that." The corner of her mouth curled in an ugly, distorted way.

She forced herself to swallow her fury, and with as much dignity as she could muster walked with the others to Maestro Tomaso's house. He plodded into the music room in his usual dour manner, and his eyes fell on her. "*Well*, Annina."

She straightened, startled. Her knees trembled.

"Have you learned your lesson?" he said, his face steely. "Did an evening without supper, banned from the company of your fellow singing students, teach you to obey your superiors? Are you ready to accept your humble lot as the most incompetent singer in my studio?"

"Yes, maestro," she said, struggling not to show her distress.

"Very well, then."

She caught a glimpse of Chiara's smug smile and felt her cheeks burn. Why was Maestro Tomaso being so hateful? She was baffled by his unprovoked severity. He'd always been stern and blunt, but never this mean. Chiara must be working on him, she thought. *She has Maestro Tomaso twisted around her little finger just like she has everyone else.*

Out of the corner of her eye she saw the other singers glaring at her. Inside, she seethed with an agony she was sure was well beyond their comprehension. No matter. Today she was determined to be a model of confidence and poise. She ignored the whispers and furtive glances and acted as if nothing unpleasant had ever happened to her. This seemed to have some effect. The maestro even gave her one or two approving looks, and Chiara seemed stumped for ways to get her riled.

CHIARA LOOKED AT the pathetic little creature and knew she had won. Through an artful scheme of secretive smiles and coy glances she had brought the old man around to her way of thinking. There was something about the girl's demeanor that worried her, though. That subtle lifting of the chin, the pert smile, put Chiara on alert. She sensed danger. She would have to inform the little minx of her punishment sooner than she had planned.

After the lesson Annina tried to hurry past her.

"Not so fast," she said, grasping her arm.

The girl turned to her with raised eyebrows and a tight, forced smile.

"Signora has asked me to inform you of your punishment for yesterday's outrageous outburst. You are to receive no coal for a month. Your *scaldino*," she said, caressing the word almost obscenely with her tongue, "will remain empty and cold. Have a *frigid* night's sleep."

ANNINA SHIVERED UNDER her quilt as she listened to the February winds roar. Her fingers were too stiff to move. Her *scaldino*, the ceramic pot that sat on top of the trunk at the foot of her cot, and should have been filled with glowing hot charcoal, lay empty—a gaping reminder of her undeserved punishment.

Again, nagging thoughts racked her mind. Why was she the victim of so much unjust treatment? For some reason Chiara had a grudge against her, and it was clear she wielded a great deal of power over this little world she'd created for herself. But she couldn't imagine why. What made Chiara so special? Was it that she was beautiful and skillfully talented, and Maestro Tomaso's star singing pupil? Why did everyone like her so much and give her everything she wanted? Even Don Antonio had given her leading roles in some of his operas. How could a nice person like him put up with a cunning witch like her?

The next day, Chiara approached her after the midday meal. She carried a score, and her face bore its usual haughty expression. "You might as well accept that you'll never be a singer," she said. "But that doesn't mean you can't be useful. Here's a motet Don Antonio wrote before he left for Rome. I want you to copy it and transpose it up a tone. I must sing it at Vespers this Sunday evening, and I need it in a higher key. I'll expect the copy to be completed by three o'clock this afternoon."

"But I won't have time to finish it before our singing lesson. If I do the copying now, I'll be late."

"Then I suppose that means you must work all the faster. Here's the motet. I want it delivered to my room by three o'clock sharp."

"Please, Chiara, I don't think I can do it that fast. Can't I start now and finish later? If I'm late Maestro Tomaso will be very angry, and I'm in enough trouble with him as it is."

"That's your problem, not mine," she snapped. "If you weren't so slow and inept you'd have no difficulty at all. Complete the copy as I've asked, or I'll have you expelled from Maestro Tomaso's studio. Have I made myself clear?"

"Yes," she muttered.

The copying was tedious, but she worked frantically. It wouldn't have been so difficult if she didn't have to transpose the key. Not only did every note have to be changed, but all the sharps and flats had to be altered as well. It didn't help that Don Antonio seemed to use a type of shorthand to indicate sharps and flats. Obviously he didn't have the patience to write them in either. She ran her fingers over the original score and longed to savor these notes he'd penned with his own hand. But there was no time to linger and daydream. She copied as fast as she could, yet by two o'clock she was only a little more than halfway through. She continued at a furious pace and by three o'clock felt she'd completed the task as best she could. She rushed the score, both the original and her copy, to Chiara's room, then dashed off to singing class. She had to creep out of the house, since Signora would be furious if she knew she was walking through the dark *calli* to Maestro Tomaso's house alone. She tried to sneak in his studio without being seen, but the maestro spotted her. He brought the lesson to a halt and glowered at her.

"Annina, what do you mean entering my class at this late hour?" he asked in his irritating nasal tone, his loose jowls quivering.

She cringed, and mumbled, "I'm sorry, maestro."

"Sorry are you? This will not do at all. Be silent, and I will deal with you later."

The other students stole smirking, sidelong glances at her, and it seemed a murky cloud had descended over the room. Even though she was late, the lesson seemed endless.

At last the maestro dismissed the class, then turned to her with a piercing glare. "Annina, stay where you are," he said, while the snickering little cluster of singers prepared to leave.

Her cheeks were in flames, and she felt pinpricks deep inside.

After the others had left, he ordered her to come forward. "This is absolutely the last straw, signorina. I suppose it is not enough that you subject us to your musical ineptitude. Now you have fully demonstrated your lack of respect for the rules of my studio. Worst of all, you've shown that you have no appreciation for the privileges that have been granted you despite your obvious lack of talent. You have forced me to make an example of you so my other students will see that disregard for rules and decorum will not be tolerated."

Her heart thumped and her knees went weak. She wanted to tell him this was Chiara's fault, but she knew that would do no good. Chiara's strange power seemed to extend over Maestro Tomaso as well as over Signora's entire household.

He continued. "I will discuss this situation with Signorina Chiara, and she will inform you of our decision."

She bristled with fear and hatred of them both.

Later that evening, Chiara appeared at her bedroom door with a smirk of triumph. "I've recommended to Maestro Tomaso that you be expelled from his studio, and he's agreed. So you're no longer a singing student and will be confined to this house until further notice."

She seethed with hidden rage and thought how much she detested that repulsive little man who reminded her so much of a twanging toad!

"Also, I've requested further punishment for your botched job on Don Antonio's score. Because of your carelessness and incompetence I'll have to pay someone more skilled to copy the score again. So I've asked Signora to reassign your status in this household to that of a servant. Tomorrow morning you'll begin to learn the art of dressmaking and assist our resident seamstress in sewing operatic costumes. That will be your fulltime job."

Crushing loneliness haunted her through the night. Again, her heart ached for home. But her mother had abandoned her and her father and sister had sent her to live with cruel strangers. Her worst fear had come true. There wasn't a single person in her life who cared about her at all. She was a prisoner in this dingy, suffocating place, and Chiara and her adoring Signora Malvolia were her prison guards. There was no possibility she'd ever have a moment's happiness again.

She crept to the foot of her cot and pulled *la moretta* from her trunk, her fingers pressing the mysterious inscription. Gazing into the mask's vacant eyes, she pleaded softly. "Save me, *moretta*. The whole world has turned against me. You're my only hope. *La chiromante* said you'd shield me from suffering. Please shield me now."

But you won't silence me, she vowed inwardly, pressing *la moretta* to her aching heart. *I will not be silenced!*

BLEARY-EYED AND SLUGGISH, she reported next morning to the sewing room. Pausing outside the open door, she warily glimpsed the cramped space. The room was crowded with bolts of colorful fabrics, stacks of dress patterns, bobbins of thread, and baskets overflowing with needles, pinkers, and bodkins. Her heart turned over and sank. The dreaded task she'd managed to avoid back in Mantua was now taking over her life. And this time there was no escape.

"*Benvenuta*, Annina, welcome!" The seamstress's smiling round face, moist with sweat, lit up the cluttered little room. She was the same young woman whose friendly smile she'd found so comforting her first day at Signora Malvolia's.

"*Grazie*," she said, dropping a quick curtsy.

The seamstress waved her hand, as if she were batting away a fly. "There's no need for ceremony with me. I'm not one of those puffed up singers. I only make their dresses and costumes. My name's Graziana."

She sat behind a long worktable, busy with needle and thread. Annina couldn't stop gazing into her pale blue eyes. They glittered like ponds in the sunlight and seemed to absorb and reflect everything around her.

"Well sit down," she said, nodding toward the stool across the table. Her eyes darted around the room. "As you can see, I'm long overdue for some help here."

"I'm afraid I won't be much help." She nervously slid onto the stool, her shoulders tense. "I'm not very good at sewing."

"Don't worry," she said, leaning forward with a sly smile. "I'll only give you the easy work. Nobody needs to know. Now why don't you cut out this *scialletto* for me."

Graziana handed her a short length of white muslin with the paper pattern already pinned to it, and a pair of scissors. She snipped carefully around the simple neck-piece outline and felt her shoulders start to relax.

"There, that's painless, isn't it?" she said, her smile turning cozy.

She nodded and tried to smile back.

Graziana peered at her with puckered lips. "You've hardly said a word since you've come in here. Are you always this quiet?"

"No, not always," she said, her cheeks warming.

Her lips eased back into a smile. "So tell me, what's a little thing like you doing all alone in Venice? You can't be more than ten or eleven."

Heat rose in her cheeks as she glanced down at her childish figure. She felt skinny and gawky. "Actually I'm twelve," she said in a small voice.

"You're lucky to be so slender," she went on, without missing a stitch. When I was your age I was round as a barrel. Still am, as you can see." She laughed good-naturedly.

She laughed with her, and the weight of her embarrassment lifted. "Truthfully I'd rather be plump," she said, thinking of Chiara's lush bosom. "Men seem to like that."

"That all depends. I'm eighteen and I still haven't snagged one."

"Oh you will, Graziana," she said, not wanting to spoil the seamstress's cheerful mood. "You're so friendly and kind. I'm sure you'll find an *amico* soon."

"And is that why you're here, Annina?" she said, her eyes coy. "In search of love?"

If only she knew how close she was to the truth. But the love her heart craved had nothing to do with romance. She hesitated a moment, then took a deep breath. "I came to Venice to study singing with a certain teacher."

"Oh? Who's that?"

"A famous violinist and opera impresario . . . They call him *il prete rosso*." She bit her lip, waiting for Graziana to laugh in disbelief.

But she didn't laugh. "Ah," she said, turning her eyes back to her sewing.

She knew something, Annina could feel it. Yet she also sensed Graziana was not one to hold gossip in for long. She kept her eyes on her work and waited for the seamstress to go on. But she continued with her sewing in silence.

She took a deep breath. "When I got here a few weeks ago, he'd just left for Rome," she finally said. "I have no idea why."

"Mmm."

Her heart beat anxiously. "Graziana, do you know why he left Venice?"

She glanced up with a shrewd gleam in her eye. "I guess you haven't heard. He had to leave Venice soon after his last opera here, *La verità*—something, I think."

"*La verità in cimento?*"

"Yes, that's it. The contested truth. Interesting title. How did you know about it?"

"My patron, the duke, told me about it right before Don Antonio left Mantua. But tell me, Graziana, what did the opera have to do with his leaving Venice?"

She sucked in her lips and her eyes brightened. "You know how the singers here talk. I heard he felt forced to leave because of the vicious pamphlet that got passed around about him and *La verità* soon after its first performance."

"Who wrote the pamphlet, and what did it say?" she asked, intrigued.

"A nobleman named Benedetto Marcello. He fancies himself a composer, and his family are part owners of the San Angelo Theater. Anyway, he decided *La verità* was too unconventional and wrote a nasty satire about it, called *Il Teatro alla moda*, The Theater of Fashion. In it he makes fun of everything about Don Antonio and *La verità*. Marcello thinks opera should be stuffy and dignified and feels *il prete rosso*'s works are too unconventional. The pamphlet spread like wildfire and caused a huge stir."

"But I thought Don Antonio's operas were very popular in Venice."

"Annina, when you've lived here long enough you'll realize Venetians love anything that's new and different. They're fickle as flies and change their tastes as often as they change their Carnival masks. A lampoon from a bigwig like Marcello can make them flip-flop faster than you can blink."

She fumed inwardly. *How unfair! Don Antonio's operas are brilliant.* It was obvious he poured so much of himself into his music, which was what gave it the power to captivate her so. If he worried about boring "convention," his music wouldn't have that power. Then she had a surprising thought: *He's like me. I don't like convention either. I feel stifled and frustrated by it.* Now she realized they both had to put up with the same kind of injustice. At once her own problems, which had loomed so large in her mind for so long, seemed trivial compared to his. This made her even more determined to stick to her convictions and not allow Chiara or anyone else to bully her.

Yet there was no escape from Chiara's taunting. Lately she seemed to be lurking around every corner, waiting for an opportunity to chide and mock her. One night she cried herself to sleep after Chiara appeared at her bedside to jeer about the stolen letters she still hoarded. Graziana noticed her red eyes the next morning, and after a bit of cajoling, she poured out her feelings about Chiara.

"Why is she so hateful to me?"

"Because as she sees it you took away her main source of income, and knocked her down a peg besides."

"Why would she think that?"

She looked up from her sewing and raised her eyebrows. "Isn't it obvious? She'd been under the patronage of the Duke of Massa Carrara since she first came to Venice, but early last month he suddenly decided to drop her."

Her lips parted as she gave a little gasp. "That's when he wrote my father offering to pay for me to come here."

Graziana smiled knowingly. "Now you're catching on."

She thought a moment. "How long *has* Chiara been in Venice?"

"About five years, far as I know. That's how long she's lived at Signora's anyway, which is almost as long as I've been here."

"What was she like when you first knew her?"

"She poured on the charm with anyone she thought she could manipulate. She's good at that."

At that moment, Marzia came in with a dress to be altered. Graziana put down her sewing and went to see what was needed. The interruption ended their discussion. She would have to wait for another opportunity to hear the rest of the story about Chiara.

The next morning she found herself alone again with Graziana. "Please, Graziana," she said, "finish what you started to say yesterday about Chiara. Why does she have so much power here at Signora's house?"

She cupped her hand around her mouth and leaned across the table. "There's a rumor that the people who raised her in Mantua adopted her as an infant, and that her real mother is Bianca Stramponi, one of the most beautiful and sought-after courtesans in Venice. All the rich nobles hanker for her. No one's supposed to know Chiara's her bastard daughter, but I've heard it whispered."

"What's a courtesan?"

"*Dio mio*, Annina. How have you managed to stay so innocent? A courtesan is a charming, highly cultivated woman who makes her living granting favors to wealthy men. Venice is teaming with them."

"What kinds of favors?"

"Has no one ever told you anything? Suffice it to say the kinds of favors courtesans bestow on their male clients have to do with romance and lovemaking."

"*Oh,*" she said, blushing.

Graziana leaned closer, eyes darting. "But let me tell you more about Chiara. They say her father's a rich Austrian nobleman and a great patron of the opera. It's rumored that he's blond, blue-eyed, dashing, and handsome, or at least he used to be. And he likes to have his way with the ladies. I've heard he even had a romance with Signora Malvolia many years ago, before he jilted her and left her *senza quattrini*, penniless."

She could hardly contain her hilarity. It was impossible to imagine Signora having a romance with anyone, least of all a handsome nobleman.

Graziana shared her barely suppressed mirth. "I know, it sounds absurd. But apparently Signora was quite alluring in her younger days, and that's how she lured the rich Austrian into sponsoring her opera career. Though now that she's old and dried out and no man will so much as look at her, she's turned bitter as wormwood." She giggled. "Anyway, when Chiara first came here she used to boast to everyone that her father was a powerful prince who'd one day appear to launch her on a great operatic career."

"Did she really believe he would?"

"She used to believe it. But as year after year went by and he never showed up, she lost hope. That's when she started to turn nasty."

"But that still doesn't explain why Chiara has so much control around here."

"Don't you see, Annina? Signora is a sour old maid, reduced to running a boarding house after a glamorous stage career. She knows Chiara's father is her former lover. And just like Chiara, she's allowed herself to believe that if and when he returns he'll take her away from all this. Ha! Wouldn't that be the day?" She gave her a sidelong glance, giggled, and went back to her sewing.

SHE LAY AWAKE for a long time that night and thought about the things Graziana had told her. She had a better idea now why Chiara had so much power, and she realized she'd have to be very careful around her. Chiara had important people on her side and would be sure to ruin any chance she might have of following her dream. Gloom shrouded her. Nothing was turning out as she'd hoped.

Chapter Five

Inside the chapel door, Antonio dipped his fingers in icy holy water and made the sign of the cross. With violin case in one hand and a large portfolio and round-brimmed hat under his other arm, he hastened toward the choir loft stairs. Shrouded in his priestly black cassock and mantle he hardly noticed the cold. It was *Mercoledì delle Cenere*, Ash Wednesday, and the Pietà's all female chorus and orchestra, the *figlie del coro*, were already in the loft, barely visible behind the iron grill that protected them from public view. At the top of the stairs he paused a moment to catch his breath. His return to Venice coincided with the holy season of Lent, which meant there was nary a break in his work schedule. No matter. His work at the Pietà was more of a ministry than labor.

The girls were in their places, awaiting him in silence. Each wore a red dress, symbolizing the Pietà's mission of "mercy." And that's exactly what the Pietà was for him. A merciful respite from the giddy rush of near constant work and pressure that plagued his life in the outside world. The girls' excitement the day before at his unexpected return had almost made it all seem worthwhile.

He glanced down at the altar, which was bathed in candlelight that flickered and bounced off the stone walls and gave the entire sanctuary a mystical glow. The rich scent of incense flooded his nostrils, and he could smell the sanctity of the little church. He gazed at the crucifix above the altar, and despite the frigid air, warmth enfolded him.

The liturgy commenced with a solemn chant:

Exaudi nos, Domine, quoniam benigna est misericordia tua.
Hear us, O Lord, for thy mercy is kind.

So peaceful. How grateful he was that the solemnity of the day's liturgy precluded rousing fanfares and sparkling motets. He savored the tranquility.

At the end of Mass the red-clad *figlie del coro*, led by their *maestra*, filed down the stairs and out the main door. Each bore a faint cross of ashes on her brow. He gathered his music scores and headed down from the choir loft. At the foot of the stairs he paused, set his violin case and leather folder on the floor and threw his mantle over his shoulders. With his violin in his left hand and his case of scores and hat under his other arm, he headed for the main door.

He heard the sound of scuffling feet, followed by a girlish cry. *"Don Antonio!"* He turned to see a slender, hooded figure standing alone in the empty sanctuary, shivering, a smudge of ashes barely visible on her forehead.

"Chi xe?" he asked, in his native Venetian, squinting in the darkness. "Who is it?"

As she drew closer he could see it was not actually a hood, but rather a shawl that covered her head and face. She pulled at the shawl and it slipped from her head.

A little thrill of recognition swept through him. "Annina?"

"Yes, it's me," she said shyly, bobbing a curtsy.

"*Annina*. Why, I almost didn't recognize you, you've grown so. How long has it been?"

"About two years," she said, her voice shaking slightly.

"And here you are in Venice. I had no idea. When did you arrive?"

"Early last month. The Duke of Massa Carrara is paying for me to live and study here."

He felt a faint lurch in his chest. "Is that so? Who are you studying with?"

"Maestro Tomaso Albinoni. I'd hoped to study with you, but you were in Rome when I got here." She hesitated. "I heard about that man who wrote mean things about you, how he forced you to leave Venice. I'm sorry."

"Who? Oh, you mean that scribbler Marcello." He chuckled. "It would take a lot more than him and his silly doodlings to drive me out of Venice. I went to Rome of my own accord."

There was a pause. She looked up at him and smiled, even as he detected the corners of her mouth twitching.

He returned her smile. "Where are you living, Annina?"

"Near here, at Signora Malvolia's house. She allowed me to walk the few steps from her door to the Church of the Pietà to attend Mass. The others came to the early morning Mass, but I couldn't, because . . . it was my practice time." She pulled her shawl back over her head and gave a little shiver.

"Well, that's on the way to my house. Come, I'll walk you home. They're probably wondering where you are."

He transferred his violin to his right hand and held the heavy wooden door for her. Outside, he placed his black clerical hat on his head. The sun had gone down and the dark waters of the San Marco Canal were aglow with soft moonlight. Ash Wednesday not only marked the beginning of Lent, but the end of Carnival, so the streets and canals were now quiet and almost deserted. *Deo gratias.*

He breathed in the tranquil air, then looked down at her. "How are your studies going, Annina?"

She stopped and stared at the cold gray blocks of pavement. He waited, sensing her anxiety, wondering what was wrong.

Her eyes met his. "All right, I suppose," she said, and her voice broke.

He moved his violin to his other hand and put a comforting arm around her. Her sweet scent brought memories of his conversation with her that evening at the Palazzo Ducale—her delicate white dress, the adoring look in her eyes. A surge of protectiveness gripped his heart. "Tell me what's troubling you," he said gently.

She leaned into him and started to weep softly. "Maestro Tomaso doesn't think I have the voice to sing opera. He and his other students are always putting down my singing, even though I practice all the time and try my best to improve. And now he's angry with me for being late and has expelled me from his singing class, and—" Her shaking voice, interspersed with choking sobs, broke off.

He squeezed his arm around her a little tighter, trying to think of something encouraging to say. She pressed closer to him for a moment, then backed away slightly, sniffling and wiping her nose with the back of her hand. He reached in his pocket and handed her his handkerchief.

"I'm sorry for making such a scene," she said, flushing and dabbing tears.

"You've had a hard time of it so far," he said quietly. "I understand why you feel so distraught. I only wish I'd been here to help you." Then an idea occurred to him. "I'll tell you what,

Annina. Why don't you come to my house tomorrow afternoon for a lesson? I'll send someone to fetch you."

"You mean, you want me to study with you? Even after what Maestro Tomaso said about my voice?"

"*Non importa*, that doesn't matter. Albinoni is old-fashioned and his concept of theatrical singing is limited. Besides, the poor wretch has been in a state of gloom since his wife died last year, so you mustn't take what he's told you to heart." He paused, remembering the fiery look of determination in her eyes that night at the Palazzo Ducale, when her sister tried to stop her from talking to him. He went on. "What's important is that you *do* have a natural flair for drama. I sensed that the first time I laid eyes on you. I can teach you everything you need to know about singing technique."

She blinked back her tears and smiled.

They were in front of Signora's house, and the old lady appeared at the door. "Annina, there you are! I told you to come home immediately after—" she started to scold, until she spotted Antonio. Her eyelids fluttered with surprise. "Maestro! What an unexpected pleasure."

"*Buona sera*, Signora Malvolia. It's all right, Annina's been with me."

"Has she, indeed?" She looked astounded.

"*Sì*. And I'm glad to have the opportunity to inform you myself, Signora, that I've asked her to come to my house for singing lessons, starting tomorrow afternoon. I'll send a gondolier around for her at four o'clock."

"Well, I—" she began to stammer.

He silenced her with a charming smile and tipped his hat. "It's been a pleasure, Signora. *Buona notte*, Annina. *A domani*, I'll see you tomorrow."

ANNINA HURRIED TO her room, giddy with excitement. Tossing her shawl across the bed, she realized she still clutched Don Antonio's handkerchief in her trembling hand. She held it to her nose and savored once more his salty, fiery scent. Tingling euphoria spread through her.

"So," came a sharp voice from the doorway, startling her back to her senses. Chiara stood at the door with pursed lips. "It seems you're craftier than I'd suspected. You've managed to use your artful wiles to persuade Don Antonio to give you a private lesson. I would never have believed this audacity even of *you*, little Miss Annina."

How in the world did she know? No doubt Signora couldn't wait to report to her.

"I didn't try to persuade him," she protested. "It was his idea."

"Indeed?" Chiara's pursed lips hardened into a smirk. "And just what do you think could have caused him to have such an absurd idea?"

"He knows my father. My father worked with his opera company in Mantua. I met him there, and he remembers me."

"Ah. But he's never heard you try to sing, has he?"

"Not yet."

"Of course he hasn't. Would he be insane enough to throw away his time on you if he had? Now think about this, you sly little imp. How will he feel about you when he realizes you've finagled him into wasting his valuable time?"

"I don't think he's going to feel that way," she said, not too convincingly.

"Oh no? I think you're wrong. So I've decided to do you a favor. I'll go to Don Antonio in advance and warn him about you. I'll be there when you arrive for your lesson. I'll remind him that you're just a foolish little girl and do my best to shield you from his annoyance." Her smile was so sickeningly sweet Annina felt like gagging.

That night she tossed restlessly in bed. Despite Chiara's threats, she was glowing with such happiness over her unexpected reunion with Don Antonio she almost didn't notice the room's icy chill. She simply *had* to tell someone about it. But who could she tell? No one, not even Graziana. As much as she trusted her dear friend, she'd die before she admitted to her how his comforting touch made her feel.

She decided to write a letter to Paolina. She'd always been able to tell her anything. Eagerly she lit a candle and rifled through her trunk for paper, quill pen, and ink. Her fingers brushed the velvety darkness of *la moretta*. "Please don't let Chiara ruin things for me," she whispered. But she left the mask in the trunk and closed the lid. She didn't want to hide behind *la moretta*, and she wouldn't be muzzled. Back in bed with her lapboard, she began to pour out her feelings:

Dearest Paolina,

Tonight something absolutely wonderful has happened! After a wretched, miserable month here at Signora Malvolia's house, Don Antonio has come back into my life. How can I express how he makes me feel? I'm tingling inside so much I can't sleep. I can't stop thinking about how I felt when he put his arm around me. And the way he looked at me, his eyes full of tenderness and understanding. The memory is so delicious I feel like I'm melting inside, over and over again. He's a burst of sunshine after a month of cold, rainy gloom!

I'll stop now, because I don't know what else to say. I want to be well rested for my lesson with him tomorrow. But how can I sleep? I'm too happy to sleep. I just want to keep reliving the sweetness of those few moments with him.

Your Loving Sister,
Annina

Her heart fluttered softly as she folded the letter and hid it in her trunk. She knew she'd never mail it. But writing it felt good. It helped define her feelings and put them in a safe, private place. She'd be able to read and relive those feelings in secret anytime she wanted.

CHIARA THOUGHT BACK to when she first met Antonio, how she'd relished the nascent stirrings of the power a woman can hold over a man. A delightful shiver ran through her at the memory. With his natural charisma and almost boyish charm he was a magnet for women, but had no amorous involvement she could detect. Yet she was so certain she had found a secret place in his heart, a place perhaps even he hadn't known was there. Without hesitation she'd slithered right in and filled it. She resurrected the ghost of passion in him, or so she thought. At the time she felt so confident she could have him. What that might entail, shadowy though it was, was intoxicating and she wanted it desperately.

She wondered what she would wear when she saw him. Should she don her flowing black lace-embellished *robe volante*, with its subtle suggestion of casual, bedchamber intimacy? Or perhaps she should choose the more formal, figure-flattering blue silk gown. Which would beguile him more? In the end she chose the blue silk, more interested in how the cut of the bodice would complement the swell of her breasts.

A smile flitted over his face when he saw her, but there was something distant in his dark blue eyes, a remoteness. He greeted her with almost frightening politeness. "*Piacere*, signorina," he said, with a slight bow, chilling in its formality. "To what do I owe the pleasure of this visit?"

Despite his coolness, at the sight of him the thrilling force that had flowed into her at their very first meeting coursed through her now, filling the cold and empty places that had been gaping inside her during his absence. Aware of her own allure, she fixed a sultry stare on him, confident she was having the effect that she had hoped for. The moment seemed right to bring up the reason for her visit.

"I understand our new little songbird, Annina, is soon to arrive for a lesson. I thought you should see this before she gets here, how she butchered the score to the last motet you wrote for me."

His slight smile wavered and vanished. "That was always your way, wasn't it?" he said evenly, and without warmth.

"I'm sure I don't know what you mean, maestro," she said, cautiously.

"I mean the way you seem to delight in sabotaging the good efforts of others, in this case undermining the musical studies of an innocent girl." His initial coolness had given way to irritation.

"I?—undermine her studies? What a thing to say, maestro. It was Maestro Tomaso who decided Annina should be punished for her careless work on your score, and for her tardiness. I tried to intercede for her, but the maestro insisted on it. It's not her fault of course, poor little thing. It was silly of her to think she could handle the rigors of musical training here in Venice. Just take a look at this," she urged, holding the score out to him.

He took the score and glanced at it briefly, then sighed with impatience as he handed it back to her. "Your foolish pretension is matched only by your ignorance, Chiara. Signorina Annina is not in training to be a copyist. If you hadn't forced her to do work she's not responsible for, she wouldn't have been late. I've already spoken to Tomaso about this, and I think I have an idea what actually happened."

Flustered by his quick perception, she licked her lips and struggled to gather her thoughts. But she was at a loss for words. She shrugged her shoulders with feigned indifference, pouting.

A smile played around the corners of his mouth that was almost mocking, yet somehow not unkind. "I like your wit more than your self pity, Chiara."

His easy ability to see through her was disconcerting, but she would not allow him to unhinge her. She merely nodded once, her jaw tight.

Her eyes darted to the studio door as it creaked open. The girl stood alone, looking pitifully pale and awkward. *Wretched, panicked little creature*, she thought, smiling inwardly.

At once Antonio's face brightened. "Annina, *buon giorno*. Thank you for coming."

How pathetic. Look at that ridiculous expression of starry-eyed wonder. The girl has no idea of the subtleties involved in gaining power over a man—especially a man like Antonio. Yet she exudes that dangerous combination of helpless innocence and worshipful adoration men seem strangely drawn to.

Surely in the end my own refined, womanly charm will appeal to him more. He had even commented, however wryly, that he liked her wit. Her eyes flitted over Annina, but lingered on Antonio. She noted his warm, almost fatherly gaze as he smiled at the girl. She didn't recall him ever looking at her quite like that. Suddenly a stinging darkness swept over her. Was it jealousy? Perhaps. The jealousy she had always felt for the tender bonds between others—between fathers and daughters, between lovers—gnawed inside her like a dull pain.

Antonio's gaze shifted to Chiara, and his smile stiffened.

"*Grazie*, signorina, that will be all."

"But, maestro—" she began to protest.

"I said that will be all," he said more firmly. "Now if you'll kindly excuse us."

The sting of his rejection smarted like a slap. Glaring at him, she raised her chin, and bit her lip to stop its trembling. Her eyes drifted briefly to the girl. Did she detect a slight smirk on little miss songbird's face?

"Oh, and one more thing, Chiara," he said. "I trust you'll make sure Signorina Annina has sufficient coal. It's not healthy to sleep in an unheated room in this dank weather."

What does he think I am, her chamber maid? Blinded by tears of outrage she dared not allow to spill, she brushed past him. She knew this should be the end, that she should put him out of her mind once and for all. But some part of her could not let him go. In the hall she grabbed her cloak, and staggering under the weight of her own fury, fled into the gold-tinged gloom of winter dusk. Numb with cold, a damp cold that chilled her to the bone, she tightened her cloak around her shivering body as she listened to the sinister echo of the seagulls' cries, an echo that resounded in the emptiness of her heart.

Then a resolution sprang to her mind with startling energy. It surprised her how much it calmed and yet excited her at the same time. An exhilarating desire for revenge clawed inside her as her plan took shape.

THE GONDOLIER HAD arrived promptly at four, just as Don Antonio promised. Chiara was nowhere in sight, and Annina shuddered to think what she might be up to.

The boat ride was brief, just a short distance up the San Marco

Canal, and down a narrow side canal to the *Ponte del Paradiso*, Paradise Bridge. She could have easily walked there herself. But it was considered improper for girls to walk the streets of Venice alone, even for short distances. Her insides felt as agitated as the canal waters that churned in the winter wind. What would Don Antonio think of her singing? What if she disappointed him, like she'd disappointed everyone else?

The gondolier helped her from the boat, and she knocked at the door overlooking the canal, her heart racing.

A slender woman answered. "You must be Annina."

"*Sì*, signora."

The lady seemed close to Don Antonio's age and had his golden hair and warm, inviting smile. "Please come in, Annina. I'm Margarita, Antonio's sister," she said, taking her hand. "He's with someone, but he's expecting you. Follow me, dear."

Margarita's friendliness eased her agitation, but she was still apprehensive about the lesson. She was also embarrassed about her childish behavior the night before. How could she expect him to take her seriously when she'd carried on like a frantic little girl?

The door of the room where Margarita led her was ajar. She rapped, pushed it open, and smiled. "Go right in, Annina."

Chiara's presence was unnerving, but Don Antonio put her in her place. Annina had to struggle to keep the corners of her mouth from curling up. What a relief when she'd finally left, though she couldn't forget the stinging glare Chiara had cast her as she swept out of the room.

Now Don Antonio was looking at her with an encouraging smile. "Well, Annina, what would you like to sing for me?"

At last she allowed her mouth to curl into a grin. "I'd like to sing an aria you wrote, *"Quanto m'alletta."*

"Ah, Cleonilla's Act I aria from *Ottone in Villa*, my very first opera. Let me see, though. I'm not sure where I put the score." He went to the credenza and began looking through a pile of thick manuscripts.

"It's all right," she said. "I don't need the music."

"No? Then we'll both make due with our memories."

He went to the harpsichord and started the aria's introduction. Her throat clenched, and she had a hard time taking a deep enough breath. But her fear started to dissipate as soon as she began to sing.

> *How alluring is the dewy grass,*
> *how pleasing that pretty flower.*
> *The perfume of one is fragrant with love,*
> *the green of the other fills my tender heart with hope.*

When the aria was over, Don Antonio looked like he was deep in thought. He sighed and frowned.

Her heart pelted her breastbone.

"Annina," he said finally, "you sing with much sincerity and conviction. But there are some problems with your technique."

A sinking feeling swept over her. She bit her lip and stared at the floor.

"Now, now," he hastened to add, "it's nothing to be disturbed about. Your technical problems are quite fixable. Here, let me show you."

He rose from the harpsichord bench and came over to her. "First of all, your jaw is much too tight." He touched the sides of her face very lightly. "Relax your jaw, and your throat will open up as well."

She felt the hardness of his left-hand fingertips, toughened by years of furious violin playing. It felt nice. Her jaw loosened, and the tightness in her face and throat began to melt.

"Very good," he said. "Now, the other problem we need to address is your breathing. You're inhaling in a shallow way, from your chest, and so you're not able to get in enough air to sustain a full, rounded tone. You need to breathe from here. May I?"

She had no idea what he meant to do, but she nodded her assent.

He stepped to her side and put his left hand on her shoulder, then placed the palm of his right hand just below her ribs. "Push my hand out while you breathe in slowly, and keep your shoulders relaxed."

She inhaled and felt the gentle pressure of his hand. She was stiff and nervous at first, but soon her breathing fell into a comfortable rhythm that emanated from deep within her.

"*Eccelente,*" he said. "Excellent." He went back to the harpsichord and played a single note. "Drop your jaw, breathe like I showed you, and sing this note on "ah."

Trying hard to remember everything he'd told her, she intoned the note very softly.

"Lovely. Now let's see if we can make it even better." He took up his violin and bowed the same note, this time drawing out the sound in a long, pulsating tone. "Close your eyes and try to match the sound of the violin. Pretend you *are* the violin."

He played the note again, and her voice and the violin's sad tremolo became a single sound. He played down a tone, and her voice moved with it effortlessly. He continued moving down, then back up to higher and higher notes. At last he put down his violin. "I hear tremendous improvement already. Let's try the aria again." He returned to the harpsichord, and she repeated the aria.

"That was so much better," he said when she was finished. "But I hear now another difficulty. The piece is too high for you. Your natural voice is centered in a lower range. Try again in a different key."

He began the aria once more, in a lower key. She glided into the opening notes, and the slight tension that lingered in her throat and jaw dissolved into velvety comfort. Her voice sailed through the aria with more ease, and more pleasure, than she ever thought possible.

"*Brava*, that was wonderful. Despite what anyone has told you, you must understand that your technical shortcomings have nothing to do with your inner talent. The difficulties you've been experiencing are merely external problems that are quite separate from your natural abilities and can be overcome with study and practice."

A thrill stirred in her.

He stood and began to walk about the room. "Now I'll tell you what really impresses me about your singing. You sing with a heartfelt fervor that brings the emotional meaning of the aria to life. That's something that can't be taught. Most singers act as if technical perfection is an end in itself and have no sensitivity for the real substance of opera. They don't understand that technique is merely a tool for expressing the feelings within. Opera is drama, not a display of vocal skills. You have a natural aptitude for manifesting emotional depth, which is the true essence of drama, and that's a priceless gift."

Her heart flurried, only this time it wasn't from fear. Her face lit up with a brilliant smile.

He paused in his pacing and smiled with her. "*Dimmi*, Annina, tell me. How do you know this aria?"

"My mother used to sing it with me. But—she went away and took her music scores with her." Her voice grew a little unsteady, but she made an effort to keep smiling. "It's all right, though, because I can sing all her music by heart."

He gazed at her, and his smile was warm. "Your talent continues to amaze me, Annina. I have students at the Pietà who've been studying for years and don't have your musical memory."

She grinned with delight, then felt compelled to ask him a question that had been weighing on her mind. "Don Antonio, with all your teaching and composing and everything else you do, how do you find time to say Mass?"

"I don't."

"But I thought all priests had to say Mass."

"Most do, but I was excused from the obligation soon after I was ordained. You see, I have an ailment that prevents me from standing and speaking for long periods of time, which of course celebration of the Mass requires."

"Is that the same ailment that kept you inside when you were little?"

He cocked his head slightly. "How did you know about that?"

"My mother told me. She used to live across the square from your family, when you lived in the Bragora district."

"I had no idea you knew so much about my past."

"That's about all I know. My mother only lived there for a short time, when you were about five."

He chuckled. "I'm sure she remembers that period of my life much better than I do."

"The main thing she told me about was your violin playing, how everyone in the neighborhood loved the sound of your music drifting across the Campo San Giovanni."

"I never realized my fame went back so far."

"Oh it does. Mamma said there was all sorts of talk about your genius, even then. She even has an album of some of your earliest opera arias. I always wondered how she got it."

"I'm sure there are many copies of my arias floating around that I have no idea of. Your mother could have found the scores at a bookseller's shop for all I know."

"I thought you might have given them to her."

He smiled kindly and shook his head. Then his brow wrinkled in concern. "Annina, what did you mean when you said your mother went away?"

She lowered her gaze. "It was three years ago. The same day I first saw you at the Teatro Arciducale. Mamma got angry that night because Papà gave my brothers money. The next morning when I woke up she was gone."

"And you haven't seen or heard from her since?"

She shook her head, then slowly lifted her eyes to his.

His gaze was steady and kind, and a comforting feeling spread through her.

SHE RETURNED TO Signora's house feeling happier than she'd felt in a very long time. She ran to her bedroom, reclined on her bed and hugged her pillow, rejoicing to see that her *scaldino* had already been filled with fresh coal. Then she heard the rustle of silk and light footsteps in the hall. She jolted to a sitting position.

Chiara stood in the doorway, smirking. "I suppose you're feeling rather good about yourself."

She could think of no response, so she waited to hear what Chiara would say next.

"You've managed to take full advantage of Don Antonio's good nature, and now you think you're on top of the world, that he'll solve all your problems and your foolish dreams will at last come true. Correct me if I'm wrong." Her smirking mouth hardened into a grim, lifeless smile.

"I haven't thought anything like that," she said, trying to quell the tremor in her throat. "Don Antonio only told me that I have a lot of dramatic potential."

"Did he now? And how will he feel about your dramatic potential when I inform him you've been writing secret letters that tell all about your crazed infatuation with him?"

She barely managed a pinched whisper. "*What?* How do you know about that letter?"

"Because I've so enjoyed reading it." Her hard smile took on a mocking look. "Private correspondence can be so deliciously revealing."

She lunged for her trunk and groped through it with shaking hands.

"Don't bother," Chiara said. "I have it." She pulled the letter from her bodice and opened it, as her face froze into a mask of feigned captivation. "Let's see, it's all so interesting. Ah, here's a particularly intriguing passage: *I'm tingling inside so much that I can't sleep. I can't stop thinking about how I felt when he put his arm around me. And the way he looked at me, his eyes full of tenderness and understanding. The memory is so delicious I feel like I'm melting inside, over and over again.*" Her smug smile worked its way into a harassing grin.

"Give it to me!" she rushed to grab the letter. She wanted to shake Chiara senseless. She wanted to scratch her eyes out!

"Oh my," she said, stepping back and holding up her free hand in mock fear. "Throwing a tantrum will get us nowhere, will it? This fascinating little gem is perfectly safe—for now. And if you're a good, obedient little girl and do exactly as I say, I'll try to see that it doesn't fall into the wrong hands." She tucked the letter into her bodice and left the room.

She groped through her trunk for *la moretta*. Yes, she was still there. Her eyes fell on the mysterious inscription, *CZL*. *"Who are you?"* she gasped, in a trembling whisper. Shaking with suppressed sobs she pressed the mask to her face and clenched the *bottone* between her teeth. *I might as well be mute*, she wailed silently. *Chiara now has the power not only to humiliate me but to make Don Antonio lose all respect for me. I'll have to do whatever she says. I can't risk having him see that letter!*

The next day, she wondered how she would get through her singing lesson. Chiara's threats clutched her heart like a vise. She wanted to tell Don Antonio what Chiara had done to her, so he could make things right again. But she knew if she said a word to him about her, she would somehow find out and make things worse than they already were. She stood outside his studio and heard the sweet strain of his violin from behind the door. Determined to put Chiara out of her mind, she took a deep breath and knocked boldly. The violin tapered to a halt, and he invited her in.

Perhaps her smile was too fixed. He seemed to notice something, and his pleasant expression faded to a look of concern. "Are you all right?" he asked.

"Oh, I'm fine." Her voice didn't sound like her own. There was a false brightness to it.

He didn't look convinced. "You don't have to tell me what's wrong if you don't want to. But I'd like you to channel the feeling you're experiencing into your singing. I want you to sing that feeling."

Her cheeks ached from her forced smile, and she blinked hard to keep tears from spilling.

"Do you know this aria, '*Solo quella guancia bella*'?" He handed her a score. "It's from one of my recent operas, *La verità in cimento*."

"Oh," she said, her interest roused. "I've heard a lot about that opera, but I don't know the music." She held the score in front of her and squinted through blurry eyes.

Only that beautiful,
charming proud face
has my love and mercy.

Taking a deep breath, she tried to concentrate on the things he'd taught her the day before—to relax her jaw and breathe from below her ribs. Before she knew it the aria was streaming from her throat, and she felt something close to ecstasy. The sobs that had threatened to spurt out transformed into glorious musical sound, and she was transported to a world far away from Chiara and her threats. The aria ended, but the spellbinding truth, the astonishing candor, of his music kept singing in her heart.

He looked at her steadily. "Whatever it is that's hurting you is fueling your singing with a dramatic immediacy that's truly extraordinary."

She shook with excitement. "Do you really think so?"

"*Assolutamente*, Annina, absolutely. You have a rare ability to fill your musical performance with an emotional sincerity that speaks directly to the heart."

She wanted to hug him, but she didn't dare move. So she just gazed at him, basking in his approval.

He smiled. "If you can develop your physical technique to match your dramatic instincts you'll have an outstanding career ahead of you."

Could she be dreaming? Was it possible she was standing face to face with the world-famous composer Antonio Vivaldi and he was saying such things to her?

"So now we'll begin your technical training in earnest." He rose from the harpsichord, picked up his violin and played a short phrase. "Repeat that on *ah*," he instructed.

She did as he said, and he listened closely. He played the phrase again. "Now on *eeh*." They went through all the vowel sounds. "Again." He started to repeat the exercise a half-tone higher. After a few repetitions on progressively higher tones she grew tired and her shoulders sagged.

"Don't let your breath support collapse." He wrinkled his brow and without missing a beat continued up another semi-tone.

She squared her shoulders and breathed deeply.

Then, "Your throat is closing. Let your jaw hang loose, and *relax*." He continued the exercise without a moment's pause, driving her to higher and higher pitch levels. When she thought her head would burst if he made her sing any higher, he stopped, lowered the violin from his shoulder, and gave her an exasperated look. "You have a long way to go with your technique." He was quite worked up, and she wasn't sure if he was angry with her or merely anxious for her to succeed.

She looked at him uncertainly. "I'm sorry."

"What's there to be sorry for? You simply must work, that's all. Talent will only get you so far. Musical perfection requires years of unrelenting practice. If you're willing to commit yourself to that, I'm willing to work with you." His encouraging smiles of just a few moments ago were gone. Now he looked intense and serious.

"I'm willing," she said, trying to sound more confident than she felt.

He gazed at her, frowning, then his mouth relaxed into a smile. "Annina," he said, sounding much calmer than he had a moment ago, "I don't want you to feel discouraged. You have instinctive abilities that'll serve you well in operatic performance, and I want to help you develop those abilities."

She felt encouraged enough to speak her mind. "I like to sing what I feel. And I want to make other people feel those things too."

"You certainly have the capacity to do that. But you'll make things more difficult for yourself if you disregard technique."

Her heart dipped, and her defensive wall sprang into place. She lifted her chin. "You mean you want me to sound like Chiara."

"No, I definitely don't want that."

"Because she was your favorite prima donna?"

"Is that what she told you?"

"Everyone says so."

"Well, that shows how wrong people can be. Chiara warbles well enough, but her style is purely ornamental. There's no fire fueling her singing or igniting her passions. She's cold as ice."

She was dumbstruck, amazed at his bluntness. For weeks she'd heard nothing but praise for Chiara's brilliant mastery of singing technique. And now Don Antonio had negated all that with his curt assessment of her vocal style.

"Technique is artificial," he said, "something learned and cultivated. But it must be mastered all the same if you're to acquire the tools necessary to fully express those violent inner passions of yours."

She felt herself blush.

Concern and amusement mingled in his smile. "What you feel in your heart can't be taught. It's part of you, and no one has the right to try to take that from you. If your talent doesn't match so-called conventional standards, so much the better, I say."

Her sinking heart swelled. To have the chance to sing onstage, sure of her voice, would be the answer to all her prayers and the fulfillment of her long-held dream. Yet she wondered how her singing could ever compete with those dazzling voices she'd heard at the opera—voices trained to the height of technical brilliance. She wanted to tell Don Antonio her fears and be comforted by his reassurance. She hid that desire. She wasn't ready to expose that much of herself to him.

Her lessons with him continued to be a fierce ritual of emotional highs and lows. His unpredictable mood swings and constant energy kept her on her toes, but also plagued her with uncertainty. One minute he'd berate her for a lapse in technique and the next he'd praise her for her dramatic expressiveness. As his look alternated between a dark, furrowed brow and a bright, sunny smile, he took her from the depths of despair to the heights of exhilaration. In some ways he frightened her. Yet she found herself growing more attached to him as the months went by.

She learned not to mind too much when he raised his voice at her. After all, he never spoke to her in a harsh or uncaring way like Maestro Tomaso so often had. He simply got worked up when things didn't go how he thought they should. That was part of his personality and a reflection of his genius. But he never stayed that way for long. He'd soon grow friendly and patient again. Mostly, though, she had to learn to be patient with *him*—to ride out his fleeting rages and wait for the calm that would return as quickly as it had left. But it was always an intense calm, never a truly peaceful one.

HER GROWING ATTACHMENT to Don Antonio led her to trust him more and more. Still, Chiara's threats about the letter gnawed at her. She wanted so much to confide in him all Chiara had done to her and put her through. But her fear that she would show him the letter prevented her. Then one day it occurred to her that perhaps she could ask him to send a message to the duke for her. They were friends, she assumed, and probably kept in touch. If the letter wasn't mailed from Signora's house there'd be no way Chiara could intercept it.

That night in bed she curled up under the covers and scrawled a hasty note to the duke, explaining the difficulty of her situation. She felt certain he'd be able to use his influence to weaken Chiara's hold over her. She planned to say nothing to Don Antonio about the contents of the letter, but she'd ask him at her lesson the next day if he'd mind sending it. Surely he'd do that for her. The following afternoon she hurried back to her room after dinner. She wanted to retrieve the letter, which she'd hidden in her satchel under the bed. She tore through the limp satchel and panic crept through her. The letter had disappeared.

Unnerved, she looked up to see Chiara at the door. "You think your noble duke and your adoring maestro will rescue you from your troubles? Think again."

She silently raged at herself for being stupid enough to allow Chiara yet another opportunity to blackmail her with her snooping. She should have kept the letter with her! "What do you mean?" she said, holding back tears with difficulty.

"My father could buy them both out in a heartbeat. And he'll do it if I ask him to."

"But why would he—why would you—want to do that?"

"I have my reasons. Just consider yourself warned."

A few hours later she arrived at Don Antonio's studio, and it was as if a dark cloud hovered over the room. Chiara stood with her arms crossed, frowning, and he seemed to be searching for something. She watched with dread as Chiara pulled him aside and whispered to him. They both glanced over at her, and her knees went weak.

Then Chiara pointed to her and said tartly, "That little girl has ruined the manuscript to one of your motets. Yes, the botched copy she made is here, but the original is nowhere to be found. I'm sure she stole it to hide the evidence. I was going to return it to you, but now it's gone."

She was stunned and mortified. She'd returned that manuscript to Chiara in perfect condition months ago, and now she was making up a lie to cause her more trouble. No doubt Chiara had hidden the score herself. But she was defenseless. As long as Chiara had her letters she couldn't dare say anything to cross her. Tears stung her eyes, and she struggled to keep them from spilling.

Don Antonio sighed impatiently. "Do I need to remind you again, Chiara, that Annina is not a copyist? You forced work on her that was not her responsibility, and if a missing score is the result you have no one to blame but yourself. Now please excuse us so we can get on with our lesson."

Chiara glared at her, then swept from the room in a flurry of anger. The dark cloud had passed, and things started to feel all right again. But her fear of Chiara was driving her to be more cautious—and defiant. She even went on the defensive with Don Antonio.

"So it wasn't good enough?" she asked, when he failed to respond with accolades to the aria she'd just sung for him. She didn't mean to be peevish. Yet despite his frequent words of encouragement, Chiara's unrelenting attacks were wearing her down.

He looked at her as if he could read her mind. "I know you're distressed about what happened here a few minutes ago. Chiara's behavior toward you is absolutely horrid. I'm beginning to understand what you've had to put up with since you came here, and I don't blame you for feeling upset and discouraged."

Her eyes misted and she bit her lip to keep it from trembling.

He came over and put his arm around her for a moment, and she leaned her head against his shoulder, savoring the warmth of his closeness. Yet almost immediately she felt ashamed. Her clingy dependence on him was childish and unprofessional. What right did she have to think he cared more about her than his other students? Why on earth would he have a special interest in her or any particular concern about her problems?

ANTONIO'S HEART ACHED for the child. He felt her suffering as he'd so often sensed the tacit suffering of the poor motherless girls at the Pietà. As brave as they were, he recognized their longings and felt their anguish, and he identified with those feelings to some extent. Not that he'd ever known a lack of parental love. Certainly he'd been covered with it since the day of his birth. But still, there was something lacking. A lack that, God forbid, this darling girl was starting to fill.

He hadn't told her yet, but he soon would have to leave for Rome again. He'd been commissioned to produce his newest opera, *Ercole sul Termodonte*, for Rome's Carnival season. He was not looking forward to it. The pope's law prohibiting women to sing in public meant he'd be forced to endure the pompous antics of those insufferable *castrati*. Their insolence was in a way understandable, seeing that as young boys they'd been handed over for castration and sold to singing schools by their parents. Technically the practice was illegal, but excuses such as *He had an accident* were typically invoked to explain the phenomenon. That parents could do such a thing to their own sons was unthinkable, but who was he to judge?

His real concern was leaving Annina at the mercy of this hoard of vultures, Chiara in particular. There was no telling what she might be up to.

IT WAS MID DECEMBER, and Annina could hardly believe she'd been in Venice nearly a year. Don Antonio had just left for Rome to put on a new opera, and she had no idea when he'd return. She felt despondent in his absence. And Chiara's menacing presence kept her nerves on edge. Chiara hadn't said much to her recently, but every time their paths crossed she looked down at her with a smug smile. What if she was planning to somehow use her secret letter against her?

Since she had no lesson she decided to visit the sewing room. She'd been relieved of her sewing duties when she started lessons with Don Antonio, but she still liked to spend time with Graziana.

The seamstress greeted her with a sly smile. "I heard about how Don Antonio stuck up for you," she said, arching her eyebrows.

"What?"

"When Chiara tried to stir up trouble for you, jumping all over you about her silly motet."

"That was days ago. How did you hear about it?"

"Because Chiara doesn't know when to keep her mouth shut." She narrowed her eyes and leaned closer. "She's still carping on about how 'that irksome child' ruined her motet score, and that Don Antonio refused to take her side against you. She's even spreading rumors that you have some kind of hold over him. She's terribly jealous, you know, of any female he takes an interest in, especially one as young and pretty as you. And when she's jealous, she can be dangerous." She said all this in a rushed whisper, flitting her eyes toward the room's open door.

She didn't care about the open door. She was too interested in something Graziana had just said.

"You think I'm pretty?"

She raised her eyebrows. "Have you seen yourself in a mirror lately? You're more than pretty—you're gorgeous."

She'd never thought herself pretty, much less gorgeous. And Graziana wasn't one to flatter. She felt a rush of pleasure, but decided she'd better go back to the discussion about Chiara. "I just don't understand why she hates me so much. It seems she's trying harder than ever to ruin things for me."

"She feels threatened by you."

"*Why?* I've never said or done anything to threaten her."

"You didn't have to. She was already fuming that the duke dropped her in favor of you. And now she's gotten worse because she can't stand the special attention you get from Don Antonio. Ever since she first came to Venice she's been trying to wangle her way into his favor, and in her view you're a major hindrance."

"But now it seems she doesn't even like him."

"She doesn't. She's too self-centered to really like anyone. But she thinks she can manipulate him into getting her what she wants."

"Why does she want to manipulate him if her father's so rich and powerful?"

Graziana looked at her with an ironic little twist at the corner of her mouth. "Like I've told you before, Chiara fantasized for years that her 'rich and powerful' father would use his money and influence to launch her into the brilliant opera career she's always dreamed of. But her brag that he'll do anything she asks is all bravado. He's never even acknowledged her. So to make up for it she keeps trying to use her beauty and charm to latch onto powerful men and use them for her selfish purposes. But they all get disenchanted with her sooner or later."

"The things you've told me about Chiara almost make me feel sorry for her," she said, frowning.

She rolled her eyes. "Don't waste your pity on her, Annina. She's brought it all on herself. And she's a snaky one, so I'd continue to watch my step around her if I were you."

An uneasy feeling slithered through her. She hesitated a moment, then said quietly, "Chiara stole a very private letter I wrote my sister. There're secrets in that letter that must never get out."

She looked worried. "You have to get it back from her. There's no telling what she'll do with information like that. At the very least she'll use it to blackmail you and control you completely."

"She's already doing that," she said, in a shaky whisper. "How can I possibly get it back from her?" She was frantic now. Graziana had spelled out plainly the shadowy dread she'd been feeling.

"Don't worry." Her calm voice was reassuring. "I'll think of something. You'll get your letter back."

A SURPRISING LETTER arrived a few weeks later that somehow evaded Chiara's intervention. But it wasn't from her family. It was an invitation to Sunday dinner at the Vivaldi home, from Signora Vivaldi, the maestro's mother. He was in Rome, of course, and she felt a bit nervous about meeting his family in his absence. The only one she knew at all was Margarita. The Vivaldis seemed to be extremely busy people, and the times she'd gone for her lessons most of the family had been occupied. But, according to Signora Vivaldi's gracious note, they were all anxious to meet her. They sent a gondola for her that Sunday afternoon, and she arrived moments later to a house fragrant with the aroma of roasted chicken and alive with the sound of friendly voices. Margarita greeted her at the door, and at once she was surrounded by smiling faces.

Signora Vivaldi took her hand. "How wonderful to meet you at last, my dear. Margarita and Antonio have told us so much about you. Come, let me introduce you to the rest of the family."

Signor Vivaldi looked like an older version of his eldest son. His flowing red-gold hair was flecked with gray, and his sparkling blue eyes and gentle mouth were framed by smile lines. She felt immediately at ease with him. He didn't just take her hand. He pulled her into his arms as if he'd known her all her life and told her what a delight it was to have such a pretty girl to dine with. Everyone smiled in agreement. No one seemed surprised at his easy display of affection.

Besides Margarita, two more of the maestro's younger siblings were present: another sister, Zanetta, and a brother, Iseppo. Zanetta was warm and gracious, but somewhat on the quiet side. Iseppo was more boisterous. He looked close to her own brothers in age and even reminded her of them a bit. Like Don Antonio, he looked remarkably like his father.

Iseppo gave her a boyish grin and winked. "I hope that slave-driving brother of mine isn't being too hard on you, Signorina Annina."

She smiled and blushed. "Well, I must admit it sometimes seems that way."

Everyone chuckled.

Unlike her family, the Vivaldis seemed completely comfortable together, and they made every effort to make her feel at home. Almost at once she felt as though she'd always known them.

She'd never been in the dining room before, and as they all sat down to dinner she stared across the room at an imposing portrait, an oil painting in warm, vivid colors. Signor Vivaldi noted the direction of her gaze. He smiled with pride. "I had that portrait painted just after Antonio took holy orders. He was twenty-five at the time. Isn't it something, Annina?"

It certainly was. The painting was almost daunting in its formality, yet at the same time full of contrasts and ambiguities. A long powdered wig flowed elegantly below his shoulder, while a stray lock of golden hair escaped down his temple. Magnificent priestly robes of crimson barely covered a simple white shirt that gaped open halfway down his chest. In one hand he grasped the fingerboard of his violin, and in the other he held a quill pen, poised over a handwritten score. His expression was impassive, yet the corners of his mouth curved up ever so slightly, as if he were on the verge of a smile. It was his eyes that most captivated her, though. The artist had captured that indescribable combination of tenderness and intensity she'd seen so often in his gaze. Although he was posed at a bit of an angle, his head was turned just enough toward a full frontal view that his eyes seemed to follow you. It was impossible to look at the painting without meeting and being held in that steady gaze. She'd never seen a portrait so fully embrace the essence of the person depicted.

Signora Vivaldi smiled over at her while she passed around steaming platters of herbed chicken and delectably aromatic polenta. "So, Annina, I understand your mother used to be a neighbor of ours."

"*Sì, signora*," she said, as her attention was drawn back to the family sitting around the table.

"I'm trying to picture her. What is your mamma's name, dear?"

"Bartolomea."

She looked thoughtful for a moment. "Hmmm. Bartolomea— Oh yes, I think I remember now. That beautiful, dreamy-eyed young girl who lived across the square from us, when we lived in the Bragora district. You remember her, don't you, Giovanni?"

"Yes, dear, I believe I do," he said, smiling at Annina. "And I see her in you, Annina. All her beauty, intelligence, and sensitivity."

His wife interjected. "My goodness, that was so many years ago." She looked around at her children. "Most of you weren't even with us yet. And Margarita, you were barely more than an infant." She returned her gaze to Annina. "And to think Bartolomea's own little girl is now back in Venice, studying with our Antonio. It's as if you were destined to be with us, my dear."

Everyone smiled and nodded in agreement. She felt so surrounded by warmth and goodwill, she could hardly keep from crying. Surely they must have known her mother had abandoned her, and that she hadn't seen or heard from her in almost three years. But they were kind enough not to mention it.

EARLY THE NEXT morning she crept downstairs to tell Graziana about her visit with the Vivaldis. To her dismay, Fiametta, Marzia, and Ernesta were crowded in the hallway outside Graziana's room, whispering among themselves. She managed to catch bits of what they said. "Have you heard? . . . I've heard something, but I'm not sure . . . I think it was something she ate . . . will she be all right? . . . poor Graziana!"

A knot formed in her stomach. "What's going on?" she asked Fiametta.

Fiametta gave her a wry look, as if she were deciding if she should let her in on their secret. Finally she whispered shrilly, "Graziana became very ill quite suddenly last night."

"Ill? How ill? What's wrong with her?" The knot in her stomach tightened.

"Food poisoning, I think," she said, looking past Annina. "Here comes Signora with the doctor."

Signora hurried down the hall, looking more somber and worried than Annina had ever seen her. She felt she would scream if someone didn't tell her what was happening.

Then Chiara appeared. Every inch of her displayed a chilling calm.

Icicles slithered up her spine. She closed her eyes and prayed silently. *Please, God. Please. Not this. Graziana's my only friend. Don't take her away from me.*

Signora and the doctor went into Graziana's room while everyone else hovered outside the door. After what seemed like an eternity, they came back into the hall. The doctor's face looked grim. Signora dropped her head and tightened her mouth and eyes. They didn't have to tell her, she knew. Graziana had died, and she was completely alone.

Time seemed to stand still. Dazed, she plodded back to her room and took *la moretta* out of her trunk. Sinking facedown into her pillow, she slipped the mask under her quilt. She tried to cry but couldn't. It was like her mother's abandonment all over again, only now there was no Paolina to comfort her. She couldn't even write to her sister, because Chiara would steal her letter. She'd been silenced. Her hands tightened into fists, and she squeezed her pillow in excruciating frustration. When would this ever end?

She felt a presence standing over her. Flipping over, she propped on her elbow. Chiara's cat-like green eyes stared into hers, and her mouth was fixed in a frigid half-smile.

"So much for your cozy friendship," she said after an agonizing moment, her voice cutting through Annina like an ice-pick. "I hope you see now that you're totally under my power and no one can help you." Her sinister smile broadened into a fiendish grin.

She shrank from her in horror. Chiara was using this tragedy to her own advantage, to make her feel helpless. And there was nothing she could do about it. Looking into Chiara's cold eyes, she knew she was defeated. She sank back on her pillow, and Chiara left as abruptly as she'd appeared.

Then she remembered that tomorrow was her birthday. But what did it matter? She was growing older, yet more powerless, with each passing day.

Chapter Six

No one seemed to know it was her birthday. Thirteen years old today, and no closer to the life she'd dreamed of four years ago, when she'd had her first glimpse of the opera. Her only friend was gone, and Chiara had turned more vicious than ever. She'd never felt so downhearted.

Just before dinner Chiara confronted her in her usual haughty manner. Annina tried to walk past her.

"Not so fast," she said, grasping her arm. "I have plans for you. I want you to transcribe another motet I'm to sing at church this Sunday."

She jerked her arm from Chiara's clutching hand. "No, I can't do that. Don Antonio told you I'm not a copyist."

"Well, he's not here, is he? So you'll do as I say." The sharpness in her voice resonated with threatening overtones. She raised her chin. "Need I remind you that you're completely under my power?"

Chiara's brazen tone was more than she could stomach. "I'm not in your power. Just because you say I am doesn't make it true. Do whatever you want to me, but I won't be your slave."

The edges around her mouth hardened, and her eyes blazed. "Don't forget that I have your treasured letters and I won't hesitate to use them against you."

"I don't care a fig about those letters." She tried to sound nonchalant, but she could barely control the tremor in her voice. "They're just the silly ramblings of a twelve-year-old girl. Who'll care what they say?"

Chiara glared at her for a long instant, the corners of her mouth twitching. Finally she said, "I think I'll show your *secret* letter to Don Antonio when he returns."

She forced herself to look calm. "Do you really think he'd be interested in a girl's frivolous writings? I'm sure he has more important things on his mind, and if you pester him to read that nonsense he'll be more annoyed with you than he already is." She braced herself for the onset of Chiara's fury.

But for the first time since she'd known her, Chiara was at a loss for words. She stared at Annina with wide, blinking eyes and tightened her mouth, as if to keep her lip from quivering.

She almost pitied her. But she enjoyed watching her squirm.

"We'll see about that," Chiara finally said, then turned on her heel and stalked off in a huff.

She felt better than she had in a long time. She was thirteen today and not a child anymore. She wasn't about to let Chiara keep her paralyzed with fear.

Later, at dinner, Signora made her grand entrance as usual. But instead of her typical stony look, today she was smiling primly. When she reached her place at the head of the table, she gave the blessing, and remained standing.

"Ladies, I have an announcement to make."

Graziana is dead. Her heart turned over and shriveled as the terrible reality flooded her mind.

"As you know, our dear seamstress, Graziana, took ill the evening before last. She grew steadily worse during the night, and early yesterday morning the physician said she would not live. But over the past few hours, praise be to God, she has shown marked improvement. The doctor examined her again a few moments ago and has informed me that Graziana is out of danger."

Her heart leaped for joy. *Graziana didn't die! She's going to live!* She was so ecstatic she nearly fell out of her seat.

Immediately after dinner she had another wonderful surprise. There was a knock at the front door, and instead of sending Bettina to answer as usual, Signora went to the door herself. She returned with a message for Annina—a note from Don Antonio telling her he was back in Venice and would like her to come for a lesson that afternoon.

When she saw him her heart swelled and she wanted to run into his arms. But she was afraid he'd be taken aback by such a display of affection. Her voice alone betrayed her joy at his return. "Welcome back, maestro!"

He smiled at her. "*Grazie*, Annina, It's good to be back. You certainly look happy today."

She couldn't contain herself. "I am, maestro, today's my birthday."

"Well, congratulations. How old are you now?"

"Thirteen."

"Thirteen? You're a young lady."

"I know." She felt giddy, anxious to share her happiness. "And the most wonderful thing has happened. My friend Graziana, who was so sick yesterday and almost died, is much better now. She's going to be all right."

"Graziana?"

"The seamstress who lives at Signora Malvolia's house. She's the only person, besides you, who's been nice to me since I've been here."

He looked at her in a very tender way. "Oh, I see. Well, I'm happy for your sake, and for Graziana's of course, that she's out of danger."

"It's the best present I could have had."

His smile grew warmer. "I have another present for you, Annina."

"Really? What is it?"

"Do you remember Rosane's aria, "*Solo quella guancia bella*" from *La verità*, that you learned last year?"

"Yes, I love that aria."

"I've rewritten it for you, with new words." The score he picked up from the harpsichord glistened with fresh ink. He held it out to her. "Now it's your very own aria."

She took the score eagerly and saw he'd renamed it "*La mia bella pastorella*." He'd even written "For Annina" at the top. She took a trembling breath and smiled at him ecstatically. "*Grazie*, maestro."

"Now let me tell you why I did this. I'm putting together a *pasticcio*, a staged performance of arias from several of my operas. It's to take place next month, in Treviso, a town just a little north of here. I'm calling it *La ninfa infelice e fortunata*, The sad and lucky nymph. I'd like you to play the part of a shepherd boy, Mirtillo, and sing this aria."

"You mean—you want me to sing in a public performance?"

"Well, considering your advancing age I'd say it's high time you made your stage debut," he said, his mouth curled in a slightly wry twist.

Again, she wanted to throw her arms around him, but she still wasn't sure how he'd feel about that. *I'm thirteen now*, she told herself. *I need to start learning to control my impulses.* So she merely clasped her hands in a ladylike way and enveloped him in the radiance of her smile.

That evening, alone in her bedroom, she ran her hands along the contours of her girlish figure. She was still quite slender but starting to develop a few curves in the right places. She dared to pass her hands over her barely budding breasts and felt a strange tingling deep inside. Quickly she pulled on her nightgown, slipped into bed, and wrapped her arms around the cool pillow. The tingling quickened. How things can change in a single day. Graziana had practically died and come back to life, she'd amazed herself by standing up to Chiara, and Don Antonio had paved the way for her opera debut. Her thirteenth birthday had turned out to be quite a day. She wasn't a little girl anymore.

The next morning she visited Graziana. "I'm so happy you're better now," she said with a cheery smile. "I have so much to tell you."

"Well what's stopping you? Tell, tell!"

"I had a really good lesson with Don Antonio yesterday."

"Yes?"

"He's written a special aria for me, and he wants me to sing it in a show he's putting together in Treviso next month. I'm going to be a shepherd boy."

"How adorable. What will you wear?"

"Oh, I don't know. I haven't even thought about that."

"Leave it to me then. *I'll* design and make your costume."

"Will you really? That'll be wonderful. Now you *have* to get better."

At that moment Signora appeared and ordered Annina out of the room. As she said goodbye, Graziana pulled her close and whispered in her ear, "I'd love to see the look on Chiara's face when she hears about this."

She stifled a giggle.

At her lesson she told Don Antonio about Graziana's offer to design and make her costume. "Is that all right?" she asked.

"Yes, I suppose that's fine, if that's what you want."

They then proceeded with what seemed like endless repetitions of the technical exercises he'd assigned her. He was so pleased by her progress he decided to let her sing a second aria in the pasticcio, another one he'd written especially for her, "*Son come farfalletta*," I am like a little butterfly. And that's exactly how she felt—happy and lighthearted as a butterfly.

TO HER SURPRISE, and much to her relief, Chiara left her alone during the weeks leading up to her debut in Treviso. Whenever their paths crossed, Chiara ignored her. It worried her that she still had her letters, and she almost felt confident enough to say something to Don Antonio about it. But a murky fear prevented her. Her debut loomed so close she could taste it, and she was afraid to do anything that might possibly ruin her big chance.

A few days before the event, Graziana had her costume ready. She sent her into the dressing area of the sewing room, eager for her to try it on. The costume was very simple: a thin cotton tunic with short, loose sleeves, in a dazzling shade of teal green, along with a brimless cap made of the same fabric. For her legs there were pale blue stockings, and for her waist a cloth belt. She slipped out of her dress and undergarments and into the strangely winsome little costume. The tunic was daringly short, reaching to just above her knees. Her body felt so free it seemed she was wearing almost nothing.

She stuffed her hair into the cap, wrapped the belt around her waist, and came out from behind the curtain to show Graziana.

With a weak smile, she said, "Um . . . do you really think my legs should be so exposed on a public stage?"

"Why not? You have lovely, slender legs. If I had legs like yours I certainly wouldn't miss an opportunity to show them off."

"How do you think Don Antonio will feel about this costume?" she asked, hoping Graziana would realize he'd find it shockingly improper.

"He'll love it."

"But don't you think he'll find it a bit indecent?"

"Of course not. He may be a priest, but he's no prude. He's created a special role for you, and he'll want you to look the part. You know better than anyone how much he values dramatic truth over stuffy decorum."

She knew Graziana was right. Over the next few days she grew more confident about the costume and tingled at the thought of wearing it onstage. It was sure to make quite an impression.

At last the big day arrived. It was late February, near the end of the Carnival season, and she and Graziana, along with Don Antonio and his entourage of singers, instrumentalists, and stage technicians, set out early that morning. They reached the mainland by boat, then coaches carried them past countless stately patrician villas along the Terraglio, the highway to Treviso. After a brief rehearsal and dinner, Graziana went to work getting her dressed and made up. Then it was show time. The orchestra played the opening sinfonia, and the curtain went up. She waited anxiously backstage for her first entrance, which was to come near the end of Act I. Before she knew it the aria before hers was ending, and Graziana rushed to her side. "This is it, Annina, you're on!"

She took a deep breath, stepped out of the wings, and walked to center stage. Don Antonio lifted his violin to start the orchestral introduction. Her eyes caught his, and he gave her an encouraging smile. Her heart swelled with excitement. Then she saw Chiara sitting near the front of the pit, her cold green eyes fixed on her with the smug assuredness that she was about to make a fool of herself. Her confidence collapsed, and her swelling heart turned to stone. At once her jaw tightened, her throat closed, and her breath constricted. *O Dio!* Every bit of the technique Don Antonio had taught her was gone in a flash, and the very worst of her old habits had come back to take its place. In an instant, Chiara had resumed power over her, and she was helpless to resist.

Don Antonio led the violins in an introduction that sounded like the graceful fluttering of little butterfly wings. She felt like those butterflies were flapping frantically in her stomach. As the flittering notes of the orchestral prelude darted toward her opening phrase, a viselike grip tightened around her jaw, throat, and chest. Her vocal entrance was only a few beats away, and she couldn't even get enough air in to sing a note. At best she might manage a shrill screech, which would send the audience into cascades of laughter and jeers. Her mind filled with stories her mother had told her about the rotten fruit and tomatoes peevish spectators hurled like missiles when they were dissatisfied with a singer's performance. She wanted to run from the stage to the safety of the shady wings. But her feet felt frozen to the stage floor, and her legs shook with such violence she was afraid if she tried to move she'd fall on her face. Oh, why did Graziana have to design a costume that exposed her trembling knees to everyone?

The introduction seemed endless. Then, just one more beat before her ultimate humiliation and the end of her career and her dreams—and, she was sure, the end of her association with Don Antonio. He'd despise her now, or worse, pity her. Gasping what little air she could, she glanced at him in desperation. Surely he knew her well enough by now to sense her terror. And surely he'd frown in disgust at her cowardice. But he didn't frown. He didn't smile either, yet his dark blue eyes shown into hers in a way that somehow fueled her determination to get past her fear. She lifted her head high and plunged into the aria.

At once her fear vanished, and in its place came a warm surge of confidence. She was no longer powerless, downtrodden Annina. She was Mirtillo, a sprightly, carefree shepherd boy comparing himself to a butterfly:

> I am like a little butterfly
> that in the middle of two lights
> ventures here and there.

The rest of the performance seemed to fly by. Between acts, Graziana took her to the dressing room to fuss with her makeup and costume. Soon it was time for her second aria, "*La mia bella pastorella*," in which Mirtillo would sing of his love for a beautiful shepherdess.

At the end of the final act the singers came out one by one to bask in the audience's applause. Since she was the youngest, and had one of the smallest parts, she came out first. The audience went wild, clapping, cheering, stomping, and throwing flowers. Don Antonio gazed up at her, his face aglow with triumph and delight. Flushed with joy, she capered off the stage amid cries of "*Brava, la bella Annina! La piccola Mantovana, Bravissima!*"

Backstage, she ripped off the little shepherd's cap, and her hair tumbled around her shoulders. Graziana rushed over and hugged her.

"Did you hear what they were saying, Graziana? They called me beautiful Annina, the little girl from Mantua."

She grinned with pride. "I did indeed. Annina, you were brilliant!"

Graziana's eyes darted, and her smile hardened into a frown. Annina turned and saw Chiara. Her face, darkened by fury, contrasted eerily with the intricate coils of her ice blond hair. Without a word she shot Annina a cutting glare and swept past her.

"You might as well get used to it," Graziana said, sighing. "Female singers are known for their haughty manner and endless intrigues. Of course, *castrati* aren't much better."

"*Castrati?*"

"Yes, male singers who went 'under the knife' as boys so their voices stay high, like a woman's. I've heard Don Antonio doesn't like to use them very much, but most opera stages are filled with them. I'm surprised you didn't know that."

She shivered at the horror of what she'd just heard. She had no idea such atrocities went on. And Graziana had no idea how sheltered she'd been all her life, and continued to be.

These gloomy thoughts flew from her mind when Don Antonio rushed backstage after the final curtain call. "*Bravissima*, Annina! You were superb. You completely enraptured the audience. Even I couldn't have imagined how beautifully you'd sparkle and bring your character to life onstage."

The mingled excitement and tenderness in his eyes melted all her reserve. With childlike impetuosity she ran to him and reached to throw her arms around his neck. Subtly, he averted her little-girlish burst of affection. Her heart sank for an instant. He smiled at her though, and gently smoothed an unruly lock from her moist forehead. Blushing, she realized his tactful guardedness was his way of showing her it wasn't appropriate to throw herself at him like that, especially in public. She looked around and saw singers and stagehands milling about, a few of them eyeing her and the maestro curiously. At once she felt ashamed of her childish impulsiveness, and she glanced up at him with a coy smile to mask her embarrassment. But her insides still fluttered with nervous energy. So she moved away from him and twirled around, her loose hair flying about. "How do you like my costume?"

"It suits you quite well. You really looked your part."

"Graziana said you'd like it. I was afraid you'd think it's too skimpy."

One corner of his mouth curled and his eyes sparkled. Then he glanced down and pressed his lips together, as if to suppress a chuckle. "Let's just say I don't think anyone but you could have gotten away with wearing it." He lifted his eyes. "Really, Annina, you were absolutely dazzling onstage. The audience was completely entranced by you."

She quivered with pleasure. Then she was startled by a vaguely familiar voice.

"Well said, maestro. I couldn't have said it better myself."

She turned and was stunned to see the duke. "Your Excellency!" she squeaked. Flustered, she tripped over her awkward curtsy, but Don Antonio caught her elbow. She felt her cheeks burn.

The duke exuded easy charm as he looked her over. "How you've grown, Signorina Annina. You are indeed a vision of loveliness."

Something about his exaggerated grin and the hard gleam in his eye made her cringe with self-consciousness. She was glad Don Antonio was there, and without even thinking she stepped closer to him.

"Maestro, you're to be commended for accomplishing such wonders with this enchanting young lady," the duke said with a cool smile.

He didn't seem impressed by the duke's oozing flattery. His smile was a bit fixed. "The credit goes entirely to Signorina Girò, Your Excellency."

The duke's grin took on a roguish quality, and he admonished slyly. "Come now, maestro, you are much too modest." But his eyes were on her. He started to move in her direction, and she detected the scent of brandy about him.

Don Antonio glared at him, unsmiling, then turned his attention to her. "You'd better change, dear, before you catch a chill."

"*Sì*, maestro." How grateful she was he'd given her a means of escape. She bobbed another curtsy and said, "So nice to see you again, Excellency," before she scurried off.

When she reached the stairs leading to the dressing rooms she glanced back and saw that Don Antonio and the duke were still talking. But she was out of earshot and had no idea what they were saying.

Graziana was waiting in the hall outside the large dressing room she was sharing with several other female singers. "Annina, there you are! Where have you been? It's chilly in here, and you're going to catch your death if you don't put something warm on."

"I know, Don Antonio just said the same thing."

"Well, he's certainly looking out for you, isn't he?" Her lips curled, and her eyes brightened. "Isn't this wonderful? Chiara's going to go mad with envy, if she hasn't already."

She tried to smile, but an uneasy feeling had crept over her.

Graziana crinkled her brow. "What's wrong? You seem worried about something."

"It's nothing, really."

"Well, it must be *something*. You were so happy a few minutes ago."

She sighed. "It's just that the duke suddenly showed up when I was talking to Don Antonio. He looked at me in a strange way that was kind of scary."

She smiled in her easygoing way. "Oh, good heavens, Annina,

you know how men are. You're adorable in that charming little costume, and you can't blame them for looking. Don't even give it another thought," she said, waving her hand past her face.

She still found the duke's unexpected appearance unsettling. It wasn't just his leering that bothered her. Seeing him again reminded her of the first time she'd met him, at her father's shop, over three years ago. The memory of that day caused the reality of her family's troubles to agitate her heart anew. These thoughts continued to flow through her head her first night back at Signora Malvolia's house. She remembered how old, sad, and helpless Papà had seemed the last time she saw him, and warm tears blanketed her eyes. A sudden fear gripped her. What if he got sick? What if he *died*? What if she never saw him again?

She thought about Chiara's shameless harassment and seethed with anger. Worst of all, Chiara had cut her off from her family. *That will end tomorrow*, she decided, with a burst of conviction. I'll confront her and find a way to make her stop stealing my mail. But how would she do it? She considered speaking to Don Antonio about the letters. Yet she knew she couldn't expect him to solve all her problems for her. If she didn't stand up to Chiara on her own, she'd never be free of her bullying.

The next morning Ernesta approached her in her usual curt manner. "Signora wishes to see you in her study immediately."

Oh dear, she thought. *What have I done now?*

Chapter Seven

Signora sat at her desk, reading glasses perched on her nose, and her mouth set in a hard frown.

"You wished to see me, Signora?"

"Be seated, Annina. I have a question to ask you." Her voice and manner were as dry as dust, but Annina noticed the knuckles of her bony fingers had gone white from clutching a small bundle of papers.

"Yes, Signora?" she said, her insides churning.

"I would like you to tell me the whereabouts of Chiara."

"I don't know what you mean, Signora."

"I find that hard to believe. Several days ago, against my better judgment, I granted you permission to accompany Don Antonio to Treviso for an operatic performance. I was against it, but the maestro was quite insistent, and he is a difficult man to say no to."

Despite her fear, she had to suppress a smile.

Signora removed her glasses, cleared her throat, and drew herself into a rod-like posture. "After you left, Chiara informed me that Don Antonio had requested her presence in Treviso as well."

She was sure this wasn't true, but she held her tongue.

"I found it quite odd that Don Antonio had not mentioned that to me. But, of course, I had no reason to doubt Chiara's word.

Of course not.

"So I hired a private coach for her in order that she might travel to Treviso in a manner befitting her station. Yesterday I received word that she was missing." She paused, as if for dramatic effect.

On pins and needles, Annina waited for her to go on.

"I would like you to tell me where she is."

"I'm sorry, Signora, but I have no idea."

"Surely you must have known she was there."

"Yes, I saw her for only a moment. But we didn't speak to each other."

"Perhaps Don Antonio knows where she is," she said, with a sly tinge to her voice.

The corners of her mouth tightened. "That I wouldn't know, Signora."

Signora pursed her lips. "You and he have become quite close, haven't you?"

She shifted in her chair. "I'm not sure I know what you mean, Signora."

"I mean it has been noted that you spend a great deal of time at his studio."

She started to feel vaguely indignant. "I'm taking singing lessons with him, as you know, and lately there's been a lot to do to get ready for the performance in Treviso."

"Has there, now?" Her mouth and jowls angled down, and she leaned toward Annina in a threatening way.

She caught her breath.

"I want you to listen to me carefully, young lady. You are to tell me immediately what Don Antonio knows about Chiara's disappearance."

She felt tightness in her chest and jaw, but she forced herself to meet the old woman's frowning gaze. "If you want my opinion, Signora, I don't think he knows anything about it. But if you don't believe me, why not ask him yourself?" He'd set the old battleaxe straight.

Signora's mouth became a pinched line, and her white-knuckled fists shook. "I am incensed at your audacity, Annina. How—how dare you presume to give me orders concerning Don Antonio, to . . . to speak to me in that way."

She looked at Signora's dried-up, quivering face and realized she was afraid of him. Even though Don Antonio was warm and friendly most of the time, she'd seen how intimidating he could be when overbearing people tried his patience. And Signora could certainly do that. But it would do no good for her to get any more on Signora's bad side than she already was. She decided she should humble herself a bit. "Please forgive me, Signora. I didn't mean any disrespect." Then she thought she'd better add, "And I certainly hope no harm has come to Chiara."

She simpered. "Indeed, we must pray to God that our dear Chiara is safe." Her eyes misted, and her voice took on a nostalgic tone. "Oh, I'll never forget the day that darling girl first came here. She has been like a daughter to me ever since."

More like a granddaughter, you mean.

"Yes, she has always exuded beauty, charm, and grace. Who could not love and admire her?"

She tried to appear wistful, though she felt like retching.

"And so gloriously talented! Her voice is like that of an angel." All of a sudden Signora snapped out of her sentimental mood. She squared her shoulders and glared at her in an accusing way. "Why, she was Don Antonio's favorite—that is, until *you* came along. Since you've been his student, he's lost interest in her."

There was a tense silence. Signora seemed to be waiting for her reaction. She couldn't think how to respond, so she simply returned the old lady's gaze with what she imagined to be a perplexed look.

Signora eyed her shrewdly. "It intrigues me, Annina, how at times you are such an open book about your emotions, yet at other times, when I would expect a revealing reaction from you, your feelings are quite unreadable."

She stifled a yawn and started to fidget. The conversation had grown tedious, and she was anxious to escape Signora's smothering presence. Yet the old woman seemed determined to stare her down until she responded to her absurd implication.

"I'm sorry, Signora, but I really don't know what to say."

"Then perhaps you'll have something to say about these." She shoved the bundle of folded papers she'd been clutching across the desk.

Her heart gave a violent jolt.

"In the hope of finding some clue to Chiara's whereabouts, I searched her room last night. I found this stack of your correspondence—some written by you, and some written to you—among her things. I would like you to explain how these letters got there."

She bit her lip and tried hard to steady her breathing. If she was to have any chance of walking out of that room with her mail she'd have to guard her tongue. She took a deep breath and looked Signora in the eye. "Very soon after I arrived here, Chiara informed me that she had the right to intercept my mail."

Signora stared at her, blinking. She opened her mouth as if to say something, then closed it. Finally she said, "Do you mean to say that you have had no communication with your family since you came to Venice?"

"No, Signora, I haven't."

"Can you tell me Chiara's reason for doing this?"

She hesitated. "I can't say for sure, Signora."

She seemed to remember herself, and her tone grew sterner. "Are you aware of the seriousness of your accusation?"

"Yes, Signora."

"I see." She paused and looked at the bundle she still held in her hands. "Perhaps I should hold on to these letters myself, until I can learn Chiara's reason for confiscating them."

She clasped her anxious hands in her lap and spoke softly. "I humbly ask your permission to read the letters from my family, Signora. It troubles me deeply that I've had no contact with them since I've been here." Stinging moisture pricked her eyes.

Signora's face had returned to its typical iciness, but she thought she detected a glint of sympathy in her glance. The old lady stared at her for a long moment. "Very well. I suppose there can be no harm in allowing you to read these letters and to correspond with your family. But be aware that I will be watching you closely. Your unwillingness to share information with me about Chiara's disappearance gives me cause to question your probity."

She was too overjoyed to be ruffled by the insult. "I'm so sorry I've caused you to feel that way, Signora. But I promise if I think of anything at all that might help you find Chiara, I won't hesitate to let you know."

What a relief to at last be freed from the prying questions of that pompous old windbag. It was nearly dinnertime, but she rushed to her room to tear into the stack of letters. Since everyone was on their way to the midday meal she could read without interruption. She passed Ernesta in the hall and asked her to tell Signora she had a headache, so she wouldn't be joining the household for dinner. Alone and trembling, she sat cross-legged on her cot with her pile of mail. The first letter was from her father. As soon as she saw his handwriting her eyes clouded, and she had to keep dabbing them with a handkerchief to see clearly enough to read.

My Dearest Annina,

God alone knows how much I miss your lively, cheerful presence. I think about you constantly, my little one, and pray that you are happy and well. Blessed as we are by His Excellency's kind generosity to you, I still wonder if sending you to Venice was the right thing to do. I worry much about you, my dear little Annina, being so far from your loved ones. Perhaps I worry too much.

Your sister arrived home safely yesterday. She and I are well, though we still have not heard from your mother or brothers. But I do not want you to worry yourself about them. They will come back to us in good time, surely. Please write to me soon, my little love, so I will know you are safe and in good spirits.

Your Loving Papà
31 January 1722

She clutched the letter to her breast and leaned against the wall, weeping. *Poor Papà. He must be frantic with worry, if he still wonders about me at all after so much time.* With tear-drenched eyes she glanced again at the letter. Paolina had added a short note at the end:

Darling Annina, since I left you in the hands of that dreadful woman I have not been able to think of anything else! Please write as soon as you can to let me know you are all right. In the meantime, I pray that someone kind will take you under their wing and protect you. It pains me more than I can say to think that you might be treated harshly. I was very uneasy about leaving you in Venice, and I regret that my anxiety made me seem impatient with you. You deserve only love and tenderness, my sweet little sister.

Your Devoted Paolina

Oh my dear Paolina. What I wouldn't give right now to have you here fussing over me. She sifted through the stack of mail and was relieved to find the letter about Don Antonio that Chiara had been using to blackmail her. Then she looked for more recent letters from home. She came across one from her sister, postmarked the month before.

Dearest Annina,

Today is your 13th birthday, and Papà and I continue to be dismayed that we have heard nothing from you in the nearly one year you have been in Venice. If it were possible to come there myself and find out the cause of your silence, I would not hesitate to do so. But your dear Papà has not been well, and I cannot leave him.

I have sent several letters to Signora Malvolia inquiring about you, but they have all been returned unopened. The reason why is a complete mystery to me. And since I have received no letters from you, I can only imagine that, for some reason, you are being prevented from sending mail. This is quite bewildering.

Since none of the letters I've sent to you have come back, I pray that you have received and read them, and that you know how very much you are missed and loved.

Wishing you the Happiest and most Blessed of Birthdays,

Paolina

She collapsed on her pillow, and her entire body shook with sobs. Her tears of anguish over her loved ones were mixed with tears of rage at Chiara. How *dare* she cause her family such pain and torment. All the letters' seals had been broken, so Chiara must have read them and known the worry and heartache she was causing. How could anyone be so cruel? She couldn't bring herself to re-read the agonized letters she'd written her father and sister during her first month in Venice, and she decided they would never read them either. She didn't want them to ever know how much she'd suffered before Don Antonio came back to Venice. She smiled through her tears as she realized he must have been the answer to Paolina's prayer that someone kind would take her under their wing.

I'll write Papà and Paolina and tell them of all the wonderful things that have happened since Don Antonio's been here, she thought. But first she wanted to destroy all her old letters to them. She gathered the letters and crept quietly downstairs to the kitchen. Bettina was serving in the dining room, so she had the kitchen to herself for a few moments. She took the letters to the hearth, threw them in, and watched them go up in flames. *What an appropriate end for the last reminders of that nightmarish period of my life!*

Just as quietly, she returned to her room and rummaged through her trunk for stationary and stamps. Her eyes fell on *la moretta*, but she didn't touch her. "I have to do this myself," she told the mask. "I don't need your smothering protection."

She took out her writing board and began her letter:

My Very Dearest and Most Adored Papà and Sister,

This is the first chance I've had to write to you since I've been in Venice. Incredible as it might seem, my routine is so busy that it's difficult to find time to write letters. I realize this negligence on my part is inexcusable, and I'm so sorry for the worry I've caused you. But I want you to know I am happy and well.

So many things have happened since I've been here that it's hard to know where to begin. The best thing is that I was fortunate enough to be accepted by Don Antonio as a private student. My studies with him have been very successful so far. And just a few days ago I was allowed to go with him to Treviso to sing in a staged performance. Papà, I don't want you to be distressed about this. It's what I sincerely want, and what makes me happier than anything in the world. Don Antonio is so kind, and a truly brilliant teacher. He's told me there's real potential in my singing, and I think he wants to do everything he can to help me.

Paolina, thank you for your birthday wishes. My 13th birthday was one of the best days of my life, and I'm sure your prayers helped make it that way.

I miss you both terribly and love you so much. I promise to write again soon.

All My Love,
Annina

Luckily it was post day, so the letter would be on its way to Mantua that very afternoon. At her lesson the next day, her first since Treviso, she didn't mention anything to Don Antonio about Chiara's disappearance or the letters. She was too anxious to talk about her triumphant debut.

"So what did you think of my singing, maestro? Was I really all right?"

"You were *meraviglioso*."

She could hardly keep from bouncing up and down with joy. "Does that mean I can make my Venetian debut soon?"

"You need a lot more study before you'll be ready for that."

"But why? You just said I was marvelous."

"A Venetian opera performance is quite different from a little pasticcio in a small town. Venice is the operatic center of the world, and audiences here expect singers to be top notch. Your time for that will come. In the meantime you must concentrate on perfecting your technique. *Ci vuol pazienza*, Annina."

I know it takes patience, she grumbled to herself. But her

eagerness to sing again onstage threatened to overcome her better judgment.

THE FOLLOWING WEEKS were eventful. She received letters from Papà and Paolina expressing their joy and immense relief that they'd finally heard from her. At long last her anxieties were eased, and she felt free of Chiara's entrapment. Chiara still hadn't returned to Signora's house, and her life had become rather agreeable in her absence. Without Chiara's meddling, her lessons with Don Antonio progressed smoothly, although she continued to wish he'd find more performance opportunities for her. But he was set on perfecting her technique and honing her acting skills.

One evening, after an especially productive lesson, she was in her room preparing for supper when she heard a tremulous cry from below, as if someone had received the fright of her life. She rushed downstairs to find everyone gathered in the front hall. Signora's hands were clasped to her heart and her eyes were as round as saucers. Chiara was at the door, bags in hand.

She entered the hall in an imperious manner, as Signora babbled anxiously. "Oh my dear! My darling! Where on earth have you been? I've nearly gone out of my mind with worry. Have we done something to vex you, my dear one? Oh please, *please* tell me what has distressed you so, that you would stay away so long."

Chiara pushed past her with a terse reply. "A sudden opportunity came up. I didn't have time to tell you."

"Opportunity?" Signora's eyes widened all the more. "Oh, tell us about it, dear."

She stopped and turned. "If you must know, I accompanied the Duke of Massa Carrara to Pesaro, where he arranged for me to star in two operas." She paused for an instant and gave Annina a chilling glance before heading for the stairs. Signora was close behind, stumbling over the hem of her gown.

During the following months, although Chiara continued to use Signora's house as her home base, she was away quite a bit without explanation. Signora wrung her hands with worry every time she failed to come home at night, but on her return Chiara would turn a deaf ear to her anxious questioning. None of this bothered Annina too much, since Chiara had apparently given up trying to torment her. She was perfectly happy to be left alone to pursue her studies with Don Antonio.

IN DECEMEBER, DON ANTONIO was to leave for Rome again to prepare for the 1724 Carnival season. His opera there the year before had been so successful he was commissioned to produce two more works at Rome's prestigious Capranica Theater this winter. Annina was thrilled for him but disappointed to be left behind. She hated being stuck in Venice without him.

He told her she should hold off singing any arias until he got back and concentrate on her technical exercises. Later, back in her room, she despaired at the tediousness of this prospect and started to brood. *I'm almost fourteen!* Other girls her age were already making their Venetian stage debuts. Why shouldn't she? Then an idea occurred to her. They had another lesson scheduled before his departure, so she decided she would bring up the subject then.

She all but skipped into his studio. "*Salve*, maestro!"

He looked up from his desk, smiling. "Well, hello, Annina. What puts you in such good spirits today?"

"I've just had a wonderful idea."

"Oh? What's that?" He'd turned his attention back to the score he was working on, but continued to smile with interest at what she had to say.

"I'll go to Rome with you. Maybe I could even sing for the Pope." A jubilant grin spread across her face.

His eyes returned to her, and his smile faded. "I'm afraid that won't be possible, my dear."

"But *why*? You said I was splendid in Treviso last year. And you haven't let me sing in another performance since."

"You *were* splendid. But Treviso was a lucky opportunity, a chance to test your skills in a safe setting. You're still much too inexperienced to face a less forgiving audience. And as for going with me to Rome, that's out of the question. During Carnival the city will be swarming with all sorts of riffraff. Not a safe environment for a young girl."

"But I'd be with you."

He put down his pen and sighed. "What do you think I am, a nursemaid? That I'll have nothing to do in Rome but look after you every minute? Be serious, Annina."

Her eyes smarted and her chest felt tight. "I don't need a nursemaid, and I don't need to be looked after every minute. I can take care of myself."

"Is that so?" The corners of his mouth curled ever so slightly, and he gazed at her for a moment, his eyes shining. Then he rose from his desk and walked to the credenza. "The best thing for you to do while I'm in Rome would be to go home to Mantua and spend Christmas with your family." He started leafing through a score, as if to end the discussion.

"But why can't I sing in Rome?"

He didn't look at her, but continued to stare at the score, his brow furrowed. "Women aren't permitted to sing in church or onstage in Rome."

"What? Then who sings the female parts?"

"Castrati, of course, or young boys."

"That's not fair."

"Maybe not, but neither you nor I make the laws in Rome. His Holiness does, and we must respect that." His eyes met hers. "In any case you're not ready for a debut in a major city. You're too young, and your voice is not yet developed enough to carry in a large church or theater without straining. Now please be reasonable, Annina, and do as I say. Go home to Mantua and rest your voice. When I return to Venice in a few weeks I'll send for you."

He left for Rome the next day, and she wrote Paolina to let her know she'd be coming home for Christmas. Maybe it's for the best, she reasoned. She hadn't seen her family or breathed the fresh air of the Mantuan countryside for almost two years. Graziana had left to visit her mother in Padua, so it would have been mighty lonely at Signora Malvolia's house. Yes, it would be good to go home.

To her astonishment, Chiara approached her that evening with a friendly smile. "Well, Annina, what are you going to do with yourself all these weeks while Don Antonio's in Rome?" Her eyes sparkled, and for the first time Annina noticed charming dimples at the corners of her mouth.

"I'm going home to Mantua, to visit my family. I haven't seen them since I've been in Venice."

"Oh, what a shame. That you won't be here, I mean. I've just heard about a wonderful opportunity that would be perfect for you."

"What opportunity?" she asked, cautiously.

"My good friend, the castrato Gaspari, has been appointed impresario and lead singer at the Teatro San Moisè for the Carnival season. I'm singing principal roles in the four operas he's presenting. But one of the singers who was engaged to sing small parts in the operas has come down with a fever, and it seems she won't be well enough to perform at all this season. I told Gaspari I thought her roles would be ideal for your voice, and I believe he'd be willing to let you try."

Her heart raced. *My Venetian opera debut.* But at once she had misgivings. "That sounds fabulous, Chiara, but I don't think Don Antonio would approve."

"Nonsense. You don't know him like I do. Believe me, he'll be pleased and proud. Just think how exciting it will be to surprise him with the news of your triumph on a Venetian opera stage."

"I don't know . . ."

"How will you ever succeed in opera if you're afraid to take a risk? To have a career you must be willing to plunge in when you have the chance. And it's not as if you've never sung in public before. Why, you were absolutely dazzling onstage in Treviso. The audience went mad for you. And everyone knows how fast you can learn new music. Even I've had to admit that." She pressed her palm to her chest and giggled, as if at her own foolishness. Then she reached over and grasped Annina's shoulder. "You know you can do it. This is a golden opportunity, and you'd be crazy to turn it down."

She flashed another winning smile, and Annina felt herself start to weaken. Then she had an uncomfortable thought. "Why are you suddenly being so nice to me? You've always told me I'll never make it as a singer."

"Oh, but you've proved me wrong. And I'm certainly willing to own up to my foolish error in judgment." She pouted. "I'm terribly sorry for all those times I was unkind to you. I'd like to make up for that by offering you my friendship. What do you say, Annina? Can we be friends?" She smiled and held out her hand. Her dimples almost glistened.

She seemed sincere about making amends, and Annina decided it would be uncharitable not to meet her halfway. She took Chiara's hand.

Her smile glimmered. "That's the spirit. Don't you feel so much better now that we've buried the hatchet? *I* certainly do." She gave a mock frown. "Now, Annina, as your friend I insist you put these silly worries aside and come with me tomorrow to talk to Signor Gaspari."

She dashed off a hasty note to Paolina, saying something had come up and she'd have to postpone her visit home.

SHE SHOOK WITH apprehension the following afternoon as the gondola glided through icy water on its way to the San Moisè. Chiara's dimpled smile and words of assurance were little comfort.

"Oh, Tonio!" Chiara called, waving, when they entered the spacious theater. Grasping Annina's hand, she pulled her toward a heavyset man sitting at a harpsichord near the stage. "Here she is, the girl I was telling you about."

The man stood and looked her over appraisingly. "She's awfully scrawny," he said, turning his eyes to Chiara. His voice was high-pitched and womanly.

She felt very uncomfortable under his critical gaze, as if she were an object to be scrutinized.

"Yes, it's true, Tonio," Chiara said. "And I'm afraid her technique is a bit underdeveloped as well. But won't you give her a chance? She's quite a little actress."

His eyes narrowed. "How old are you, my girl?"

"Thirteen, sir. I'll be fourteen next month."

He raised his eyebrows and ran his eyes over her again. "You look more like twelve." He groaned and turned his eyes to Chiara. "She's a baby. I don't have time to wet-nurse a neophyte."

She felt her jaw tighten.

Chiara simpered. "Really, Tonio, how you exaggerate. Annina is far from a beginner. She's been studying for quite awhile—first with Maestro Tomaso Albinoni, and most recently with Don Antonio Vivaldi."

He still looked doubtful. "Does she have any experience?"

She smiled cheerfully. "Oh yes. She sang splendidly last year in Treviso, in a pasticcio Don Antonio organized."

"Performing a pasticcio in Treviso is a far cry from singing an entire season on a Venetian opera stage. I don't think this is a good idea, Chiara."

"But, Tonio, I'm sure she'll do fine. Just wait till you see how she comes to life onstage. Don Antonio has said as much, and you know he never says anything he doesn't mean."

He sighed and frowned down at Annina. "All right, all right. Let me hear you sing something." He picked up a score. "Sing this."

He sat at the harpsichord, and she faltered her way through the piece, her voice shaking. When she finished he said nothing. He pressed his lips together and glared at Chiara. Her smile almost glowed.

He looked at Annina again. "Can't you sing any louder than that?"

"I, um," she stammered, her knees quavering. "Don Antonio told me I'll strain my voice if I try to sing too loud."

He laughed. "Well let me tell you something, little miss. If you can't manage to generate more volume than you've just demonstrated, you won't be heard beyond the footlights."

"Oh, but she will," Chiara said. "I'll work with her. She's very nervous, poor thing. But she'll get over her fear, you'll see. I'll have her singing with strength and confidence in no time."

He stared at her a moment, then returned his gaze to Annina. "Does your teacher know about this, young lady?"

She bit her lip and looked at Chiara.

She spoke up quickly. "Don Antonio is in Rome for the Carnival season and it would be difficult to reach him. But I'm certain he'd be pleased for his student to help us out in this time of need."

He didn't look convinced, and a dull panic crept through her.

Quite suddenly, though, he seemed to resign himself to the situation. "You're right, Chiara," he said, shrugging his shoulders and sighing. "It would be nearly impossible to find a more experienced singer to fill in for Rosa at this late date. I suppose we'll have to make do with this little mite."

"At last you're being sensible, Tonio." Her eyes shone with triumph.

IT WAS OPENING night of Maestro Tomaso's *Loadice*. Annina was to sing the very small role of Clistene. She'd brought *la moretta* along in her satchel for good luck. But when it was time for her entrance she walked onstage with her heart thudding in her ears and her knees shaking so violently she thought she'd collapse. She looked at the audience and then at the maestro's toad-like face behind the harpsichord. Remembering what Don Antonio had said about Maestro Tomaso's wife dying, she felt a flicker of pity for him.

She knew this wasn't right. Without Don Antonio's approval and support she felt frightfully vulnerable. This was the terror and humiliation of performing in front of Maestro Tomaso's singing class a thousand times magnified. How could she have been foolish enough to think she could pull this off? She alternated between dread at what lay ahead and elation that she was making her Venetian stage debut. Her dream was about to come true. But would that dream become a nightmare?

Somehow her voice became disembodied as she sang her one and only aria that night. Her throat ached with the effort to get the sound out, yet it seemed like someone else was singing. She glanced toward Maestro Tomaso at one point and caught his eye. He looked older and more tired than ever, and his somber expression gave no clue what he was thinking. By the time she finished her aria, the audience's curious looks had turned to angry grimaces and mocking sneers. The light applause and much louder catcalls while she was making her bows made her feel she never wanted to sing onstage again.

Back at Signora's house, she sobbed on Chiara's shoulder. "I was *awful*. Did you hear how they scoffed at me? I just can't go on. I can't sing the rest of the operas."

"There, there, darling," she said, stroking her hair. "You're being much too hard on yourself. It really wasn't as bad as you think. All you need to do is learn to project your voice a bit more, and you'll be fine."

"No, I can't. My throat already hurts from singing louder than I should. Tomorrow I'll tell Signor Gaspari he has to find someone to replace me."

"But it's much too late to find anyone to replace you. You can't let everyone down by backing out now, dear. Don Antonio would be most displeased to hear you behaved so unprofessionally."

"He's going to be even more displeased when he finds out I sang these roles behind his back!" She choked on her last words as a new flood of tears welled up.

"Nonsense. Why on earth would he want to hold you back from the very thing he's been training you for? Your worries are for nothing, Annina darling."

She swallowed a gasping sob. "Are you sure, Chiara?"

"Of course I'm sure. You must think of tonight's performance as a learning experience. The first time is always the most difficult. Why, you should have heard *me* the first time I sang on a Venetian stage. But the worst is over now, and you're going to do much better next time. I'll help you. That's what friends are for, right, Annina?"

She nodded warily and wiped her eyes with the backs of her hands.

THE FINAL OPERA for San Moisè's Carnival season was *Il Nemico Amante*, The Hostile Lover, by Giuseppe Buini. Annina was to sing the part of Idalma, a bigger, more demanding role than her previous three had been. Chiara had coached her for the part, encouraging her to sing with even more power than before and to push her voice as forcefully as she could. She assured her that all singers had to do this to be heard over the orchestra.

As the sinfonia signaled the beginning of the opera she felt a chill in her stomach. Her last three performances had not gone well, and the role she was about to sing was by far the most challenging. It was only a week before the beginning of Lent, and Don Antonio was due to return any day. How would she be able to face him if she failed? She sang that night with all the passion and strength she could muster, but her voice felt so strained she was barely able to make it through her final aria. Surprisingly, the audience seemed much more enthusiastic about her performance than they had before. *I must have awed them with my acting skills*, she thought.

After the final curtain call, as the audience started to scatter and leave, she peeked out from the wings and saw a man approach Signor Gaspari. The castrato seemed to know him, and after they exchanged a few pleasantries she realized the man was a journalist. His loud voice sailed across the stage to the far dark corner where she stood. "I must comment on Signorina Girò's performance."

Her ears perked up as she hovered in the shadows.

"Seldom have I seen or heard such an unbridled emotional display onstage. There is something quite unsettling about her singing. She shows an appalling lack of mastery of vocal technique."

Gaspari shook his head and murmured something she couldn't hear, but his tone and expression told her he was equally displeased with her performance. Her heart plunged as she realized her haste to make her Venetian debut had caused her career to be over before it started.

The journalist went on. "Yet I must say, signore, that the girl's dramatic execution displays a crude power and vitality."

She snapped to attention and strained her ears.

"I suppose I should congratulate you," he said, slapping the castrato's back with his large paw.

Gaspari looked taken aback but fixed his mouth into a tight smile.

"I admire your courage in allowing this little sprite to make her professional debut with your company," the journalist said. "If I was not required by tradition to confine my critical acclaim to singers of the utmost technical excellence, I would not hesitate to offer my endorsement of Signorina Girò."

Despite the journalist's private approbation of her last performance, her reviews were terrible. Chiara was delighted. "Well, well, little miss prima donna, what a disappointment. I never imagined you could sing so badly. You're a laughingstock. You'll never be able to appear on a Venetian stage again." The sparkle had left her eyes and the charming dimples had retreated behind the corners of her smirking mouth.

"Chiara, you tricked me," she rasped in a voice almost too hoarse to speak. "You pretended to be my friend and talked me into doing this, knowing all along I'd fail!" She felt her face crumple. "How am I going to face Don Antonio after this? When he comes back and hears about it he's going to be furious with me."

She sneered. "How you fool yourself, Annina darling. Do you really think he cares that much? That you're the most important thing in the world to him? Believe me, you're not. It's pathetic how you overestimate his concern for you and your stupid little problems." The corners of her pert mouth curled. "Of course, you know this means he'll drop you as a student. He won't work with people he can't trust."

"Why should I believe anything you say, Chiara? *You're* the one who can't be trusted. I'll never trust you again. *Ever!*"

Chiara responded with her most sparkling laugh as she drifted airily out the bedroom door.

She ripped *la moretta* from her satchel, which she'd thrown on the bed. "And you!" she said, her voice a rasping croak. "You've finally got what you want, haven't you? I have no voice! My voice will never be heard on a Venetian stage again!"

THE NEXT DAY, Graziana returned from Padua to find her brooding in the parlor.

"Annina, what's wrong? How was your trip to Mantua?"

"I didn't go." She barely managed to gasp the words out.

"Why not? And what's wrong with your voice? You sound raspy as a sanding file."

"My plans changed."

"Really? Well tell me about it."

"I don't know what went wrong. Everything was going so well for a while, and now things just couldn't be worse."

"What do you mean? Annina, you must tell me what's happened."

"After Don Antonio left for Rome, Chiara persuaded me to stay in Venice and fill in at the San Moisè for a singer who'd become sick."

"Oh dear. You didn't actually do it, did you?"

She looked down, nodded, and tears blanketed her eyes. "And it all turned out awful. I don't know how I could have been so stupid. Now Don Antonio won't want to have anything more to do with me."

Graziana looked concerned but tried to comfort her. She took Annina in her arms and patted her shoulder. "Come now, I'm sure it can't be all that bad."

She sobbed into her friend's neck. "He's going to hate me now. I just know it."

"Nonsense. He could never hate you."

"Why didn't he take me with him to Rome, like I wanted him to? Then none of this would've happened."

Graziana took hold of her shoulders and looked into her eyes. "How could he have done that, Annina? He wouldn't have had time to look after you. And remember, Rome is the center of the Catholic world. Don Antonio is operating right under the Pope's nose there and is expected to act like a priest. How would it look for him to go about Rome and the Vatican with a beautiful young girl clinging to him?"

She glared back at her and frowned. But she knew her friend was right. Faithful, wise Graziana. If only she'd been there when Chiara started tempting her with empty promises. She sighed, exasperated. "Why does Chiara keep torturing me? Why is she so determined to see me fail?"

"Because she imagines you're succeeding where *she* failed."

"What do you mean?"

"I might as well tell you. I recently heard a very interesting story about Chiara and Don Antonio, from one of the other singers who starred in *La verità in cimento*, Anna Maria Strada. She came to me for a dress fitting just before I left town."

"What did she tell you?"

"Well, as you know, Don Antonio helped Chiara get her start. He gave her roles in several of his operas. And she adored him. But unlike you, she was always more interested in herself and her own personal ambitions than in him or anyone else. It didn't take long for her pompous opinion of herself to completely take over her better judgment."

Her eyes widened. "Go on."

"According to Signora Anna Maria, after all the applause on *La verità*'s opening night, Chiara was so full of herself she proposed to Don Antonio that he should leave the priesthood and marry her."

"You can't be serious!"

"Apparently she bragged to the other singers that he was in love with her."

She felt an unpleasant jolt but pressed on with her questions. "What happened then?"

"He rebuffed her, of course, and she's been fuming ever since. In fact, according to Signora Anna Maria, Chiara was so outraged by his rejection she was determined to spite him in some way."

"How awful. What did she do?"

"Remember the nasty satire I told you about? The one written by that hack Marcello?"

She nodded anxiously.

"Once the pamphlet got around, the owners of the San Angelo lost confidence in Don Antonio and he was forced to give up his management of the theater. Marcello and his toadies moved in, took over, and replaced Don Antonio's program with a slew of boring, old-fashioned operas. Then Chiara signed a contract with the new management to sing in all those operas. Can you imagine it, Annina? After everything Don Antonio had done for her?"

So those were the "five operas in a row" that had strained her voice so much she had to stop performing for a season. And she'd alienated Don Antonio in the process. Served her right. *Only now she's trapped me into sharing her fate.*

"I can't imagine how she could turn her back on him like that," she said, bristling with mingled shame and contempt.

"Well here's the really interesting part. All this led to a falling out between Benedetto Marcello and his older brother Alessandro, who really *likes* Don Antonio and his music."

"So then what?"

"Alessandro Marcello wrote a glowing letter to Princess Borghese in Rome, recommending that she arrange for Don Antonio to produce his latest opera there."

"And did she?"

"Yes. Which put Chiara in a real stew. Then she fumed because he didn't beg her to break her contract with San Angelo and come with him."

Her jaw dropped. This was unbelievable. So Chiara imagined herself a scorned woman. If it weren't so shocking, it would almost be laughable. *But why is she taking it out on me?* "So . . . do you think this has anything to do with the way Chiara's treated me?"

"I think it has everything to do with it."

"*Why?*"

"She feels threatened by you. She's seen how much Don Antonio likes you, and she can't stand to see him even look at another female. It makes her crazy."

"But that doesn't make sense. She'd already turned against him before I even came here."

"It backfired on her, and she's still smoldering," she said, with a gleam in her eye. "Think about it this way. He's obviously done fine without her, and now he's shifted his interest to you. That's enough to drive her over the edge and make her really deadly. Like I keep telling you, Annina, you have to watch your step with her."

Coldness crept through her. It was the cold truth of Chiara's words: *Of course, you know this means he'll drop you as a student. He won't work with people he can't trust.*

ON POST DAY she received a forwarded letter from Mantua. It was from Don Antonio, telling her he'd be back in Venice by mid February. Much as she dreaded it, she knew she had to face him.

The day after his return she managed to slip out of the house when no one was looking and hurry through the maze of dark *calli* that opened onto the Campo Santa Maria Formosa. She scurried across the square and along the Rio del Mondo Novo until she reached the Vivaldis' house, at the Ponte del Paradiso. She knocked at the door, her stomach twisting with fear. Margarita seemed surprised to see her. She was gracious as always, but her smile seemed fixed. That wasn't a good sign.

As she approached his studio she considered throwing herself at his feet, bursting into tears, begging his forgiveness, and blaming the whole thing on Chiara. But that would be the coward's way

out. It might spare her his anger, but it would cost her his respect.
She wasn't willing to pay that price.

Chapter Eight

Antonio sat at his desk, his reading glasses perched on his nose, staring at the newspaper in disbelief. A sick feeling swept over him that quickly transformed into anger. Raging thoughts raced through his head. *How could she? The minute my back is turned! Good God, she's Chiara all over again.*

Margarita stood by with a worried look on her face, then hurried from the room to answer the bell at the door. A moment later she returned. "It's Annina," she whispered.

He took a deep breath to steady his nerves. "Send her in."

She had never looked so pretty, and for some reason that angered him all the more. Her eyes were radiant, and her cheeks were flushed from the cold. She smiled brightly, too brightly. "*Salve*, maestro, welcome back!"

There was a hoarseness to her voice he'd never heard before. And her false cheeriness annoyed him. He tightened his lips and clutched the paper more forcefully. "Hello, Annina," he said coldly. "I'm surprised to see you never left Venice, as I'd suggested."

She glanced uneasily at the papers on his desk, "Well, um," she stammered, "things didn't go as I'd expected."

"Yes, I can see that," he said, looking down at the newspaper he held in his hands. "I'd asked Margarita to save all the Venetian opera reviews while I was away. It's a good thing she did, because I wouldn't have believed this if I hadn't seen it with my own eyes."

Her smile faded and she stood in silence, blinking, her eyes pitiably wide and bright. He felt a slight tug at his heart, which was quickly expunged by his growing agitation.

He removed his glasses and sighed with impatience. "How on earth did this come about? How could you consent to such a foolish thing without my knowledge or approval?"

She stared at him steadily, but he could see her hands were shaking. She clasped them together. "I—the opportunity came about very suddenly. The singer who was supposed to do the parts became ill, and Signor Gaspari asked me to take her place."

He was speechless for a moment. Did she really expect him to swallow such a shallow explanation as that? He struggled to keep his temper in check. "I can't believe Gaspari would expect such a thing of you. There must be more to this than you're telling me," he said as evenly as he could manage.

Her lip began to tremble, and she seemed at a loss for words.

He could no longer hold back his anger. "Whatever the reason, this was absolutely foolhardy. You've damaged your voice. I could hear it the minute you opened your mouth. To think you could just breeze in and take over these roles, with no experience, no preparation—on a Venetian opera stage! You must have known I never would have allowed it. You weren't ready for this. I can't tell you how disappointed I am, Annina. I thought I could trust you."

Her face clouded and she looked like she was about to cry. But he was too angry to feel any pity for her. Part of him wanted her to suffer for her insubordination. He glared at her and continued his tongue-lashing. "If you'd followed my advice, I would have soon been able to keep you steadily employed with minor engagements that wouldn't tax your current capabilities, as I did last year in Treviso. Now you won't be able to make an appearance in Venice, or anywhere in the province, for at least another year. Audiences here have long memories, and you wouldn't be well received."

She was staring at the floor, her cheeks glowing bright red and her quivering lips pressed together. There was a tense moment of silence. Then she raised her eyes to his and lifted her chin slightly. "But I heard that newspaper man tell Signor Gaspari my singing had dramatic power."

He had to admire her spirit. She was contrite, but she wasn't groveling. Yet he wasn't ready to let go of his anger. He frowned at her. "Then he's more astute than I would have thought. But your admiring journalist also knows the current fashion does not value dramatic expression over technical brilliance. He certainly wouldn't put his career on the line by saying what he really thinks in print. And as for Gaspari, I can promise he'll never use you again. He's far too cautious to risk going against his audiences' tastes."

She said nothing, but her eyes glistened with agony. She looked so frail and vulnerable, and he felt himself begin to soften. He came around to the front of the desk and leaned against it, his arms folded across his chest. "I know you didn't bring this about yourself, Annina," he said, a bit more gently. "Someone put you up to it. Who was it?" There was little doubt in his mind who was behind this, but he wanted to hear it from her.

She dropped her head, pulled a handkerchief from her sash, and twisted it with trembling hands.

Impatience rose in him again. He sighed. "Was it Chiara?"

Her shoulders began to quiver with little sobs. She nodded without looking up. He maintained his composure with difficulty.

"May I ask how she managed to persuade you to go so completely against my wishes?"

Tears streamed down her crumpled face, and her words were interspersed with choking sobs. "She said she wanted to make amends for all her unkindness to me. Then she advised me that I'd be foolish to pass up such a chance, that I'd never make it as an opera singer if I was afraid to take risks. She said if I didn't take the roles it would be all over Venice that I'd refused to step in when help was needed. She assured me she was only telling me all this as a friend. She filled me with confidence that I could do it, and that you'd be pleased."

His anger surged back with burning force. Only now his rage was directed at Chiara, and memories of her treachery. *That little minx. Is there no end to her intrigues?* "How could you be so gullible, Annina? By now you should have learned she's no friend of yours. She's no friend to anyone, not even to herself. She's her own worst enemy." When he stopped to catch his breath, he saw that she'd lowered her head and covered her face with her hands. She was weeping and trembling like a helpless child who'd been mercilessly punished. He felt like a heartless bully. At once his anger vanished. He stepped toward her and drew her to him. Her little body was quivering like a violin string, and her tears were warm on his chest. She felt so soft and delicate in his arms, he was afraid he'd crush her if he held her too tightly.

"Don't cry, you'll only strain your voice more," he murmured. *Mother of God, that wasn't what I meant to say.* He meant to say something gentle and comforting.

She sobbed all the harder and he felt the delicate weight of her pressing more firmly against him, as the sweet scent of lavender soap filled his nostrils. He didn't know what to do. He'd never had to deal with a situation like this before. At the Pietà the students were so structured and manageable. Disruptions were rare and were always handled by the *maestre*, the female supervisors. But teaching and mentoring a naïve, spirited girl outside the confines of an institutional setting was another matter entirely. What on earth had he gotten himself into?

As if she could read his thoughts, she pulled away and gazed up at him. "Do you still want to be my teacher?"

The simplicity and directness of her question startled him. He didn't answer right away, but gazed back at her in silence. Her eyes were filled with innocence, anxiety, and pain. It was as if her whole world, her very life, depended on his answer. For a long moment, he considered his options. He could simply say, "I think it best if you find another teacher," and have an end to it. But would he be able to get her out of his mind? No, he'd continue thinking and worrying about her, and about the unscrupulous impresarios and patrons who are all too eager to get their hands on a lovely, vulnerable young singer. The thought was unendurable. She'd already dug her way too deeply into his heart. He felt his chest tighten, and turning his head aside for an instant, held a fist to his mouth to stifle a cough.

"Yes, I do," he said finally.

The smile that lit up her face left no doubt he'd made the right decision.

Then he thought he'd better add, "I don't mean to be harsh, Annina. I only want the best for you. I've seen too many over-anxious young singers burn themselves out before they had a chance to get started. I don't want that to happen to you."

"Will you help me?" she asked, dabbing the corners of her eyes with her drenched handkerchief.

"Yes, I'll help you. But you must be willing to commit to a regimen of intense technical study. We already know you have a dramatic gift. That will still be there when you've perfected your craft. If you'll do my bidding, adhere to my instruction, and allow me to help you develop your vocal skill to match your natural talent, you'll have the critics at your feet."

"Do you really think so?" Her sweet little face glowed with renewed hope. "Oh, I'll do anything you say, maestro, I promise."

He looked at her thoughtfully, then said, "I can see I'm going to have to keep a close eye on you from now on."

Her eyes and cheeks were still moist, but the corners of her mouth curled up. "When shall we start our lessons again?" she asked, wiping her nose with the back of her hand.

"I have some business to take care of today. We'll start tomorrow. Plan to come at your usual time." He looked at her half reprovingly, half curiously. "I won't ask how you got here today. But I'll see you home."

He made a point of being patient with her over the following months, a virtue that did not come naturally to him. At her lessons he took her gently through easy technical exercises to repair her strained voice and restore its clarity and suppleness. His patience paid off. Slowly, not only her voice but her lost self-confidence came back. And so did her hold on his heart.

"ANNINA, YOU HAVE an important visitor."

She nearly jumped from her skin at the sound of Signora's hissing voice. It was late evening, and she'd been so engrossed in studying the lyrics to a new aria Don Antonio had given her she hadn't heard Signora open her bedroom door. She parted her lips to ask who it was, but Signora was already bustling down the hall toward the stairs. She took a quick glance in the mirror, smoothed her hair and dress and hurried down to the parlor. Her heart lurched when she saw the duke.

A grin lit up his face. "Signorina Annina, what a delight." Oozing charm and elegance, he bent and kissed her hand.

"Your Excellency." She lowered her eyes and curtsied.

"I only just arrived in town and decided to take this opportunity to pay a call on my enchanting protégée." Gripping her hand, he ran his eyes over her.

She felt her cheeks redden.

"I didn't think it possible, Annina, but you grow lovelier every time I see you."

"Thank you, Excellency." His hand felt hot and moist around hers. She pulled it away and dropped another curtsy.

"Now, now, you needn't be bashful. After all, you're not a little girl anymore. You're practically a woman."

Signora appeared with a carafe of brandy and glasses on a tray. "Your Excellency!" she gushed, her voice uncharacteristically high pitched. She set the tray down and flittered about. "May I pour you a glass?"

"Thank you, Signora Malvolia, I would like to speak with Signorina Annina alone."

"Oh, of course, certainly, Excellency." She scuffled out of the room and pulled the parlor doors closed.

Annina clasped her hands in front of her. "This is certainly an unexpected pleasure, Excellency."

"Yes, it is a pleasure indeed." He poured a glass and held up an empty one to her, his eyebrows raised.

She shook her head.

He sauntered back over to her with his drink in hand and his mouth set in a confident smile. Taking her hand again, he very lightly stroked her palm with one of his clammy fingers. She stiffened and felt her flesh creep. He downed his brandy in a single gulp and went to refill his glass.

Resisting the urge to wipe his sweat from her palm, she clasped her hands again, her knuckles rigid with tension.

"Let us sit, my beautiful one, and I'll tell you why I've come." He sank onto the only upholstered piece of furniture in the room, a settee covered in faded damask. He patted the cushioned seat and gave her an inviting look. Reluctantly, she slid in beside him.

"I heard you made quite an impression at the San Moisè last winter. I'm sorry I had to miss that."

She stared at her clenched hands. "Well, I—"

"Don't be modest, my love." His fingers were caressing her shoulder. She shrank from him, and he glanced at her in mock reproach. "There's no need for alarm, sweet girl. I think you'll be pleased at what I have to say."

An inkling of curiosity made her look his way.

"A fledgling cantatrice such as yourself should have her own private domicile. Thus I've decided to remove you from this gloomy boarding house and set you up in a private apartment, under my protection of course."

"By your *protection* you mean . . ."

"That I'll pay your rent and all your expenses, naturally."

Her heart fluttered with excitement. "Oh, Your Excellency, this is much too generous."

His smile was gallant. "Nothing is too generous for such a beautiful, talented young lady as you, Signorina Annina."

She dismissed all her foolish fears. He really did mean well, she felt sure of that now.

ANTONIO TURNED AND smiled at Annina as she entered his studio. Her cheeks were prettily flushed, and she grinned happily.

Before he had a chance to greet her, she spoke up excitedly. "The duke wants me to move out of Signora's house. He says he'll pay for me to have my own apartment."

He stared at her, alarmed, and placed the score he'd been perusing on the credenza. "I don't think that's a good idea."

"Why not? You know how much I hate that wretched boardinghouse. The duke has offered to give me a place of my own to live and money to live on."

"You can't take money directly from him! Do you know what he'd then expect of you?"

She blinked. "What do you mean?"

He sighed. "You're very innocent, Annina. Let me make this clear. He'll expect to share your bed as well as your operatic triumphs."

Her flushing cheeks turned crimson.

"I'm sorry to be so blunt, but it's important you understand this."

She tighted her lips, defiantly it seemed. "I'm not a child. I'm old enough to have my own home."

"Annina, you must listen to me. Venice is not a safe place for a young girl to be alone. Who would protect you?"

She crossed her arms and frowned, her lip quivering.

He sighed again. "Be reasonable. Do you want to end up like Chiara?"

She lifted her chin. "You know I'm nothing like her."

"The duke doesn't, though. If you accept payment from him on those terms, he'll think he owns you."

Her discomfort was palpable. She pulled her handkerchief from her sleeve and squeezed her fists around it. "You're wrong, maestro, he's not like that at all. He really wants to help me build my opera career."

He almost laughed at her naïveté. "Annina," he said, trying to calm his voice, "for your own good I must tell you this is wrong. The arrangement he's proposed would be ruinous for you. Your operatic success is not his first priority. He wants to use you for his own ends, and if you insist on remaining under his dubious protection I'm afraid I can't help you."

She stared at him in wide-eyed silence, and he noticed she'd twisted her handkerchief into a knot.

He frowned, shook his head, and turned back to the score he'd been studying. "Do as you please, then. You don't need my permission to leave Signora Malvolia's house."

She spoke softly, her voice trembling slightly. "I know I don't need your permission . . . but . . ."

"You'd like my approval," he said, turning back to her.

"Yes."

"I'm afraid I can't give it."

She looked defeated, then her face brightened. "I'll write to my sister. Maybe she could come live with me and be my chaperone. What about that, Antonio?" She had dared to drop his priestly title. He somehow didn't mind.

"Well . . . I suppose that's a possibility."

"I'll write to her today. I'm sure she'll be willing when she realizes how important this is to me."

"Hmm." He thought a moment. "Whatever your living arrangements, you must agree not to sing in any more public performances until I decide you're ready."

"Oh, I promise."

"And if the duke is to continue being your patron, he must understand this and consent to it."

"He will, I'm sure. I'll make him understand. Or . . . maybe you could talk to him, maestro. He likes you, and he'll listen to you."

He smiled at her innocence. "I think he likes my music more than he likes me. Nevertheless, I'll speak to him if you wish. I'll try to explain to him the folly of pushing you into a career before you're ready."

The duke left town again before Antonio had a chance to talk to him. But the next day a messenger delivered a banknote to Antonio, signed by the duke, to cover Annina's expenses for the next six months.

"Does this mean I can move into my own apartment?" she asked him eagerly at their next lesson.

"You'd better wait on that. I've just received an invitation to produce my new opera in your hometown."

Her eyes widened. "You're going to Mantua? When?"

"Prince Philipp has asked that I begin rehearsals just after the New Year. The opening performance is scheduled for mid January."

She looked sad. "I wish I could go. It's been so long since I've seen my family."

"You haven't given me a chance to ask."

"Ask what?"

"If you would do me the honor of accompanying me."

Her ecstatic smile warmed his heart.

Chapter Nine

The minute they made port, Annina hurried from the boat, the slant of the gangplank nearly causing her wobbly sea legs to falter. She clung to the rope with one gloved hand to steady herself as the January wind whipped around her legs.

"Annina, *ma petite!*" her father cried, as he rushed to greet her. She threw herself into his arms, and he held her in a firm embrace. Taking her by the shoulders he backed away for a bit and gazed at her with tear-filled eyes. "Look at you, my little one, I almost would not have known you, you have grown so. And how beautiful you have become. So like your mother, but in some ways even more love*ly*." Tears welled in his eyes all the more, and he drew her into another warm embrace. She clung to him and bit her lip to keep from sobbing.

Antonio had seen to their luggage, and soon joined them.

Pierre grasped Antonio's hand in both of his. "How wonderful to have you with us again, monsieur maestro! And how can I thank you enough for your kindness to my little Annina?"

"There's no need to thank me, Signor Girò. Annina is a gifted student and a pleasure to work with."

"But she is a hand*ful*, no?"

Her joy was disrupted by mild annoyance. "*Papà*. Must you talk about me as if I'm five years old?" She glanced at Antonio and saw he was making an effort not to laugh.

"Forgive me, my little one. I forget you are a young woman now. I am just a foolish old man, and I say foolish things."

"It's all right, Papà." She snuggled against his arm. Truthfully, she was so happy to see him that his scatterbrained chatter was like music to her ears.

"She is a good girl, maestro, but of course. It should please you to know that as a little girl she pestered me al*ways* about the theater. Oh, how she would go on. I never heard the end of it." He threw up his free hand in his distinctively French way.

Still on the verge of laughter, Antonio smiled and nodded.

Her patience grew thin, and she squeezed her father's arm. "Papà—"

"But, natura*lly*, I was concerned about my little daughter falling under the influence of the sordid types that populate the theater world. I am sure you must know what I mean, monsieur maestro."

"Yes, signore, I understand exactly what you mean," he said, crossing his arms and looking more serious."

"And yet now I can see she is a natur*al* for the theater and that is what makes her truly happy. Realizing this, it is such a comfort to me, monsieur, that my little Annina has you to look after her."

She sighed and glanced at Antonio. If Pierre was trying his patience, he made no indication of it.

"You, monsieur maestro, clearly are not like these other people of the theater. You are a holy man of the Church, and my precious little daughter could have no better guide and protector, sure*ly*."

Antonio smiled respectfully. "I appreciate your vote of confidence, Signor Girò."

Pierre invited Antonio to supper that evening, but he declined politely, saying he believed he was expected to dine with the prince. So they made their goodbyes.

As the carriage pulled in front of the old, familiar house, Paolina rushed out the door, an apron covering her simple dress. Annina leaped from the carriage before anyone could assist her and ran to her sister.

"Annina, Annina! Look at you! Where is the frightened little girl I bid farewell to in Venice three years ago? Oh, my sweet baby sister!" She hugged her, then pulled back to look at her. She was smiling, but her eyes were filled with tears. "All I see is a lovely, confident young woman. I can't get over how you've changed. Oh, my little Annina," she said, drawing her sister to her again.

The last time she saw Paolina she had to look up to meet her eyes. Now their eyes were nearly level, which made her sister seem smaller than she remembered. She also noticed faint lines in her face that weren't there before and a few strands of gray in her dark hair. But her soft brown eyes were as full of love and tenderness as they'd ever been. She was too choked up to speak, so she held Paolina tightly.

When she stepped in the house her heart gave a violent leap. Laurent emerged from their father's study with a glass of wine in his hand and a charming grin on his face. At the sight of her, his eyes widened, and he put down his glass. "This can't be little Nannina!"

She flew to him, and he swept her into his arms and twirled her around.

The next thing she knew, Marcel came from behind and pulled her from his brother's arms. "Well, well, who is this fine lady who's come to visit us?" he said, feigning an aristocratic accent. He held her firmly around the waist and her feet dangled off the floor. It tickled, and she squirmed and giggled. Her stylish little tri-cornered hat dropped to the floor, and her hair came loose and fell around her shoulders.

Paolina admonished impatiently. "Will the two of you never learn to act your age? Your sister is a young lady, not a little hellion to roughhouse with. And just look! You're spoiling her lovely outfit."

Marcel put her down and gave her an elaborate bow. "My deepest apologies, Your Ladyship."

She wrapped her arms around her middle, and her eyes teared with laughter.

Laurent took up his wineglass. "A toast to our dear little sister's homecoming!"

"*Mais oui!*" Pierre interjected as he entered the hall, carrying as much of her baggage as he could manage. He set her bags on the floor and gasped for breath, then said, "Paolina, my dear, bring the wine flask and glasses. We must drink to our Annina's return and rejoice that she is safely home with her family."

Paolina sighed and did as he asked, and the rest of the family moved into the parlor. The wine was poured and Pierre, with moist eyes, glanced around at everyone.

"I cannot say what a joy it is to have all of my children about me once again. It has been much too long." He raised his glass. "To my loved ones, my dear ones. May you all have happy, prosperous lives."

Annina was already feeling tipsy. Drunk as much with emotion as with wine, she set her glass down. Running to her father and then to each of her siblings, she sobbed and hugged them as if she'd never let them go.

Her brothers left soon after dinner, and Pierre went to bed. But she was too restless to sleep. In the kitchen she and Paolina sat at the old wooden table. The hearth's glowing flames made the faint lines she'd noticed on her sister's face seem more pronounced.

"Is everything all right, Paolina?" she asked with a quiver of worry in her voice.

"I won't mislead you, darling," she said, sighing. "You're old enough to hear the truth."

She felt a little jab in her heart. "What is it?"

"Papà is in serious financial straits. With you and Mamma gone, he's been too dispirited to run his business effectively. And to make matters worse, your brothers come around regularly to divest him of every *soldo* he manages to earn. I hate to disillusion you, but I think you should know this."

Her stomach churned with unease. "But *why*, Paolina? Why do they do that to Papà?"

"Because he allows it. He's so desperate for their love he can't bring himself to say no to them. He refuses to see how they're using him."

"Why haven't you mentioned this in your letters?"

"I didn't see any point in causing you distress, darling, when you were so far from home. There would have been nothing you could do about it."

"But there *is* something I can do about it. I'm going to be earning a lot of money soon, when Antonio starts giving me roles in his operas."

"*Antonio?*" Paolina looked at her sharply, her eyebrows raised.

"Yes, that's what he wants me to call him."

"I see. I didn't realize you and he had become so familiar."

"Oh, we have. I mean, I'm very comfortable with him. He treats me like family."

"Well, I suppose that's a good thing. Now what were you saying about opera roles?"

Her insides bristled with excitement. "Antonio has said that in a few months I can start singing in private salon concerts and by next year I'll be ready to sing onstage in his operas. I'll be earning my own money, and nothing would give me more pleasure than to use that money to help my family."

"That's awfully generous of you, Annina. You've always been so sweet and loving. But you're only a child. You shouldn't be burdened with supporting our family."

"But it's not a burden. I *want* to help. Don't you see? Here in Mantua there's nothing I can do to help Papà. In Venice I have the opportunity to prosper with my music. And—if you'll go back there with me we can move into our own apartment, where I can have privacy for my practicing, away from the distractions of Signora Malvolia's boardinghouse."

"Yes, you mentioned that in your last letter, but I haven't had much time to think about it." She gazed at her sister, then looked down thoughtfully. "There's something else I should tell you."

"What?"

"I've heard from Mamma."

"*What?* When? Why haven't you told me this before? What did she say?" Her insides were a whirlwind of joy and anxiety.

"I received a letter from her last week. You're the first person I've told."

"You mean you haven't even told Papà?"

"No. I was too ashamed for her."

"Ashamed?" Her heart had a sinking feeling.

Paolina kept her eyes cast down and seemed to be choosing her words carefully. "Mamma is in Venice. She's living in the house of a man named Francesco Cavalarizzo."

"Do you mean . . . she's left Papà for another man?" Her voice quavered, and she started to feel ill.

"I don't really know for sure. But it certainly seems that way."

She couldn't believe it. In all these years of worrying what had become of her mother, it never occurred to her that she was being unfaithful to Papà. *Why, Mamma is no better than one of those courtesans Graziana was telling me about*, she thought, as angry tears filled her eyes.

Paolina glanced at her, blinked, and smiled. "There is some encouraging news, though."

"What's that?" She tried to feign enthusiasm, but her voice sounded sad and dejected.

"Mamma would like to see us. I think she might even be hoping for a reconciliation with Papà."

She felt a faint surge of hope. "I think you should tell Papà about this. And now you have even more reason to come back to Venice with me. We can meet with Mamma there, talk to her, and help pave the way for her reunion with Papà. Oh, it's perfect!"

"I don't know, Annina. How would we afford it?'

"The duke has offered to pay my rent and all my expenses. Antonio didn't like the idea until I thought of asking you to live with me. And then his sister Margarita heard about an apartment for rent in the Santa Maria Formosa district, not far from the Vivaldis' house." She looked at her sister with pleading eyes. "Won't you please, *please* consider it?"

Paolina was thoughtful for a moment or two before she responded. "I think it might be a good idea."

At once her sinking heart leapt for joy. "Oh, this will be wonderful. I can't wait to tell Antonio."

Paolina's expression grew more serious. "You mustn't tell him, or anyone, our suspicions about Mamma's conduct in Venice. Most especially, you must not tell Papà. It would kill him if he thought Mamma had been untrue to him."

"Yes, it would."

"As distraught as we've been about her long absence, we must allow her the chance to have her say before we jump to conclusions. So I'll go to Venice with you. We'll leave as soon as possible. I don't know if my nerves can take much more of the turmoil around here, anyway."

Her heart soared, but then she had a worrisome thought. "What about Papà? Will he be all right if you leave him?"

"Marcel and Laurent are home most of the time now. They'll continue to squander his money, of course, but I can't stop that even if I'm here. At least they'll be around to keep him company. And as you said, we can probably do more to help Papà if we're in Venice. Perhaps even persuade Mamma to come back to him."

Antonio had to rush back to Venice ahead of them to meet with the owners of the Teatro San Angelo. Before he left, he promised he'd have Margarita arrange the apartment rental for them. The sisters left Mantua a few days later.

On the long boat ride, she told Paolina about Chiara's recent trickery and her troubles at the San Moisè.

Her sister gave her a reproving look. "*Santo cielo*, Annina, what mischief you get into if you don't have someone to look out for you every minute. I'm surprised Don Antonio isn't at his wits' end with you by now."

This scolding was to be expected and didn't bother her in the least. She grinned and shrugged.

AS THEIR BOAT entered the Venetian lagoon, she breathed deeply and savored the salty smell of the sea, and her ears feasted on the cries of gulls overhead. She felt a rush of elation. They were to move into their new apartment that same day.

The furnished lodgings Margarita had found for them were on the second floor of a building that rose above the calm waters of the Rio Maria Formosa. The windows on the opposite side overlooked the *campo* Santa Maria Formosa, which opened out before the church of the same name. Like every square in Venice, this *campo* was a tiny village unto itself. The ground floors of the surrounding buildings housed shops and markets of all kinds: an apothecary, blacksmith, shoemaker, coffee shop, greengrocer, baker, butcher, and barber. Their *appartamento* was small, just three rooms and a kitchen, but to Annina it seemed like a palace. Singing to herself, she hung her dresses in the wardrobe cupboard that stood near the bed she and her sister would share. When Paolina left the room for a moment she quickly took *la moretta* from her trunk. "I'd better hold on to you, just in case," she whispered, as she tucked the mask in the back of the cupboard, behind her clothes.

After they'd unpacked, she gazed out their bedroom window and watched glittering patches of sunlight dance on the dark green waters of the canal. She sighed with pleasure. At last her dreams were coming true. Best of all, her mother was nearby and wanted to see her. She could hardly contain her delight at all her recent good fortune. Yet despite her happiness, she started to brood. She'd never discussed her conflicted feelings about her mother with anyone. But doubts about her mother's love for her festered at the very core of her being. That was her dark secret. No one, not even Antonio, knew of the pain her poor unhappy mother had caused her. It was too mortifying to admit she'd been denied the most basic need of any human being—a mother's unconditional love.

That night she lay awake, trying to persuade herself that everything would be fine once they were together again. During the six years since she last saw Bartolomea she'd fantasized more times than she could count how it would go. She'd convinced herself that as soon as her mamma saw her, her face would melt with emotion and she'd gather her daughter into a warm embrace and tell her how sorry she was for hurting her. At that moment all her accumulated anguish would melt away, and she'd bask forever after in the secure knowledge that she was loved and cherished by her mother.

By eight o'clock the next morning the *campo* buzzed with activity. She opened the parlor window to a colorful view crowded with balconies, shutters, and chimneys. Cages of chirping canaries, crowing blackbirds, and squawking parrots dangled over nearly every balcony. Housewives hung their laundry and gossiped from window to window. Below, rosy-cheeked water girls chattered and laughed as they drew buckets from the well, the neighborhood cats prowling about eager for a sip. An old peasant woman, bent from carrying baskets of bottled milk, glowered at a rowdy pack of boys who surrounded her and rudely mimicked her hunched posture and crooked gait. She upbraided them in the name of all the saints and powers of darkness, and they scampered off, laughing uproariously. A carpenter made fragrant whittlings with his knife and flirted with a shop girl, and a fisherman wandered across the *campo*, hawking baskets of sole and mackerel with a melodious cry of "Beautiful and all alive!"

She stepped out on the balcony, breathed in the crisp winter air, and peered across the square toward the *Rio del Mondo Novo*, New World Canal, which led to Antonio's house. Her heart spilled over with happiness. This "new world" was her dream coming true. Paolina soon joined her, carrying a tray of steaming coffee with milk. They sat in comfortable companionship and sipped from their mugs, while streams of sunlight bathed them in the winter morning's chill light.

"I have a bit of news," Paolina finally said, her gaze fixed on the nearby Rio del Mondo Novo.

Her slightly grim tone caused Annina's stomach to agitate, and the sip of coffee she'd just swallowed turned bitter. She set her cup down. "What is it?"

Paolina reached into her apron pocket and pulled out a folded sheet of paper. She hesitated a moment, then handed the paper to her sister. "This arrived just this morning."

Anxiously she unfolded the paper and read:

> *To my daughters:*
> *I have considered your suggestion and will*
> *come to your apartment this afternoon.*
>   *Your mother*

Her heart leaped. Clutching the note possessively, she looked up at her sister. "How did she know where to find us?"

"I didn't tell you yesterday because I was afraid she might not respond. Soon after we arrived I had a note delivered to her at Signor Cavalarizzo's address, suggesting that she come and stay with us for a bit."

Her agitation turned to exhilaration. "Paolina! This is the most wonderful news you could have given me."

She smiled kindly and reached over to squeeze her little sister's hand. "I'm glad, darling. But you mustn't get your hopes up too much. You know how temperamental Mamma can be."

"Yes, yes, I know," she said, as her soaring heart started to flounder.

Bartolomea arrived later that day, dragging a trunk behind her. She gave each of her daughters a perfunctory kiss on the cheek, then, with critical eyes, she proceeded to scan their sparsely furnished parlor.

"Annina," she said tersely, "what sort of patron is this duke of yours? He hasn't even provided a spinet."

"Oh . . . well, Mamma, we only moved in yesterday. I'm sure with time . . ." Her voice trailed off. She prayed she didn't sound as nervous as she felt.

"Hmmph," her mother responded. She didn't seem terribly interested.

Paolina spoke up. "Mamma, come see the lovely room we've prepared for you. Annina and I will share the other bedchamber so you can have your privacy."

"That's very thoughtful of you, dear," she said with indifference.

The following Sunday, Antonio invited the three of them to a concert his students were giving at the Pietà. These concerts were held every Sunday and holiday, and Venetians from all walks of life, along with visitors from far and wide, came in throngs to hear the famed *figlie di coro* whenever they performed. As they entered the crowded hall, Annina looked up to see about two dozen girls and young women, all in red gowns. They were only partially visible behind the latticework that shielded their performance loft, but she could see that each of them held an instrument. Straining her eyes, she noticed violins, cellos, mandolins, flutes, oboes, bassoons, and several other instruments she couldn't name.

Soon Antonio appeared in the priestly cassock he always wore at the Pietà. Movements behind the latticed screen looked shadowy, but she could see everyone position their instruments to begin. The music that started a moment later was anything but shadowy. Brightly colored and wildly exciting tones filled the room and moved at such a lively pace her ears could hardly keep up. More instrument sounds than she'd ever heard flooded her eager senses. It sounded so invigorating and fun. Yet these young women's technical precision and professionalism were astounding. She almost envied them, but the joy their music stirred in her heart prevented her. Antonio was indeed a gifted teacher, and she was grateful his gifts could be shared with so many.

AT HER LESSON the next day she was surprised when Antonio handed her a banknote for sixty *zecchini*.

"What's this?" she asked.

"The duke sent this for you. One of his minions, Count Savioli, delivered it to me last night."

She stared in astonishment at the unimaginable riches she held in her hand.

He smiled at her. "So, what are you going to do with your newfound wealth?"

"Well . . . I'd like to buy a harpsichord. I really need one for practicing at home."

"I think that's an excellent idea."

"When Paolina and I went shopping this morning I saw one I liked very much, at the shop of Andrea Bonazza. The sign on top said it was built by Domenico da Pesaro and includes a four-foot stop."

"Sounds like a good instrument."

"Do you think sixty *zecchini* would be enough to buy it?"

"More than enough. You could probably get it for a lot less."

"Really? But I don't know what to do. I've never bought anything like this before. Could you help me?"

"Hmm. I know a man, Giovanni Gallo, who's negotiated instrument purchases for me before. For a small percentage he'll get you the best price. I'll talk to him."

"Oh, would you? Thank you, Antonio."

Within a few days it was all arranged. Signor Gallo met her at Antonio's house and informed her that Signor Bonazza had agreed to sell the harpsichord for thirty *zecchini*. So if she would kindly give him that amount, plus five more for his negotiating fee, he would finalize the purchase that afternoon and have the instrument delivered to her apartment immediately.

Her heart swelled with happiness. She'd never felt so grownup and professional. But her life soon took an unexpected turn.

Chapter Ten

Early one morning Paolina was in the kitchen making coffee. Bartolomea had gone to the market for fresh bread. Annina was in the bedroom she and Paolina shared, brushing her hair and musing about how well things had turned out. Their mother had not yet told them anything about her life in Venice these past years. But even though she remained distant, Annina found her presence reassuring. She was so happy to once again have a real home, in comfortable companionship with her mother and sister. No more Signora Malvolia or Chiara to harass her. Best of all, she was finally making significant progress with her music. Soon she'd be singing onstage again and earning money to help her family. Things couldn't be better.

Still in her nightgown, she went to the parlor and sat at her harpsichord. On the rack was the new aria she and Antonio had been working on together. She plucked away at the stirring melody and hummed along. Then she dreamily mouthed the aria's words and basked in the sweet agony of a girl betrayed by her loved one:

My suffering spirit . . . speak no more of love!

Her reverie was interrupted when her mother returned, empty-handed. Something was wrong.

Bartolomea stalked over to the harpsichord and glared at her daughter.

She felt an unpleasant quiver inside. "Mamma, what's happened?"

Her mother's eyes were cold and hard, and her jaw was tense with anger. "Do you know what they're saying about you?"

"No . . . I . . . what do you mean, Mamma?" she stammered, flustered.

"Women at the marketplace were saying insinuating things about *L'Annina del prete rosso*—the red-haired priest's Annina."

"I don't understand. Why would they call me that? Why would they be talking about me at all?" She tried to sound calm, but the little quiver she felt inside had gripped her voice.

"They're talking about you because you are making a bold spectacle of yourself."

Her mother's voice had taken on a caustic tone, and Annina's inner quivering was taken over by sharp jabs of fear. She sprang to her feet, and tears filled her eyes. "Mamma, *please* tell me what you're talking about. What have I done wrong?"

"Very well, I'll spell it out for you. They wouldn't call you that unless there was reason to believe some sort of intrigue is going on."

"That's ridiculous. How could anyone think such a thing?"

"You have set yourself up for it, Annina. Everyone knows the opera business in Venice is a den of vice, and now that you're so conspicuously involved with a well-known impresario, people are going to assume the worst."

"But they're wrong. They have no right to say things like that."

"It doesn't matter whether they're right or wrong. The fact that they're saying it is enough."

Her insides burned with indignation. She tried to quell her growing rage by crossing her arms and tightening her lips. Finally she said, "Well I'm not going to allow my life to be ruled by a few meddling busybodies."

"Your life and your reputation will be tinged by public opinion whether you decide to allow it or not. And I won't tolerate it. No daughter of mine is going to be talked about that way in the fish markets of Venice. Can you imagine what your father would have to say about this? You're to pack your things right now, young lady. I'm taking you back to Mantua where you belong."

"No, Mamma, I won't go. My life is here now."

"I'm your mother, and you'll do as I say."

"But this is what I've always wanted. This is what *you* taught me to love."

"I never taught you to behave like a shameless hussy."

Her words stung, and salty tears rolled down Annina's cheeks. "How can you say that, Mamma? I've never behaved like that."

Paolina came out of the kitchen, wiping her hands with a dishtowel. "What on earth are you two going on about?"

Bartolomea had worked herself into a frenzy. "The neighborhood gossips are talking about your sister as if she were a brazen harlot."

Paolina's mouth fell open. "*What?* Mamma, you can't be serious."

"Would I joke about something like that?"

"No, of course not. But I find it very hard to believe."

"I know what I heard with my own ears. And as a mother I have the duty and the right to remove my underage daughter from this hotbed of slanderous incriminations."

Annina's indignation escalated into bristling rage. She glowered at her mother through tear-clouded eyes and shrieked, "I believe you gave up that right when you abandoned me six years ago! Have you forgotten, Mamma? I was nine years old, and without warning you walked out on me. You left me to languish in agony, not knowing where you were or why you'd rejected me. Where was your motherly concern for me then? I could have been lying dead in the gutter, and you never would have known or cared. And what's more, you've been living in sin. Do you have any idea of the shame and agony you've caused? So don't give me this lofty speech about your duty and right as a mother. You've never been a proper mother to me!" She couldn't say anymore. She was shaking, sobbing, and gasping for breath.

Paolina tried to interject, but Bartolomea cut her off. She grasped Annina painfully by the shoulders. She tried to squirm away, but her mother held her fast. "I won't have my own daughter speak to me in that way, do you understand? I won't stand for it. Now pack your things as I told you."

She glared back at her mother. "No, I won't."

Bartolomea's face went white with fury, and her voice had a biting edge. "You refuse to obey me? Then you are no longer my daughter. It would have been better if you'd never been born."

Her icy calmness was much more terrifying than her shrill anger of just a moment ago. Annina stared at her in stunned disbelief.

Paolina spoke up quickly. "Stop, Mamma, you can't mean that. You don't know what you're saying."

Bartolomea glared at her with chilling composure, then cut her eyes to Annina. "I know exactly what I'm saying." She turned and walked calmly toward her bedroom.

Annina stumbled after her, sobbing. "Mamma, please, *please* don't say that."

Her mother began filling her trunk with her belongings.

She clutched her arm and pleaded, "No, Mamma, please don't leave me. You mustn't do this to me again. You *mustn't*. I can't bear it."

She jerked her arm from her daughter's clinging hands and continued packing her things, her features set in stone-cold rigidity.

"Please, Mamma. Can't we be sensible and talk about this?" said Paolina, who had followed them into the bedroom.

"There's nothing more to talk about," she snapped, without looking up.

Annina stood as close as her mother would allow, trembling and whimpering. "Don't you love me even a little, Mamma? Does my happiness matter at all to you?"

Her mother ignored her.

Paolina put her arm around her sister. "Mamma, haven't you the least bit of pity for the pain you're causing? Annina is only a child. I don't see how you can be so hard and cruel." Her usual calm voice shook with distress.

Without a word, Bartolomea grasped the handle of her trunk and pulled it out of her bedroom toward the front door.

Annina was overtaken by uncontrollable rage. She ran after her mother and screamed, "Go then, *go!* I hate you and I hope I never see you again! You are the cruelest, most hateful mother in the world! I wish my mother was *anyone* but you!"

Paolina followed and tried to restrain her. "Annina, don't say things you'll regret."

Bartolomea had already slammed the door behind her. She never even looked back.

Pressed to the closed door, Annina slid to the floor and dissolved into tears of anguish. Paolina sank down beside her and gathered her into her arms. She pressed her face into her little sister's hair, and Annina could feel her gentle sobs.

SHE NEVER FELT like getting dressed that day. After a meager lunch of vegetable soup, which she couldn't bring herself to eat, Paolina prepared a bath for her. The warm moisture helped relax her bodily tension, but the water's soothing mist brought fresh tears to her eyes. After her bath, she wrapped in a dressing gown and returned to the parlor.

"Aren't you going to get dressed for your lesson?" Paolina asked.

Her eyes were still stinging and hazy, and her voice was hoarse from crying. "No, I can't go. I couldn't possibly sing today. And I don't want Antonio to see me like this."

"All right then, I'll go over shortly and tell him you're not coming."

During Paolina's brief absence, she mulled over the dreadful morning. How had things gone so wrong? Why were the women at the marketplace saying such vicious things about her? And why was her mother so willing to believe them? What would Antonio think of all this? She clutched her middle and bent forward as another heaving sob welled up.

"WHAT DID YOU tell him?" she asked anxiously when Paolina returned from the Vivaldis' house.

"That you didn't feel up to coming to your lesson."

"What did he say?"

"He asked if you were ill."

"*And?*"

"I told him a bit of what happened."

"How did he react?"

"He's very concerned. He said he'll come see you later."

That evening after supper she sat with her legs curled beneath her on the small divan in the parlor. She heard a light knock at the front door, then Paolina's footsteps in the hall. She wrapped her arms about herself.

There was murmuring in the front hall, then Antonio appeared in the archway, smiling at her sympathetically. He came over, sat beside her, and took her hand.

"Are you all right?" he asked. "I've been worried about you."

She nodded. "I think so."

"Would you like to talk about it?"

Burning moisture stung her eyes, and she bit her lower lip. He pressed her hand. Then, stopping every few moments because of her tears, she told him everything.

Paolina had come into the room and was seated in a high-backed wooden chair opposite them. Antonio looked at her, and she nodded soberly, confirming the story.

He looked back at Annina with a tender glow in his eyes. "Your mother heard some foolish gossip and overreacted, that's all. You mustn't take it so to heart."

"But she told me she wished I'd never been born," she wailed.

"That was a terrible thing to say. But people often say cruel things they don't mean when they're angry, usually to the ones they care about the most."

She closed her eyes, and her lip trembled uncontrollably. "I know. I said some rather awful things myself."

"There, you see? And you didn't mean them, did you?"

With her eyes still closed, she shook her head.

"Your mother was right about one thing, though. When you're in the public eye, you will be talked about. And the talk usually won't be flattering. Venetians thrive on malicious gossip and rumors of intrigue. It's their favorite form of entertainment, next to the opera. If there's nothing real to base their tongue-wagging on, they'll make things up."

Paolina looked at him with an exasperated expression. "How can we put a stop to it?"

"We can't."

"Then what should we do?" she said, her voice uncharacteristically shrill.

"Ignore it."

She sighed and slumped against the back of her chair.

"But what about Mamma?" Annina said. "How can we get her to come back?"

He turned his eyes back to her. "I think you should write her a letter and explain how all this has made you feel."

"A letter? What would I say? I don't even know where to begin."

He gave her hand a gentle squeeze. "I'll help you. Paolina, we'll need your input too."

He led her to the dining table, while Paolina fetched paper, pen, and ink. First, they talked through the overall situation, and he jotted notes. They discussed the problems back home, especially Pierre's financial situation and their brothers' wild extravagances. Based on all their comments, he composed the letter, then read it aloud to them:

Dearest Mamma,

The love between parents and children is a law of nature, sanctioned by God Almighty. We, your daughters Paolina and Annina, beg you not to sever this loving bond, which is God's will, over a momentary displeasure caused by evil rumors. Your daughters are suffering overwhelming sorrow over your absence from our home, and we are exceedingly sorry that we were the cause of your decision to depart. Above all, we regret that this alienation occurred over such a small matter, and not for any truly important reason. We beg you to come home to us and not cause such sorrow to two daughters who love you more than themselves. So we hope you are equally loving and, rather than listen to wicked gossip, will follow God's law and please him by granting your pleading daughters' request.

We also hope you will understand why we cannot return to Mantua with you. I, Paolina, have over the course of many years struggled in vain to hold things together at home. I have decided to make my home in Venice now, where I can look after my little sister. And I, Annina, am doing the best I can with my music and enjoying the honor of noble patronage. I'm hopeful for continued good fortune and for more performance opportunities. As long as God grants me these things, I will not hesitate to help my parents financially. There are other reasons why I cannot return to live in my father's house, but the main one is that it's important I not live near my brothers. With their wild, extravagant ways they have squandered all Papà's assets and left him in poverty. How then could I prevent them from squandering the little bit of affluence I've found?

We pray that you will know we sent you this letter in good faith, in keeping with our humble Christian sentiments and the countless feelings of love and respect we have for you. We long to live in harmony with you and to show you we are obedient and reconciled to God's law and to worldly honor.

Your Loving Daughters,
Paolina and Annina
7 June 1725

"It sounds so formal," Paolina said.

"Your mother will take this more seriously than something soft and sentimental," he said. "If this letter doesn't get her attention, nothing will."

Paolina sighed. "Yes, you're probably right."

Annina smiled her gratitude to Antonio.

The next day he had the letter notarized, then he consulted city authorities about Bartolomea's whereabouts. It was discovered she'd taken up residence again at the home of Signor Cavalarizzo. The letter was delivered, but Annina and Paolina waited in vain for a response.

Annina began to realize her mother's departure and decision to live in compromising circumstances was largely her fault, and this realization left her overwhelmed by melancholia. For days she was unable to eat or sleep. Nothing could give her pleasure or comfort. Antonio was patient with her. At her lessons, he'd greet her with a compassionate smile and go through simple vocal exercises with her. Then one day she detected a gleam in his eye that told her he had something more in mind.

His studio effused an unusually warm glow that afternoon. Sun rays bounced off the sparkling canal waters and sprang through his windows like nimble sprites. His blue eyes gazed into her dark ones with genial intensity, and sparks of sunlight illuminated his golden hair.

"Annina, I understand why you feel so sad," he said, "but you mustn't continue blaming yourself for your mother's departure."

Her eyes burned with tears. "But it's my fault. She wouldn't have left if I hadn't made her so angry."

"That sort of thinking is useless, because you haven't done anything wrong. What concerns me most is how this whole business has sapped your energy and dampened your will to apply yourself to your music."

"How can I help it?"

He took her hand. "Life is filled with misfortunes and disappointments, most of which we can do very little to change. You're a very sensitive girl, Annina, and you feel powerless to stop the pain your mother's behavior has caused, and so you feel drained of all your strength."

She bit her lip and nodded.

He clasped her hand more firmly. "You can't get rid of the pain, but you can get your strength back."

She looked up at him. "How?"

"By pouring your feelings into your art."

"But . . . I'm not sure I can do that."

"Of course you can. I've heard you do it before."

"This is different, though. This time my feelings are so . . . deeply personal."

"So much the better." He let go of her hand and went to his desk. "I was awake half the night trying to think of a way to help you turn your sadness into something positive, something beautiful."

She blinked. "You were?"

He smiled and nodded. "Here's the result." He handed her a freshly written score. "I wrote this for you, my dear, the words and the music."

She took the score with trembling hands and looked it over. Across the top were the words *Sovente il sole*. She blinked harder to clear her eyes as she read:

Often the sun shines in the sky
with greater beauty and allure
if before it was obscured by a dark cloud.
And at times the calm sea
seems to have hardly a wave
if a terrible storm agitated it before.

She glanced up. "You really wrote this just for me?"

Without a word he took up his violin and played a melody of such sweet sadness and melting beauty that she thought her heart would burst. She was about to dissolve into fresh tears, but before she had a chance he stopped playing and spoke gently. "Don't cry, Annina, *sing*. Direct that crying feeling into your singing."

He began the aria's introduction again. She straightened, cleared her throat, and started to sing. At once she felt a warm, fluid sensation flow from somewhere deep within. The notes and words glided effortlessly through her throat and filled her head with an almost numbing dizziness. Her voice intertwined and blended with the violin's trembling cry as if they were a seamless sound, an indivisible expression. The feeling was painful, yet the pain was sweet, not bitter—a plaintive yearning that broke into sobs and sighs.

When the aria was finished, he lowered his violin and gazed at her with a triumphant glow in his eyes. "That was exquisite."

She hardly knew what to say. She was gripped by a strange sense of joy that was more unsettling than her former sadness. She tried to steady herself with a quivering sigh. Finally, she managed to say softly, "That's the most wonderful thing anyone's ever done for me."

He smiled. "All I did was put spots of ink on paper. You brought them to life. Until a few minutes ago that song was just an abstract idea. Now it's real, infused with pathos and genuine emotion."

Her eyes clouded and the score slipped from her hand. She rushed over to embrace him, barely able to contain her tears of happiness. He didn't resist this time, but clasped her in a firm, fatherly hug.

She was beginning to have a true appreciation for the power of Antonio's music. She thought about his students at the Pietà, all of whom had been abandoned by their mothers in infancy. Yet the music he wrote for them gave them happiness and a sense of purpose. She'd seen that at the concerts she had attended there. She felt neither pity nor envy for those young women. She felt only admiration for them and joy that he was able to transform his sensitivity to the pain of others into music of such astonishing beauty and energy. Now he'd done the same for her. And his unselfish act of love brought her to a startling realization. For over three years he'd been there for her when her mother wasn't. Even when she'd disappointed him, he hadn't turned away. With him she'd come to feel a sense of security, an aura of unconditional love she'd never felt with her mother. Secretly, she prayed he and she would always be together.

Then, in mid August, she received a document that caused all her confidence to crumble.

Chapter Eleven

She rushed to Antonio's house with the letter in her hand and tears in her eyes. He was busy at his desk working on a new concerto, but he looked up when she came in.

"What on earth is the matter?"

"This!" She shoved the letter at him. "Signor Bonazza's accusing me of cheating him out of half his money. Somehow he found out about the sixty *zecchini* the duke gave me, and now he's demanding I give him another thirty for his harpsichord."

"Oh that. Yes, I know, I got a letter from him too."

"Aren't you at all concerned? He's going to take me to court if I don't give him the money." Her face crumpled and she started to sob.

He put down his pen, came over, and put a reassuring arm around her. "Leave this to me, Annina, and put your mind at ease. There's absolutely no foundation to Bonazza's accusation. Count Savioli probably spread some gossip, and Bonazza heard about the sixty *zecchini* after the fact. So now he thinks he can bully you into giving him the other thirty. The man is a scoundrel and an extortionist. But he has no case, so there's no need to worry."

She sniffed and wiped her nose with the back of her hand. "How do you know he doesn't have a case? You're not a lawyer."

"It doesn't take a lawyer to see how absurd and unfounded Bonazza's charge is. Now don't be upset. I'll handle this."

Two weeks later, they stood outside the courthouse.

"What should I say?" she asked him.

"Not a thing. I'll do the talking."

"But . . . what should I do?"

"Just sit there and look innocent."

Inside the courthouse, she sat anxiously before the magistrate while Signor Bonazza ranted about misappropriation of funds. He even dropped a few malicious hints about her relationship with Antonio.

Antonio sat beside her, a thin stack of papers resting on his knee. He listened impassively except for an occasional tightening of his mouth and slight shaking of his head.

When Bonazza had had his say, he returned to his seat in a huff.

The magistrate turned to Annina. "Signorina Girò, how do you respond to Signor Bonazza's accusation?"

She bit her lip in panic, and Antonio quickly rose to his feet. "Signor *Magistrato*, I will speak for Signorina Girò."

"You are Reverend Vivaldi?"

"I am."

"What is your relationship to this young lady?"

"She is my student, signore."

"Has she no male relative to speak for her?"

"No, signore."

The magistrate looked at her again. "Signorina Girò, is it your wish that Reverend Vivaldi speak on your behalf?"

"*Sì*, signore," she said softly, her eyes wide with apprehension.

"Very well, Reverend Vivaldi. You may proceed."

"*Grazie*. First of all, I want to make it plain that Signorina Girò had very little direct involvement with the transaction in question. She is fifteen years old and asked me, her teacher, to arrange the purchase of a harpsichord for her. I then engaged the services of Signor Giovanni Gallo to negotiate the said purchase with Signor Bonazza."

His composed expression became animated as he went on. "Signor Bonazza's charges are no more than fabricated chimeras and fanciful inventions, Signor Magistrato. There is no truth to the charge that the Duke of Massa Carrara has ever dealt with or possessed the harpsichord in question, and even more false that sixty *zecchini* were handed out or paid by the duke for the purchase of the same.

"Yet Signor Bonazza claims he has been treated unjustly. In truth, the only injustice that's come from this whole affair is that brought on by Signor Bonazza's reckless pretensions, through which he's endeavored to obscure the facts. Let me enumerate them for you."

He walked over to the magistrate's bench and handed him the papers he'd been holding, then continued. "I demand that Signor Bonazza retract his unbelievable presentation, or I will take legal action against his damning slanders, based on the following:

"It was and is true that some months before last March, Signor Andrea Bonazza wanted to sell his harpsichord with four-foot register constructed by Domenico da Pesaro, at a price to be negotiated with the purchaser.

"The Duke of Massa Carrara left Venice on the second of last March, immediately after which I was given sixty *zecchini* by Count Angello Savioli, which I consigned in full to Signorina Girò as commissioned by the Duke of Massa Carrara.

"Signor Gallo, at my request, confirmed the sale of the above mentioned harpsichord with Signor Bonazza for thirty *zecchini*, plus five for his mediation.

"The thirty *zecchini*, the price of the sale, were given to Signor Gallo by Signorina Girò.

"Immediately after the sale was concluded, the harpsichord in question was taken to the house of Signorina Girò in the *contrada* Santa Maria Formosa, where it still is."

The magistrate studied the papers. Annina wrung her hands in her lap, and Antonio returned to her side.

Finally, the magistrate looked up and directed his eyes to Signor Bonazza. "Signore, considering the facts Reverend Vivaldi has presented on the young lady's behalf, which these documents bear out, your charge appears to be groundless. I declare this case dismissed."

Annina clutched Antonio's sleeve and whispered, "Does that mean we won?"

"It does indeed," he said, smiling.

She breathed a sigh of relief, then glanced over at Signor Bonazza. He rose from his seat and stormed out of the courtroom, but not before directing a hostile glare at Antonio.

She held onto his arm and felt very light on her feet as they stepped outside.

"Do I still get to keep the harpsichord?"

"Of course, it's yours."

"And I don't need to give Signor Bonazza any more money?"

"Not a *soldo*."

"Oh, Antonio, you're so smart. I could never have thought of all those things to say."

"Didn't I tell you I'd take care of it?"

"Yes you did, and you were right. You're always right."

Her lighthearted mood was disrupted when she heard him gasp

for air. She turned to him and saw him clutch his chest and his face contort in pain. Her heart was in her throat. "Antonio!" Afraid he'd fall to the ground, she grasped his arm more firmly and led him back to the stone steps at the courthouse entrance. "Let's sit for a minute," she said as calmly as she could, though her heart was beating wildly. As they sat on the cool stone step, she could see he was breathing with difficulty. She held his free hand in both of hers and asked gently, "Antonio, are you all right?"

He looked at her and nodded. His face was flushed but had relaxed, and he was breathing with more ease. He smiled weakly. "Sorry about that, Annina. My chest ailment flares up sometimes without warning."

"Please tell me what just happened."

"Every so often my chest tightens unbearably, and all I'm aware of is a crushing pain and inability to breathe. It's a condition I've had since birth."

She'd almost forgotten. That was the illness that kept him indoors as a child, why he had so many hours to practice. She felt an overwhelming surge of compassion for him. "I'm so sorry. Does it happen very often?"

"No, not very often anymore, thank heaven."

She took a trembling breath. "I've caused you so much trouble recently. That must be what brought this on."

He smiled and squeezed her hand. "Nothing could be further from the truth, my dear." He stood and pulled her to her feet, apparently recovered, although his breathing still sounded a bit jagged. "I'd better get you home before Paolina wonders what's become of you."

THAT NIGHT SHE was kept awake by cramping pains in her belly. She thought perhaps it was because of her worry about Antonio, coupled with the oppressive August heat. After finally drifting into a fitful sleep she awoke the next morning to find spots of blood on her nightgown.

"Paolina!" she shrieked.

Her sister, who was already dressed and in the kitchen, came running into the bedroom.

"What's happening to me?"

Paolina smiled knowingly and gave her a hug. "You've become a woman," she said calmly.

"What?"

"Don't you remember when I told you about this several years ago?"

"Is this what you used to call *the curse?*"

"Yes, but it's only a small inconvenience. Nothing to get worked up about."

Ugh, what a mess, was all she could think. "How can I go anywhere or do anything with blood seeping out of me?"

"It's not so bad," her sister said as she busied herself with rolling up lengths of bleached cotton she'd just pulled from a drawer. "I'll show you how to take care of it. No one will know. Now let me go heat up some water. You'll feel much better after a warm bath."

Fortunately it was Saturday, so she had a couple of days before her next lesson with Antonio. She wondered if he'd notice anything different about her. When she arrived at his studio Monday afternoon he greeted her in his usual genial way, his strength apparently restored after the weekend's repose. She smiled with relief that things were back to normal, and that Paolina was right. He knew nothing of what was going on beneath her skirts.

She had no idea that in barely a month he would see her doused in blood for another reason.

IT WAS A DISMAL Saturday afternoon in late September. A damp chill hung in the air and dark clouds loomed overhead. Paolina had gone to the market, and Annina sat gazing out the parlor window. Dusk blanketed Venice's spires and domes with a creeping gray mist. Darkness quickly overtook the lingering afternoon light, and a tremor ran up her back as if a cold wind had blown through the house. She lit the oil lamp in the hall and carried it to her bedroom. Soon a hard rain began to fall, and she wrapped in a thin shawl and sat on the wooden window seat that overlooked the Rio Maria Formosa. *Poor Paolina.* She hated to think of her caught in this downpour. Shivering, she watched the gush of rain and listened to the rhythmic sound of icy drops pattering against the window pane. Her gaze fell on the turbulent waters of the canal, stirred to a frenzy by the gushing torrent.

A sharp knocking at the front door startled her. She picked up the lamp and hurried back to the hall. It must be Paolina, she thought. She's forgotten her key again.

But it wasn't Paolina. It was the duke.

"Your Excellency! I had no idea you were back in town."

"Yes, I'm sure you're quite surprised to see me," he said, without smiling. Before she could think how to respond, he'd stepped inside and closed the door. "I'll get right to the point." He removed his dripping mantle and shook it out on the rug.

She shivered, but not from the dank cold he'd brought in with him. Again, she smelled liquor on him, and his usual roguish manner was darkened by an angry tinge. She felt a pricking sensation deep inside.

"Not only did you leave Venice last winter without my knowledge, but I understand you've turned down all the operatic engagements I've arranged for you. May I ask what you have to say for yourself?"

The pale light of the oil lamp flickered, as did her insides. She placed the lamp on the hall table. "I went to Mantua to visit my family. I didn't think you'd mind. And Anto—my teacher has advised me not to accept any more opera engagements for the time being. He wants more time to work on my technical skill."

"Yes, I'm sure he does," he said, sneering. "Don't you know it's all over Venice what's going on between *il prete rosso* and his Annina? Have you any idea how much of a chump you've made me look?"

"*What?* What do you mean? I don't understand."

The color rose in his face. "I think you understand perfectly. Don't even bother with your innocent little girl act. I've seen it before. I'm no longer fooled by your clever dramatics. By the way, how much of my money are you paying him?"

"I'm not paying him anything. He doesn't want money from me."

"Then what *does* he want? Do you expect me to believe the great Antonio Vivaldi would give up so much of his valuable time for a little nobody like you—for *nothing*? Come now, signorina. You insult my intelligence."

She wished Paolina would come home. She had a feeling something bad was about to happen.

The duke ground his teeth and his eyes blazed. "Aren't you going to say anything?"

"I think you should go," she said, trying to stay calm, but the tightness in her throat made her voice crack.

"Let me remind you, young miss, that your presence here in

Venice is financed by *my* generosity. You have no right to dismiss me from the house I'm paying for, or from your presence." He grabbed her arm and roughly pulled her to him.

She writhed and fought to free herself from his strong grip. "Let me go! My sister will be home any minute!"

There was no stopping him. He crushed her body to his and fastened his hot mouth on hers. She felt him throbbing and trembling, and panic overtook her. Pressing her fists to his chest, she managed to push away from him. Before she could catch her breath, he smacked her hard across the mouth with the back of his hand. She staggered backward and shrieked in pain as tears flooded her eyes. Her hand flew to her mouth, which was already wet with blood. She stared at him, stunned. No one had ever struck her before, not even her mother in her blackest of rages.

Instantly his fury seemed to vanish, and panting, he reached for her. "Annina, I'm—"

She didn't wait for the rest of his sentence. She ran to the front door, hurled it open, and darted down the stairs and into the frigid downpour. The usually busy *campo* was practically empty, except for a few cloaked figures who were running for cover. Blinded by cold daggers of rain in her face, she collided with a man who grasped her arm and said, "Can I help you, signorina?" Terrified, she pulled away from him and continued her flight across the now deserted *campo*.

At last she stopped at the Rio del Mondo Novo, gasping for breath. Rain poured harder than ever and it was starting to thunder. The waters of the canal churned with a terrible violence, and there wasn't a gondola in sight. She was alone, completely drenched, and so chilled she could hardly move. She stood for a moment hugging herself, her teeth chattering. Blinking the rain out of her eyes, she realized she was only a short distance from the

Ponte del Paradiso.

Sloshing through icy puddles she approached the bridge. The wind off the canal nearly blew her over as she gripped the bridge's concrete railing and inched her way across. Soon she was on solid ground again, and just a few steps from the Vivaldis' house. She made her way to the front door and pounded with all her strength.

Margarita opened the door, and her jaw dropped. "Annina! *Dio mio*, what has happened to you?" she said, pulling her out of the rain.

She was shaking too hard to speak.

"*Antonio!* " she called, her voice shrill with fright. "It's Annina! She's been hurt!"

He appeared from his study in shirtsleeves, his sandy hair falling around his face. His eyes widened with panic when he saw her.

She ran to him and pressed her face into his shoulder. "You were right, I should have listened to you," she said in a muffled voice.

"About what?"

"About the duke."

He held her close for a moment then gently clasped her upper arms and stepped back to examine her face. The blood oozing from her lip, which had already seeped down the front of her bodice, had soaked through his white shirt, as had the wetness from her dress and hair. But he didn't seem to notice. With a troubled look, he took out his handkerchief and dabbed carefully around her lips.

The corners of his mouth twitched. "Did he do this to you?"

Her throbbing lip made it impossible for her to speak, so she merely nodded.

His jaw tightened.

Margarita stood nearby, making the sign of the cross and

wringing her hands. "*Antonio*," she said, "I must get the poor child out of these wet clothes before she catches her death."

"Yes, find her something dry to put on," he said.

She allowed herself to be guided by Margarita's firm hands into a little bedchamber off the kitchen. With much fretting and tongue clucking she had her dry, cleaned up, and wrapped in a soft dressing gown within minutes. Then she combed out her damp hair and left it hanging loose around her shoulders.

As they walked back through the kitchen, Annina looked around. "It's so quiet here. Where is everyone?"

"Mother went to bed early with a headache and Zanetta is with her. My father had a late rehearsal at San Marco, and the good Lord only knows where my younger brother is." She sighed and shook her head.

Annina touched her hand. "I'm sure all the commotion I've caused isn't helping your mother's headache."

"Nonsense, she's fast asleep by now. You did the right thing coming here after that devil of a duke assaulted you. Now go talk to Antonio while I fix you a nice pot of tea," she said, patting her arm.

Teary-eyed and shaky, she returned to the parlor to find Antonio pacing about and fastening up a fresh shirt. "I'm sorry about your shirt," she said.

"Never mind about that. Come, my dear, have a seat and tell me what this is all about."

She curled up on the sofa, tucking her shoeless feet under her and wrapping her arms around herself to ease the bone-rattling chill that shook her body. He picked up a *copriletto*, a coverlet, from a nearby ottoman and tucked it around her shoulders.

"Thank you, Antonio," she said, shaking as much from her stinging lip as from the cold. Margarita had managed to stop the bleeding, but it still smarted.

"Try to tell me what happened," he said, sitting on the ottoman, his hands clasped between his knees.

She looked at him with eyes that felt like they were melting in salty liquid. "Paolina went to the market, and I was home alone. Then the duke showed up, asking me a lot of questions. I was scared and asked him to leave, but he wouldn't."

His brow darkened. "What did he do exactly?"

She started to cry, and he rushed to her side. He took her hand, and she leaned her damp face against his shoulder. Her quivering lip brushed the crisp, fresh smelling fabric of his shirtsleeve as she went on. "He grabbed me and tried to kiss me, and when I pulled away from him, he hit me. Then I ran out the door and came here." Her body trembled anew at the memory of the duke's sweaty hands on her and the smell of liquor on his breath. She clutched Antonio's sleeve and squeezed her eyes against the tears that welled once again.

"Is that all?" he asked.

She nodded and pressed her cheek to his shoulder.

"It's all right now," he said, patting her hand. But there was an edge to his voice, and she could feel his body tense with anger.

Margarita came in with a tray of steaming tea. "Here we are, my little lamb, this will help warm you up." There was an anxious knocking at the front door, and she put down the tray and hurried into the hall.

"That must be Paolina. I sent a gondola to fetch her," Antonio said as he rose to greet her.

Paolina looked like she was going to burst into tears when she stepped into the parlor. Annina reached for her, and her sister hurried over and took her in her arms. "My poor, poor darling!"

She allowed herself to melt into Paolina's protective embrace.

"That monster! What are you going to do about this?" she said, glaring up at Antonio.

He looked at the sisters as if he were deciding what to say. He sighed and ran his hand through his hair. "I could have him charged with assault and arrested tonight."

"Would he go to prison?" Annina asked, between sniffles.

"Most likely. And there'd be a trial."

"Would I have to go?"

"Yes. And since this is a criminal case, I'd hire a lawyer for you. But you'd have to tell the judge yourself exactly what happened."

"Would other people be there?"

"I'm afraid so. Criminal trials are open to the public, and something like this could turn into quite a spectacle."

She gazed at him in dismay. There was a brief silence, save for Margarita who sat nearby murmuring over her rosary beads.

Paolina squeezed her hand. "Do you really think that's advisable?" she asked Antonio.

He sighed again and rubbed his forehead. "No, I don't. As much as I hate to see that brute get away with this, I wouldn't want to arm the scandalmongers. They could cause far more harm than he has."

"Then how can we protect Annina from him?"

"Don't worry, I'll take care of it," he said.

"*How?*" Annina asked.

"I'll write to the duke and inform him that you'll no longer accept his patronage. That should end the problem, God willing."

Tears of panic filled her eyes. "But Antonio, how will Paolina and I pay our rent? How can we live? How can I help our parents, like I've promised?"

"Relax, Annina. You'll be earning your own income soon enough. In the meantime, I'll cover your expenses."

She sighed shakily.

Later that night, her mouth bruised and swollen, she pulled *la moretta* from her secret place in the wardrobe cupboard. Paolina was in the parlor, busy with her stitchery. Her fingers caressed the plush darkness of *la moretta*'s velvet face, and she murmured to her. "If I were wearing you, would you have protected me from the duke?" But the mask's silent stare gave her no answer. She turned the mask over and her eyes fell on the puzzling *CZL* inscription. Perhaps solving the letters' meaning would release *la moretta*'s protective powers. But how could that be done? Closing her fingers around the muzzling *bottone*, revulsion came over her. She flung *la moretta* back into the wardrobe, closed it firmly, and pressed her forehead against the cupboard's wooden door. "You do nothing to protect me, but you plot to silence me. You've crippled my lip—my voice's threshold to the world. I should throw you into the canal and forget I ever laid eyes on you." But the memory of *la chiromante*'s words kept her from carrying out that threat: *The silence of la moretta will shield you.*

SHE MADE PAOLINA promise not to tell a soul about what had happened. Not Papà, Mamma, Graziana, or *anyone*. She wanted to put the shameful incident behind her as quickly as possible. But if anything at all valuable came out of her unfortunate run-in with the duke, it was the realization that she was attractive to the opposite sex. The idea began to form in her mind that this could be helpful. And she certainly needed help. Ever since the "incident," she'd felt like *she* was in prison. The warm comfort she'd felt at Antonio's house the night the duke assaulted her had become stifling. She wasn't allowed to go anywhere, and she could never be alone. She knew she had to find a way to free herself from these suffocating restraints, or she'd go mad. A few days later she found a way.

Paolina usually accompanied her on the short walk across the Campo Santa Maria Formosa for her lessons, but on this particular afternoon she had a headache and decided to let Annina go on her own.

"I suppose you'll be all right," she said. "But I don't want you walking alone. You can go by gondola."

"Of course I'll be all right. I'm not a baby, you know."

Paolina pressed her hand to her aching head and went down the back stairs to hail a gondola. Annina stood at the door with her pile of scores while her sister gave the gondolier Antonio's address and payment for the gondola ride. The boatman lifted his cap and grinned. He looked familiar. After he'd handed her and her stack of music into the boat and they were off, she realized who he was.

"I know you," she said.

He seemed pleased. "Is that so, miss?"

"Yes, you gave my sister and me a ride from the boat, when we first arrived in Venice . . . um . . . over three years ago."

"Hmmm." He eyed her curiously. "I'm not sure—"

"Don't you remember? I wanted my sister to take me to the opera, and you helped me talk her into it."

His face brightened. "You can't be that little girl who told me she'd come here to study music and to sing in the opera."

"Yes, that's me."

"Well what do you know, miss. I never would have recognized you. You've become quite a young lady."

"And everything you predicted that night has come true. Well, almost. I've been studying with Don Antonio. That's where you're taking me right now—to his house for a singing lesson. I've already sung in several public performances, and I'll probably make my debut soon in one of his operas here in Venice."

"Is that a fact? Well I'll be, miss."

The man seemed so nice, and so trusty. She gave him what she hoped was her most charming smile. "Do you mind if I ask your name?"

"Not at all, miss, I'm Fortunato."

"What a nice name. I'm very pleased to make your acquaintance, Fortunato. I'm Annina."

He almost seemed to blush. "Likewise, Miss Annina."

"Fortunato, I can see you're a true gentleman, the kind of man a girl can trust."

He drew himself up proudly. "I'd like to think so, Miss Annina."

"So I hope you won't mind if I ask your advice about something."

"If it's advice you need, miss, you've come to the right fellow."

"I knew it. Do you think it's safe for a girl like me to go around Venice unescorted?"

"A pretty young thing like you? Oh no, miss, that would be most unwise. You have no idea of the shady characters out there just waiting to . . . uh . . . take advantage of a sweet girl like you, Miss Annina."

She said nothing, but merely cast her eyes down again.

"If you don't mind my asking, Miss Annina, how did you get that swollen lip?" He sounded genuinely concerned.

She'd almost forgotten about her hurt lip. She raised her fingertips to it. "Oh, that's nothing. Just a silly accident."

"You should be more careful, miss. It wouldn't do at all to mar that pretty face of yours." He peered at her with a vaguely worried look. "If you'll allow it, miss, I have a suggestion for you."

"Oh?"

"You need someone to look out for you. Your teacher is a very busy man, obviously. And as far as I can see, you have no other man in Venice to escort you around. I can also see you're the kind of girl who doesn't take to being cooped up at home."

"You're so right. How clever you are, Fortunato."

He straightened, and squared his shoulders. "I don't like to brag, miss, but I must say I've been known to have a few bright ideas from time to time."

"Of course you have, you're so astute. So tell me, what's your suggestion?"

"Well, miss, I'd like to offer you my humble services. I can take you to and from your lessons and escort you wherever you'd like to go. And mark my words, miss, you'll be perfectly safe with me. If any lewd looking fellow bothers you, I'll pound him into the pavement!"

She looked at his muscular, sun-darkened arms and had no doubt he was capable of keeping his word. She wondered how old he was, but decided it would be impolite to ask. Studying his face, she realized his weathered skin probably made him look older than he actually was.

"Why Fortunato, you're too kind. And so brave. But are you sure it wouldn't be too much of a bother for you?"

He gave her his brightest smile. "Certainly not, Miss Annina. It'd be a pleasure."

"I'll pay you, of course."

He grinned. "Truth be told, I hadn't even thought of that, miss. But a few *soldi* now and then might help keep me honest," he said, chuckling.

She smiled at him and giggled. Then she realized they'd arrived at Antonio's house.

Fortunato leaped off his perch and with great gallantry handed Annina and her stack of music out of the gondola. She turned toward the door, but he rushed ahead with her scores in his arms, and said, "I'll announce you."

When Margarita opened the door, he took off his red cap and lifted his chin with an air of importance. "Announcing Miss Annina . . . uh . . ." He looked back at her helplessly.

"Girò," she whispered, leaning toward him.

"Miss Annina Girò is here for her lesson with Don Antonio Vivaldi."

Margarita ushered them into the hall. "I'll let him know Signorina Annina has arrived," she said, giving her a curious glance.

She thought Fortunato would have left by now, but he continued to stand in the hall, grinning, and holding her pile of music. Margarita hurried toward the study, and a moment later Antonio appeared, adjusting his collar.

"Annina, what—Oh, hello," he said when he spotted Fortunato.

"What an honor this is, maestro! I've long been an admirer of your operas. Please allow me to introduce myself. I am Fortunato, sir, at your service as well as that of your charming student, Miss Annina."

"Well, thank you, um—"

"I know you two have important work to do, so I'll take my leave." He turned to her and smiled. "Miss Annina, when shall I return for you?"

"In two hours, please."

"I'll be here." He handed Antonio her stack of scores, bowed ceremoniously, and departed.

"What on earth was all that about?" he asked. "Who is that man?"

"That was Fortunato, my gondolier," she said, trying to sound nonchalant.

"*Your* gondolier?" He gave her a reproachful look. "Annina what are you up to now? And why are you out alone? Where's Paolina?'"

She was feeling too good about things to be put off by his stern questions. "Paolina's home with a headache, and—"

"Oh, I see. I'm sorry she's not well."

"So she hailed a gondola and decided it was all right for me to come here by myself. And as soon as we were off, I realized I knew the gondolier. He's the one who brought Paolina and me into Venice my very first night here."

The corners of his mouth tightened. "This isn't convincing me that—"

"Wait, let me finish. He and I started talking, and he remembered me too. He realizes I don't like to be cooped up, so he offered to escort me around Venice wherever I want to go."

He closed his eyes and sighed. "After what happened last week, I'd think you'd have learned to be more cautious. We don't know anything about this Fortunato character—"

"But I *do* know him. We talked a lot. He's really nice, and a gentleman, and he wants to protect me."

She was getting more wound up, and he was losing patience. "Annina, this conversation is absurd and has gone far enough. When the gondolier returns, I'll tell him you won't need his services after all."

"No, Antonio, please don't tell him that. Won't you at least talk to him? *Please?* Once you do, I'm sure you'll agree he's completely trustworthy. I just can't live like this anymore. It's making me crazy. I might as well be in prison."

He looked at her, frowning. Finally he said, "All right, if it means that much to you, I'll talk to him. But I'm not promising anything."

Antonio's talk with the gondolier later that afternoon went well, and Fortunato soon became a trusted protector and friend. With him to escort them, Annina and Paolina decided to risk a visit to their mother.

Chapter Twelve

Fortunato silently turned his gondola into a dark, remote canal. The house where Bartolomea lived was in a rather rough part of town, and the sisters looked about in dismay. Women with painted faces leaned from windows, their bare arms trailing over the sills. Dissipated idlers hung about the filthy *calli* and stared at them with dull, cunning eyes. A wizened hag spewed a profusion of maledictions on a coal peddler because of his prices, reviling him as having sprung from a race of ugly old curs. *"Maledizione! Cagnaccio vecchio!"* she croaked as she scratched her face with claw-like fingers and gave the peddler a withering glare.

Fortunato lamented the pitiful state of the neighborhood. *"Proprio un campo di sospiri!"* he cried with heartrending pathos. "Indeed this is a field of sighs!"

Bartolomea was astonished to see them. Her mood had mellowed since their last encounter, and she even seemed sorry things had gone so badly. She was still a bit stiff and distant, but she no longer seemed angry. After a somewhat awkward chat, they managed to persuade her to go back to Mantua and attempt a reconciliation with Pierre. Paolina agreed to go with her and stay for a short visit. As much as Annina yearned to go along, she couldn't leave Venice because she and Antonio were engaged for a series of private concerts. The first of these events was to take place the following week, at the Venetian home of Antonio's Bohemian patron, Count von Morzin.

Graziana, who'd come to stay with Annina while her sister was away, spent that day fussing over her. Early in the afternoon Graziana washed her hair, rinsed it with lavender water, and brushed it dry by the kitchen hearth. One advantage to her fine, silky hair was that it dried fairly quickly. As she sat by the fire wrapped in a warm dressing gown, worrisome thoughts nettled her brain.

"Graziana, my throat feels awfully dry. What if my singing's terrible?"

"Don't be silly. Of course you'll sing beautifully. Don Antonio wouldn't let you do this if he wasn't sure you're ready."

"I don't know why I'm so nervous."

"You should feel excited."

"I *am* excited, but I'm also afraid."

"Now stop this, Annina. I'm going to make sure you look so beautiful the audience will be mesmerized by you. Your singing will only dazzle them all the more."

"I wish I could feel as confident as you do."

When her hair was dry, Graziana brushed it till it shone, then coaxed her wayward locks into ringlets with the curling irons she'd been heating over the fire. While Annina put on her underclothes, Graziana brought out the new dress she'd designed and made for her—a silk gown of eggshell white, with a lace bodice and rose-colored sash. The bodice angled down from her waist, in the latest fashion, and the skirt fell in graceful folds to the floor. The dress's slightly off-the-shoulder sleeves were snug around her upper arms and flared gracefully just above the elbow, falling about halfway down her forearms.

After she'd helped her into her dress, Graziana went back to work on her hair, pulling most of the curls back and up and tying them with rose-colored silk ribbons, allowing a few loose tendrils to fall around her face. She felt quite elegant. She was sorry she owned no jewelry, but Graziana assured her she looked fine without it. "Never mind, Annina, jewelry is for faded old matrons. Pretty, fresh-faced maidens like you have no need of it."

Fortunato was bringing Antonio to fetch her, so they could go to Count von Morzin's *palazzo* together. When she came into the front hall, he had just arrived. He was dressed simply but tastefully, in a black broadcloth frock coat and priest's collar. His reddish-gold hair fell past his chin in loose waves.

"Annina, you look lovely. The count's guests will be completely enchanted by you," he said.

"I hope you're right." Her stomach flittered as he placed her cloak around her shoulders.

Graziana stood at the door to see them off, and Annina noticed her and Fortunato exchange bashful smiles. But she was too anxious about the concert to give them much thought. She was thinking about the audience's reaction to the first aria she'd sung at the San Moisè that fateful January. The grimaces. The mocking sneers. She tried to give Antonio a confident smile. But fear crept through her, and she felt every muscle in her body go rigid.

SHE WALKED INTO the grand salon of Count von Morzin's palazzo on Antonio's arm and gaped at the sumptuousness that surrounded her. Her eager eyes drank in the throngs of elegantly dressed people who seemed to float about the room, chattering, laughing, and clinking glasses. The men's embroidered waistcoats, trim knee breeches, and powdered wigs paled in comparison to the lavishness of the women's finery, which glittered in more colors and designs than she'd ever imagined. The room's towering walls and soaring ceiling were clothed in even more splendor. Almost every inch was covered in ornament or fresco.

Many curious eyes turned their way, and she noticed hand-guarded whispers, particularly among the women, accompanied by flashing glances directed at her. Then she spotted the duke across the room. He held a glass of brandy and eyed her coolly. She looked away and clutched Antonio's arm more tightly. Out of the corner of her eye she saw a glamorous, bejeweled blond woman step close to the duke. She turned her head slightly in their direction and couldn't believe her eyes. It was Chiara. She flashed Annina a scornful smile and slipped her hand through the duke's bent arm.

The room became stifling. Her heartbeat quickened, and sweat dripped down the inside of her bodice and between her breasts. She pressed closer to Antonio and looked up at him anxiously. His attention was completely taken up by his many admirers, who swarmed around him like bees to honey, prattling compliments and witticisms. Lately she'd tended to forget how famous he was. His fans must have wondered who this frightened looking ingénue was clinging to him. She prayed they'd forgotten about her bungled performances at the San Moisè.

Antonio slowly worked his way through the crowd, pulling her along. When they reached the performance area he patted her clinging hand, gently unfastened her from his arm, and ushered her to a nearby seat. He'd told her earlier that before her aria he would introduce one of his new concertos. She watched him joke with his musician friends, while her thoughts drifted back to Chiara and the duke. The image of their threatening glares loomed in her mind like a gathering storm.

Her attention shifted back to the musicians as Antonio took up his violin and bowed a long, shimmering note. The room fell silent. The other players lifted their bows and matched the tone, and the harpsichordist played a sweeping flourish. Antonio gave the musicians a subtle but precise gesture to start the piece. The concerto began with slow, peaceful music, tinged with an ominous calm. She felt herself being lulled into a dreamy, yet slightly edgy state.

After a few phrases he raised his violin to his shoulder and started a frenzied solo that jolted her out of her dreamlike mood and took her breath away. His fingers flitted across the strings with dizzying speed, and his facial expression was so intense he almost looked as if he were in pain. Suddenly the rest of the string players joined him in a furious unison. Just as abruptly he lowered his instrument, and the orchestra returned to its earlier peaceful theme. For a fleeting instant he looked like he was trying to catch his breath. Then he lifted his violin to his shoulder again. This time he played a solo that floated above the other instruments in a melody of such excruciating tenderness she thought her heart would melt. Before she could bask too long in that euphoric state, the music exploded once again in an even more turbulent frenzy. She felt she'd been swept up, helpless, into a violent storm. Only this storm was thrilling, not terrifying.

The corners of his mouth twisted and beads of perspiration dribbled down his temples. He was in such a furiously impassioned state she felt she hardly knew him. She glanced around and saw people sitting on the edges of their seats, spellbound. Wide-eyed women panted, their chests heaving as they fanned themselves. A girl of about sixteen swooned and nearly fainted. Annina returned her gaze to Antonio and felt something close to adoration. Her eyes misted, and she sucked in her lips and blinked against the stinging moisture.

When the piece was over, he took out a handkerchief and mopped his face. The spectators were frozen in silence for an instant before they burst into applause. He smiled his appreciation, gestured toward his musicians, and bowed. The applause went on.

Finally their host, the count, stepped forward, clapping vigorously. He laid an appreciative hand on Antonio's shoulder. "*Bravo*, maestro! Thank you for that sampling of yet another musical triumph from your prodigious pen and dynamical bow."

Antonio smiled and bowed courteously.

The count turned to his guests. "My friends, what you just heard is the first movement of Don Antonio's "Summer" concerto, from his brilliant new set of works, *The Four Seasons*. And now if I may, maestro, I would like to introduce your enchanting protégée to my guests. My friends, may I introduce La Signorina Annina Girò."

All eyes turned to her, accompanied by curious smiles and polite applause. Her stomach twisted into a knot. She glanced at Antonio and saw that he too was smiling at her, and she felt a faint surge of confidence. He stepped over, and she slipped her trembling hand into his. He gave it an encouraging squeeze as he led her to the front of the little ensemble. She wondered how he had the strength to go on. And how could she possibly match the dazzling performance he just gave? Sharp pangs of anxiety jabbed her stomach when her eyes met Chiara's and the duke's smug stares.

The harpsichordist played the opening chord, and she burst into a stormy recitative:

> *Ah, the traitor will not listen to me!*
> *Treacherous stars!*

Have I not suffered enough to satisfy you?

She felt the words swell and burn inside her. Antonio lifted his violin to his shoulder and with a quick nod to the musicians began thrusting away at the aria's ritornello. His music swept her into its embrace and held her fast. She poured every ounce of herself into her solo verse, then her voice mingled with the ritornello:

> *My suffering spirit!*
> *How can I break the arrow in my heart*
> *since I adore the one responsible?*

Tingling energy hung in the air, and for a moment the room was cloaked in deafening silence. The aria was over. Her eyes darted to Antonio. His face shone with rapt serenity, as if he were still caught in the magic of his own musical mind.

The room exploded with applause. People leaped to their feet with cries of *Brava! Bravissima!* Antonio took her hand, and she sank into a deep curtsy. The applause showed no sign of letting up. *Ancora una volta! Ancora una volta!* many shouted.

"They want us to do it again!" He dropped her hand, snatched up his violin, and dove into the ritornello with renewed fury. She barely had time to catch her breath before she plunged once more into her opening verse.

Antonio wanted to leave as soon as possible after the concert. They'd just stepped outside and were walking toward the gondola when the duke appeared. Her heart flinched, and she clutched Antonio's arm.

His hand fastened on her wrist. "Leave this to me," he murmured.

She stepped back obediently and crossed her arms, clutching

the edges of her cloak.

The duke staggered slightly, and his voice was too loud. "Well, maestro, I couldn't let you leave without congratulating you on yet another musical triumph!"

Antonio eyed him coldly. "You are too kind."

"Not at all, maestro. And please allow me to pay my compliments to your charming protégée."

An icy wind suddenly blew off the canal, and she pulled her cloak more snugly around herself.

"I was under the impression you were here with another lady," Antonio said, his lips tightening.

The duke grinned sloppily. "As if I'd give that slut the time of day?"

Antonio frowned.

"She's amusing, I'll grant you. But no, my real interest is in the young lady standing just beyond you," he said, cocking his head, his grin widening. "What a vision of loveliness, such purity and innocence." He sighed dreamily. "And such incomparable talent, so filled with passion. One can only imagine the many ways that passion— "

"Signorina Girò desires neither to see nor speak to you, sir," Antonio interrupted. "So please have the decency to leave us."

"Surely you don't mean that, maestro." The duke's fuzzy tone had an angry edge.

Antonio turned to Fortunato, who hadn't taken his eyes off the two men. "Please help Signorina Annina into the boat."

"With pleasure, Don Antonio," he was quick to respond. He leaped off his perch and took her by the elbow. She let him hand her into the gondola, while she stared wide-eyed at Antonio and the duke.

The duke began to swagger closer to Antonio. "So I see you're determined to keep her all to yourself."

He visibly stiffened. "What is your meaning, sir?"

"I think you know what I mean, maestro," he said, his grin turning cocky. "Do you expect me to believe you've never partaken of the charms of that enticing young lady, when she's obviously so attached to you?"

This was too much for Fortunato. With blazing eyes he made a move to get out of the boat, but she grabbed his arm and pulled him back. Her instincts told her it was better to let Antonio handle this.

Antonio glared at the duke for a long moment, and she saw his fist clench. She held her breath. Finally he said in a low, tense voice, *"May God forgive you for having such a thought."*

The duke backed off without a word and sauntered toward the house. Antonio tightened his lips, shook his head, and turned to join her in the gondola. Fortunato rushed to assist him. Once they were afloat, she felt safe and happy under the starry sky with her two protectors. Antonio was distant, though. He stared to the side, frowning, as if his thoughts were as deep and dark as the murky green waters of the Grand Canal.

She broke the silence. "What a pest he's turned out to be."

"He's more than that. He's absolutely incorrigible," he said, still gazing into the canal's gloomy depths.

"You're so right, Antonio. But you intimidated him. You always know how to put troublemakers in their place."

He turned to her with a half-smile.

She raised her eyebrows. "And did you see who he was with?"

"I did."

"What do you think about that?"

"I think they deserve each other."

The blunt wisdom of his remark sent her into peals of giggles.

He smiled at her giddiness, then laughed with her, softly. In truth, she was tingling with the afterglow of the evening's success and bursting with eagerness to talk about it. The frosty night air pricking her face sharpened her excitement. She grinned ecstatically at Antonio. "Your new concerto is amazing. It's the most thrilling, exciting music I've ever heard. Everyone was completely enchanted. I'm sure they've never heard anything like it."

His smile brightened. "They haven't. No one has."

She hugged herself. "I knew it. Oh, Antonio, you're a genius. How do you think of music like that? I'm just astounded by how creative you are. I don't know how you do it."

Her gushing praise seemed to please him, but he replied modestly. "I don't know how I do it either. My music simply comes to me. It's a gift from God."

"You're too modest, Antonio. That music comes from *you*. It *is* you.

He smiled again. "Which is another way of saying I'm abiding by God's will. But enough about me. Let's talk about your performance this evening. I can't tell you how moved I was by your singing tonight, you were stunning. When you sing my arias before a crowd you positively sparkle and shine. You breathe life into my music and make it your own. It's as if you become the music."

Her heart fluttered violently, and she hugged herself even tighter. It was the most wonderful thing he could have said to her. This was no empty flattery. He was likening her to his music, the thing that meant more to him than anything in the world. Her heart overflowed with tenderness for him. "I'm so glad I pleased you, Antonio."

"I'm more than just pleased. I'm very proud of you. You sang with such fire and sincerity, you charmed everyone in the room and completely won them over. It won't be long before you're ready to go onstage again—in one of my operas."

Her whole body sizzled with joy.

GRAZIANA WAS WAITING up for her. "So how did it go?" she asked, her eyes bright with curiosity.

"It was wonderful." She went on to tell her friend every tantalizing detail. When she got to the part about Fortunato's zeal to defend her honor when the duke became offensive, Graziana grinned and blushed.

She paused. "What are you thinking, Graziana?"

"Oh . . . It's just that I find Fortunato so appealing, in a rugged sort of way." She giggled nervously.

"Are you trying to tell me you've taken a fancy to Fortunato?"

"Well . . ." Her blush deepened. "I don't know. But I do get a strange tickly feeling inside when I look at his brawny arms."

She was fascinated. "I noticed he gave you a certain look when you stepped outside earlier."

"Did you? Oh, Annina, do you think he likes me? I mean . . . well, he's not married or anything is he?"

"Not that I know of." It had never occurred to her to ask him.

Graziana was excited now. "You're so friendly with him. Do you think you could, well, you know, find out how he feels about me? Without letting him know I asked, of course."

She was delighted. She'd never been asked to play *Amore*, Cupid, before.

The following afternoon, on the way to her lesson, she looked at Fortunato with a breezy smile. "What did you think of the dress Graziana made me for my concert appearance last night?"

"It was splendid, Miss Annina. You looked lovely as an angel."

She beamed with pleasure. "Isn't she talented?"

"She is at that."

"Oh, Graziana's good at everything. I don't know what I'd do without her. No one could have a better or more loyal friend."

"Graziana's a dandy girl, I won't deny it."

His candid grin told her all she needed to know.

ANTONIO GREETED HER with exciting news. "My negotiations for regaining managerial control of San Angelo are complete. I'll launch the new season a week before Christmas with a pasticcio, *L'Inganno trionfante in amore*."

"Oh Antonio, how wonderful. Will I be singing in it?"

"Not this time. I'm planning your debut for next autumn, after you and I have had time for a lot more intense work."

She tried not to show her disappointment.

He looked at her with a wry smile. "I have another piece of news I'm sure you'll be pleased to hear."

"What's that?"

"A retired singer from Venice, Signor Denzio, is putting together an opera company in Prague. He wants to hire Venetian singers and has asked for my help. I'm going to send him Chiara."

Her jaw dropped. "How are you going to do that?"

"I've already asked for a meeting with her. Once she sees what a good opportunity this is she won't hesitate to sign the contract."

"I don't understand. Why should you do her such a favor?"

"To get her on the other side of the Alps, of course, where she can't cause us any more trouble."

She gazed at him in wonder. "That's so clever, Antonio. I never would have thought of it. But what if she won't go?"

"She'll go." His smile radiated confidence.

"How can you be so sure?"

"Because she's shrewd enough to realize Denzio's company is her best option. She has no prospects in Venice right now, or anyplace else for that matter. She's depraved herself to get back in favor with the duke, but she knows he's already grown weary of her. Trust me, Annina, she won't turn down this opportunity."

In her mind's eye, she pictured the magnificent mountain range on Venice's northern horizon. "Antonio, you said Prague is across the Alps? Where, exactly?"

"Far to the north, in Bohemia."

"How far?"

"Many hundreds of miles."

"It must be cold up there."

"Extremely. The climate should suit Chiara's temperament well, don't you think?"

They shared a smile.

SHE HAD JUST finished her morning bath and was starting to dry her hair by the kitchen hearth. There was a knock at the front door, and Graziana went to answer. She heard muffled voices in the hall, then Graziana came back to the kitchen. "It's Chiara," she said in an anxious whisper. "What would you like me to tell her?"

Her heart quavered. "Invite her to sit, and tell her I'll be right there." She looped the sash of her dressing gown, wrapped her damp hair in a towel, and went to the parlor to face Chiara. She had a look of desperation in her eyes, and her pinched mouth told Annina fury was lying just below the surface.

She tried to look composed. "Well, Chiara, what a surprise."

"I suppose you weren't expecting to see me again."

"No, I wasn't."

"I'll keep this short. I've come to warn you. To open your eyes to what you're getting into."

"I have no idea what you're talking about."

"You think you've finally triumphed. That you have defeated me and now, at last, everything will go your way." Her voice had a tense, almost strangled sounding edge.

She hesitated. "I hadn't thought about it like that."

Her eyes spit fire. "Then let me educate you. You think Antonio is some kind of saint. Well he's not. Just look what he's done to me."

"What he's done to you? He's done you a favor. Which is more than you deserve, if you ask me."

"A favor? Is that what you call it? I call it throwing his weight around to render me powerless. Shipping me off to his crony in Prague, as if I were a piece of livestock."

"What nonsense. No one's forcing you to go."

"You mean, you actually think I have a choice? Are you blind? Haven't you figured out yet how these impresarios, these smug tyrants, take control of our lives when we're young and vulnerable? How they use us for their own purposes then pass us around among themselves when it suits them? And your adored Antonio is no different. If I refuse to go to Prague, he'll make sure I'm blacklisted at every theater in Italy."

"Did he tell you that?"

"Not in so many words. But thanks to his meddling even that codger Albinoni won't work with me anymore, the spiteful old fool." Her face took on the crimped expression of a peevish child. "I've been used, I'm telling you. Nobody cares about me." Angry tears filled her eyes, and she dabbed at them with a frilly lace handkerchief.

She felt more disgust than compassion for Chiara's sniveling self-pity. As if *she* hadn't used others for her own ends, not to mention made her life a living hell for the better part of two years? She tightened her lips. "I don't see how you can say that. Antonio did everything for you—and you betrayed him."

She lowered her handkerchief to her lap and glared at her, her green eyes catlike. "What are you talking about?"

"You know exactly what I'm talking about. When he was forced out of his position at San Angelo five years ago you turned your back on him and sided with the people who were out to destroy him."

"And who, may I ask, told you that?"

Her throat tightened. She wasn't about to betray Graziana's confidence. "No one had to tell me. I figured it out for myself."

Chiara's mouth twisted into a sinister smile. "Well, Miss Genius, let me tell you something. If you don't learn to look out for yourself in this business, *you* will be the one who's destroyed. Oh, I know you think you're safe and protected because you're the Great Maestro's little darling right now. You think you're special to him, don't you? Well think again. You're just one in a long line. When you're no longer useful to him he'll pass you on to one of his cohorts. How do you think you'll feel then?"

She'd had enough. Chiara could say whatever she wanted about her, but listening to her talk about him that way was more than she could stomach. She stood abruptly. "I'm afraid I must end our visit. I have to finish drying my hair."

Chiara breezed out with a cold, glittering laugh. Annina watched her silk skirts trail away as she closed the door firmly behind her. Leaning against the closed door, she sighed with mingled revulsion and relief. The sting of Chiara's venom was softened by the near certainty that she was now out of her life forever.

SOON AFTER CHIARA'S departure for Prague, Antonio told Annina about the opera he was planning for the autumn season. "It's called *Dorilla in Tempe*. It's about a princess, Dorilla, who against the will of her father and the gods is in love with a shepherd, Elmiro."

"Is Dorilla my role?"

"No, you're to play Eudamia, a nymph who's also in love with Elmiro and who spends most of the opera scheming to win him for herself."

"And does she get him?"

"She doesn't. But neither does Dorilla. Elmiro's accused of abducting Dorilla and is executed in the end by being chained to a tree and shot through with arrows. So Dorilla ends up marrying a herdsman, Nomio, who's really the god Apollo in disguise. Eudamia marries another shepherd, Filindo, who's been secretly in love with her and loyal to her throughout the story."

"How many arias will I have?"

"Three, one in each act. In the first, Eudamia expresses her yearning for Elmiro's love. In the second, she bemoans the hopelessness of her yearning. And finally, in the third, she pours out her rage to Elmiro for his rejection of her love."

She sizzled with excitement. But the following autumn, after the first rehearsal, she realized her role was not as significant as Antonio had made it sound. As *seconda donna* she was relegated to a rather low status in the opera's hierarchy of characters, and the higher ranking singers looked down their noses at her. To make matters worse, they seemed jealous of her close relationship with Antonio and determined to put her in her place. The most trying of them was Maddalena Pieri, a contralto who specialized in singing *en travesti*, male roles. Antonio had hired her to sing the part of Elmiro.

About two days into rehearsals she found herself alone

backstage with Maddalena. The contralto eyed her coolly, with barely concealed contempt. "I had a letter from my friend Chiara Orlandi recently. She told me how you've bewitched Don Antonio into making you his exclusive protégée, to the point where you were able to persuade him to have her exiled to Prague."

Her heart skipped a beat. "You know Chiara?"

"Yes indeed. And she's told me all about you and your secret relationship with *il prete rosso*."

"There's nothing secret about our relationship," she said stiffly. "He's my teacher, and that's all there is to it."

Her smile showed her disbelief. "If you expect anyone to believe that, you must be even more foolish than you are cunning."

She bristled with indignation, and her cheeks burned. "I don't have to listen to this," she said, and turned to walk away.

Maddalena's next words brought her to a halt. "I find it interesting that after all the fuss the maestro apparently has made over you, he's only given you the secondary female role in *Dorilla*."

Now her indignation was compounded by stinging humiliation. She was speechless, and to her horror, tears sprang to her eyes. Maddalena returned to the stage, clearly pleased with herself.

She knew she couldn't talk to Antonio about this. After all he'd done for her she was afraid her petty complaints about Maddalena would sound like the whining of a spoiled brat. If she tried to get Paolina's sympathy, her sister would only frown and shake her head in that *Didn't I try to tell you so?* way. So she went to visit Graziana, who she hadn't seen much of since Paolina's return to Venice. Ever since Chiara left for Prague, she'd avoided Signora Malvolia's house. She was sure the old woman blamed her for Chiara's departure, and she had no wish to face her overblown accusations.

Fortunato delivered her to Signora's door, and she was greeted with the old lady's cold, quivering stare. She quickly made her way to the sewing room. At the sight of her, Graziana's face lit up and she rushed to embrace her. Annina poured out her story.

She smiled knowingly. "Most opera singers are self-centered, backbiting, and just downright mean-spirited. I learned that a long time ago when I started making costumes for them. Chiara, I must say, is an extreme case. But they're almost all like that to some degree. I think one of the reasons Don Antonio likes you so much is because you're *not* like that."

She felt the flicker of a warm glow inside, which almost immediately was clouded by doubt. "Then why has he given me a secondary role?"

"This is only a start. You're still very young. Those other singers are much more experienced, and you can only expect they're going to try to lord it over you."

"It's just so hard to take."

"Ignore them. Look at it this way—you're finally getting to sing onstage in Venice, in one of Don Antonio's operas. That's what you've been wanting, isn't it?"

"Yes, you're right," she said, sighing.

Her eyes brightened with curiosity. "What sort of role are you playing?"

"I'm a nymph."

"A nymph? How appropriate. I'll design and make a costume that'll keep every eye on you, I guarantee it. Those high-flown singers will be so astounded when they see how gorgeous you look their jaws will drop to the floor."

Now she was talking. Annina was starting to feel better already.

ON A CHILLY November morning, Graziana appeared at Annina's door. "I have a surprise for you," she said, pulling from her haversack what looked like a filmy piece of loose fabric.

"What's this?" she asked.

"Your costume, of course."

She held before her a sleeveless gown, whitish in color, made of a very thin, almost sheer fabric.

"That's just the main part of it," Graziana said with a smile. "Here's the rest." She handed her a pale, flesh-colored silk chemise and matching stockings, a gauzy pink sash, and silk slippers the same shade as the stockings. She grinned eagerly. "Why don't you try these on?"

She held the lovely but flimsy pieces of clothing in her hands and felt their delicate sensuousness. Days before, Graziana had measured her carefully for the costume but hadn't allowed her to see it yet. She wanted to surprise her. She was more than surprised—she was stunned.

"Go on," Graziana urged. "I can't wait to see this on you."

Reluctantly she went to her bedroom and slipped out of her clothes. Shivering, she donned the wispy little nymph costume. She had to admit that the clinging silk chemise, which barely reached halfway down her thighs, tickled her skin in a thrilling way, as did the thin stockings that hugged her legs so snuggly. The diaphanous outer garment, cinched at the waist with the pink sash, draped softly around her body and fell in delicate folds down her legs to just above her ankles. The sheerness of the fabric made everything subtly visible that wasn't covered by the chemise. The little silk slippers completed the delicately alluring ensemble. She gazed at her image in the mirror. How, she wondered, could she wear this in public, on stage, in front of hundreds of people—in front of Antonio? Hesitantly she stepped out of her bedroom, hoping

Graziana would agree the costume was too daring.

Graziana glowed with pleasure when she saw her. "You look absolutely *gossamer*."

"Gossamer?"

"Yes. Light, delicate, ethereal. I asked around about nymphs when I was planning your costume and learned they're beautiful, fragile, semi-divine maidens who dwell in forests and country meadows. And that's you, Annina. As I look at you now, I'm convinced you *are* a nymph."

She wasn't sure if the goose bumps popping out on her skin were from the cold or the thrill that swept through her.

Graziana looked down with a demure smile. "I had supper with Fortunato last night."

"Really? Where?"

"At the tavern near Signora's house."

"And?"

She blushed. "I think he's sweet on me."

"That's wonderful!"

"I know he's a bit rough on the outside. But he's really quite charming, don't you think?"

"Oh, I do. Fortunato's one of the kindest, bravest, most loyal men I've ever known. You and he are perfect for each other."

Her smile was euphoric.

THE DAY OF *Dorilla*'s premier, Graziana spent most of the afternoon arranging Annina's hair, applying her makeup, and making sure every tantalizing thread of her costume was perfectly in place. Her hairstyle was simple. Graziana tied the sides back with a pink silk ribbon and let the loose strands fall around her shoulders, then placed a dainty wreath of pale pink morning glories on her head. She decided her makeup should be light and understated so it wouldn't contrast too much with the graceful filminess of her costume. No one, not even Antonio, had seen the costume yet, and she tingled with anticipation of the reaction she'd get.

Shortly before the opening sinfonia Antonio came backstage to make sure everyone was ready. He looked at her almost in awe. "Annina, you're beautiful," he said, smiling boyishly, while the other female singers, especially Maddalena, glared at her. She reminded herself that Maddalena's character, Elmiro, was to be chained to a tree and shot dead with arrows near the end of the opera. The thought made her smile.

The opera went off without a hitch, and the audience clapped and hooted their praise when she made her bows. But she couldn't help feeling miffed about the little-girlishness of her role. She decided to speak to Antonio about it at her lesson the following Monday.

Chapter Thirteen

When she arrived at Antonio's studio he was writing furiously with ink-stained fingers, and his haste showed he was in a state of fevered inspiration. She had always respected his need for solitude when he was in the throes of creative frenzy. But today she felt too keyed up to be that considerate. She crossed her arms and fixed her eyes on him. The room was silent except for the rapid scratch of his pen across the music paper.

"Will you please listen to me?" she said.

He was oblivious to everything but the notes that seemed to want to fill the page faster than he could move his pen.

"Antonio!"

"Hmmm? What?" He glanced at her, abstractedly.

"I'm trying to talk to you."

"What is it, dear?"

"Why do you keep putting me in these little child roles?"

"Because you *are* a child."

"I'm almost seventeen!"

"Are you? I thought you were still fifteen."

She gave a loud sigh and raised her eyes heavenward.

He put down his pen and smiled. "All right, why don't you sit and tell me exactly what it is you're trying to say."

She was too restless to sit, so she strode about and gestured manically with her hands. "I want to play someone glamorous and sophisticated. Not only that, but someone who's fighting injustice and not afraid to stand up for herself. I don't want to be some meek little nymph or shepherd who sings sweet little songs about love and nature. I want to play characters with violent, mixed up feelings and sing music that's full of passion and movement. I know you can compose music like that, I've heard it. So why won't you create music like that for me? You've always said I fill my performances with sincere emotion and energize your music like no one else can. I want the chance to do that onstage!" Out of breath, she paused, her heart in a flurry.

He gazed at her with fascination in his eyes. She felt herself soften under his gaze, but she wasn't ready to let go of her agitation. She crossed her arms again. "Well?"

He cleared his throat. "Well—you've certainly made your point." He stared down at his manuscript and seemed to be deep in thought. Finally he said, "I have some ideas I think you'll be pleased with, Annina. But I'd like to wait and continue this discussion tomorrow, if you don't mind."

She was impatient to hear his ideas but realized she'd probably pushed things far enough for one day.

THE NEXT DAY she couldn't get to her lesson fast enough.

When she arrived, he wasted no time getting to the point. "Annina, I feel you're almost ready for a truly challenging role."

She waited anxiously for him to continue.

"There's something you need to understand, though. As I've

told you so often in the past, you have all the dramatic tools you need to portray emotionally complex characters convincingly. But your vocal technique still needs work."

Her heart sank, and she felt her face droop.

His tone and expression became more animated, and he started to pace about. "Don't be downhearted, Annina. Opera singing is an art, and all art is a struggle between expressive freedom and craft. I'm caught in that struggle all the time with my composing. Why do you think I called my latest set of concertos *Il cimento dell'armonia e dell'inventione*, the contest between harmony and invention?"

She thought a moment. "Because your creative urges clash with the rules of composition?"

"Precisely. And that's the way it should be. The more intense the conflict, the more exciting the artistic product. Expressive instincts are a goldmine, but without the discipline of technical precision they remain formless and therefore useless. Do you understand what I'm saying?"

She nodded. As hard as it was to admit, she knew he was right. "But what about the challenging role you were getting ready to tell me about?"

"There's an opera I wrote several years ago, *Orlando furioso*, based on the epic poem by Ariosto. Do you know the story?"

She shook her head.

"It's about a Christian knight, Orlando, whose mission is to disempower an enchantress from the underworld, Alcina. In my original version, Orlando was the central character. Now I want to revise the opera for next year's autumn season at San Angelo, only this time I'll put Alcina at the heart of the story. To do this I'll have to rewrite all her texts and music in order to make her a more complex character, who the audience will sympathize with. I'm envisioning you in that role, Annina."

Her heart started beating so wildly she thought it would leap out of her chest.

He went on. "You can turn the painful experiences you've had to your advantage with this role."

"How can I do that?"

"By channeling your feelings, painful as they may be, into your art. You must allow your emotions to become the energies they really are."

"I'm not sure I understand."

"Well, for example, how did you feel when Tomaso denied you the chance to express your emotions in your singing?"

"Angry and frustrated. Also terrified I'd always have to hide behind a mask—that my true self would never be understood or accepted."

"And what about when Chiara pretended to be your friend, then betrayed you?"

"I hated her. I wanted revenge."

"This is difficult, I know, but think about your mother. What was your emotional reaction when she listened to false accusations and turned her back on you?"

She hesitated. Her jaw tightened and her eyes stung. "What I felt at the moment she walked out the door was a level of fury like I've never known—rage and despair rolled into a single feeling."

He eyed her steadily. "I want you to summon those feelings when you play Alcina. Sing the role through the filter of your own experience. You must become Alcina, but don't think of yourself as a wicked sorceress. Think of yourself as a misunderstood young woman with ardent yearnings that are doomed to remain unfulfilled. Your reactions to those unfulfilled longings alternate between grief and rage and culminate in the kind of fury you've just described."

Excitement built in her until she thought she'd explode. That moment marked the beginning of one of the happiest times of her life. She eagerly tackled all the technical exercises he assigned her and practiced with a fresh sense of purpose. With his help, all her painful memories became tools to shape and hone her vocal technique into something that transcended mere craft and sparkled with artistic splendor. Together, they developed a method of vocal expression that had the dramatic power needed to portray Alcina's stormy passions and tragic downfall.

OPENING NIGHT WAS magical. Earlier that day the grey mist of mid November had been driven away by a cool but sunny brilliance. By evening the cloudless heavens cast a luminous aura over Venice's San Angelo district that almost matched the gentle radiance of the theater's interior. Shortly before curtain time Annina peeked from backstage at the dazzling *mise-en-scène* of Alcina's enchanted island. The painted backdrop portrayed a scene of such exquisite beauty it could only be compared to paradise. Alcina's enchanted palace, with its surrounding gardens and distant view of a raging sea, was the setting for Act One. The soft, muted light of oil lamps gave a dreamlike atmosphere, while sparkling candelabras from above depicted a starry sky. She'd never seen anything so exquisite.

She was already dressed and ready for her big entrance. Her costume was a wasp-wasted gown of alluring violet. The dress's bodice featured a daring, off-the-shoulder décolletage to which were attached filmy sleeves that flowed to her fingers. The skirt was made of many layers of the sheerest silk, some of which clung to her hips and legs enticingly, and some of which fluttered about her freely. The gown made her feel as light and sparkly as a cloud of fairy dust. Graziana had brushed her hair to a high sheen and arranged it in an elegant twist on top of her head. A silvery crown studded with glittering faux amethysts completed the costume. The overall effect was exactly as Graziana had intended: seductively regal. In the third act, an element of mystery would be added to her costume when she donned a hooded black cloak, lined with purple satin.

Thrill and anxiety stirred in her, and she sighed deeply. Then she heard familiar footsteps. It was Antonio. The orchestra was gathering in front of the stage, and in a few moments he'd join them to begin the introductory sinfonia.

His eyes and smile glowed. "Annina, you're absolutely stunning."

She was so happy she was afraid she'd get teary-eyed and ruin her makeup if she tried to speak.

He touched her cheek in a very tender way. "You're going to astound them."

His smile and his touch filled her with confidence. She took a deep breath, smiled, and nodded.

"See you in a few minutes." He kissed her forehead lightly and hurried off.

From the shadows came a silky-toned voice. "What a *touching* scene."

She turned, and her blood ran cold. "*Chiara.*"

Her smile glistened with charm, but her eyes were hard. "Yes, it's me. Can you believe it? Here we are, together again. You thought you were rid of me for good, no doubt." She clucked her tongue and shook her head. "And your devoted Antonio not even here to hold your hand and protect you. How unfortunate."

Her fingers stiffened and folded into fists "What are you doing here?"

Chiara's smile became smug. "Prague is dreary, so I decided to return to Venice once my contract with Denzio was up." She looked her over with cool, appraising eyes. "It looks like I got here just in time." In the dim backstage light her eyebrows took on a diabolical slant, and deep lines seemed to be etched around her mouth. Both gave her a frighteningly sinister look.

Her fists tightened. "What do you want, Chiara?"

Her lovely, cold face came close to Annina's, and her voice was a sharp whisper. "To see you fail, of course."

Her skin crawled at the feel of Chiara's hissing breath.

The orchestra was tuning up. The other singers were still in their dressing rooms but would soon be coming out for their entrances.

She glared at Chiara with burning eyes. "*Get out.*"

"Oh, I wouldn't dream of it," was her smooth reply. "To see you humiliated—brought low in all your radiant finery, hooted and jeered by a hostile audience—will be so thrilling." Her eyes brightened. "Best of all will be the look on Antonio's face."

She had a sick, quivering feeling. She could only think of a single question. "*Why*, Chiara?"

"Because I have nothing but contempt for you. You and your clever schemes. You're no singer, and everyone knows it." Her eyes narrowed and chilled, and her lips spread into an icy smile. "And deep down, Antonio knows it too. Tonight will bear that out."

"That's absurd." Her voice was pinched.

"Is it? You're nothing but a trickster who's managed to bewitch him all these years with your crafty wiles. It's no coincidence he was prompted to create for you the role of that evil seductress Alcina. She characterizes you perfectly. You have no real talent. Through a combination of guile and little girl charm you managed years ago to wheedle Antonio into taking you under his protection.

And you'll be the ruin of him. So I intend to teach you a lesson. Tonight you'll be exposed for the fraud you really are."

She stared into Chiara's icy green eyes, speechless, as the shadow of terror descended over her with all its malevolent power.

The sinfonia began and singers started to assemble backstage. Chiara strolled off with a smile of glee.

Dazed with fear, she walked onstage behind the closed curtain. Chiara had won. She'd shattered her confidence. With cold precision she had roused all her worst fears. And how well Chiara knew: Fear would ensure her failure.

Her opening aria was the most brilliant and technically challenging piece Antonio had ever written for her. Exactly the kind of aria she'd been pleading for. She wouldn't be able to sing it. Her throat and jaw were welded shut. Terror pricked her insides with the piercing sharpness of a thousand spearheads. All her strength had been sucked out of her. She felt weak and helpless.

Channel your feelings, painful as they may be, into your art. Allow your emotions to become the energies they really are.

Antonio's voice was in her head. He was telling her to use her fear to fuel her dramatic power. All at once she knew: Chiara's evil plan had backfired. The rage and terror she'd ignited in her heart would give Alcina life and make her real. The curtain rose, and Antonio raised his violin to launch the brisk introduction to her first aria. She gathered her skirts and moved with an imperious stride toward the footlights. Her quivers of fear turned to tingles of delight as flickering candlelight from above danced in the folds of her gown and gave it a shimmering quality. She caught Antonio's eye, and the fire in his gaze shot through her. She became Alcina. With queenly confidence she asserted her power, while revealing her underlying fear of Orlando:

His warlike gaze,
that spreads terror,
brings fear to my heart!

The aria sprang from her throat, from the very core of her being, with more vehemence than she ever knew was in her. All her anxieties melded and flowed through the words and music in a way that felt wonderful and excruciating at the same time. She soared through the opera's first two acts, swept up in a fever of inspiration. She schemed to weaken Orlando's power by seducing his fellow knights, Ruggiero and Astolfo. Secretly, though, she grieved at her inability to find true love:

If only I too could enjoy with the one I love
the peace my heart cannot find.
But tied to my fate, both treacherous and rebellious,
the god of love threatens only torment.

In the third act her lament transformed into fury at the injustice of the gods:

My bow wishes to break you,
my torch to extinguish you,
savage, tyrannical god of love!

At the end, defeated by Orlando, she donned her hooded cloak and raged:

Oh unjust gods! O fates! O adverse stars!
My grief and my shame are too bitter!
Everything is against me!
Even my magic has lost its power!
I will go down and call out of the depths

the evil furies from the ghastly abyss,
and I will ask the depths for vengeance
for my betrayed love!

Swooping her cloak about herself with a violent flourish, she descended into the underworld in a cloud of smoke.

She came out for her first curtain call to the most thunderous applause she'd ever experienced, or ever could have imagined. Palms clapped, feet stomped, voices whooped. She curtsied deeply, smiled until her face hurt, and blinked back tears of happiness, while starry-eyed young men showered the stage with flowers and love sonnets. After more curtain calls than she could count, she came back onstage with the rest of the cast. Antonio had come backstage and walked out with them, and they all joined hands. Strands of hair had come loose from her careful coiffure and stuck to her forehead and the sides of her face. She was drenched with sweat, but so was everyone else. It felt wonderful.

The thunder of applause mounted. She spotted Graziana and Fortunato, standing together near the front of the pit. They smiled up at her, and their candid faces shone with the love of true friendship. Her eyes darted to the box Paolina and the Vivaldi family were sharing. She couldn't make out their facial expressions, but she saw them spring to their feet and clap wildly.

In the midst of the cheering throng she caught a glimpse of Chiara. She neither stood nor clapped. But even in the dusky candlelight she could see her ivory cheeks blaze red with helpless rage. She seemed to fade into the crowd as the applause became all the more deafening. For a fleeting moment her heart ached that her parents weren't able to share her triumph. Yet her soul rejoiced that they were together again, and that her good fortune would help free them from their financial worries. She closed her eyes a moment and prayed that someday she might find a way to help her mother free the love that had so long been buried in the dark depths of her heart.

Soon the clamor was punctuated by cries of *Bravissima L'Annina del prete rosso!*

She leaned close to Antonio. "Did you hear what they called me?"

He didn't answer, but merely clasped her hand and kept smiling.

Chapter Fourteen

Antonio had begun to notice something about Annina—she wasn't a little girl anymore. Those big adoring eyes still pulled at his heartstrings as they always had, but now the fire that so often flashed in those eyes gave him an unsettling thrill as well. And that smile. So sweet, innocent, and irresistible. Yet did he detect something a bit more "knowing" in her smile than had been there before? And her enticing little figure in that Alcina costume. But he couldn't allow himself to think of her in this way. He simply could not. Nothing good could possibly come of it—only scandal, disgrace, corruption, and heartbreak. So he would be her friend. Her dearest, closest friend, and protector of her honor and her innocence. She herself had chosen a career over marriage, and he would make certain that was a safe choice for her. No one with any lustful ideas would get near her.

TWENTY-TWO-YEAR-OLD Count Landi thought he'd never seen anything so ravishing. Everything about the girl delighted him—her lovely face, expressive eyes and mesmerizing voice, the way the flickers of candlelight sparkled and danced about her. He couldn't stop thinking about the filmy layers of silk that floated around her and moved with her like a cloud of fragrant lavender, while other layers clung alluringly to her slender body. He smiled as he pondered the clinging layers.

L'Annina del prete rosso. What the devil did that mean? Did she somehow belong to him? In what way? He had to find out. After the final curtain call he sent his manservant, Roberto, backstage to ask for a meeting with her.

"*Well?* " he asked anxiously, when Roberto returned looking regretful.

"The young lady is accepting no visitors," was the servant's reply.

"Damnation!" His disappointment knew no bounds. What he wouldn't give for even a moment of the alluring Signorina Girò's company—to have her smile at him, inflame him with those fiery dark eyes.

I'll write her a note, he thought. Something gallant and just enticing enough to rouse her interest. After all, young prima donnas relish the attentions of noblemen, do they not?

"I believe the priest-composer shields her from the overtures of potential admirers, sir," Roberto said dryly.

"Vivaldi?"

"*Sì*, Excellency. He guards her carefully, I'm told."

"Guards her? Whatever for? What's his stake in the girl?"

"I'm afraid I do not know, Excellency."

"Well for the love of heaven, find out!"

ANNINA SOON GREW used to being called *L'Annina del prete rosso*, the red-haired priest's Annina. When she and Antonio took notice of the nickname at all, they laughed about it. "I think you're more famous now than I am," he'd say with a chuckle.

On the evening of the *Orlando* premier she was given another nickname. Antonio's family gathered at the Vivaldis' house later that night, and she joined them after stopping home to quickly bathe and change into the new lemon silk party gown Graziana had fashioned for her. When she arrived, the atmosphere was festive. Everyone was laughing and talking excitedly about the evening's triumph. As soon as she entered the parlor, Giovanni came over and clasped her in a warm embrace.

"I think Antonio has finally found his Muse. My darling, you were sensational."

Before she could respond they were joined by an attractive, well-dressed woman. "Papà, you must introduce me to this charming young lady. I can't believe I'm the only one in the family who hasn't met her."

The woman smiled at her as Giovanni put an arm around each of them. "Annina, my dear, this is my daughter Cecilia Mauro." He looked around. "Her husband and two scamps of sons are around here someplace too, I believe," he said, winking at her.

Cecilia frowned and took Annina's hand. "Don't listen to him. Come, I'll introduce you to them." They walked across the hall into the dining room. At the opposite end of the room two red-haired, freckle-faced boys about ten and twelve years of age were at the sideboard, stacking wine goblets into a precarious pyramid.

"Pietro! Daniele! Stop that before you destroy your grandmother's best glassware!" Cecilia scolded.

They carefully un-stacked the goblets and turned to face their mother, smiling sheepishly.

"Where is your father? He was supposed to be watching the two of you," she said, looking about sharply.

"He's talking to Uncle Antonio," the older boy said, turning his head toward a far corner where the two men were immersed in conversation, wine glasses in hand.

Cecilia gave the boys a reproving look. "Your grandfather just called you scamps, and I think he may have been right. Now act like gentlemen so I can introduce you to this lovely lady. Signorina Annina, these are my sons, Pietro and Daniele."

Both boys grinned widely and bowed. "Pleased to meet you, signorina," they said.

She smiled at their awkward attempt at civility. "Pleased to meet you both," she said, trying not to laugh

Their mother looked pleased. "Now go to the kitchen and play with your cousin."

They grinned again at Annina, then darted off.

"And stay out of trouble!" Cecilia called after them. She looked back at Annina and sighed. "Boys. What can you do? Now come meet my husband," she said, taking her hand again.

Antonio beamed with delight when he saw her, and his joy seemed to light up the room. To her surprise, he wrapped his arm around her, and pulled her to him, in an almost possessive way. "Wasn't she the most enchanting thing you've ever seen or heard?" he said.

"She certainly was," said Cecilia.

Her husband smiled politely.

"Oh," said Antonio. "You haven't met our brilliant set designer. Annina, may I present my brother-in-law, Antonio Mauro." He grinned. "It confuses everyone having another Antonio in the family, so we simply call him Mauro."

"A pleasure, Signor Mauro," she said.

"The pleasure is mine," he said, bowing slightly.

"Your sets were exquisite, Signor Mauro." She looked at

Antonio. "You never told me your brother-in-law designed them."

"He not only designed the sets but managed the painting of the backdrops and the lighting."

"Really? What a talent you have, Signor Mauro."

Cecilia broke in, giving her husband a sharp look. "Talented at painting, perhaps, but not at keeping an eye on our boys. While you two were over here chatting away, your sons almost broke every glass in the house."

Mauro glanced around. "I don't see any broken glass."

She groaned. "I'm going to see if Margarita and Zanetta need any help." She gave her husband another reproachful glance. "And why don't you go back to the parlor and talk to my father. He was looking for you."

He nodded and did as he was told.

Cecilia smiled again at Annina. "So lovely to finally meet you, my dear," she said, before heading for the kitchen.

Antonio took another taste of his wine and squeezed Annina to him even closer. She felt her cheeks flush with self-consciousness, but also with a strange little thrill. Never had she felt so accepted and admired, at the center of something so important. She was still quivering with the heady ecstasy of having triumphed against all odds. She wasn't sure if he realized Chiara had been there but decided not to bring it up and risk spoiling his radiant mood.

"I enjoyed meeting your sister and her family," she said. "I'm surprised I've never seen them before."

He turned to face her. "They live across town and don't come here very much. I think Mauro is a bit overwhelmed by my family. Too much commotion for him."

"Yes, he does seem a little reserved. But his work is outstanding. Has he ever done work for you before?"

"Only once. He did the sets for *Dorilla* last year."

"Oh, I hadn't realized. Speaking of your family, where is your mother?" She glanced around. "I'd like to thank her for this lovely party."

His expression grew more sober. "She's upstairs resting. I'm afraid the excitement of the opera was a bit wearing on her. She hasn't been feeling her best lately."

"Oh dear, I'm sorry to hear that." It occurred to her that she hadn't seen Signora Vivaldi more than a few times since the Sunday dinner when they'd first met.

"She'll be fine after a good night's sleep, I'm sure. There's no need to worry." He sighed, then smiled as his spirits seemed to lift. "Enough talk about my family. You're the star of the evening, and everyone's celebrating except you. The least I can do is pour you a glass of wine."

As he went to pour her wine, she felt her skirts being tugged. Looking down, she saw a tiny, red-haired girl. The child gazed up at her with blue eyes as big and round as saucers. "Chee-na!" she squealed. "Will you take me to your magic island?" Then she stretched her little arms up. Not knowing what else to do, she reached down and lifted the little girl into her arms. She was light as a feather and her little body was soft and lean. She locked her legs around Annina's waist and her arms around her neck and looked straight into her eyes. "I love you, Chee-na. You're a beautiful magic queen. I want to be like you when I grow up."

She realized the child was trying to say "Alcina." She smiled in spite of herself as the little girl tightened her tiny arms into a stranglehold around her neck. "Well," she said, "I don't know when I've ever felt so admired. What's your name, sweetie?"

"Gee-gee!"

"Gigi? What a pretty name."

The girl's hair and eyes left no doubt she was a Vivaldi. Antonio returned with a glass of wine in each hand. She gave him a questioning look as Gigi tightened her grip around her waist and neck.

He smiled in amusement and set down her glass. "Her name is Giovanna. She's Iseppo's daughter."

She remembered that Iseppo was Antonio's younger brother. She had no idea he had a child, or even that he was married. She decided not to ask any questions in front of the little girl.

"I'm Gee-gee!" she insisted, when she heard Antonio tell Annina her real name. She reached for him, and he took her in his arms, handing Annina his glass of wine. Gigi wrapped herself around him and smothered his face with kisses. Then she wiggled free and scampered across the room.

"What a little bundle of energy," she said.

"Full of mischief too," he said, smiling.

She handed him back his glass and picked hers up. "How old is she?"

"Three years old."

She looked around. "Where are her parents?"

He took a taste of wine and sighed. "The poor girl my brother dishonored died giving birth to the child. The girl's parents had planned to raise her but have decided she's too much for them, so now she's with us. And as for my wayward brother, he's off looking for work, or so he says."

She gazed at him, incredulous he'd never told her any of this before. She didn't know what to say, so she asked a neutral question. "What sort of work does Iseppo do?"

He smiled, ironically. "He doesn't seem to have figured that out yet."

At that moment there was a startling noise, and everyone's heads turned. "Giovanna! I warned you if you acted up one more time—!" an exasperated Margarita scolded as she entered the dining room.

Little Gigi dodged her aunt's grasp and scurried away. "*Nonno, Nonno!*" she shrieked. Giovanni had just come into the dining room and she attached herself to his leg. "Save me! Save me!" He scooped her up, and she clung to him, her head on his shoulder.

Meanwhile, Margarita and Zanetta were on their knees, cleaning up the platter of food Gigi had knocked to the floor.

"That child should be in bed," she heard Margarita mutter.

"How on earth do you think we can get her to stay in bed with all this going on?" Zanetta said.

She thought she should help them, but Gigi had already slithered out of Giovanni's arms and was tugging her skirts again. She smiled down at the child.

"Chee-na!" Her head was bent all the way back and her eyes were fastened on Annina's. "Are you Uncle Antonio's wife?"

Antonio nearly choked on his wine.

She felt her face go red as the shock of Gigi's innocent question caused her to burst into nervous laughter. She looked at Antonio. He was wiping his mouth with the back of his hand and struggling to suppress an uneasy laugh.

She knelt down to Gigi's level and smiled at her patiently. "Gigi, sweetie," she said softly, "your Uncle Antonio can't be married. He's a priest."

Gigi considered this a moment. "Oh," she said at last, apparently satisfied with the explanation. Then she said, "Are *you* married, Cheena?"

"No. And my name isn't really Alcina. It's Annina."

You're *Cheena*," she said with a pout of determination. "You're a beautiful queen and live on a magic island."

"Only in story land. In real life I'm just a regular person, not a magic queen."

Gigi's face broke into a huge grin. "*Chee-na!*" She giggled and scurried off. Her cousin Pietro, who seemed to have appeared out of nowhere, was at her heels.

Poor little thing, she thought. She seemed so desperate for love and affection, but almost afraid to cling to it for too long. She sighed as she rose to her feet.

Antonio was still at her side. "You handled that very well," he said, smiling. "You'd make a good mother."

She looked at him, amazed. "Me, a mother? I never imagined you saw me in that way."

"Truthfully, I never have until just a moment ago."

She gave him a wry look. "So what are you saying? That I should get married and start having babies?"

"Not if you want to continue your opera career."

"Well, since there should be no doubt in your mind that that's exactly what I want, I don't know why you're even bringing up the subject of motherhood."

His smile mellowed. "I only made a passing observation, Annina. I wasn't suggesting you change the course of your life."

His startling remark may not have changed the course of her life, but it launched a disturbing trend in her thinking.

LATE THAT NIGHT, while Paolina was sleeping, Annina crept out of bed and pulled *la moretta* from her hiding place in the back of the wardrobe cupboard. She wrapped a shawl around her shoulders, slipped into soft shoes, and tiptoed down the stairs to the Campo Santa Maria Formosa. Padding across the square, her nightgown whipping around her, she made her way to the Ponte del Paradiso. She paused on the bridge and held *la moretta* at arm's length over the railing. "You can't shield me, and you've failed to silence me," she said, her words ringing in the night wind. "My voice is free, and so am I!" She opened her fingers and watched *la moretta* plunge into the rippling dark waters of the Rio del Mondo Novo.

SHE FINALLY HAD everything she'd ever wanted. Yet a vague longing told her something was missing. Exactly what, she wasn't quite sure. She only knew an elusive desire was tormenting her deep inside. For the time being, though, a much more pressing matter weighed on her mind.

When she and Antonio met at his studio the following Monday afternoon to discuss her Alcina performance, she decided to bring up what was bothering her.

"Did you realize Chiara was at the opera Saturday night?"

"Yes, and I've already received a letter from Denzio. She never showed up in Prague, and he wants me to swear out a warrant for her arrest."

She stared at him, dumbfounded. "Are you going to do it?" she said finally.

"I hope I won't have to. I'll try to talk to her first and make her understand the seriousness of what she's done. Reneging on a signed contract is a criminal offense."

"But she told me she'd fulfilled her contract."

"She lied."

She felt nothing but disgust for her. "Oh, why don't you just have her arrested and sent to prison? That's what she deserves."

"Because I'd rather get her as far away from Venice as possible."

"Will Denzio still take her?"

"I think so. He's a decent fellow, and I'm sure he'll listen to reason once I've talked to Chiara. That is, assuming she cooperates."

The door creaked open, and she turned. "I think we have a visitor."

Gigi peered timidly around the edge of the door.

Antonio smiled at her. "It's all right, Giovanna. You can come in." Then he looked back at Annina. "You don't mind, do you?"

"Of course not."

Gigi scuttled into the room with an impish smile and attached herself to Annina's skirts, as she directed coquettish little glances at her uncle. He gave her funny looks, and she giggled and buried her face in the folds of Annina's dress. Then she turned to him and giggled again.

This was a new situation for her. There was a child in the room, and she and Antonio were the adults. She was no longer the little girl, looking up to him in a hero-worshipping way. Without her realizing it, their relationship had become more equalized. She felt closer to him, yet at the same time more aware of the inevitable distance between them. The vague longing that had recently crept up on her was beginning to define itself with alarming precision.

Later in bed, she wrapped her arms around herself and stared through the window at the clear night sky. She struggled not to let herself think it. An untenable desire had overtaken her. Complete happiness was so close at hand, yet untouchable. That realization only increased her agony. It was wrong. It was Satan tempting her. It was the same desire that had caused Chiara's falling out with Antonio seven years before. She curled up on her side and hugged her knees, letting out a trembling sigh as her heart raced. Part of her reasoned that the gossips were saying it about them anyway, so why not *really* give them something to talk about? Another part of her recoiled at such an idea. The worst part of all was that she couldn't discuss this with anyone. She was determined that no one suspect her forbidden yearning. But it was there. She managed to suppress her foolish fantasies for awhile by reminding herself that those sorts of thoughts put her in the same league as Chiara, the last person in the world she wanted to emulate. She caused nothing but problems and misery for everyone around her.

The next day Antonio met with Chiara and persuaded her to return to Prague. Then through a series of letters he managed to smooth things over with Denzio. What a relief. Annina's life always flowed so much more easily when Chiara wasn't around. She just hoped she wasn't about to follow in her footsteps.

COUNT LANDI'S JOURNEY from his hometown of Piacenza had been tiresome, yet his first glimpse of the sun shimmering on the icy waters of the Grand Canal had sent a delicious shiver through him. As a boy, he'd visited Venice with his father, but the thrill of finally venturing to *La Serenissima* on his own was unmatched. Venice, the Most Serene, rising wondrously out of the sea with its boundless network of land and water. There was nothing like it. Now, the incomparable beauty of the Venetian sunset set his loins afire as his thoughts filled with the vibrant young woman he longed to see again. Only last week, at the premier of the red priest's *Orlando furioso*, he'd fallen prey to her charms as she stood at the edge of the stage, her lovely face and tantalizingly lean figure aglow in the footlights. He couldn't deny the allure of her purposeful stride onto the stage, the passion and, yes, sensuality that pervaded her every movement. He'd sat there awestruck, washed by wave after wave of intoxicating sights and sounds. That night a strange desire took possession of him and now, as darkness shadowed the city's vast cluster of spires and domes, the gold-tinged gloom of winter dusk only increased his desire.

He was to see her again tonight. She and the priest were giving a private concert at the home of his host, Signor Piero Pasqualigo, a distinguished member of the *Signoria*, Venice's aristocratic ruling body. He felt fortunate to be staying in the magnificent palazzo of his father's old friend, with its sprawling mosaic tile floors, layered with sumptuous carpets. One of the best houses in Venice, and a perfect setting for suavely making the acquaintance of the enticing Signorina Girò.

Strolling through the Piazza San Marco he gazed at the Campanile. Its pointed green and white rooftop towered above the vast square, illumined by the blazing lights of the Basilica. The piazza was becoming more and more crowded with masked revelers as cascades of fireworks filled the night sky. Most fascinating were the ghostly white *pulcinellas*, with their huge beaked noses catching the fireworks glow. Here and there he caught a glimpse of an even more mysterious *moretta* mask. He chuckled. Only last week he'd found one floating in an obscure canal and had reached from his gondola to retrieve it, deciding it would be an apt memento of his Venetian adventure. *Probably tossed into the water by some spirited girl*, he'd thought, as his fingers caressed the stifling *bottone*.

He was startled from his thoughts by the loud clanging of the *Marangona* bell of the Campanile, signaling the late hour. *Blast*, he thought, *the party is underway*. Signorina Girò would be swamped by admirers and he'd have no chance to approach her.

When he arrived at the Palazzo Pasqualigo, he hurried through the milling crowd in the foyer and up the massive staircase to the second floor—the *piano nobile*, the floor used by the Venetian aristocracy for entertaining. And there she was, smiling politely and nodding as two dowagers prattled on about something. *This is going to be easier than I thought. She'll be grateful to me for rescuing her from those hags.* Then he spotted the red-haired priest, only a few paces away. Like a dragon at the gates. But the priest was absorbed in an animated conversation with a jovial nobleman.

He thought he'd better seize his chance. Plucking two glasses of champagne from the tray of a roaming servant, he approached her from behind. "*Signorina mia—*"

She wheeled about and stiffened as a savory wisp of scent tickled his nostrils.

"My dear lady," he said, bowing. "Please don't be alarmed." She looked younger than she'd appeared on stage, her face framed by wispy tresses of chestnut hair. Such tender, pure beauty. She couldn't be more than sixteen or seventeen. He felt a tug at his heart.

Her astonished stare turned suspicious.

The dowagers seemed flustered by his sudden appearance. He smiled at them charmingly and bowed again, glasses of champagne still in either hand. "Enchanted, ladies," he said. "If you would be so kind, I would like to have a word with Signorina Girò."

"*Piacere,*" one of them murmured, looking a bit put out. He watched as they wandered off, heads together.

"Allow me to offer you libation, signorina, and to introduce myself," he said, turning his attention back to Annina and handing her a glass. "I am Count Landi, of Piacenza."

"*Piacere,* Excellency," she murmured as she gave a small curtsy.

There was a brief silence. She dropped her eyes.

He took a long draft of champagne. "I must tell you, signorina, that I attended the premier of your maestro's new opera last week. I only wish I could find words to tell you how magnificent your performance was."

She met his eyes for a moment, and the faintest shadow of a smile crossed her face.

Encouraged, he went on. "All I can do is marvel at how the maestro's music has the ability to express the inexpressible through your fiery tones. It expresses more than words can say."

The brilliance of her smile startled and delighted him, igniting for a moment the spark of that spirit she'd demonstrated onstage.

"I'm afraid you've given my two friends something to talk about," she said, glancing toward the dowagers, who stood a short distance off, watching them and whispering to each other.

"Poisonous windbags," he muttered.

She broke into a cheerful laugh, and her laugh was genuine, rather than some simpering titter or fluttering of eyelashes. "Don't worry," she said cozily, "this isn't the first time I've been the victim of petty gossip."

He took another generous sip of champagne. "Well, I say let them gossip away if they have nothing better to do."

She laughed again, softly, then lowered her gaze.

He looked at her with searching intensity. "You're not like other opera singers, are you?" He paused and smiled at the look of childish incomprehension on her face. "What I mean to say, signorina, is that you seem so . . . lacking in the artifice one tends to expect from those in the theatrical world."

"I only know how to be myself," she said simply.

He gazed at her with fascination, imbibing in her delicate, enchanting loveliness, and her endearing artlessness. Glancing warily toward the maestro he noticed the priest turn a stern eye on them for a moment. *Damnation.* What *is* his stake in this girl? He had to find out. He thought of challenging the priest directly, but no. That would be bad form.

He cleared his throat. "Without any offence to the honor and respect that is owed your celebrated maestro, signorina, I must ask . . . how shall I say it . . . it's just that I've heard so many stories of how badly the impresarios treat their singers."

A fleeting wave of indignation crossed her face. "He's never been anything but kind and good to me, signore."

"Ah, but in the heat of passion men sometimes forget themselves and do foolish things."

The corners of her mouth tightened, and she lifted her chin. "Are you talking about him or yourself, signore?"

The cool directness of her question startled him. Feeling vaguely chastened, he chuckled uncomfortably and took another quaf of champagne.

His host was tapping his glass. "*Attenzione, per favore*. My two illustrious guests, our own Don Antonio Vivaldi and the Marchese Guido Bentivoglio of Ferrara, wish to entertain you with a concerto for two mandolins. Please continue your merrymaking, but I assure you you'll want to hear this magnificent new composition from the hand of our esteemed maestro."

Blast, now I must pretend to be riveted while I endure some pastoral ditty written to flatter this fop of a marchese. Where the devil is that waiter? I need another drink.

Pasqualigo turned toward the two men. The marchese was seated in front of the orchestra, his mandolin resting on his knee, the chair beside him empty. The priest stood before the orchestra, mandolin dangling in one hand as he gestured the musicians to begin. The orchestra sprang into a bright, energetic ritornello, and the maestro took his seat beside Bentivoglio for the entrance of the mandolins. What ensued was no pastoral ditty. While the priest's mandolin part was decidedly more complex, the marchese's counter melody was skillfully performed. This music was anything but staid and static. It lived and moved. It was a manifestation of action. He had never heard anything like it.

He glanced at Annina as she watched the performance. Her rapt expression exuded love and pride. At the end of the first movement, she turned to him, handing him her untouched champagne. "I can't drink this, I have to sing in a few minutes."

He took it gratefully. "How does the maestro know the marchese?" he whispered.

"They met in Rome a few years ago, when Signor Bentivoglio was studying for the priesthood."

He turned his eyes to the marchese as he took up his mandolin to begin the second movement. "Why doesn't he wear a clerical collar?"

"He was called home to take over as head of his family in Ferrara when his older brother died, and had to give up his career in the Church."

"I see—"

"Shhh. They're about to start the next movement."

Oh, signorina mia, was all he could think, struggling with desire for her untouched, innocent beauty mixed with twinges of envy over her obvious devotion to her maestro. But his petty jealousy was quickly being overtaken by the utter exquisiteness of the priest's music.

Chapter Fifteen

Annina hurried across the *campo* toward the Ponte del Paradiso, nearly slipping on the slick pavement. It had been a damp, overcast day, with patches of fog hanging like a pall over the spires and domes of Venice.

Antonio's studio was immersed in stillness, a stillness so palpable it seemed to tremble and whisper, broken now and then by the faint sound of his cough. She felt a cold chill as the twilight sky outside the window faded to somber grey. She wanted to rush to his side and hold him in a tight embrace. But her guilty longings prevented her. She glanced about the darkening room. Dusk had drawn its shadowy veil, and she could barely make out the figure of Antonio, his worried hands clasped on the desktop, his head bowed in silent prayer.

As she approached his desk he looked up, almost imploringly, and fixed his troubled eyes on her. His face appeared younger in the shadowy light, and even in the near darkness she could see his eyes were bleary with hovering tears, bringing tears to her own eyes and a clenching pain to her heart.

She took a trembling breath. "I just heard your mother has taken a turn for the worse. How is she?"

The air between them grew very still as something hovered, shadowy and unspoken.

He shook his head slowly, and a sad smile flitted over his face. "She's with God now," he said, his voice thick with unshed tears.

His words seemed to hang in the still air for a moment, glowing with a ghostly luminescence. She'd heard the strangling lump in his throat and felt an unbearable pull on her heart. She took another deep breath. "God rest her gentle soul," she murmured. It was all she could think to say. She was at a loss how to help him, yet she felt a great surge of love.

He averted his eyes, a desolate look clouding his face. Slowly, she reached her hand across the desk to touch, gently, the pale skin of his temple. For an instant, neither of them moved, her fingertips cool and dry on his moist skin. He reached up and gently clasped her outstretched hand, his grasp firm. But it was the gentleness that really got to her. Again she saw the tears looming in his eyes, and all her reserve vanished as she rushed around the desk to put her arms around him. She bent to hold him as tightly as she could. He patted her shoulder as she clung to him.

There was a rustle in the darkness, and the room was suddenly lit by a dusky radiance. Startled, she backed away from him.

Margarita stood in the threshold, the wild flicker of her taper casting eerie shadows on the wall. "Oh Annina, thank heaven you're here," she said, as the empty outline of a smile wavered across her lips.

Annina hurried over to her. "I'm so terribly sorry about your mother," she said, trying to quell the trembling in her voice.

"Thank you, dear," Margarita said, blinking back tears. Then she leaned toward her and whispered. "I'm grateful you're here to comfort Antonio. I've been so worried about him. You know how his ailment flairs up when he's distressed."

"Yes, he was coughing earlier, but he's calmer now," she said, relieved that she didn't detect even a hint of reproof in Margarita's tone.

"Please stay with him awhile," she said in a choked whisper. "I should go tend to my father."

She nodded, pressed Margarita's hand as she kissed her softly on the cheek, then returned to Antonio. He was hunched over a leaf of manuscript paper, writing furiously, suddenly oblivious to her presence. She glanced at the title across the top: *Ave Regina Caelorum*, Hail Queen of Heaven. An intense ballad-like prayer, addressed to the spiritual mother. He paused a moment and glanced up at her, his eyes moist. She gazed at him. This was a side of him she'd never seen, this profoundly emotional man with tears in his eyes.

"God is inconceivable without music as a medium, something we can embrace without fully understanding," he said softly, his voice dark with pain.

His words were enigmatic—frightening, yet oddly comforting. *Something we can embrace without fully understanding.* Her mind churned for a moment. He was expressing his intense relish for life combined with his ardent response to things of the spirit, conveyed so eloquently through his music. These things had always drawn her to him. Yet how little of him she understood, how little she knew him. His music alone allowed her to glimpse the secrets of his soul.

He smiled at her a moment, then his smile wavered and vanished as he turned his attention back to his musical prayer.

ANTONIO WAS SICK at heart over his mother's death, but with his impending production schedule he had little time to grieve. He was to produce his newest opera *L'Atenaide* at the Teatro di Via della Pergola in Florence for the upcoming Carnival season. Annina would take the part of Pulcheria, a seconda donna role. Even though she had smiled cheerfully and pledged her support in this endeavor, he knew she was disappointed not to have the title role. But he couldn't risk it. He couldn't chance putting a seventeen-year-old girl with limited theatrical experience, especially one he cared for so deeply, at the mercy of those Florentine vultures. No, he'd taken the advice of that aging, cantankerous marchese turned impresario, Luca Casmiro degli Albizzi, and engaged the celebrated Florentine soprano Maria Giustina Turcotti for the role of Atenaide. He made a mental note to appease Annina by composing the most sparkling, brilliant aria of the opera for her.

Albizzi had invited him to compose and produce operas for him twice before, and he'd always obliged, due to the prestige of the Pergola theater. But Albizzi had always been a trial to work with. Antonio had in fact given up on the Pergola two years before, seeing that their programs were slowly beginning to change under pressure from the *gusto nuovo*, the new Neapolitan fashion in opera. Yet Albizzi was now asking him back. He was grateful this time he had Annina to help him prepare—and that she would be there by his side at the Pergola. Yet he feared she would be a prize target for the sanctimonious gossips who comprised Florence's opera patrons.

On opening night she dazzled the audience with the special aria he'd written for her. His heart swelled with love and awe at the sound of her voice intertwining with his furious violin ritornello, as she lamented the forced separation from her true love:

> *I protect myself as much as I can*
> *Against wounds and chains,*

But I am afraid
That against love
It may be too fragile a defense
To be prudent and strong.

As it turned out she was very happy with the treatment she received in Florence. Indeed, she'd been generously received by everyone. Her splendid performance even furnished the occasion for a sonnet, which had been distributed anonymously in the theater, extolling her singular merit:

Ode to La Girò
Neither the wind that blows among the leaves
Nor the nightingale that sings its love
Touches my heart like your sweet tones
With their countless charms and loveable caresses.

He tried to dismiss the pang of jealousy he felt upon reading those words. Yet the pride that swelled in his heart overcame his envy. She was his creation, in a way. The instrument that conveyed his musical ideas as no other could. She alone had worked her way into his creative mind, and his heart. He made a tacit promise to seek out any opportunity that would nurture her developing talent and advance her career.

Such an opportunity came four months later through his friend and patron, the elderly and distinguished Piero Pasqualigo. Long a champion of Antonio's music, Piero had recently taken an interest in Annina's growing accomplishments. Through his influence a visiting nobleman, Count Sicinio Pepoli, was seeking to arrange a contract with Antonio to produce a season of operas in Bologna, his native city. The count's older brother owned and managed

Bologna's only opera house. Antonio's mind had been churning for days with the possibilities such a contract might offer both him and Annina.

When the four of them met at Antonio's house the following Saturday afternoon, his hopes soared. To his relief, the rest of the household was out for the day, on a visit to his sister Cecilia and her family.

ANNINA WAS ANXIOUS to get to Antonio's house early that Saturday. When Pasqualigo and Pepoli arrived she greeted the count with all the poise and charm she could muster. After he showered her with compliments she sang her dazzling new aria for him, to Antonio's accompaniment at the harpsichord. The count was so entranced by her talent and beauty he declared he would write to his brother immediately and urge him to engage her and Antonio for the following season. While he went to the study to compose the letter, Antonio happily poured wine for everyone.

"This calls for a celebration," he said, squeezing his free arm around her for a moment and raising his glass in a toast toward Piero.

Smiling, Piero raised his glass in return. Soon Pepoli joined them.

The count finished his wine in several large gulps. After a generous swig of his second glass he moved closer to Annina. "And you and I will have our own private celebration later, will we not, my beautiful one?"

The change of mood in the room was palpable. She shuddered inwardly and stepped away from him, her eyes darting to Antonio and Piero. Their smiles had vanished, and they stared at Pepoli with a mutual air of indignation. The count looked from her to them with a perplexed smile.

At last Piero spoke up. "I think you owe this lady an apology, sir."

Pepoli looked incredulous, then downed his second glass. "An *apology*? You want me to apologize to *her*? Whatever for? She's an opera singer, for God's sake. I was only offering to show her a good time. Isn't that what her type likes? And doesn't she owe me a little courtesy, considering all I'm doing for her?"

She could see Antonio was controlling his temper with difficulty. "I'll not have you speak that way, sir."

The count's confused smile became a cynical sneer. He gave a scoffing laugh as he eyed each of them. "What kind of dupe do you take me for?" His eyes narrowed. "Ah, I understand now. You gentlemen consider this little stunner to be your personal property."

His insolence was more than she could bear. She glared at him. "I'm no man's property, Excellency. These gentlemen are my friends."

His look was smug. "And have you no room in your life for another *friend?* "

Piero took a threatening step toward him. "Now see here. You are offensive, sir. I think it best if you leave now."

The count visibly bristled with wounded pride. He shifted his eyes to Antonio. "Is this how it's to be then?"

"It is," was his curt reply.

"I must say, you have a very strange way of doing business." He turned to her with a piercingly cold look. "And as for you, young woman, you are treacherous and deceitful. I shall write another letter to my brother directly and inform him of the truth about you."

She was too shocked to speak. She stiffened, as tears stung her eyes.

Antonio's composure crumbled. "Be silent, sir, and get out!"

Pepoli gave him one more furious frown before he stormed into the hall and grabbed his cloak. He turned once more to Antonio. "You will never produce an opera in Bologna, maestro, I guarantee it."

As soon as the count had left, Piero put his hand on Antonio's shoulder. "Astonishingly rude fellow. I never would have thought it. I swear to you, Antonio, I had no idea what a contemptible louse he is."

"This is in no way your fault," he said bitterly.

Piero sighed and shook his head. "Damnable business, the theater." Then he came over and took her hand. "And you, my dear, how he could have the gall to say or even think such things, I can't imagine. The idea." He pressed her hand. "You're well rid of him," he said, looking back at Antonio. "You both are well rid of him. And now, I suppose I should be going as well." He released her hand and gave Antonio's shoulder a squeeze. "*Arrivederci*, my friend."

She followed him to the door, and he smiled at her in a fatherly way. "The man is nothing more than a blackguard, Annina. He's course and utterly lacking in tact, and you must put him out of your mind at once. Will you promise me that?"

Her eyes were still moist, but she smiled at him. "Yes, I promise."

He kissed her forehead and departed.

Antonio had retreated to his studio and was by his desk, rifling through a pile of manuscript papers. He was in the kind of agitated mood that made him difficult to approach.

She stood in the doorway. "I'm so sorry, Antonio."

He didn't look at her. "Sorry for what?"

"Well, obviously I must have said something to give the count the wrong impression."

He continued to search through the stack of papers. "You said nothing of the kind, and you have nothing to be sorry for."

"Then why do I have the feeling you're angry with me?"

"I'm not angry with you, I'm angry *for* you. The way that bastard looked at you, the things he said to you. And his outrageous presumptions. I've never felt such an urge to kill someone."

She sighed and gazed at him steadily, although he seemed to be avoiding her eyes. "I can't help feeling responsible. I know how important this deal was to you," she said softly.

He set the papers down and looked her in the eye. "Pepoli and his opera commission can go to the devil for all I care. He's of the breed of the spoiled, idle rich who think we're here for their amusement. They have no honor, and they assume we have none either."

"Still, you'd have the commission if it weren't for me."

"Do you really think that matters after the way he treated you? Don't you know you're more important to me than any opera commission?"

She pressed her lips together and blinked back a fresh mist of tears. She didn't know what to say, so she merely smiled and nodded. There was a moment of comforting silence as they gazed at each other.

Finally she said, "I should leave now. Paolina's expecting me for supper. Will you join us?"

"Thank you, but I have to finish this concerto tonight for the Pietà." His eyes drifted to the window. "I'll walk with you across the *campo* though. It's getting dark."

They walked in silence, and at her door he kissed her lightly on the forehead. "Get some rest tomorrow. We need to resume our work in earnest on Monday."

She decided not to tell Paolina how unpleasantly the day had ended. "It didn't work out," was all she said at supper, before excusing herself to go to her bedroom. Paolina didn't press, that wasn't her way. Grateful for the solitude, Annina sat on the edge of her bed, mulling over the day's events. Her guilt over the lost commission still tormented her. She was glad Antonio was already looking ahead to new projects. But she knew the reason he'd been so keen for the Bologna contract was because his prospects in Venice were dwindling. The *gusto nuovo* for opera in the simplistic, predictable Neapolitan style had been eking its way into Venetian theaters for nearly two years. Antonio's brilliant musical style, the music that had drawn her to him so many years ago, was quickly going out of fashion in Venice. *Graziana was right*, she thought, *Venetians are unbearably fickle!*

WHEN SHE ARRIVED at Antonio's studio Monday afternoon he greeted her with a shrewd smile. "You won't believe what I found out yesterday about our friend."

"Who do you mean?"

"Count Pepoli."

She bristled. "Tell me."

"He's here in Venice because he was exiled from Bologna, for trying to kill his wife."

Her jaw dropped. "How did you find out?"

"Piero heard about it yesterday outside San Marco, from one of his colleagues in the Signoria."

"So we were entertaining a would-be murderer?"

He nodded. "So it seems. At the very least he's a hothead with no respect for women, which explains his despicable behavior toward you."

"Is he still in Venice?"

"Yes, as far as I know."

"What if he tries to see me again?"

"I don't think he will, but be on your guard. Keep your doors locked and don't answer to anyone, unless you're certain who it is."

She sighed and sank into a chair. "How can we know who to trust? First the Duke of Massa Carrara, and now this murderous count. Where does it end?"

"It doesn't. Aristocrats are a decadent and dangerous lot. The only ones I fully trust are Pasqualigo and Bentivoglio. They've proven their decency many times over. But they are the exception, I'm afraid." He paused and gave her an encouraging smile. "Speaking of Piero, I do have a bit of good news. He's planning another *serata* and would like you to sing."

"Will you be performing too?"

"Of coarse. I'll debut my new concerto for two oboes and two clarinets."

"The one you've been working on day and night?" She clasped her hands as a thrill sang through her. "I can hardly wait. When will the party take place?"

"Early next month."

"What do you think I should sing?"

"Why don't you put together a portfolio of your favorite arias and we'll plan from there."

Over the next few weeks they worked almost daily on her music for the *serata*.

HER MEDLEY OF ARIAS and Antonio's new concerto were received with wild applause at the Palazzo Pasqualigo.

"I have some business to discuss with Piero," he told her as the applause abated, and the crowd of nobility resumed their drinking and chatting. "Why don't you mingle with some of his friends? I'm sure many of them would be delighted to meet you."

Panicked, she grasped his arm.

He gave her an encouraging smile. "Don't worry, I'll be nearby."

Her insides trembled like the fluttering of wings at the thought of having to face these puffy aristocrats on her own. But before she had a chance to protest he was off, raising his hand to flag Piero's attention.

Her eyes darted about. And then she saw him, the handsome young count, watching everything with that cool, self-possessed air young men put on when they're trying to impress. She felt prickly all over. Suddenly his eyes were on her, but she quickly glanced away, pretending not to notice. Eager to escape his searching gaze, she fought the urge to bolt from the room.

He approached her with a faint glimmer of humor at her startled look and bowed in courtly fashion. "*Mi fa molto piacere vederla ancora*, signorina, I'm so very pleased to see you again."

Her face was burning. She knew it must be scarlet. Trying hard to ignore the anxious flutter in her stomach, she lowered her gaze and gave a small curtsy. "*Il piacere è mio,* signore, the pleasure is mine."

"Please allow me to tell you, signorina, how overcome I am once more by the dazzling beauty of your maestro's music, but even more so by your incomparable artistry. During my recent tour of Italy I've heard nothing like it."

Although his words sounded rehearsed, she flushed with pleasure at the compliment. But she was careful not to appear overly excited. She gave him her most bold look. "*Grazie*, signore, but you can hardly be very familiar with my work. You haven't heard me sing since Signor Piero's last *serata*, well over a year ago."

A little smile played around his lips, as if he were contemplating something he couldn't share. Again she felt her skin prickle.

"I must confess that I attended your splendid performance in Florence this past winter. Regrettably I never had the chance to pay you my compliments."

She felt a little shiver of excitement.

He reached his hand toward the tray of a passing servant, replacing his own glass of champagne and offering one to her. She accepted with a grateful nod.

He took a long quaff. "It seems your devoted maestro has left you to fend for yourself this evening."

Her eyes darted uneasily as she sipped her champagne. "He had to talk to Signor Piero. He'll be back any moment."

He laughed, his eyes warm and unexpectedly gentle. "So are you that dependent on him, that you can't do without him for more than a few minutes?"

"No, I wouldn't say that," she said, her eyes cast down and her cheeks burning.

"Don't be defensive. I'm sure there are reasons why you're so attached to him. Everyone can see how close the two of you are." His grin verged on cocky. The champagne seemed to be making him overly confident.

"He protects me. He's empowered me to live the life I've always dreamed." She lifted her chin. "He's even defended me in court."

He took another swig of champagne. "Women have their own power, not by law but in their sway over men." He smiled gamely. "And it's my understanding that here in Venice laity and clergy alike fall prey to every temptation of the flesh and spirit."

Did he have the gall to suppose she and Antonio were

romantically attached? Memories of Massa Carrara's and Pepoli's impudent presumptions coursed through her mind. She straightened her shoulders and took a deep breath. "You presume too much, signore. Do you really think I'm one of those strumpets of the theater, here for your pleasure and everyone else's?"

He shrugged, smiling sheepishly, then waved off her question with a grin. At least he had the good grace to show a flicker of embarrassment. She was flattered by his fleeting discomfort. It made her feel mature, worldly.

His smile mellowed. "I'm sorry if I spoke out of turn. He's obviously devoted to you, and you to him. And fidelity is even more precious than love."

"That's very true."

"And you're right about strumpets in the theater. They're cheap and temporary. He took her hand and pressed it firmly as he gulped another sip. "But true friendship is a rare treasure."

She pulled her hand from his as a shameful thrill coursed through her.

He smiled in his disarming way and bowed. "Again, my deepest apologies if I have offended you in any way, my dear signorina."

After the party, Antonio was clearly not pleased with her. "I suggested you mingle with Piero's guests, not allow that young count to monopolize you for the entire evening."

He'd caught her elbow as they stepped onto the *fondamenta* outside Piero's house. The balmy May air, coupled with the soft glow of moonlight, was an unsettling contrast to the agitated mood she felt brewing.

She bristled with annoyance. "What is it you want from me? You want your independence as a priest, yet at times you act like you own me."

He was quiet a moment, and a slightly wounded look crossed

his face. "I simply want to protect you."

"You want to control me," she said, feeling a small quiver of guilt.

He tightened his lips. "That's absurd. If I weren't here, who'd look out for you? The theater is a treacherous business, and I'm the one who got you into it, so I feel responsible for your welfare."

She sighed. "That doesn't explain why you always try to prevent me from talking to other men."

"You don't understand their motives. You're too innocent and trusting to see beyond their charming guises."

"Oh Antonio, you worry too much. I'm old enough to know what I'm doing."

"Annina, please listen to me," he said, more gently. "Weren't your bad experiences with Massa Carrara and Pepoli enough to convince you that these pompous noblemen are nothing more than thinly disguised lechers? They're only interested in one thing, and it's not your career. I've seen this before. It's been the ruin of many young singers, and I don't want that to happen to you."

She paused. Perhaps he was right. But she wasn't ready to admit that openly. She couldn't reveal her true longing to him. She lifted her chin. "I'm sure I can take care of myself."

"That attitude will only get you into trouble. We've been through this before."

"I was much younger then."

His face softened. "It doesn't matter. You're still as lovely and youthful as you ever were."

Feeling the rush of blood to her face, she turned from him. Then she felt his hand gently touch her shoulder, and she turned back to him. She saw his eyes glint in the moonlight, and there was a trembling in her middle. "Why do you always do this to me?" Her soft voice faltered a bit, and tears stung her eyes.

"Why do I do what?"

"Make me feel so . . . baffled about things."

"What on earth is there to be baffled about? You have everything you want."

She lowered her eyes to hide her hovering tears and gave a quavering sigh. "It's not enough." Her voice was so faint she doubted he heard her.

But he did hear her. He took her hand and spoke softly. "There's something you want badly, isn't there? Can you tell me what it is?"

She shook her head without looking up, desperately trying not to let her tears fall. She felt him squeeze her hand gently, and she thought her heart would burst.

HER HEART FLUTTERED with confused feelings. But her agitation soon faded into the background as the demands of her life with Antonio mounted. Barely a week later, their lesson was interrupted by a commotion in the front hall. Antonio hurried from the room, and she followed. She froze with apprehension at the scene she beheld. Two uniformed policemen flanked a desperate looking Iseppo and held his arms firmly. Antonio rushed over to assist Giovanni, who was pleading with the officers. A few yards away, five-year-old Gigi cried frantically and stretched her arms toward her father. "*Babbo, Babbo!* I want my *babbo!*" she shrieked, while Margarita and Zanetta struggled to restrain her.

Annina went to her. "Let me try," she said quietly to the aunts, and they loosened their grip on her. She knelt before Gigi and took her hands in hers, squeezing them gently. The little girl looked at her with helpless, panicked eyes, and her shrill sobs slowly gave way to trembling snivels.

She gave the child an encouraging smile. "How would you like to come with me to Uncle Antonio's studio and look at pictures of Alcina and her magic island?"

Still quivering and sniffling, she nodded.

The two sisters looked at each other, then Margarita smiled and mouthed to Annina, "Thank you."

She smiled back at her, then returned her eyes to Gigi. "Come with me, *dolcezza*." She rose to her feet, and Gigi clutched her hand as they proceeded down the hall.

Glancing at Gigi out of the corner of her eye, she scanned Antonio's bookcases. The little girl climbed onto the sofa and curled up, hugging herself. *Poor little lamb*, she thought. At last she found what she was looking for—Ariosto's epic poem *Orlando furioso*, with illustrations. She pulled the heavy volume from the shelf and went to the sofa to sit beside Gigi. The child watched as she opened the book on her lap and leafed through until she came to a picture of Alcina, ensconced in celestial splendor and looking ravishingly self-assured.

Gigi gasped softly and stared at the picture with wide eyes and parted lips. She lifted her gaze to Annina. "Is that *you*, Nina?"

She laughed impulsively. "Good heavens, no. I've only pretended to be Alcina in the opera. I'm really nothing like her at all."

Gigi studied the picture again, then looked back up with a slightly furrowed brow. "I think it *is* you, Nina. There could be no one else as beautiful."

Her innocence and candor were touching. Annina hugged her and gently ruffled her soft golden curls. At that moment Antonio appeared at the door, looking somewhat disquieted. Gigi broke from Annina's arms, scurried off the sofa, and ran to him. "Where's my *babbo*?" she asked, looking up at him anxiously.

He smiled at her and smoothed her hair. "Your father had to leave for a little while."

Her lip started to quiver, and she clutched his hand. "When will he come home?" she asked in a trembling whimper.

"Oh, before you know it," he said with a confidence that belied the concern in his eyes. With Gigi still clinging to his hand, he came over and, with a sigh, sat by Annina on the sofa.

She felt vaguely uncomfortable, as if she were intruding on a private family matter. "Maybe I should go," she whispered to him.

"No, stay," he murmured.

Gigi climbed into his lap and nestled against him, her blue eyes round with worry.

A frightened little girl in need of male reassurance, she thought. She glanced at the book that still lay open on her knee. Alcina's smoky eyes gazed back at her with sultry intrepidness. Then she looked at Gigi. The child's anxious stare was fixed on her. Her cheek still pressed against Antonio's chest, she reached over and clutched Annina's hand. A little riot of feeling erupted in her that was both delightful and disturbing. The triad of love that resonated among them at that moment felt so natural, yet at the same time unsettling. Still, she savored the moment, and wanted it never to end.

THE DAY'S EVENTS did not turn out well. It came to light that Iseppo had seriously injured the grocer's errand boy in a brawl. He was arrested, charged with vicious assault, and ordered to appear in court, where he was sentenced to five years exile from Venice.

"He claimed the boy had been tormenting his little Gigi," Antonio told her later that day. "But the judge didn't see that as just cause for the crime."

"I can't believe it. Certainly he has a right to defend his daughter."

"If she were in any real danger, that would be true. But Iseppo has always been a hothead, ready to trounce anyone he imagines has offended him. This time I'm afraid he went too far."

Gigi, still distraught over her grandmother's death, was inconsolable at the prospect of her father being sent away. So Giovanni took a leave of absence from his post as violinist at San Marco and accompanied his youngest son and granddaughter to their new home on the western mainland. Antonio, she learned, made a substantial financial contribution to the venture. It was hoped that this arrangement would maintain as intact a family environment as possible for Gigi.

Chapter Sixteen

The following autumn Antonio received a thrilling invitation. "I've been called to the imperial court of Vienna. His Highness, Holy Roman Emperor Charles VI, has invited me to direct a series of concerts this winter." He was ecstatic. It was the happiest she'd seen him in a long time.

She smiled with him, but her heart sank. This meant he'd be gone for many months, possibly a year or more. "That's wonderful," she said, with as much enthusiasm as she could muster.

His eyes sparkled with excitement. "I'd like you to come too, Annina."

She couldn't believe it. He was inviting her to accompany him on one of his extended trips. She felt her face light up with joy. "Oh Antonio, that would be fabulous. Will I be able to sing for the emperor?"

His smile brightened. "You'll enthrall Charles and his court just as you've enthralled all of the Veneto with your stunning performances. You'll sweep them off their feet."

The thrill was almost too much to bear. "This is so exciting—

when will we leave?"

"Soon after Christmas. I'm going to ask my father to come along too. He's never been to Austria, and I think the change of scenery will do him good."

"What a marvelous idea. But do you think Iseppo and Gigi can get along without him?"

"Oh I think so. My brother's going to have to grow up one of these days, and what better time than now?"

She tingled with anticipation at the prospect of their upcoming adventure. To travel to a mysterious foreign land and perform with Antonio at an imperial court was an unimaginable honor. How proud she was of him, and how filled with wonder at the magnitude of his fame. He easily won over princes, emperors, and *everyone*, with his captivating charm and miraculous music. He'd met the emperor a year before, when Charles was visiting the nearby town of Trieste during his tour of allegiance through the southern provinces of the Habsburg monarchy. The emperor was so impressed with Antonio that he knighted him and commissioned him to compose a new set of violin concertos, *La Cetra*, "The Lyre." One of Charles's courtiers told Antonio the emperor had talked more with him in two weeks than he had with his ministers in two years. She wasn't a bit surprised.

She ached to tell him how she felt—how she loved him, how she wanted him. Her fear of how he'd react overpowered that ache. So she silently endured the demons that raged in her, as she sizzled with wonder at what lay in store for them across the Alps.

IN VENICE SHE had grown used to the magnificent mountain view to the north. But she'd never imagined what a transalpine journey would actually be like. The coach ride was treacherous and seemingly endless. They'd reach the top of an icy slope, often with the coachmen having been on foot pulling the horses, only to see what looked like an infinite series of peaks and valleys ahead. Coming down the slopes was even worse, since there was the danger the carriage would collide with the horses and go barreling downhill. Sometimes they all had to get out of the coach, and Antonio and Giovanni would help the drivers push the carriage over rocky terrain. They wouldn't allow her to exert herself, so she merely stumbled along behind them.

The views were breathtaking. Green valleys, woodlands, and sparkling lakes were flanked by towering summits of rock and snow-covered peaks. But there was no civilization in sight, much less even a semblance of bearable lodging. Consequently there were no warm beds or fresh food. All they could do was make camp at nightfall, sleeping in the coach for the bit of warmth it provided. As for food, there was the basket of provisions Margarita and Paolina had packed for them, which consisted of bread that had already gone stale, dried sausages, figs, and wine. Worst of all, there were no lavatories. This seemed to be less of a problem for the men than it was for her. She tried to minimize the difficulty by eating and drinking as little as possible. Her stomach was too queasy from the bumpy ride to get much down anyway.

Before long she felt weak and sick from lack of food and liquids, and she thought she'd die if she didn't have a bath. One afternoon, after an especially harrowing excursion along a craggy tract, they reached a grassy dale, and the coachmen stopped alongside a stream to get fresh water and rest the horses. Everyone got out to stretch their legs. She felt stiff and cranky and told Antonio and Giovanni she needed some private time. They asked no questions. She had the drivers get her trunk down from the top of the coach, and she rooted through it for soap, towels, and clean clothes. Then she followed the stream until she found a secluded spot. She stripped, and with shivering body and chattering teeth eased her way into the frigid water. Her fingers went numb as she quickly lathered herself from head to toe and rinsed. Then she stepped out of the stream and rubbed herself with the towels. Her skin was turning blue from the cold, and she could see her breath stream from her mouth and nose in smoky clouds. She put on clean underwear and clothes and shook out her wet hair. By the time she got back to the coach her hair was nearly frozen.

As they continued their Alpine journey she couldn't quite shake the chill she'd gotten from the icy water. Soon her throat started to hurt and her head became so stuffed she could hardly breathe. It occurred to her that the cold and discomfort they were all experiencing couldn't be good for Antonio's health either. But strangely, this rugged existence seemed to invigorate him. "The air is so clean in the mountains," he'd said on more than one occasion during their trip, breathing deeply and smiling with confidence. He and Giovanni urged her to eat a little something and drink some wine. She managed to get down a bite or two of bread, and the wine eased her sore throat and warmed her a bit. She slept fitfully that night, and by the next morning she was burning with fever. The rest of their mountain trek was little more than a blur in her mind.

She was vaguely aware of having cool, damp cloths held to her face and wrists, as she drifted in and out of consciousness. At one point she awoke to darkness and stinging cold. Her teeth chattered uncontrollably, and her body shook so violently she could feel her bones rattle. She was coughing and wheezing, and her chest hurt. She had a hazy awareness of Giovanni snoring softly at her side and Antonio dozing across from her. The next thing she knew he was beside her, holding a tumbler of strong red wine to her lips.

She drank thirstily and felt the comforting liquid sooth her parched throat and spread its warmth through her body. Then he wrapped her in his cloak and pulled her close to him, rubbing her arm briskly. She heard him murmur something like, "*Stai con me,* Annina, stay with me. This misery will be over soon." She leaned her head against his chest. The steady rhythm of his heartbeat and the surf-like waves of his breathing lulled and soothed her as she drifted back to sleep.

ANTONIO AND GIOVANNI sprang to their feet as she slowly made her way into the dining room, her dark blue travel dress loose around her waist and shoulders.

"There she is," Antonio said with a smile.

"She almost looks as good as new," said Giovanni.

She wavered a bit, and they rushed to either side of her, guiding her to their table. As they lowered her into a chair, Antonio flagged a waiter. "More coffee, please."

Giovanni gave her a warm smile. "What a joy that you've come back to us, my dear."

In confusion, she looked at Antonio. "Where are we?"

"We're just across the Alps, in Graz. You gave us quite a scare."

"I remember feeling sick in the coach . . ."

"You were coughing uncontrollably and deathly feverish. We did everything we could for you, but it wasn't enough. We were desperate. Fortunately our drivers knew about a hostel where we could stop to rest. The godly proprietress took over your care."

She coughed lightly. "I wish I could thank her, and I'm so sorry I caused you such trouble. We must be way behind schedule."

"Nonsense," said Giovanni. "Antonio and I needed the respite as much as you did."

Moments before, she'd looked at herself in the mirror for the first time in nearly two weeks. She was appalled at how alarmingly thin and pale her face appeared and at the bluish shadows lurking under her eyes.

The waiter returned with a tray of coffee. *"Für die Fräulein."*

After a few sips she felt faint. "I think I need to rest," she said, rising unsteadily to her feet.

Antonio stood quickly and took her arm. "I'll help you back to your room."

Outside her door he clasped her wrist gently. "I thought I'd lost you. I didn't think I could bear it."

She turned to him and took his hand. "The last thing I remember clearly is your asking me to stay with you."

"That was all I could think about at that moment."

She smiled wanly. "I'm here."

He pressed her hand and kissed her softly on the forehead as she opened her door.

THEIR STAY IN GRAZ was longer than expected. But with good food, warmth, and cleanliness she soon regained her strength. The rest of the trip was much easier. Though they were traveling north and the weather getting progressively colder, they at least were on level ground and passing through towns and villages where they could stop to refresh themselves.

At last they reached Vienna. Nothing could have prepared her for the grandeur of the imperial palace. She was given her own suite of rooms, along with a chamber maid. After the harsh journey, this unimaginable luxury was like a piece of paradise.

Antonio was the only one of the three of them who could comprehend at all the guttural noises coming from everyone's mouths. To her, the German language sounded like it was constructed entirely of hard consonants hissed from the throat, unlike her native Italian with its liquid vowels rolling gently off the tip of the tongue. Slowly, though, she picked up a few words: *bitte, danke, guten tag . . .*   A few people she met claimed to be able to speak Italian. But when she spoke in her own language they'd say she talked too fast and all her words ran together. To be understood she had to slow down her speech and separate each word as if she were talking to a simple-minded child.

One afternoon she watched Antonio rehearse the court musicians. Giovanni was playing along as well. She couldn't understand much of what was being said, but she could tell there was some friction between Antonio's musical ideas and what the players were accustomed to. After the rehearsal, he told her what had gone on. The players of the *continuo* instruments—the harpsichord, double bass, and cello—complained that he hadn't written out the bass parts note for note. "Blockheads," he complained. "And they call themselves musicians."

He went on to explain that the violinists were miffed about the lack of counterpoint between their parts. "Why are we so often playing in unison?" one of them had asked. "So the melody sings above the lower parts with crystal clarity," he'd responded. "But our great German composers, Bach and Handel, pride themselves on their learned mastery of contrapuntal technique," another had said.

As if to belittle Antonio's more songlike musical style, she thought.

"Counterpoint may be the language of the intellect," Antonio had said evenly, "but melody is the language of the emotions. In Italy we sing from the heart, not from the head." The Austrian musicians had no response to that, and the rehearsal had gone on smoothly.

While Antonio and Giovanni rehearsed with the court orchestra she found herself with a lot time to think about things. Her feelings for Antonio had intensified. She looked around at the handsome young noblemen who populated the court. Not one of them measured up to him in her eyes. Exactly what Antonio thought about their relationship, she had no clue. She knew he cared for her. He'd shown her in so many ways. But she had no idea *why* he cared. It wasn't the type of thing they ever talked about. She wondered what her life would be like right now if he'd never taken notice of her, which he might not have if she hadn't disobeyed her father and snuck into the Teatro Arciducale that day so long ago. After that things had just happened, one after another, until here she was, ten years later, at the imperial court in Vienna, about to sing for the Holy Roman Emperor. She should have been ecstatically happy. What more could she want? She had everything she'd ever dreamed of, and more. It wasn't enough.

THE IMPERIAL PALACE seemed to reverberate with anticipation as she took her place in front of the orchestra. Antonio and Giovanni were seated nearby, their violins raised to their shoulders. The stirring, emphatic introduction to the aria Antonio had written just for this occasion filled the room. She glanced at him and he cued her entrance with an almost imperceptible nod.

> *I followed him happily when the sky was cloudless,*
> *I shall still follow him when there are storms in his breast.*

The heights of pleasure and depths of determination, the sheer passion he'd built into the aria were intoxicating, and the truth of the words burned in her own breast as she sang. With each new vocal entrance their mutual private glance signaled a new eruption of emotion. It was almost as if there were no one else present.

At the reception after the concert she tried to distract herself from her foolish thoughts by focusing her attention on Giovanni. He still hadn't gotten over his wife's death, and she felt terribly sorry for him. She noticed him sitting alone. As usual, Antonio was surrounded by throngs of admirers, so she went over and sat by Giovanni. She took his hand. "May I join you?"

His smile was kind but sad. "Now why would a lovely young thing like you want to spend time with an old man when the room is filled with dashing young noblemen?"

"Because not one of them is as dashing as you, Giovanni." She gave him her most flirtatious smile. "I want to enjoy the jealous looks on all the ladies' faces when they see I'm keeping the most handsome man in the room to myself."

He grinned happily, and his eyes crinkled at the corners exactly as Antonio's did. He put his arm around her shoulder and leaned close. "I've been looking around at these Austrian beauties, but I'll tell you something, Annina. Not one of them can hold a candle to you."

She blushed and simpered. "Oh Giovanni, you do know how to flatter."

"It's not flattery, my darling. And I'll tell you something else. Antonio would never say it, but I know he thinks so too."

She looked at him with a fixed smile and blinked. Was he trying to tell her something? She decided to make light of it. "How silly. Antonio never gives a thought to how I look."

He winked. "I wouldn't be too sure of that."

She smiled and rolled her eyes, then looked around. "A lot of these women remind me of Chiara Orlandi. They have her look. Do you know her?"

"I bit." He sighed. "I know she's caused plenty of trouble for Antonio."

A vague fear swept through her, and she said impulsively, "Oh, I hope I'm nothing like her."

He looked at her with a tender smile. "There's not a chance of that, *cara mia*. The difference between you and women like Chiara is that you know how to make a man feel good about himself. And you're loyal. Those are two qualities she couldn't begin to understand."

She blinked back a tear. How wise and kind he was. She had meant to comfort him, and he'd ended up comforting her.

AFTER VIENNA, the threesome visited Dresden, where a former student of Antonio's, the violinist Johann Pisendel, was now concertmaster for the Saxon court. This beautiful city, known as the *Schmuckkästchen*, Jewel Box, was a feast for their eyes with its exquisitely ornate buildings and dazzling artistic splendor.

When Pisendel returned to Dresden after his studies in Venice he'd brought a lot of Antonio's scores with him. Dresden's musical connoisseurs were so enchanted by Antonio's music that his name had taken on practically godlike proportions there.

In Annina's mind, and in her heart, he'd become godlike to her as well. And the pain of the inevitable distance this put between them was excruciating. She longed for the comfortable companionship they'd always shared. Now things were different. She saw him in a new way. The Eden-like bliss of their previous relationship had faded away along with her childhood. If Antonio was at all aware of the turn her feelings for him had taken, he gave no indication. He treated her much the same as he always had.

One evening after dinner Giovanni retired early, and she and

Antonio took a walk around the sprawling palace grounds. It was the first time in weeks they'd been alone together. She shivered in the cold night air. As they walked, she hugged his arm and pressed against him for warmth. A pricking thrill stirred in her.

"Are you cold?" he asked. "We could go back inside."

"No, no. It's nice to be out in the fresh air. I like the peace and quiet."

"Yes, it's good to escape the commotion of the palace for a few minutes."

"They really love you here, Antonio. Their adoration of you and your music is almost like a cult."

She felt him smile. "Surprising, isn't it?"

"Not a bit. No one else's music is as exciting and full of energy as yours. I don't think you realize how much it enchants people, and how much happiness it brings."

"You flatter me too much, Annina."

She smiled at him coyly. "Now when have I ever flattered you? Don't I always tell you the truth?"

He nodded his agreement. "That you do."

They walked a while longer in silence. Then he said, "I've been meaning to tell you how much I appreciate your kindness to my father. You've really lifted his spirits. Thank you."

"I *love* your father. He's the sweetest man in the world." *Except for you*, she thought, but didn't dare say.

"I can't argue with that," he said.

She pressed into him all the closer, and his familiar scent drenched her senses. How could she describe it? It was like the smell of a lightning storm over a salty sea. She felt his energy, and it excited her physically. She wished these few blissful moments could go on forever.

THEIR RETURN TRIP through the Alps was much easier, since they were traveling in early summer. After a year and a half in Austria and Germany it was wonderful to be back in Venice. To have more privacy for composition, Antonio moved from his family home to a house on the Riva del Carbon, which overlooked the Grand Canal, near the Rialto Bridge. Annina and Paolina had given up their apartment on the *contrada* Santa Maria Formosa when she left Venice the year before, and Paolina had gone back to Mantua. Now she'd returned to Venice, and they rented an apartment in the San Angelo district, just a few blocks west of Antonio's new house. Graziana and Fortunato, who were now married, moved into a small apartment on the back of their building.

Annina was busier than ever. On their return from the north a whirlwind of activities awaited her and Antonio. Private concerts in Venice and opera commissions throughout northern Italy kept them constantly occupied. Time seemed to spin out of control. To her delight, they spent the winter of 1732 in Mantua, at the invitation of Prince Phillip. As visiting artists the prince offered them his hospitality, but she preferred to stay at home with her family. She was to sing the title role in Antonio's opera *Semiramide*, and to revive a role she'd sung in Venice several years before— Tamiri in his *Farnace*. To her dismay, Antonio had hired Maddalena Pieri to sing the leading *en travesti* roles in both operas. But she wasn't about to cause problems by complaining.

At the first rehearsal, Maddalena was no more friendly to her than she'd been the last time they'd sung together. If anything, she'd grown more unpleasant. "So, I see you've finally made it to prima donna status," she said, with a catty tone in her voice.

She forced herself to smile. "Yes, I've been singing leading roles in Don Antonio's operas for over five years now."

"Well," she said, snorting. "You've obviously played your hand well, keeping the maestro happy, that is."

Her smile faded. She folded her arms and held Maddalena's eyes with a steady stare. "I've played my hand well by studying hard and perfecting my art."

Maddalena gave her a sultry look. "The art of seduction, no doubt."

Hot indignation seized her, but she refused to succumb to Maddalena's nettling. She frowned and shook her head. "Is that all you think about?"

"Is there anything else?" she said huskily.

She scoffed. The conversation was pointless, so she excused herself.

Maddalena was a constant irritant during the weeks of rehearsal and straight through both performances. The only thing that made Annina's Mantuan sojourn tolerable was the comfort of being home with her family again. Paolina had traveled to Mantua with them, and for the first time since Annina was a little girl, her entire family was together. Their evenings were lively. She and Bartolomea sang their favorite opera arias, Marcel and Laurent laughed, joked and kept the wine flowing, Papà chattered happily, and Paolina basked in her familiar role of family nurturer. She'd never seen everyone in such good spirits all at once, and she resolved to enjoy it as long as it lasted.

Antonio's obligations at the Pietà soon called him back to Venice, and she planned to follow at the end of the summer. Paolina decided to stay behind and join her later. On her journey back to Venice she was filled with vague apprehension. The joy of the summer she'd just spent in happy companionship with her family made her realize how hectic her life had been for the past ten years. The thrill of singing onstage was so often overshadowed by the sheer exhaustion and harrowing difficulties of theater life. Singers and other show people could be nasty and cutthroat. Antonio had much more tolerance for such people than she did, and for some reason this made her angry at times. She realized her occasional bouts of anger likely had something to do with her tacit feelings for him, which had not diminished. More and more, she felt a strain in their relationship that he seemed oblivious to. But the unbridgeable chasm between them was growing increasingly painful for her.

Chapter Seventeen

Prompt as the sunrise, Fortunato rowed up to meet Annina's boat as it entered the lagoon. "How was your trip to Mantua, Miss Annina?" he asked, grinning cheerfully as he handed her and her baggage into the gondola.

"It was lovely, Fortunato, a welcome respite. But I'm glad to be back. So what's been going on here? I haven't heard a word from Don Antonio."

"Well, miss, he's been busy with his new opera."

"New opera?"

"Didn't he tell you? He's written a whole new opera, *L'Olimpiade*, on a libretto by that famous poet Metastasio. And he's hired a slew of the most popular new singers. In fact, I believe he's meeting with them right now."

Her mouth tightened as she felt her blood slowly boil. Obviously he'd been too busy composing this new opera to write her even a single letter. "Where are they meeting?" she asked, struggling to maintain her composure.

"At San Angelo."

"Fortunato, can you give me a little time to freshen up at home and then take me there? I'd like to surprise Don Antonio."

"Of course, Miss Annina. I know he'll be thrilled to see you."

At the theater she saw nothing but a mass of unfamiliar faces clustered on and near the stage. There was no sign of Antonio.

Finally she spotted someone she knew. "Signor Mauro!" she called, approaching him briskly.

"Well, Signorina Annina," he said mildly, "welcome back. What a surprise this is."

"Yes, I'd say so," she said, barely able to contain her growing fury. "Where is Antonio?"

"At the notary's, drawing up some paperwork."

"Do you know when he'll be back?"

"No idea. It could be a while."

She looked around, frustrated. "So when will *L'Olimpiade* premier?"

"Not until mid February. But since this is a new production, Antonio wanted us all to meet here today so I can start planning the sets."

"I see. Can you tell me where he's put the score to the opera?"

"I believe he left it on the conductor's stand."

As she searched for the score, a tall, effeminate young man strutted up to her. "May I help you, signorina?" he asked, in a patronizing tone. His voice was unnaturally high-pitched, and she realized he was a castrato.

"Yes you may," she said, eyeing him sharply. "I'm looking for Don Antonio's score to *L'Olimpiade*."

"Are you now? And might I ask who you are?"

"You might indeed. I am Anna Girò. And you are?"

"Signorina Girò, what an unexpected pleasure," he said, almost ironically. She wouldn't have thought it possible for him to raise his nose any higher. But he looked like he was sniffing something on the ceiling as he continued. "Allow me to present myself. I am Mariano Nicolini, virtuoso singer, known professionally as Marianino. Surely you have heard of me?"

"No, I can't say I have."

He pursed his lips primly, then simpered, as if he decided she must be joking. Looking past her, he wiggled and waved excitedly. "Angela! There's someone here you simply *must* meet."

She turned to see a large, intimidating looking woman approach her, holding a thin score.

"Signora Angela Zannuchi, may I present La Signorina Anna Girò," Marianino said with fussy formality. Angela looked down her nose at her, and without cracking a smile practically shouted, "How interesting to finally meet you, Signorina Girò. I must say, you are much more—delicate looking than I had expected."

Her booming voice would have startled even Fortunato. What she meant to imply, Annina couldn't begin to guess. She smiled stiffly.

As if she read her mind, Angela went on. "What I mean is that your famous teacher has written a role for me, that of Licidas, which I would almost have thought suitable for you." She looked her up and down. "Although considering how dainty you are, I can now see the role would not suit you at all."

Her jaw tensed. "Is that it in your hand?"

"Yes, it is."

"May I see it?"

She handed her the score, and along with the castrato watched her smugly as she perused the words and notes. With rising vexation, she could see that Angela was right. Antonio had written Licidas's part precisely in her vocal range and in the same kind of intense, declamatory style he always used for her roles. She bit her lip to prevent it from shaking and forced herself to smile as she handed the score back to Angela. "It's been a pleasure meeting you both," she said, with forced dignity, "but I must be going."

The two singers looked down at her with pompous smiles. "The pleasure has been all ours, I'm sure, Signorina Girò," Marianino said, as he gave her a vaguely contemptuous bow.

Back in the gondola, she fumed. *Has Antonio gone completely mad? Why in heaven's name would he choose to work with those unendurable boors and not with me?*

Fortunato looked concerned. "Is everything all right, Miss Annina?"

She felt ready to explode. "No it's not. How could he do this to me?"

His brow darkened. "Has someone hurt or offended you, Miss Annina? Just tell me who and I'll make him wish he'd never been born!"

"Oh it's nothing like that. It's Don Antonio. He's written this new opera, and instead of using me he's hired a passel of the most unbearable snobs to sing in it. Why would he do this to me, Fortunato?"

For once she'd presented a problem that was beyond his ability to cope with. He knit his brow and shifted uncomfortably. "Well, uh, I'm not sure I can say, Miss Annina. Maybe you should give him a chance to explain things to you himself."

"Oh, yes, he'd better explain. Take me to his house right now." She crossed her arms and stared off to the side, and they rode to Antonio's house in silence.

She waited for over an hour in his parlor, pacing furiously. By the time she heard him walk in the front door she'd worked herself into a fury.

"Annina!" he said, clearly delighted to see her. "Mauro told me you were—"

"How could you do this?" she practically screamed, before he could finish his sentence.

"How could I do what?"

"I can't believe you're doing this new opera without me." Now she was close to tears. "And why am I the last to know about it? I had to hear about it from Fortunato."

"How could I tell you about it? You were in Mantua."

"You could have written me. You never responded to my letters, yet you found time to write a whole new opera and hire a pack of foreigners to perform it."

"Annina, please," he said, sighing, as he removed his coat and threw it across a chair. "You have no idea of the headaches I've had to endure with those people."

"Then why *are* you putting up with them?"

"Because it was the only way I could get back control of San Angelo. Venetian audiences have gone mad for this new breed of Neapolitan singers, so I must use them, even though they're insufferable. Their haughty attitudes are driving me nearly insane." He sighed and raked his fingers through his hair. "And that castrato Nicolini! My God, if my sanity survives working with him it'll be a miracle. But I have no choice if this opera's going to have any chance at all."

Her wounded feelings continued to fuel her anger. "I could learn to sing like them and help make *L'Olimpiade* a big success. When I was at San Angelo this afternoon looking for you, I saw part of the score. Why can't I sing the role of Licidas? It's perfect for me."

"Because it's a male role."

"But you have that Zannuchi woman singing it."

"Have you seen her? I'm not even sure she's a woman. If she were in breeches I'd think she were a man."

She covered her mouth and coughed, fighting the urge to laugh. "Does that make her more qualified for the part? You know I could sing it better than she can."

He sighed. "You probably could. I believe you can sing anything. But even if it were feasible I won't put you in a male role. You couldn't pull it off."

"That's not fair. You're trying to limit what I can do. How do you know I couldn't pull it off?"

He sighed again, but he was smiling now. "Because you're too petite and pretty—too feminine looking for a trouser role. Now don't pout. You should take that as a compliment. Would you really want to look like one of those female battleaxes who sing male roles?"

"But in my very first opera with you I had a male role."

"That was different, you were playing the part of a shepherd boy. Licidas is a heroic male character. Those types of *en travesti* roles are better left to viragos like Angela Zannuchi."

It was getting more difficult to stay angry with him. But she folded her arms and tightened the corners of her mouth, staring at the floor.

"Don't be angry, Annina. Trust me, you don't want to get involved with those voguish fanatics. You'd be like a lamb among wolves. Besides, I have a couple of more important projects in mind for you."

He'd caught her interest, and she looked up, trying hard not to let her anger dissipate completely. "What?" she asked, guardedly.

"I wasn't going to tell you about this quite yet, but now I suppose I must. Never mind *L'Olimpiade*. I'm taking the risk of my life this autumn, premiering an opera on a subject that's far afield of the standard Venetian repertoire."

"What is the opera?"

"*Montezuma*. It's on a libretto by an obscure poet, Alvise Giusti."

"I've never heard of it. What's it about?"

"It's an historical subject, based on the conquest of Mexico by the Spaniard Harnán Cortés, in the sixteenth century."

"Mexico?"

"Mexico is part of the Americas. The conquest caused the downfall of the Mexican emperor Montezuma. A fascinating piece of history."

She tried to appear as fascinated as he was. "I'm happy for you, Antonio. So will the Neapolitans be performing this one too?"

"Zanucchi and Nicolini will take minor parts, and I've already hired two German singers for the title and seconda donna roles."

"And who will take the prima donna role?"

"You, my dear."

She tried not to show her excitement. She took a slow, deep breath. "And you're just telling me about this now? When does *Montezuma* open?"

"November 14. It'll be San Angelo's *opera prima* this season, and my first new work for the Venetian stage in five years." He smiled apologetically. "I know I should have written to you about all this, but I've been incredibly busy."

"Yes, I can see that. Composing two new operas and arranging the casts and production details in such a short time. I suppose it's no wonder you had no time to write a letter."

"I knew you'd understand."

She sighed. "So what is this prima donna role you've reserved for me?"

"I'd like you to take the part of Mitrena, Montezuma's wife. It's an intensely dramatic role, one I wouldn't entrust to anyone but you."

She felt overcome by gratitude and remorse. She smiled stiffly and nodded, then suddenly teared up, her mouth trembling. "I'm sorry I was so awful to you just now. I must have sounded like a nagging shrew."

He chuckled. "No you didn't. You were just expressing your feelings. Nothing wrong with that."

She groped about her waistband for a handkerchief. He reached in his pocket and handed her his.

"I have more news I think you'll enjoy hearing."

She dabbed her eyes with his handkerchief. "More news? I already feel overwhelmed."

"I'm planning a revival of *Dorilla in Tempe*. And this time I'd like you to sing the title role. That production will premier in late January."

She fought the urge to shout for joy. "I never imagined singing that role."

"You weren't ready for it eight years ago. You are now."

She started to relax a bit. "I'll never forget when you first told me the story of *Dorilla*. It was the same day you told me you were sending Chiara to Prague."

He raised his eyes. "A short-lived proposition."

She giggled. "Let's just be glad she's finally out of our way."

He sighed. "Yes, thank God."

"When can I see my Mitrena role?"

"Why don't you go home and get a good night's rest. We'll start work tomorrow."

THE FOLLOWING AFTERNOON she marveled at the new music Antonio had written for her. He'd filled her Mitrena role with sparkling arias and fiery recitatives, exactly the kind of music that brought out her dramatic instincts. And the opera's plot proved to be much more exciting than she'd imagined, featuring a host of adventures involving disguises, oracles, and threatened human sacrifices.

"If the rest of the music you've composed for *Montezuma* is anywhere near this brilliant, the audience will be absolutely dazzled opening night," she said, when she paused in her singing to pour a glass of water.

His smile was confident. "Between the story, the music, costumes and sets they'll be dazzled all right."

"Is Signor Mauro designing the sets?"

"Yes. This is the first time I've worked with him in six years, since *Orlando*."

"What is he planning"

"Act I will open to a magnificent scene depicting a Mexican lagoon, which will divide the imperial palace from the Spanish quarter."

"Why have you waited so long to work with him again? His work is outstanding, as I remember."

"It certainly is, but he wants to do more and he's not satisfied with the standard fee. Ever since *Orlando* he's been pestering me for a financial share of my productions."

"What would that mean?"

"It would mean he'd essentially be my business partner."

"Wouldn't that help you?"

"I have my doubts. He's partnered with impresarios of some of Venice's best theaters over the past eighteen or so years. But he's run into some trouble."

"What sort of trouble?"

"Money troubles, which has led to several legal battles. For all his artistic talent he's proved himself inept with financial matters and a bungler at management. He can't even manage his own children." He sighed. "I'm doing what I can to help those boys. After the New Year, Pietro will be apprenticed to me as a copyist."

She remembered with a smile the mischievous, freckle-faced boy she'd met briefly on the opening night of *Orlando* and had seen only a few times since.

"The truth is, Mauro's deep in debt. And it's no wonder, the way they live."

"Where exactly do they live?"

"Near the southern end of the Grand Canal."

"That's an expensive area, isn't it?"

He frowned. "It is, much more than he can sustain financially. But my sister has lavish tastes."

It had been quite a while since she'd seen Cecilia, but she remembered her extravagant clothes and jewels. Much finer attire than she herself could afford. She didn't allow these thoughts to occupy her mind for long. The exciting work of preparing her Mitrena role soon consumed her again. The work paid off. *Montezuma* was a rousing success, and the triumph lifted Antonio's spirits more than she'd seen in quite a while. Soon it would be time to begin rehearsals for the revival of *Dorilla*. Her heart soared. She was about to sing her first title role on a Venetian stage.

FORTUNATO DELIVERED HER to Antonio's house on a chilly evening in early January. There was to be a meeting with the singers he'd hired for *Dorilla*. To her surprise, she was greeted at the door by a handsome, smiling young man.

"Annina!" he said excitedly, drawing her into his arms, then pulling back to look at her. "You haven't changed a bit. I would have known you anywhere."

She looked into his vaguely familiar face and struggled to

remember who he was.

"Don't you remember me?" he said, still smiling and without a flicker of offense at her lack of recognition. "I'm Pietro. Uncle Antonio's training me to be a copyist. I've been here all day writing out the parts for *Dorilla*."

"Pietro? The last time I saw you, you were a little boy. How did you grow up so fast?" She couldn't tear her gaze from his blue eyes and sandy hair. The family resemblance was unmistakable.

He laughed. "I suppose it's been a long time since we've seen each other. Or maybe you're mixing me up with my little brother, Daniele. I plan to hire him as my assistant, by the way, as soon as I can afford to set up my own shop."

"Then you're quite serious about making this a career."

"I am indeed. My parents see music copying as a worthy trade."

"And right they are. How old are you, Pietro?"

"Nineteen. And you are, let me see, about sixteen now?"

She burst into a sparkling laugh. "Good heavens, no, I'm twenty-four."

His face registered disbelief. "*Non è possibile!* You can't be a day over seventeen."

She smiled flirtatiously. "You certainly know how to flatter a girl."

"I never engage in flattery, signorina. I only tell the truth." The smile that spread across his face and lit up his eyes was genuine—and irresistible.

She felt thrilling little ripples in her middle. Then she rebuked herself silently. *He's just a boy. I can't allow myself to have such feelings for him.*

"Annina, there you are." Antonio had just stepped into the hall and was walking toward her, smiling. He gave her a hug, then put an affectionate hand on his nephew's shoulder. "Our Pietro here is the finest copyist I've ever engaged. He's been toiling over my score all day, and his work is outstanding. And he's never complained once." He winked at Pietro and gave his shoulder an affectionate squeeze.

The young man smiled his appreciation.

"The others should be arriving any minute," Antonio said. "Annina, dear, will you help me greet them?"

"Of course." As the singers started streaming in, she acknowledged each of them with a gracious smile. Even Marianino and Angela couldn't ruffle her confidence. She was the star.

"Is everyone here?" Antonio asked, after the little band of singers had been ushered into the parlor. He looked around. "I don't see Marta. Annina, has she arrived yet?"

"Marta?"

"Marta Arriggoni, the girl who's to sing your old Eudamia role."

At that moment the bell sounded at the door, and Pietro went to answer. The young lady flounced into the room as if the world were her stage. All heads turned in her direction. She seemed delighted. Her gaze swept them, and Annina felt the girl's sharp glance take her on. She then directed her fringed eyes to Antonio and clasped a tiny gloved hand to her bosom. She dropped a small curtsy. "Maestro," she purred. "Such an honor."

He walked over with a smile and took the girl's hand. "Signorina Arriggoni, what a pleasure."

Annina couldn't help noticing how her dress was cut low enough to show the curve of her delicately rounded shoulders, as well as a stimulating view of her cleavage. Every male in the room was agape.

The ensuing rehearsals were vexing. Marta managed to bore under Annina's skin like a thorn, while beguiling Antonio with feigned adoration and silly compliments. At one particular rehearsal she tossed her head toward him when Annina started to sing, shooting him a private look, her blond curls bouncing. He smiled at her. This drove Annina beyond the limits of endurance.

"I don't like her," she confessed to him, after everyone had left.

"Who?" He was studying his notes from the rehearsal.

"Marta. Haven't you seen how she preens like a peacock, as if she were the star?"

He looked at her. "Why should that matter to you? We're here to put together an opera, not judge people's characters."

There wasn't a glimmer of reproof in his words, but she felt chastened all the same. Her vexation began to fester.

At the next day's rehearsal, her voice cracked in the middle of an aria. Her eyes darted to Antonio. He sighed and frowned. Marta smiled. Later, when Antonio paused the rehearsal for a break, Marta approached her.

"Perhaps it's not the best role for you." Her face looked hard.

She glared at her. "What do you mean?"

"I think Dorilla's range is too high for you, I can hear the strain in your voice."

She controlled her anger with difficulty. "I don't think you need to concern yourself with the vocal range of my role."

The hard corners of Marta's mouth curled into a pert smile. "You don't need to be so defensive. I was only trying to be friendly."

Her jaw tightened. "How sweet. If you'll excuse me, I'd like to get a drink of water before we resume."

Marta's hard look returned. "You know, you really should try to be more friendly with the other singers. You never know when you might need the help of one of us."

She nodded stiffly and headed for the credenza, where there was a pitcher of water and glasses. The rest of the rehearsal did not go well for her. Her tight jaw and throat made her voice sound pinched, especially on the high notes. Antonio gave her several impatient looks, which only increased her tension. By the end of the rehearsal her voice was hoarse from the strain. She left quickly. She had no desire to endure Marta's gloating.

The next day she arrived early, hoping to talk to Antonio about her growing agitation. She never had the chance. When she arrived at his studio he was busy at his desk, frantically editing the *Dorilla* manuscript.

Unpleasant feelings stirred in her belly. "What are you doing?" she asked, her voice still hoarse from the strain of yesterday's rehearsal.

He looked up. "I've had to make a difficult business decision, I'm sure you'll understand."

A sharp fear curled her stomach. "What decision?"

"I've decided to give the role of Dorilla to Signora Della Parte. This will allow you an opportunity for a repeat performance of Eudamia, which I trust will be agreeable to you."

Agreeable? Rage swelled in her breast, but she held her tongue. "And what of dear little Marta?" she asked. "Won't she be crushed to hear you've reassigned her role to me?"

"Marta has already kindly agreed to step down and take the lesser role of the solo chorister."

You discussed this with her before you did with me? "How magnanimous of her," she said aloud, with a stiff smile.

"I hoped you'd see it that way. Annina, you're an angel," he said, smiling his most charming smile as he came around the desk and kissed her forehead.

Her face hurt from her forced smile.

Chapter Eighteen

Antonio's patience with Annina was quickly dwindling. On the surface she seemed agreeable to taking back her Eudamia role, but it was obvious her heart wasn't in it. In a way he felt guilty about taking Dorilla from her, after his promise to finally give her a title role. But he had no choice. The part was obviously too much for her, and her voice had been giving way under the strain. He couldn't have that, not with his current precarious position at San Angelo. And he wouldn't subject her to the ridicule that would surely rain down on her if her voice faltered onstage. He sighed. Thank goodness for Marta, who after expressing concern to him about Annina's vocal strain had so graciously offered to step down from her role.

The next day during a rehearsal break he retreated to his studio to make some adjustments to the score. There was a timid knock on the door. "Who is it?" he asked, while leafing through a pile of scores.

"It's Marta."

He stood quickly and went to open the door. "Oh, Marta, come right in. What is it, my dear?"

She cocked her head shyly. "I'm so sorry to disturb you, maestro, but there's something I feel you should know."

He furrowed his brow. "Well what is it?"

She lowered her fringe of black lashes and turned from him slightly. "I really shouldn't tell you this, I so hate to see you deceived."

"What on earth are you talking about?"

She turned back to him and lifted her blue eyes to his. "I overheard Signorina Annina and Signor Nicolini talking earlier, before the rehearsal started. He was telling her of an opportunity with an impresario friend of his in Verona, at the new Teatro Filarmonico. But she would have to go right away. She told him she was interested and asked that he write her a letter of introduction."

He had a sharp sinking feeling that quickly turned to anger. "How did you manage to overhear all this?" he asked, feeling his chest tighten.

"I was in the parlor, where they were talking. I was going to leave, but Annina asked me to stay. She wanted a witness to Nicolini's proposition."

His sweet, loyal Annina. He never imagined she could be so smooth and calculating. His chest tightened painfully. Turning his head, he held his fist to his mouth to stifle a cough.

"Was anyone else in the room?" he asked, when he'd recovered from his bout of coughing.

"Only your nephew. But he was off a ways, working on one of your scores. I don't think he heard anything."

"I see. Is that all that was said, what you've told me?"

She lowered her eyes again and spoke softly. "Well . . .there was something else. But I hesitate to say."

He tightened a fist. "Please tell me."

"Annina told Nicolini that she's tired of being controlled and manipulated by you. That she wants to break out on her own. She finally promised Nicolini she would accept his offer." She whisked a lacy handkerchief from her waistband and dabbed her eyes as she touched his arm lightly. "Oh maestro, I so hate being the one to tell you this. I know what it's like to be betrayed by someone you trust."

"Thank you, Marta," he said, turning back to his desk. "Please tell everyone we'll resume in a few minutes."

"Of course, maestro." She went to open the door, then turned to him again, smiling sweetly. "And please don't take this too hard. You know what most singers are like."

Yes, I know what most singers are like. I've had to deal with more than my share of self-centered, conniving prima donnas over the years. But not her. Never my Annina. But her attitude had been slipping lately. Ever since she'd returned from Mantua things had not been quite right. He coughed again, struggling to catch his breath.

Marta was still standing at the door, her hand on the knob, watching him. "Are you sure you're all right, maestro? Can I get you anything?"

He shook his head, coughing again as he gestured her to leave. He sank down at his desk as the door closed gently behind her. He didn't know how he'd continue the rehearsal. His chest felt like it was on fire, and he couldn't breathe. Pressing a fist to his chest, he stumbled to the credenza to pour a glass of wine. After a few generous quaffs he was able to breathe again. He stood very still for a moment, his eyes closed, feeling his chest rise and fall as he savored each satiating breath. After a few moments, a bit calmer, he returned to the parlor.

He couldn't stop watching Annina, but she seemed to make a point of avoiding his eyes. *No wonder,* he thought bitterly, *she's ashamed to look at me.* Her singing was lackluster, and his annoyance was growing. His chest started to tighten again, and he slammed a dissonant chord on the harpsichord. All eyes turned to him in astonishment.

He glared at her. "Maybe you could learn a thing or two from young Marta here. Surely her performance would be filled with a passion and professionalism your sad attempt doesn't even approach." He felt the sharp bite of his own words and hated himself for saying them. He'd said them for one reason: to hurt her, to shame her into reneging on her promise to Nicolini.

She didn't flinch. Instead, the chilling steadiness of her gaze burrowed into him and wrapped his own heart in the hurt he meant to inflict on her. The room was agonizingly silent.

Finally she said, "Then by all means, let her sing the role," with a calmness that stung him more deeply than her angriest tears ever could. She didn't even blink as the score she'd held in her hands fell to her feet and hit the parquet floor with a sharp clap.

Pietro rose to go after her as she headed for the hall.

"Pietro, stay where you are," Antonio ordered.

He reluctantly returned to the small table where he'd been working.

Antonio's breaths became short gasps. He pressed his fist to his chest again. "I'm sure we're all tired," he said huskily. "Why don't you all go home, and we'll resume tomorrow afternoon."

He retreated to his studio and closed the door. He poured another glass of wine and sat at his desk, trying with all his might to quell the agonizing feelings that surged in him. He reached for a pile of correspondence and began scribbling responses. After a while, he had no idea how long, there was a knock at the door. *Who the devil can that be,* he groaned to himself. *I thought everyone had left.* "Enter," he said.

The door creaked open, and Pietro stepped into the room.

"I thought you'd gone home. What is it?" he asked impatiently.

"It's about Annina."

He went back to his scribbling. "What about her?"

Pietro came over to the desk and leaned forward, the palms of his hands pressed to the surface. "Uncle, please, listen to me. I must tell you the truth of what happened."

He tightened his mouth and continued scribbling. "And what truth is that?"

"The truth about what transpired between Annina and Nicolini this afternoon. I was there. I heard the whole thing."

"I've already heard what transpired. I don't need to hear anymore," he said without looking up.

"You heard it from that conniving little hussy, Marta. I overheard her telling Nicolini all about it only a moment ago. What she told you was a brazen lie, Uncle."

He looked up, startled by the vehemence of Pietro's words. "What are you saying?"

"I'm saying that Marta has been waiting for an opportunity to discredit Annina ever since she arrived here. She's insanely jealous of her and has been plotting and scheming to undermine her relationship with you. Everyone has seen that clearly except you, Uncle."

He had a sudden, terrible sinking feeling. He put down his pen and sighed wearily. "Tell me what you know, Pietro."

"It's true Nicolini tried to tempt her to go to Verona. He made the opportunity sound very enticing and even gave her a letter of introduction to present on her arrival. But she told him she wouldn't consider it, that her place was with you and she wouldn't accept any opera engagement without your blessing. When he jeeringly reminded her that you'd taken away her Dorilla role, she assured him she would never allow her personal feelings to get in the way of your artistic decisions. She adores you, Uncle, and she'd die rather than betray you. Why have you failed to see that?"

He slumped forward, his head in his hands. "Dear God." In the next instant he felt his nephew's comforting hand on his shoulder.

"Please don't despair, Uncle. I'm sure this can be worked out."

He stood and embraced his nephew. "Thank you for telling me all this. If only you'd said something sooner."

Pietro stepped back and smiled gently. "It's not always easy to tell you things, Uncle. There never seems to be a moment when your mind isn't simultaneously creating and grappling with complex business decisions. I understand that. And so does Annina."

He felt tears blanket his eyes. He drew his nephew to him again. "I must go to her."

Chapter Nineteen

Paolina greeted Antonio at the door.

"Sorry to disturb you at this late hour," he said, "but I must see Annina."

"She's not here," she said, unable to hide the worry in her eyes.

His heart lurched. "Not here? Where on earth would she be at this time of night?"

"She left for Verona well over an hour ago."

"Verona?"

"Yes. She came home more distraught than I've ever seen her, but she wouldn't tell me what was wrong. She ran to her bedroom and started throwing things into her trunk, which she then had Fortunato carry to his gondola. Graziana and I tried to stop her, but she said she had to get to Verona a soon as possible, that it was urgent."

He stared at her, drained and speechless.

"Can you explain what that was all about? I'm worried sick about her."

"So am I," he said, as he turned to leave.

"Wait, where are you going?"

"To Verona."

She had apparently caught the last post-chaise, and there wasn't another leaving until the following week. He tried to hire a private coach, but there were none to be had. He'd have to wait for the next public transport.

THE REHEARSAL HAD drawn to a close and the singers and musicians were beginning to disperse. Antonio waited restlessly at the rear of Verona's sparkling new Teatro Filarmonico until nearly everyone had left. Annina remained on the stage, the fat little impresario prattling on to her about something. Antonio approached the stage, and her eyes suddenly met his. Her face froze into an expression that could only be described as evincing pride tempered by acute pain. He struggled to ignore the guilt pangs that tormented his heart. He sighed deeply and tried to smile.

"Can it be? Oh, maestro!" The impresario threw up his pudgy hands and half ran, half waddled, down the stage steps. "Why, Signorina Annina didn't tell me her esteemed *professore* was so soon to arrive!"

Antonio looked down at him with a combination of curiosity and distaste. The sentiment behind the man's grin was as artificial as his wired-together false teeth. He managed a curt nod. "A pleasure, maestro."

"The pleasure is all mine, *reverendo*," the man gushed, as he stooped into a pompous bow.

He returned his gaze to Annina, who continued to stare at him with the same ardent look. She said nothing.

"Perhaps we can share a dram or two in my office and become better acquainted," the irritating little impresario effused, his chubby cheeks expanding even more to display his hideous dental work.

"Thank you, but no. I've only just arrived and would like time to get settled." His eyes returned to hers.

"Oh, I see. Of course, maestro. You and Signorina Annina no doubt have, um, intimate matters to discuss." His eyes shifted to her. "*Buona sera*, signorina."

"*Buona sera a Le*, maestro." She was looking down on the man with a tight, half-smile. Antonio saw disgust behind that smile.

As soon as the impresario had left the theater, he walked to the edge of the stage and gazed up at her. *My God, she looks more beautiful than ever.* At once he was reminded of the things that so endeared her to him: the wisps of hair that refused to be tamed, the fiery eyes that failed to mask her affection for him—despite her anger. He cleared his throat. "Could you come down, please?" he said, in as friendly a tone as he could muster. "So I don't have to shout up to you?"

"Very well," she said stiffly.

He extended his hand to help her down the stage steps, but she refused to take it. At that instant, the toe of her shoe caught the hem of her gown, and with a shrill gasp she stumbled down the steps, and into his arms. Immediately she backed off, smoothing her skirts and hair and avoiding his eyes. "I'm sorry," she murmured. "I didn't mean for that to happen." A little spot of flaming red sprang to the surface of each cheek.

"It's quite all right. Are you hurt?" he said, reaching over and touching her arm.

She pulled it away. "No, I'm fine." She was still avoiding his eyes.

He glanced around, uncomfortable with the theater's sharp echo. "Is there someplace we can speak privately?"

"We could go across the street to my room. But who knows

what people might think." Her tone displayed her bitterness, but her eyes were looking up into his now.

"I don't care what people think. I only know I have to talk to you, away from prying ears."

"All right then. Follow me."

HE GLANCED ABOUT at the tiny room's scant furnishings. "May I sit?" he asked.

"Please." She gestured toward the room's only chair.

He chose the edge of the bed, leaving the chair for her. But she remained standing.

He sighed and looked up at her. "I'm sorry about our misunderstanding, Annina, and that you felt you needed to leave Venice so abruptly."

"Misunderstanding?" she said, her eyes dangerously bright.

"Yes," he said, averting his eyes. "I realize now it was all a misunderstanding. I reacted too quickly, before I'd fully considered everything I'd been told."

She crossed her arms. "*Misunderstanding?* The reason you didn't stop to consider what you'd been told was because you were blinded beyond all sensibility by the insidious charms of that shameless Arriggoni wench."

Her stinging words put him on the defensive. "I wouldn't say I was blinded by her charms—but I'll admit I was wrong about her."

"And what finally brought you to that realization?"

He frowned, uncomfortable. "After you left, Pietro told me everything. He'd overheard your conversation with Nicolini."

Her eyes softened for an instant. "Dear Pietro. My only friend these past weeks."

"I'm sorry you can't say the same about me, but I certainly

understand the distress you must have felt. I can't tell you how glad I am to put this unpleasantness behind us."

She eyed him intently for a long moment. Finally she said, "So be it, then."

He pressed the palms of his hands to his knees, took a deep breath, and smiled. "Good. Thank God that's settled."

She turned her back to him and began flipping through a score that rested atop the chest of drawers.

He rose, came over to her and put his hand on her shoulder. It felt tense, and he squeezed it gently. "Tomorrow night's your last performance here, isn't it? I trust you'll return to Venice with me the following morning."

She spun around, and the fire in her eyes startled him so much he stepped back. "So you think a few clever, guarded words is all it's going to take to make amends for what happened? Do you think I'm so docile and contrite that I'll obediently follow you back to Venice the minute you order me to do so?"

He was at a loss for words. "I'm . . . not ordering you to do anything, Annina. I'm simply asking—"

"You're asking me to submit to your dictates, as you always have. You expect me to return with you to Venice and sit dutifully by while you give the most coveted roles in your operas to an unending line of opportunistic strangers. And I—I who have stuck by you and been nothing but loyal to you for well over ten years am expected to yield cheerfully to the roles no one else wants. Have you seen how they look down their noses at me? How they laugh behind my back?" Her voice was getting louder as she shook with rage.

He took her firmly by the upper arms. "Annina, calm yourself, please, the neighbors—"

She jerked away from him. "The neighbors be damned!"

The shock of hearing such language come from her mouth stung him fiercely. "Annina—"

"You *humiliated* me! You *shamed* me—in front of the very people who'd love nothing better than to see me disgraced. Oh, what pleasure you gave them, Antonio, you gave those pretentious boors exactly what they wanted. Why didn't you just slap my face? That wouldn't have hurt nearly so much as your cruel words!"

He felt crestfallen. He gazed into her pain-filled eyes and finally said, "If anyone should feel shamed it's me, not you, Annina. I was completely out of line speaking to you the way I did. There was no excuse for it. The only reason I can offer is that the lie Marta told me—and I should have known it was a lie—flooded my mind with memories of other singers who've turned their backs on me when they thought they had better opportunities. At that moment all I could think was that I could bear anyone's betrayal but yours. The thought of you turning against me made me crazy."

Her eyes filled with tears. Suddenly she looked frail and vulnerable, and he felt a surge of protectiveness rise in him. He pulled her to him, and she leaned her head on his shoulder, weeping softly. "How could you ever have thought I would turn my back on you?" she said, between sighs. "I love you. And not only that, I think you're the greatest composer alive. I don't just think it, I know it. I've always known it."

He could feel the delicate curves of her body, pressed to his, trembling. He held her even closer. Finally he murmured, "I'm so sorry. Can you forgive me?"

"I already have." She pulled back and looked up at him. "I told you I love you, Antonio." Her eyes glistened with tears.

He gazed at her, speechless, and nodded, his own eyes smarting.

She sniffed and wiped her nose with the back of her hand. "Do you . . . love me as well?"

He hesitated. "You know I do."

"Then why won't you say it?"

He sighed. "The way I feel about you, Annina, I don't even know how to explain it to myself, much less to you."

She wiped away her tears with her fingertips and looked at him with that tolerant, knowing smile peculiar to women—the smile that says *Isn't that just like a man?* He knew she wanted to talk about this more. Females always did. But that smile told him she was willing to let the matter drop. For that he was grateful.

He took another deep breath. "You need to eat something, you're probably starving."

"Which probably means *you're* starving," she said, her smile growing more wry, despite her sniffles. "Leave it to a man to think of food at a time like this."

He smiled. "All right, I'll admit I'm hungry. Is there anyplace decent to eat around here?"

"There's a tavern at the corner that's fairly decent."

"Sounds fine."

"But I'd like a minute to freshen up before we go."

"Go ahead, I'll wait." He stood with his hands clasped in front of him.

Again, the patient smile.

"Oh," he said, "you need privacy. I'll wait outside."

"Thank you, Antonio. I'll only be a few moments."

As he paced the pavement in front of the inn, long-buried thoughts flooded his mind. He had loved many women in his life and in many different ways, although he'd forsaken carnal pleasure when he took holy orders. It hadn't been easy. His passions had often tempted him to break his sacred vows. But he'd poured his longings, his deepest desires, into his music. And then there was Annina. The pretty little girl who had won his heart and before his eyes grown into a stunning woman. How, indeed, could he describe his feelings for her? She, who understood the secrets of his soul better than anyone, who shared his passions and brought those passions to life with her incomparable artistry. At that moment he made a tacit vow: Never again would he pass her over in favor of a more "fashionable" singer. Her singing style, so filled with drama and fire, exemplified the music of his heart. She was his *prima donna assoluta*, his Muse, and central to his creativity.

It had been quite a bit more than a few moments, but worth the wait. She stepped out on the walkway, fragrant and glowing as a rose in first bloom. At twenty-four she was still as slender and fresh-faced as a seventeen-year-old. Just being in her sparkling presence made him feel young. How he cherished her.

"SO I SUPPOSE Marta took back the role of Eudamia," she said, after they were seated at the tavern.

He sighed and nodded. "Yes, and she sang terribly. In fact the whole production was dreadful and not well received. I just can't do this anymore without you, Annina."

The waiter came with a carafe of wine and two glasses. Antonio poured a glass for her and then one for himself.

She didn't comment on the failed *Dorilla* performance, but smiled sweetly at him across the table between sips of wine. To his relief, she seemed to be growing much more relaxed.

"What did *signor impresario* mean when he said I'd come sooner than expected?" he asked her.

"Oh, I meant to tell you. He's looking to commission Venetian composers, and I suggested he contact you."

He felt a surge of excitement—and gratitude. "You did that for me? As angry as you were with me?"

"You know I never let my personal feelings get in the way of artistic matters."

He noticed her wine glass was empty and poured her a second.

She raised the glass to her lips, then lowered it to the table as she burst into a throaty laugh. "Thank goodness you arrived when you did, to rescue me from the clutches of that insufferable troll."

"What was he saying to you?"

"Not much in particular. A lot of blathering flattery, mostly. He's disgusting."

"He wasn't making indecent advances was he?"

"Not exactly. But I'm sure he would have soon enough if you hadn't shown up. I've seen him make slathering but unsuccessful attempts at intimacy with nearly every female singer who's crossed his stage."

He frowned. "What's his name, by the way?"

She took a long sip of wine. "*Cicciottello* is what everyone calls him behind his back."

"They call him Chubby?"

She nodded, then puffed out her cheeks in mockery of the hapless Cicciottello.

He grinned and chuckled. There was no one funnier—or more honest about their feelings—than Annina after she'd had a glass or two of wine. He decided this would be a good time to bring up the other matter he'd come to talk to her about.

"There's another project I'm considering, one I think you'll be quite pleased about."

She smiled brightly. "What is it?"

The Grimani brothers, who own the Teatro San Samuele, have approached me about writing a new setting of Zeno's *Griselda*, to be performed next year, on the eve of Ascension. I'd like you to sing the title role."

Her smile vanished, and she lowered her glass. *"Griselda?* I saw the libretto when Albinoni did it a few years ago. You want me to play that cringing doormat? That pathetic excuse for a woman? Is that how you see me? As that foppish rag doll whose husband treats her like dirt, humiliates her, casts her aside, and all she can say is, 'Do whatever you want to me, great Master, I'll always love you no matter how cruel you are to me!'? Well I won't do it. You can't make me play a part like that."

Heads were starting to turn, and Antonio glanced around uncomfortably. A group of women across the room seemed to take particular interest. *Isn't that the prima donna from last week's opera?* he heard one of them whisper shrilly. *Arsace, wasn't it? . . . She was that Statira character . . . striking performance.* Then the remarks came fast and furiously. *Yes! . . . And do you know who that is she's with? . . . Are you sure? . . . Look at the red hair and the priest's collar! . . . That's il prete rosso and his Annina!*

Mater Dei, he groaned inwardly, Mother of God.

He turned his eyes back to Annina and responded to her in a low voice. "I know. That's why I've already told the Grimanis I won't do it unless they hire a poet to rewrite the libretto."

Her fiery eyes did not relent. "Rewrite it? How? How would you have it changed?"

A titter from across the room: *Must be a lovers' quarrel!* Annina didn't seem to hear. He ignored the barb.

"First of all, it needs to be shortened," he said, lowering his voice even more. "As it is, there's so much recitative the audience would be asleep before the first aria. Mainly, though, I'd have the story restructured so Griselda's inner turmoil, her outrage at her unjust treatment, is at the center of the drama. As you've pointed out, Zeno's depiction of Griselda's character is unrealistic. No woman in her right mind would be that passive under such circumstances. I want to make her more believable—to show her taking action and displaying real, human emotions. That would require superior acting skills, and you're the only singer I know of who could do it convincingly."

The fire in her eyes had softened to a hazy glow. She took another sip of wine. "Do you really believe I can do it?"

"Of course. You just demonstrated it for me a moment ago, and even more so earlier this evening."

She smiled and cocked her head, her elbow resting on the table and her wineglass propped midair.

"That's the kind of energy and vigor needed for the Griselda I have in mind," he continued. "I actually plan to model her after you."

She looked overjoyed. She set her glass on the table. "Will you write arias for me that are passionate and full of action and motion?"

"Absolutely. And I won't agree to work with any poet until he proves he can write the kinds of texts such arias require." He looked at her for a moment, with a partial smile. "Do you feel better now?"

"Do I feel better?" She lifted her glass and downed the last drop of wine. "I feel wonderful."

A sharp whisper from across the room: *Look, they've made up!*

He cut his eyes in the direction of the whisperer, then looked back at Annina, frowning and raising his eyes heavenward.

Her laugh sparkled. "The gossips here in Verona are worse than in Venice, believe it or not. Ignore them, Antonio. Let them have their fun, I say." She seemed to enjoy the notoriety. She held out her glass for a refill.

He cleared his throat. "Maybe we should order something to eat now."

AFTER SUPPER HE walked her back to the inn. At the door, she turned to him. "Where are you staying? I didn't even think to ask."

"The abbot of San Zeno Maggiore was kind enough to offer me accommodations. He's well acquainted with my royal friend Emperor Charles and always hosts him when he travels through here."

She smiled. "It helps to know important people, doesn't it?"

"Indeed it does."

"Is San Zeno far from here?"

"No, only a short walk."

She peered up and down the street. "We should hail you a coach."

"No need, I'll walk. I enjoy the night air."

She touched his arm. "Are you sure you'll be all right?"

"Of course." He kissed her lightly on the forehead. "I'll meet you at the theater tomorrow."

"Good night, then. See you tomorrow." She smiled, and turned to go in.

He caught her arm gently. "There's something else I've been meaning to ask you, a favor, actually."

She gazed at him, her eyes wide with curiosity. "What is it?"

"I know how you feel about the singers who are starring in my *L'Olimpiade*. But . . ." He paused, sighing, staring at the ground briefly. Then he lifted his eyes to hers. "It would mean so much to me if you were there opening night."

She said nothing for a moment. She raised her chin slightly. "Why should it matter if I'm there or not?"

"It matters to me. I'm going out on a limb with this opera, and the critics will delight in devouring me if the least thing is amiss. I'd like you there because I trust your opinion, and I know you'll tell me the truth." He took a deep breath. He'd opened his heart to her, admitted how much he'd come to depend on her.

She looked at him steadily, her expression serious. Finally she said, "If Licidas's rage aria is any indication of the opera as a whole, I have no doubt it'll be a huge sensation." Her face relaxed into a confident smile.

He smiled with her, marveling again at how beautiful she'd become, and at how he'd grown to adore her.

THE SAN ANGELO THEATER sparkled with magnificence on the opening night of *L'Olimpiade*. Antonio had reserved a box seat near the stage for Annina and Paolina.

Toward the end of the second act there was a knock at the door to their box, and Paolina rose to answer. Annina turned as she opened the door to two young girls, who looked at her excitedly, giggling. One of them pointed at her, and she heard her whisper to the other, "*Annina del prete rosso!*" They both tittered with laughter. Paolina gave them a stern frown as she closed the door firmly.

"How dare they," Annina said. "Why can't people mind their own business?"

Paolina came back to her seat and gave her a vaguely reproachful look. "Well what do you expect?"

"What do you mean?"

"The way you cling to Antonio in public, what do you expect people to think?"

"Paolina! What are you saying?"

"That you are too old to carry on with him the way you do. It was different when you were a young girl. But you're a woman now and must be more discreet. I know you don't mean anything by it. You're vivacious and affectionate, and those are the things people who know you love about you. Others see it differently, though. They don't understand your relationship with him, and so they're going to think the worst."

"But . . ." she said, flustered. "He doesn't seem to mind how I act with him in public."

"Of course he doesn't mind, he's a man isn't he? What man wouldn't enjoy going around with a beautiful, adoring young woman hanging on his arm?"

"That's ridiculous. He's not just a man. He's a priest, and—my teacher, and a brilliant composer."

"Yes, he is all those things. But he's a man first. You must never forget that, Annina."

"You're not suggesting . . ."

"Of course not. He cares about you and respects you too much to compromise you in any way. I know that about him, but others don't."

She sighed, exasperated. "So you think I should suddenly start acting cold and distant around him?"

"No, certainly not. I'm just suggesting you exercise more decorum when you're out in public with him."

Onstage, Angela Zannuchi was poised to begin her stirring "rage" aria. The orchestral strings become raging furies. Gripped by a terrifying yet indefinable premonition, Annina shivered and hugged herself as Angela began to sing:

> *I groan and shudder,*
> *the day seems dark to me,*
> *a hundred specters surround me,*
> *a thousand furies rage in my breast!*

The emotional tension of the music was palpable, and she felt gripped by an energy that transcended her own selfish pride and desires. Suddenly it didn't matter who was singing the aria. Antonio's music was all that mattered. Yet by the time the curtain fell on the final act, she still wasn't able to shake the ominous feeling that had overtaken her at the end of Act II. She'd been courting danger, allowing her feelings for him to show themselves in public. She trembled. Like Licidas, a thousand furies raged in her breast. She forced herself to put her fears aside as she joined the rest of the audience in a burst of furious applause. The singers came out one by one to feast on the near hysterical accolades.

Finally Antonio emerged from the wings, and along with many others in the theater she sprang to her feet and clapped all the louder. Many hooted and threw flowers onto the stage. Antonio looked ecstatic, and she smiled down at him and clapped until her hands hurt. Her former anger at being excluded from *L'Olimpiade* had been undermined by the sheer beauty of his music.

Suddenly he looked up at her. She smiled all the more brightly, hardly able to hold back the tears of love and pride that were ready to spill out.

DESPITE *L'OLIMPIADE'S* SUCCESS, Antonio's Venetian comeback was short-lived. The upstarts from Naples indeed had a stranglehold on Venice's opera theaters, and several of his most trusted singers had jumped ship to join their ranks. He was so irate, he almost began to doubt Annina's loyalty once again.

"Are you going to leave me too?" he asked irritably one evening, when he stopped by her apartment with a freshly copied score for her to preview. He handed her the score and sank down on the sofa.

She felt a stab in her heart. The question hurt. But she knew she'd only make things worse if she overreacted. She took a deep breath, and sat beside him, the score resting on her knee. Putting her hand on his, she spoke patiently. "We've already been through this. Don't you remember our conversation in Verona? I told you I'd never turn my back on you, and I meant it. You mean more to me than anyone else in the world. And you're a hundred times more talented than these newcomers. That's obvious to anyone with intelligence and good taste."

He sighed, then put his arm around her and drew her to him. "You're an angel, Annina. I'm sorry. I didn't mean to be short-tempered with you."

She tingled with warmth, but decided she'd better turn her mind to more practical matters. "What those turncoats have put you through would make anyone short-tempered. I say we forget about them and move on. And what about your commission to do *Griselda* next spring at San Samuele? The Grimanis asked *you*, remember? Not one of those hacks from Naples."

"You're right, we do have that to look forward to." He looked at her and smiled, his eyes suddenly bright. "Oh, and I almost forgot to tell you. I heard from your friend Cicciottello. He's commissioned me to write two operas for Verona's 1735 Carnival season."

She pulled away from him. "He sent you a contract? When?"

"A couple of weeks ago."

Her eyes widened. "And you're only telling me about it now? What are the operas?"

"He's left that up to me. I was thinking of a new setting of *Tamerlano*, which is about a Mongolian tyrant. Only I'd like to restructure the story to focus on the Turkish sultan Bajazet, whose throne Tamerlano usurps."

She narrowed her eyes and smiled. "Sounds like the situation you're facing now with the Neapolitans."

"Do you think so?" His smile told her that was exactly what he had in mind.

"Yes I do," she said. "And is there a part in it for me?"

"Of course. I want you to sing the role of Asteria, Bajazet's daughter."

"Oh Antonio—"

"I'll also debut my new opera *Adelaide* there. That's what I stopped by to show you. In this one I'd like you to sing the title role."

She gazed at him, overwhelmed, then glanced down at the score that still rested on her knee.

"Pietro only just finished copying your part this evening," he said, his voice growing more animated, "and I wanted to bring it to you right away. I'm not even sure the ink is dry yet."

She scanned the score, her insides churning, then looked up at him. "How do you write all this music so fast? And how will I have time to learn it?"

His smile was confident. "There's no need to worry about that. You learn new music faster than any singer I've ever worked with."

She sighed. "We do have our work cut out for us. I don't think we'll have time to give another thought to these upstarts from the south."

He chuckled and squeezed her hand. "No, I don't suppose we will."

She gave him an arch look. "Does it worry you at all that Cicciottello will be in charge of your Verona projects?"

"He won't be in charge. The man's a fatuous fool and would make a mockery of the productions. I wrote the theater owners and told them I wouldn't take the commission unless I was given full managerial control of the Filarmonico for the 1735 season."

She looked at him in awe. "And they agreed so quickly to hand it all over to you?"

"Certainly, why wouldn't they?"

"I don't know why you were so moody when you got here," she said, frowning slightly and shaking her head. "You're as much on top of things as you've ever been."

"You're right, and I'm sorry for what I said earlier. I was tired." He smiled and squeezed her hand again. "But you've renewed my energy, Annina."

Things were good again. Until she found out he was planning to hire Maddalena Pieri to sing the role of Tamerlano. She fumed, but said nothing.

As they were going over her recitatives one afternoon at his house, he noticed her unease. "Is something wrong, Annina?"

"No, nothing."

"Something *is* wrong. Now tell me what it is."

She sighed loudly and frowned. "All right, if you must know, I'm not too happy about the prospect of sharing the stage again with that Pieri woman."

He looked surprised. "Why not?"

"Because she's a witch. The last time I sang with her she was rude and hateful to me."

"You never mentioned anything about it then."

"I didn't want to be a nuisance."

He rubbed his forehead with his fingertips. "I'm afraid it's too late to get out of it now. I've already made a deal with Albizzi."

She raised her eyebrows. "Albizzi?"

"Don't you remember? He's the impresario of the Pergola theater in Florence. He and I go way back."

"What does he have to do with Pieri?"

"He's, um, rather involved with her."

"In what way?"

He cleared his throat. "They say she's his mistress."

She crossed her arms and gave him a sharp look. "They say that about us too."

His jaw tensed and the color rose in his face. "Annina—"

"So what's the deal you made?"

He sighed. "Albizzi wants me to compose two operas for his theater, for the 1736 season, and he's asked that you sing the *prima donna* roles. Apparently when Pieri heard about it she was quite upset. So to appease her, he's asked that I give her a lead role in one of my operas elsewhere."

"So you and this Albizzi are now procurers, exchanging your women? Treating us like chattel? Making deals behind our backs?"

"Don't be ridiculous."

"Chiara warned me about this sort of thing years ago. I suppose I should have listened to her."

His mouth tightened. "What on earth are you so worked up about? I thought you'd be happy to be the star of the Carnival season in Florence."

"I'm just wondering why this is the first I've heard about it."

He frowned. "You know I never discuss deals with you while they're still in the making. I wouldn't think you'd want to be bothered with the tedious details of negotiating a contract."

"You mean because I'm a woman you don't think my mind could grasp it."

"I didn't say that."

"You didn't have to."

He looked baffled, and restive. "I don't understand what's gotten into you, but we have work to do. And as for Maddalena Pieri, I know she's difficult, but you're going to have to put up with her. That's what we do if we want to survive in this business."

How could he not understand why she was so miffed? Now she dreaded the Verona project. But how could she ever explain that to Antonio? The complexity of it was perplexing, even to her. How would it be to him? Why couldn't things go back to the innocent simplicity of her early relationship with him? He obviously still thought of her as he had then, while her feelings had gone far beyond her former girlish adoration of him. But that was her burden to bear. Not his.

ANTONIO WAS NOT himself over the next few days. He remained moody and distant, and Annina was hurt by his sudden indifference to her feelings. But she swallowed her pain and forced herself to go through the motions of preparing for the *Bajazet* project. He'd decided to make the opera a *pasticcio*, combining his own music with that of other composers. This surprised her, until she realized why. He planned to use popular arias by the Neapolitan composers for Tamerlano and his evil minions, and his own music for Bajazet and Asteria. The idea of identifying his own artistic fate with the political fate of the noble sultan and his daughter, and the arrogance of the Neapolitans with that of Tamerlano's conquering forces, was too tempting for him to resist. She thought it was a clever idea. But she was still annoyed about the whole Maddalena Pieri situation and the way it had come about. Antonio's silence on the subject only increased her vexation.

Then one day the source of his moodiness became clear. She arrived at his house early one morning to go over Asteria's recitatives for Act 1. He was still upstairs, and his housekeeper let her in. While she waited in his studio she noticed his desk was littered with music papers. She stepped over to take a look. The fevered handwriting of the scores and glistening freshness of the ink told her they'd been written hurriedly and quite recently. She picked up a sheet. It was the first page of one of Bajazet's arias, in which he pours out his rage at the injustices and frustrations that have been thrust on him. Her eyes swiftly scanned the score. Percussive, lightning-fast notes alternated with abrupt pauses. The aria's words matched the fury and agitation of the notes: *I am desperate, I no longer have a daughter, I have no throne!*

Her heart turned over as the aria's meaning pierced her awareness. Antonio was much more devastated by the "Neapolitan invasion" than she'd realized. And the recent friction that had sprung up between the two of them had deepened his despair. A question entered her mind. Did he think of her as a daughter? She certainly didn't think of him as a father. But then again, she had a father, and he had no daughter. The ambiguity seemed to complicate their relationship.

She picked up another page where he'd dashed off a fragment of Asteria's music: *All his injuries meet in me!* The same fury and vehemence that characterized Bajazet's music was mirrored in his daughter's desperate outburst. The symbolism was too glaring to miss. Antonio was doing exactly what he'd always taught her to do. Instead of allowing his stormy emotions to defeat him, he'd poured them into his art. And he'd done it brilliantly.

She glanced up and saw him standing in the doorway. He looked exhausted, yet at the same time brash and agitated. She felt her eyes glisten and a warm smile light up her face. "You've outdone yourself, Antonio. This is the most stirring work I've ever seen you do. No other opera composer can write like this. Not one of them can capture the essence of human feeling the way you can."

For the first time in days, he smiled at her.

Chapter Twenty

Her Asteria costume was one of the most striking Graziana had yet designed for her. It was in traditional Turkish style—a layered silk skirt of the palest turquoise, with a silver embroidered, dark blue border at the hem. A matching velvet, silver trimmed jacket snuggly encased her arms and torso, while a jewel-studded fes topped with a filmy veil completed the ensemble. The costume's exotic foreignness filled her with tingling anticipation.

At the conclusion of the premier performance the audience went into a frenzy. Antonio had found a young Venetian baritone, Marc'Antonio Mareschi, to sing the title role. The young man's warm, rich voice was so thrilling, and his dramatic delivery so captivating, the women went mad for him. He and Annina received so much applause, they each had to perform several encores. *Adelaide* was equally well received.

On her return to Venice, she visited Graziana for a long chat.

"So tell me how it went," she asked anxiously.

"It was wonderful, I don't know when Antonio's ever had such a triumph."

"And?" She eyed her questioningly. "How did things go with

Maddalena?"

"Fortunately she didn't cause too much trouble, outside of a few insolent remarks, which I managed to ignore."

"Good for you. You're learning, Annina. You can't let these high-flown divas get the better of you. You can out-sing any of them."

She smiled wryly. "I don't know about that. But I did notice a new quavering in Maddalena's voice."

"Well, she's no longer young, you know. Her years of singing all those demanding *en travesti* roles must be taking their toll."

"I think you're right. Strangely, though, her vocal problems didn't seem to bother Antonio."

"Of course not. Didn't you tell me he was using this opera to show up the Neapolitans? I'd think he'd be delighted that her weaknesses diminished the appeal of their arias. That would make the music he wrote for you and the Bajazet character all the more dazzling."

"You're right, I hadn't thought of that. And to think I was angry with him when I realized he'd hired Maddalena."

Graziana gave her an ironic look. "It sounds like you should have more faith in his decisions."

She sighed. "I know. It's just that I get so exasperated sometimes when he plans things behind my back."

"I'm sure he doesn't see it that way. Aren't you pleased he takes such pains to write music for you that suits your voice so perfectly? He wouldn't do that for just anyone, you know."

She felt a wave of shame and had to blink back a tear. Graziana sensed her distress at once and gave her a reassuring hug. She wanted to pour out all her feelings to her friend, but she couldn't. She didn't dare.

A few days later, she and Antonio dined at a lovely tavern on the Grand Canal. As wine was poured, his face beamed with happiness. It was wonderful to see him in such high spirits again. He downed a draft of wine then smiled at her. "I've been thinking about something you said a few weeks ago."

"What's that?"

"You indicated you'd like to be more involved in the planning process of our opera performances."

"Oh I would."

"Good, because the Grimanis have hired a young poet to rewrite the *Griselda* libretto. He's coming to my house tomorrow evening to discuss the project, and I'd like you to join us."

She could feel the radiance of her smile as she gazed at him. At long last he was inviting her to be a collaborator in the creation of one of his operas. When she arrived at his house the following evening she was surprised to find him in his priestly garb, his breviary in his hand.

"Am I too early?" she asked.

"Not at all. I just want to have an excuse to get rid of this young tyro if I decide he's not up for the job, which I imagine he's not."

"Why do you say that? Who is he?"

"His name is Carlo Goldoni. He's had no experience writing opera librettos—I checked. I suppose the Grimanis decided to try to save money by hiring a novice. I'll probably end up having to write it myself, so I'd like to get this over with as quickly as possible."

The bell sounded at the front door, and she went to answer. "Bring him to my study, won't you dear?" he said, as he disappeared down the hall.

She opened the door to a bright-eyed young man, about her own age. "Signor Goldoni?" she asked.

He bowed. "*Sì*, signorina. *Buona sera.*"

"Good evening, signore, please, come in. I'm Anna Girò."

"*Grazie*. Such a pleasure, Signorina Anna. You are to be the prima donna of the opera I'm here to discuss with Signor Vivaldi, I believe," he said with a twinkle in his eye and a slightly cocky smile.

"Yes, I am. Please follow me. I'll take you to him."

She rapped lightly at the studio door and peeked in. "Signor Carlo Goldoni is here."

Antonio nodded.

As she ushered young Carlo into the room, Antonio stood with the open breviary in his hand and greeted him without smiling. "What is the reason for this pleasure, signore?"

"*Buona sera, reverendo*," the young man said, with a sweeping bow. "His Excellency Grimani has entrusted me with the alterations that you think necessary in the upcoming opera." He glanced briefly at the piles of music scores spread everywhere, then squared his shoulders and returned his eyes to Antonio. "I came here to see what your wishes are."

Antonio feigned bewilderment, and there was an awkward silence. Finally he said, "Oh. Do you mean to say you've been asked to make the changes to the opera *Griselda*? Is the Grimani's house librettist, Signor Lalli, no longer connected with their theater?"

Carlo took a deep breath and pulled himself to his full height. "Signor Lalli is quite old, sir, and will always profit from the dedicatory letters and the sale of the librettos. But this doesn't concern me. I have the pleasure of busying myself with work that ought to please me, and I have the honor of being under the direction of Maestro Vivaldi." He gave Antonio another bow.

Unimpressed with this boyish bravado, he returned his attention to his breviary and made the sign of the cross.

Carlo looked stricken at the obvious rebuff. "I didn't mean to disturb you during your religious exercises, *reverendo*. Perhaps I should come back at another time." He looked at Annina, and she smiled sympathetically. Then he turned to leave.

Before he reached the door, Antonio spoke up. "I'm well aware of your talent for poetry, young man. I've seen your play *Belisario* and it pleased me very much. I know you can write spoken tragedy and epic poems. But writing a musical quatrain and adapting an opera libretto for specific singers is something else entirely. It's quite difficult and requires a special talent."

Carlo pursed his lips and put on a proud demeanor. "Do me the honor of showing me your drama, sir."

"Yes, as soon as I can find it," he said dismissively. Then he took up his breviary and began reciting: "*Deus in adjutorium meum intende . . . Domine . . .*"

Carlo's mouth tightened with impatience. "Sir—"

He looked up from his prayer book. "Yes, yes, I'm looking. Now what did I do with *Griselda?*" He shuffled absentmindedly through a pile of papers while still holding the open breviary in one hand.

Annina felt sorry for Carlo. He didn't realize he was being taunted.

At last he found the libretto. "Ah," he said, holding it up. "Here it is." He caught her eye, and she frowned at him, annoyed he was giving poor Carlo such a hard time. *Be nice*, she mouthed to him. He winked at her subtly, then turned his eyes back to the young poet.

"Come, Signor Carlo, let me show you this scene at the end of the first act. It's a compelling and moving scene. Griselda has just been rejected by her husband, and now she's being harassed by an evil predator. But the original author put a doleful aria here, and Signorina Girò doesn't like the languid style of singing." He glanced over at her. She smiled, and he went on. "She'd prefer an aria with expression and excitement. One that shows emotion in different ways, such as by interrupted words and heaved sighs. That is to say, we need this aria turned into one that's full of action and agitation." He watched for a moment as Carlo studied the libretto. "Perhaps you don't understand what I mean."

"Yes, sir, I understand exactly what you mean," the young man said, with a smile of assurance. "If you'll be so kind as to lend me the libretto, I shall see what I can do with it."

"I'm afraid I can't do that," he said, frowning. "I need it myself, since I'm under pressure to get this opera written."

"Very well, sir. Then if you'll allow me a few moments, I'll write the type of aria you've just described while you wait."

For the first time since Carlo arrived, Antonio broke into a smile. He laughed lightly and shook his head. "You clearly have no idea what you're saying, young man."

Carlo's jaw tightened. "Perhaps you should reserve your laughter until you've seen what I can do," he said stiffly.

He continued chuckling and put his hand on Carlo's shoulder good-naturedly. "All right, all right. Don't be angry. Here, make yourself comfortable at my desk and write me a verse."

He took up his breviary again and started pacing the room. Annina picked up a score to peruse. They exchanged an amused look, while Carlo wrote furiously.

After about fifteen minutes, Carlo rose from the desk and handed his work to Antonio. With his prayer book in his right hand and Carlo's sheet of paper in his left, Antonio read softly:

> *My heart is torn*
> *by a thousand anxieties,*
> *Cruel people are*

conspiring to hurt me,
I want to hide,
I want to run away,
Lightning from heaven
makes me tremble.
I'm dazed by dreadful blows,
I have no more tears,
I have no more voice,
I cannot cry,
I cannot speak.

He dropped his breviary to the floor, and his face lit up with a brilliant smile. He threw his arms around Carlo, then turned to her. "Did you hear that, Annina? Can you believe what this young man has done? He did it right here, in less than a quarter of an hour."

Anxiously, she took the poem from him and read it through again.

He grasped the poet's hand in both of his. "I must congratulate you, Carlo, I'm truly amazed. My God, that was fast work. And it's perfect for the Act 1 finale. Exactly the type of aria to bring out Annina's dramatic capabilities. Isn't that so, my dear?"

She'd never seen him so excited. She smiled and nodded. "Indeed it is."

Carlo beamed. "Does this mean I have the commission?"

"Do you have the commission? Of course you have the commission. We'll begin work tomorrow. Annina, I'd like you to be here too. We'll need your input."

She basked in happiness over the next few weeks. She and Carlo met at Antonio's house every evening to transform Griselda from a stoic martyr into a woman of intense feeling and impassioned sensibilities. Ornamental vocal displays were replaced with directness and simplicity. Languid arias gave way to passionate declamations. Aided by Carlo's poetry, Antonio's music, and Annina's dramatic instincts, the passive victim became an active resister. Together, they created a new type of operatic heroine.

On opening night she shook with suspense. At the end of Act I she stood alone onstage, in a simple dress. Her hair was unadorned, and unruly wisps fell around her face. Her eyes, her entire demeanor, blazed with resistance and desperation. She cast a furtive glance at Antonio, and his dark blue eyes shone back at her as he lifted his violin to start the aria's introduction. At once the audience snapped to attention as cascading torrents of notes foreshadowed the "lightning from heaven" to which Griselda would compare her desperate situation.

Antonio caught her eye again and gave a quick nod. She began to cry out in anguish at how her heart was being torn apart by fear and despair. The pattern of rhythmic tension and release in the vocal melody mirrored the jolts of agony expressed in the words—*I want to hide, I want to run away!* In the second stanza, her anxiety turned to profound sadness. She was drained of emotion, and her voice faltered—*I have no more tears, I have no more voice, I cannot cry, I cannot speak.* The soft eeriness of the music reflected the chilling intensity of her inner torment. An abrupt reprise of the "lightning from heaven" ritornello signaled her return to an even more intense state of outrage and desperation. She felt she was on fire. She blustered and raved. She abandoned all pretense of dignity and restraint. At the end of the aria the audience exploded with cheers and ovations. She felt drained but ecstatic. Her gaze fell on Antonio. His eyes and his smile exuded something she couldn't quite describe—a sort of combination of love, esteem, and gratitude. But there was something else in his look, she couldn't quite say, that filled her with excruciating excitement.

ANTONIO HAD TRIUMPHED. And so had she. *Griselda*, their first true creative collaboration, was a resounding success. She'd never felt closer to him, and the thrill was intoxicating.

Following the performance they celebrated over supper and wine at his house, along with Carlo, the Grimanis, and several members of the cast. They congratulated each other and talked about future projects. The wine and the heady excitement gave her a feeling of invincibility she'd never known before. It was nearly three in the morning before the last of the guests departed. Exhausted, but still exhilarated, she walked to the parlor arm in arm with Antonio.

Her head awash in hazy euphoria, she felt her body press against his, and before she knew it, their mouths met, and he held her even closer—but only for a moment. Quite suddenly he tensed and pulled away.

Her head cleared in an instant. She held both hands to her mouth, and whispered, "Antonio, I'm so sorry."

He looked shaken. He stared at her and said nothing.

She stood frozen in shame and fear. The spell was broken. Now she knew for certain the secret fantasy she'd harbored for so long and tried in vain to suppress could never be fulfilled. The words she'd sung with such heartfelt passion that night came back to torture her like hammer blows: *My heart is torn by a thousand anxieties . . . I want to hide, I want to run away, lightning from heaven makes me tremble!*

"I should go," she said shakily, as she turned toward the hall to fetch her cloak.

"Annina, wait, please." He followed her and grasped her elbow. "I think we should talk about this."

Her heart pounded with dread, but she let him lead her back into the parlor. He directed her to the sofa, then pulled up a wooden chair. She shuddered with fear of what he might say.

He sat near the edge of his seat and leaned forward, his elbows resting on his knees and his hands clasped between them. For a long moment, he stared at the floor thoughtfully. Finally he said, "I think we've known each other long enough to be honest about our feelings."

"I really don't know what came over me. I'm—"

"It's not just you, Annina. I've probably given you the wrong impression."

"No, you haven't. You've never said or done anything improper."

"Perhaps not. I hope not. But the fact is, my dear, you're a very attractive young woman. Not only in looks, but your personality as well. You're so . . . ardent and spirited, and I love that about you." He was smiling at her now. But it was a sad smile. "The truth is, if I were twenty years younger, and not a priest, well—things might be different."

She stared at him, stunned. She'd never dared imagine he thought of her in that way, much less that he'd admit it. She blinked and smiled back at him as a guilty thrill fluttered through her.

He sighed. "But what happened just now must never happen again. I'm not blaming you—I just want to be sure we understand each other. You know full well what the gossips are saying about us. If something like this ever got out, God only knows what would come of it."

She looked at him through the mist of anguish that floated between them. "Yes, I know," she finally said. "And you're right, of course. I'm really sorry, Antonio. Can you forgive me?"

He reached over and took her hand. "There's nothing to forgive."

She felt burning moisture well up behind her eyes. Clutching his hand, she raised it to her cheek as a tear started to fall. She fixed her clouded gaze on him. His eyes were full of love and empathy—but also distance and loneliness. Strangely it was at times like this, when he seemed so vulnerable, that she loved him the most. She felt almost unbearably sad and frustrated, but she forced herself to smile at him as she lowered her hand, still clutching his, to her lap. "It's late. I really should go."

He smiled back, squeezed her hand, and nodded.

At the door she turned to him. There was a question she had to ask, and now seemed the opportune time. "Are you sorry you took holy orders?"

"No."

"Why?"

"Because I decided many years ago to serve God with my music. If I'd married and had a family, it wouldn't be possible to accomplish all the things I do."

Or for us to have the kind of relationship we have, she thought but didn't say.

IF THINGS WERE DIFFERENT. He'd finally acknowledged it to her, and she to him. No doubt he'd hoped she would never put him in that position, where he'd have to confess what he really felt. Such a bittersweet moment. So now they had a private, if partially unspoken, understanding. They loved each other. They were drawn to each other. But their relationship could never go beyond friendship. She sighed as the futile notion tortured her mind. *If only things were different. But they're not,* she thought to herself as she and

Fortunato rowed home in silence. She longed for physical intimacy with a man. But Antonio was inaccessible in that way, and what man could ever measure up to him? Even if she found someone she cared for enough, marriage would probably mean the end of her career. And most likely the end of her association with Antonio—an unimaginable prospect. That was her dilemma. It seemed she was doomed to celibacy in this strange yet wonderful bond he and she shared.

But her yearning did not let up. *I can't allow myself to think of him in this way. I simply cannot.* Besides, that kind of love doesn't last, she reasoned, thinking of Chiara, and her parents. No, the lesson and mystery of her bond with him lay elsewhere. Not in the realm of romantic love, but in the realm of friendship. After all, true friendship is harder to come by than romance, and in the end it is far more precious. She resolved to keep reminding herself of this.

ANTONIO WAS IN AGONY. He couldn't sleep. There was a tension in his chest, and his lungs would not let him take in enough air. In the black gloom of predawn he rose from bed and tried to pray as he paced his bedroom. But the thoughts that churned in his mind were as torrid as his tightening chest. He raked his hand through his hair as he was reminded of his self-imposed admonition of eight years before. Her seductive performance of Alcina had triggered his first stirrings of desire for her, which he'd quickly dismissed, pledging inwardly to be her friend, and protector of her young innocence. But the sweet intensity of that young innocence—the irresistible youthful energy that had been his inspiration for so long—had slowly given way to a womanly allure he felt helpless to resist. *God help me.*

He clasped his hands and raised his eyes to the dark ceiling. *Are my feelings for her a sin?* After all, nothing had actually happened. He'd always been a friend to her, and her to him. And true friendship is a rare treasure, a special kind of love. His tacit desire had grown out of his love for her, a love that was pure and chaste. What sin was there in that? He clasped his hands all the more forcefully and squeezed his eyes shut as the uncompromising words of Christ flooded his mind: *Whosoever looketh on a woman to lust after her hath committed adultery with her already in his heart.*

And then he was struck by such a pang of loneliness and longing that he thought he would weep. *Blessed Savior*, he gasped as an explosion of pain clenched his chest. *Release me from the chains of the devil!*

THE STREETS OF VENICE were crammed with people, and Annina struggled to inch her way through. After a sleepless night she'd felt so overcome by shame she had hurried to Antonio's house as soon as she'd bathed and dressed. She wanted to apologize for her inexcusable indiscretion the night before. He wasn't home, and in her panic she decided to venture alone across town toward the Piazza San Marco. Perhaps he was there watching the Ascension Day festivities.

She neared the piazza and blaring music filled her ears as the crowd grew thicker and more boisterous. In the distance, along the Canale di San Marco, streams of colorful tapestries and silken banners, festooned with seemingly endless garlands of flowers, hung as far as the eye could see. The crowds and music, along with all the pomp and glitter associated with this most festive of holidays, centered around *il Palazzo Ducale*, the palace of the Doge, the supreme authority of the Venetian Republic. She caught sight of the red velvet canopy of the glimmering *bucintoro*, the great ducal barge, as it lay in wait at the quay of the Doge's Palace. Countless boats of all sizes crowded the Canale di San Marco, waiting to escort the ceremonial barge to the Lido. There the Doge would perform the centuries old Ascension Day ritual of casting a wedding ring into the Adriatic, symbolizing Venice's metaphorical "marriage to the sea."

As she made her way across the piazza the music and din of the crowd, coupled with the cacophony of bells that continually extolled the rhythms of Venice's daily life, made her dizzy. Frantically she looked about for Antonio, but he was nowhere in sight. Desperate to escape the crush of the crowd, she worked her way east along the Riva degli Schiavoni. After a short distance she found herself in front of the Chiesa della Pietà, its graceful white façade beckoning her into the tranquility and solitude she knew she'd find within. Carefully she opened the heavy wooden door and stepped into the church's inviting coolness. It took her eyes a moment to adjust to the darkness. And then she saw him, on his knees before the Virgin, his lips moving in silent supplication. Her heart paused a beat as she stifled a gasp. He was so engrossed in prayer he hadn't heard her come in. She watched him for a bit, her eyes moist with tears, longing to go to him. But she couldn't intrude on such a sacred moment. Slowly she backed toward the door and quietly exited.

Chapter Twenty-one

Antonio was being secretive again. Annina could tell by the look on his face every time he received a letter from Albizzi that their continued negotiations were thorny. But he wouldn't share with her any of the reasons why. She knew, though. It was that impudent wench Maddalena Pieri. She was indeed Albizzi's mistress. She'd bragged about it at the *Bajazet* rehearsals. And she'd been in a fury of jealousy ever since Albizzi had asked for Annina as prima donna for Florence's 1736 Carnival season. She knew in her heart Maddalena was giving Albizzi a hard time about it, and therefore he was giving Antonio a hard time. She suspected Maddalena was spreading all kinds of evil rumors about her, and Antonio didn't want to tell her about it. He kept silent about the problems and assured her he was "taking care of it."

When they arrived in Florence, she and Antonio were given rooms next door to the theater, in one of the centuries-old buildings that flanked the narrow Via della Pergola, in the center of town. The accommodations were comfortable enough, but thanks to Maddalena, the atmosphere in the theater was as bleak as the piercing January air.

She never saw Maddalena during their stay. But according to

whispers she heard among the other singers, she'd been carping on about her before her arrival, bashing everything from her voice to her morals. Just as she'd suspected. *The shameless witch!* Maddalena had publicly refused to accept anything less than a leading role. When Albizzi told her Antonio was composing and directing the operas at the Pergola that season, and therefore Annina would be the leading lady, she threw a colossal tantrum in front of everyone, and Albizzi had sent her home to sulk and fume. *Good for him.* So now she was too mortified to show her face at the Pergola.

As for Albizzi, he was old as the hills and crotchety besides. It amused her to think of him having to put up with Maddalena's saucy henpecking day and night. She wondered what on earth she saw in him. She started to realize this was what most female opera singers had to do to survive in the cutthroat world of theater— prostitute themselves to a wealthy patron or influential impresario. The thought made her shudder, and she reminded herself how fortunate she was to be under Antonio's protection.

But Albizzi's growing surliness was not helping Antonio's mood. One evening after a particularly trying rehearsal, during which it had been clear to her that Albizzi's churlish interference had brought Antonio to the limits of his patience, he stormed outside in a fury. She hurried after him into the frigid evening air and down the narrow Via della Pergola.

"Antonio, why do you do this to yourself?" she said breathlessly as she caught up with him and grasped his arm.

He kept up his brisk step. "Why do I do what to myself?"

"You're a kind and decent person, yet you constantly put yourself in company with lowlifes and talebearers."

"How do you mean?"

"Albizzi is a sullen oaf, and his girlfriend is a shrew who's been spreading vicious lies about me."

He sighed and slowed his furious pace. "Such people go with the territory of the opera business. I have a passion for drama expressed through music, just as you do. That's all that matters to me where the theater's concerned."

"But sometimes I wonder if it's worth the headaches—the scandalous gossip we're forced to endure, from people who themselves are no better than pimps and harlots and shameless traitors."

He stopped and put his hand over hers, and his voice became gentler. "Christ didn't shun sinners. Not that I'm comparing myself to Our Blessed Lord. I'm certainly no saint. But he and his Holy Mother have helped me resist Satan's damnable enticements on more occasions than I can count. They've taught me that to do any good in this world one must face evil and transcend it, not hide from it."

She thought of him at the Chiesa della Pietà last Ascension Day, how he'd humbled himself before the Virgin in ardent prayer. Prayer strengthened him, was his armor against the trials he constantly had to face. She wished she had his depth of faith.

AFTER THEIR STAY in Florence, she was anxious to get back to Venice. On their return, they were saddened to find that Giovanni had taken ill. According to Antonio, he'd never been sick a day in his life. She wasn't able to see much of him, but Antonio spent almost every waking moment at his father's bedside. On the morning of May 14 she got word that Giovanni had passed away. Fortunato delivered her and Paolina to the house on the Riva del Carbon, where Giovanni had been residing with his son. Antonio looked teary-eyed and vulnerable, his grief so weighty, too stubborn even to allow the tears to fall. Her heart melted when she saw him, and she rushed to put her arms around him.

He hugged her in a clinging way. "He was my best friend."

"I know," she said, sniffing back her sadness.

Poor Margarita and Zanetta sobbed helplessly, and Paolina spoke soothing words to them. The rest of the family had been sent for, and Antonio immediately set to work arranging the funeral.

Giovanni's death, following so quickly and unexpectedly the unpleasantness in Florence, left Antonio uncharacteristically dispirited. And she found herself plagued by guilt. It seemed that ever since her "transgression" the night of the *Griselda* premier things had gone steadily wrong. She blamed herself for his creative slump, which went on for month after month.

Then on a crisp November morning he stopped by her apartment unexpectedly, his face aglow with its old, familiar sparkle. "I've just come from a meeting with Abbé Bollani, the impresario of the Ferrara Opera. My Ferrarese patron, Marchese Bentivoglio, sent him to discuss negotiations for putting together a series of operas there for this coming Carnival season."

Her heart leapt for joy. "Oh Antonio, how wonderful."

"There's a problem, though. I'm tied up with a project that's just come up at the San Cassiano Theater. Perhaps you could go ahead of me, to oversee preparations for the productions."

She hesitated. "Of course, I'll do whatever will be most helpful."

His smile was infectious. "This is a golden opportunity for us. We're going to put together a company the like of which has never been seen on the stage at Ferrara. Singers, dancers, musicians, set designers and lighting specialists—it all has to be arranged." He pulled her to him and held her in a firm embrace. "You and I will make this happen, Annina. I couldn't do it without you."

"I don't know what to say—"

He stepped back and gave her an encouraging smile. "And you don't need to worry about being in Ferrara alone. Bentivoglio has graciously agreed to take you under his protection until I arrive. If you have any difficulties at all he'll be there to help you."

"When would you like me to go?"

"Next month." He grinned, almost sheepishly this time. "And I almost forgot to tell you. Your friend Cicciottello has invited us back to Verona next spring. He's anxious for a repeat of the sensation you made there last year."

"What? When did you hear from him?" Her mind was a whirlwind.

"Last week."

"Why didn't you tell me—oh never mind. This is all so overwhelming."

"It's all so fantastic! We're back in business."

"Yes, but . . . How will I have time—"

"I'll need you back here by March at the latest, so we can begin work on the Verona project."

"March?" Her stomach was churning. "That's nearly four months, such a long time to be away."

"With everything we have to do the time will fly."

She sighed. "I hope so."

"Why don't you ask Paolina to go with you? Then at least you'll be in familiar company."

"I don't think she can. My father hasn't been well, and she left for Mantua yesterday to help with his care."

"I'm sorry to hear that. I'll pray for him."

"Thank you, Antonio."

She felt guilty not going to Mantua with Paolina. But her life had become so entwined with Antonio's, and so dense with commitments, she felt she had no choice. Her father needed her, but Antonio needed her more.

THINGS DID NOT go as well in Ferrara as they'd hoped. The Abbé Bollani was condescending to her, and dismissive of her efforts to carry out Antonio's instructions in the production planning. The marchese sympathized, but offered little practical help in dealing with the impresario. She felt useless, and poured out her frustrations in a letter to Antonio. His response was prompt:

From what I hear, Bollani has shown himself to be a complete incompetent. He keeps changing his mind about the operas to be performed, continually pestering me with demands that I send him new manuscripts. And I understand that his idiot assistant Lanzetti has taken it upon himself to make changes to L'Olimpiade, ruining the manuscript in the process. That was my original score, and I sent it reluctantly with specific instructions that copies could be made, but only under your supervision, Annina. The original was not to leave your hands. And now the fool has changed his mind and decided he doesn't want L'Olimpiade after all! As if that weren't enough, Bollani spends money like a drunken sailor, jeopardizing the solvency of the entire enterprise. I can see there's no point in your staying in Ferrara any longer. Nothing is going to be accomplished until I can get there next fall and try to clean up this mess.

Although he didn't blame her directly for the continuing problems in Ferrara, the letter's angry tone showed his disappointment in her. He'd entrusted her with his two most valuable possessions—his manuscripts and his money. *And I've failed him on both counts*, she thought miserably. On the journey back to Venice, all she could think was how she dreaded facing him. Not that she feared him. Far from it. She just couldn't bear to disappoint him after everything he'd done for her.

He was waiting for her at the dock of San Angelo, and greeted her with a warm embrace. "I didn't realize how much I'd miss you," he said.

"I missed you too." She glanced at him as the gondolier lifted her luggage onto the dock. She saw no anger in his eyes. Only joy at her return.

He took her elbow as they walked to her apartment building. Once inside, she sank into a chair.

"How are you feeling?" he asked.

"Exhausted."

"I can imagine." He remained standing, looking at her with concern.

She looked up at him. "I'm so sorry I made such a mess of things."

"You did no such thing. I blame myself for too readily putting my faith in that blockhead Bollani."

She sighed heavily. "I tried to talk to him, Antonio, to reason with him. I really did. But he wouldn't listen to me. He apparently thinks women have no brains."

"He's the one without a brain. Don't worry, we still have almost a year to plan this. I'm going to see to it that Bollani's fired from the project, so we won't have to worry about him doing any more damage. Once I can get to Ferrara in the fall everything will be straightened out." He smiled at her reassuringly. "It'll all be fine, no need to fret about this."

She smiled back at him, breathing a gentle sigh of relief.

"I'll leave you to get some rest," he said. "Will you join me for supper later? I was thinking of going to our favorite tavern on the Grand Canal."

"Yes, I'd like that."

"All right, then, I'll be back for you around seven."

She followed him to the foyer. "Most of these are yours," she said, nodding toward the pile of boxes the gondolier had just carried up. "I managed to salvage all your manuscripts. I thought you'd want them back."

The glow in his eyes showed his appreciation. "I certainly didn't expect you to do that, Annina. Thank you. This will save me a lot of headaches."

"I'm sorry about *L'Olimpiade*. I hope the manuscript's not beyond repair."

"Whatever that simpleton Lanzetti did to it, I'm sure Pietro and I can fix." He came over and kissed her forehead. "Thank you again for this. I'll send someone to pick these up tomorrow."

OVER THE NEXT few months they were swept up in a flurry of activity. After the completion of the Verona project in May, Annina was anxious to go home to Mantua to spend the summer with her family. She especially longed to see her father, whose health had not improved. But the Ferrara enterprise weighed heavily on her mind, and she didn't feel she could leave Antonio alone to deal with the plans and arrangements. She also knew how terribly she'd miss him if she was away from him for so long. Their separation during her two months in Ferrara had been bad enough. He needed her, and she him.

ON SUNDAY MORNING, September 22, she was home alone, enjoying a few moments of solitude before going to Mass. Paolina was still in Mantua, and Graziana was visiting her mother in Padua, along with Fortunato. A brisk rapping at her door sent her rushing to answer. It was Antonio. He looked sad and worried. Her heart felt heavy.

"What is it?" she asked, as he stepped inside.

"Perhaps we should go to the parlor and sit down."

"I don't want to sit. Tell me what this is about."

His eyes glistened. "Your father has died."

Something terrifying tore open inside her, and she collapsed into his arms, sobbing. With his arm around her, supporting her, he led her to the sofa in the parlor. Her lip trembled and her teeth chattered. "How—how did you find out?" she asked, her voice pinched and shaking.

He spoke gently. "I just got word from Paolina. She didn't want you to be alone when you heard."

Fresh tears flooded her eyes, and Antonio held her for a long time as she wept and sighed.

"I should've gone to him," she said finally, between sobs. "But I let other things get in the way. I took for granted that he'd always be there."

"None of us knows how long we or our loved ones will be on this earth," he said soothingly. "You've been doing what you had to do. It was God's will."

"I have no one now," she said, choking. "Except Paolina—and you."

"You have your mother."

"She doesn't love me. She never has."

He held her closer and sighed. "God knows, sharing the same blood is no guarantee of love."

She crumpled against his chest and wept helplessly.

She learned something that day. She loved Antonio more than anyone else in the world, and she could endure losing anyone except him. It didn't matter anymore that there were limits to their relationship. She savored her time with him, talking to him, and making music with him. He'd always been so good to her, making her feel safe and valued. He was the only person on earth she could not do without.

AFTER A WEEKLONG trip to Mantua for her father's funeral, she was back in Venice. It was only six weeks before she and Antonio would leave for Ferrara, and she buried her grief in the bustle of preparations. At last the day arrived. It was mid-morning, and she was still in her dressing gown, just having bathed, busily packing her trunk. She was startled by a rapid knocking, and she rushed to the front door.

"Antonio—"

He looked like he was about to explode with rage. His eyes were blazing and his mouth was set in a hard frown.

Fear gripped her heart. "What's happened?"

He stepped in the door and proceeded into the parlor. She followed him, tense with worry. He turned and fixed his gaze on her. "We're not going to Ferrara."

She stared back at him, blinking. "What? Why not? Will you please tell me what on earth is going on?"

"I've just come from a meeting with the papal legate. I received a summons from him early this morning. He's ordered me in the name of His Eminence Cardinal Ruffo not to come to Ferrara to produce the operas."

"I don't understand. Who is Cardinal Ruffo?"

"The archbishop of Ferrara."

"Why would he forbid you to go there?"

"Because I'm a priest, and I don't say Mass."

"But that's no reason. Everyone knows why you don't say Mass.

You'll just have to write to him and explain about your illness."

"I'll try," he said, sighing. "I have to do something. Do you realize I'm burdened with six thousand ducats in contracts for this enterprise, and I've already paid out more than a hundred zecchini? I simply cannot entrust such a large sum of money to other hands. If the season's a failure, it could mean my financial ruin."

"I'm sure this can be resolved. And in the meantime there's no reason why I can't go ahead of you to Ferrara and try to get preparations underway for the final rehearsals."

"I'm afraid that won't be possible."

"Why not?"

"Ruffo won't allow you to come to Ferrara either."

"What?" She stared at him, incredulous.

He looked at her uncomfortably for a moment, then sighed and looked away. "It's—absurd. And it doesn't matter. This is really about me, not you, Annina. Ruffo simply disapproves of priests being involved in the theater."

She folded her arms and continued to stare at him. "If a Cardinal of the Catholic Church has forbidden me to go to Ferrara, I think I have a right to know why."

He put his hands in his pockets and his mouth twitched. "Cardinal Ruffo claims that you and I live together—and that you're my mistress."

Her mouth fell open. It was one thing for the neighborhood gossips to make such an accusation—*but a Cardinal of the Church?* She had never felt so much humiliation and shame. She glared at Antonio. "Do you realize what this means? It means that—that high-ranking Church authorities are talking about me as if I were the very worst kind of harlot. A seducer of a Catholic priest! It's probably all over Ferrara and who knows where else by now." Tears of rage sprang to her eyes, and she collapsed into a chair.

He took a seat across from her, and his jaw tightened. "You know who we have to thank for this, don't you? The stupid, meddling gossips who can't mind their own business, much less keep their vicious tongues from wagging. They apparently have no lives of their own, so they must dream up fantasies about ours." He leaned back in his chair and sighed heavily. "Annina, I can't tell you how sorry I am that these evil rumors have traveled so far. Of all the problems Ruffo's decree has caused, what grieves me the most is the stain he's put on your honor. I promise I'll find a way to set him straight."

She wrapped her arms around herself and met his gaze. "What are you going to do, Antonio? He's a Cardinal, for God's sake. Are you going to take on the whole Catholic Church? And what will it matter even if you *do* set him straight? How is that going to undo the damage that's already been done?"

He didn't answer.

She looked down, sighed, and raised her eyes to his again. "I can't understand how such a lie could have spread so far."

"You underestimate the Venetian gossip mill, Annina. They possess slander capabilities unknown in any other place or time. Yes, the citizens of this fine Christian republic have cultivated the vice of defamation to a fine art."

She eyed him angrily. "And you told me years ago to ignore the gossip, to let tongues wag. That idle talk couldn't harm us."

He frowned at her a moment, then rose to leave. "I'll go home and write to Bentivoglio. Maybe he can talk some sense into this Ruffo."

She reached her hand out to him as he passed her chair. He took it, and she looked up at him. "Forgive me, Antonio. I didn't mean to take out my anger on you."

He squeezed her hand, but his smile was bitter. "I know."

"It's just that I'm so distressed about this whole situation."

He nodded. "So am I." He pressed her hand again, then released it. "I'll see you later."

She smiled, sadly. "See you later."

She couldn't shake the idea that this whole dreadful situation was her fault. Others had tried to warn her about how her relationship with Antonio was perceived. And she'd courted disaster herself when she instigated that fateful moment of passion two years before. If only she'd been more discreet and kept her guilty longings to herself. She was as bad as Chiara. Worse, because she'd brought him to the brink of financial disaster, and disgrace. She'd even compromised his position in the Church.

His letters were to no avail. Bentivoglio was unable to persuade Cardinal Ruffo to budge from his position, or to cancel the opera season in Ferrara. A new impresario and prima donna were to be brought in.

Antonio was livid. "I wrote the lead roles of those operas for *you*, Annina. There simply isn't another singer who can do them justice. And from what I've heard, the new impresario they've engaged has little if any experience and no idea what he's doing. What Ruffo has done is unconscionable. This is a nightmare!"

She tried her best to soothe him. "I know, I know. It's outrageous. But if you keep on like this you're going to make yourself ill. All we can do is pray, and hope for the best." Truthfully, she was as worried as he was—not so much for the Ferrara enterprise, but for him.

He sighed. "At least my brother-in-law Mauro will be there and can keep me abreast of what's going on."

"Signor Mauro is involved in the project? I didn't think you trusted his management practices."

"He won't be managing anything except the set designs, which I have no doubt he'll do exceptionally well."

It occurred to her that in Antonio's absence Mauro might try to step outside his bounds. But she held her tongue. She didn't want to add more worries to his already agitated mind.

A FEW WEEKS LATER, as she was finishing getting dressed, there was again a frantic knocking at the front door. It was Zanetta, looking wide-eyed and frightened.

She tensed with alarm. "What's wrong?"

"Annina, you must come with me at once. It's Antonio. He just received word from Mauro about the opera production in Ferrara. Apparently it was a disaster, and now he's fit to be tied."

"Dear God."

"In the state he's in, I'm terrified he'll do serious harm to his health. Won't you please come talk to him? If anyone can calm him, you can."

"Of course, I'll come right now."

When they arrived at Antonio's house a few minutes later he was storming about, holding a letter in one hand and gesturing wildly with the other hand. Margarita was pleading with him. "Antonio, *please*. You must calm yourself before you have one of your spells."

"How can I be calm after what they've done to my opera? Those idiots have completely massacred my work!" In despair, he pressed the palm of his free hand to his forehead.

Annina rushed over to him. "Tell me what's happened."

"This is not to be believed. Just look at this." He handed her the letter and waited agitatedly while she studied it carefully. She sighed, frowned, and shook her head as she read the dreadful report:

. . . the orchestra members sounded as if they were drugged with opium. The singers emitted little more than squawks, squeals, and screams on the high notes. As for tempo, the fast arias moved at about the speed of a crippled snail, and the slow ones didn't move at all . . .

"Oh, Antonio, this is incredible. It's inexcusable."

"Have you ever heard of such incompetence? And not only that, the church organist they hired to play the harpsichord is so inept he took the liberty of changing all my recitatives at the last minute, because they were too difficult for him to play. Can you even imagine it, Annina? The gall, the idiocy! That moron destroyed my opera."

It was painful to see him this way. She struggled to think how she could help him. "You're absolutely right, Antonio. This is so unfair and simply wrong."

He looked at her sadly, his rage spent. She put her arms around him, and he held her tightly. "My reputation is ruined."

"Nonsense. I must disagree with you." She took his hand and drew him to the sofa. "Ferrara is miles away and only one town out of many where your music has flourished," she said gently, holding his hand. "What's happened there with your opera is horrible. But it's not the end of the world. How many times have you told me yourself that life is full of disappointments? But we always bounce back, don't we? And we will again."

He sighed deeply and almost smiled. "I hope you're right, my dear."

"Of course I am. We simply have to put this behind us and move on."

"Yes, I suppose we must accept that this is God's will." He seemed a bit more resigned, but she was still worried about him.

Over the following weeks she watched sadly as he sank into

another creative slump. Nothing she said or did helped. He seemed resigned to the Ferrara disaster, and he was spending a great deal of time in prayer. But he wasn't composing. Then in mid May her worries about him escalated to near panic when he disappeared for the better part of a week.

ANTONIO PACED ANXIOUSLY the vast *atrio* at the offices of the Archdiocese of Ferrara, his black clerical hat under his arm, the hem of his cassock whipping around his ankles. He'd requested an audience with the archbishop and had been kept waiting for hours.

He'd left Venice quite suddenly, telling no one. This was something he had to do, and he had no intention of giving anyone the chance to dissuade him. The only person he'd contacted was Bentivoglio, who warmly welcomed him into his home.

A young priest stepped into the *atrio*. "The archbishop will see you now."

Cardinal Ruffo sat behind a sprawling desk, his blue-veined hands clasped in front of him. The scarlet piping and buttons on his black cassock shown brightly in the afternoon light, as did the scarlet zucchetto that crowned his thick white hair.

Antonio paused just inside the door and bowed. "Your Eminence."

"At last we meet, Reverend Vivaldi. But let us not waste each other's time. If you think a personal appeal is going to change my mind about your opera ventures here, you're sadly mistaken."

"That's not why I'm here."

Ruffo narrowed his eyes. "I see. Please, have a seat." He gestured toward a chair on the other side of his desk.

"*Grazie*, Your Eminence."

"I suppose then you're here to bemoan the financial setback my decree no doubt caused you."

"Money can be recovered, but one's reputation is not so salvageable."

"So your reputation is what concerns you. Perhaps you should have thought of that before going into the theater business."

The corners of his mouth tightened. "I wasn't speaking of myself, but of someone else whose name has been wrongfully smeared."

Ruffo sighed and leaned back in his chair, his folded hands resting on his rounded belly. "Who is it you speak of then?"

"I'm talking about Signorina Anna Maddalena Tessieri, known as Annina Girò."

He smiled wryly. "Ah, your singer friend. What exactly are you asking me to do for her?"

"I ask that you retract the unfounded accusations you made against her."

He raised his eyebrows. "Unfounded?"

"With all due respect, Your Eminence, your presumptions were based on idle gossip. I've known Signorina Annina since she was a young child, when I was court composer at Mantua. After that she came to study with me in Venice, when she was only twelve. That was sixteen years ago, and I can tell you with certainty she is a chaste, honorable young woman, completely devoted to her art. I will not have her name tarnished."

The archbishop's smile faded, and he looked at Antonio thoughtfully. "Your ardor is impressive, Reverend Vivaldi. But I'm not convinced."

"If my word isn't enough for you, there are many others who know her well who would attest to her good character."

"But the rumors . . ."

"Were rumors, and nothing more," he said firmly.

Ruffo tapped a finger against his lip. "She lives with you, though."

"She does not and never has. I lived with my family until a few years ago, and now I live alone. Signorina Annina lives with her sister, several blocks away. If you need proof, I can send copies of the property censuses."

He leaned forward, adjusting the skirts of his cassock, the chain of his large pectoral cross clinking the edge of his desk. Clasping his hands again, he closed his eyes, as if in prayer.

Antonio waited impatiently for him to say something.

Ruffo slowly raised his eyelids. "This girl means a great deal to you, doesn't she?"

The poignancy of the question startled him. He cleared his throat. "She does."

"I see. She is like a daughter to you, then."

He paused, then nodded slowly. "In a manner of speaking."

The archbishop's eyes grew sad. "Perhaps I was too rash in my judgment. I'll admit it's one of my worst faults." He wrinkled his brow. "Unfortunately I can't retract my decree. What's done is done. But I'll tell you what I will do." He reached for a sheet of stationary and dipped a pen in the inkpot. "I'll write a personal letter of apology to your young friend, along with a promise that if she ever needs an advocate in the Church, she can count on me."

"Thank you, Your Eminence." He waited, listening to the quick scrawl of the archbishop's pen.

He closed the letter with his official seal and handed it to Antonio, smiling regretfully. "You may be gratified to know, Reverend Vivaldi, that I've resigned my position here at Ferrara and will return to Rome next month."

He stared at him in surprise. "This seems rather sudden."

"It is, I decided quite recently. But as you well know I tend to make rash decisions. In any case, I feel it's for the best. My work is done here."

Antonio rose and bowed. "Godspeed, Your Eminence."

THE DAY AFTER he returned to Venice, he paid a visit to Annina.

"Antonio, where in the name of heaven have you been? I've been worried to death about you," she said, as soon as she'd answered his knock at her door.

He stepped into the hall. "I went to Ferrara, to meet with Cardinal Ruffo."

Her mouth fell open. "You didn't."

"I did indeed, and I have something for you." He pulled the letter from his breast pocket and handed it to her.

She stared down at it. "What's this?"

"A letter for you, from Ruffo."

She looked back up at him warily. "Should I open it?"

He smiled. "By all means. I'll leave if you wish."

"No, I want you to stay." With nervous fingers she broke the seal and read the letter aloud:

My Dear Signorina Tessieri,

Your friend Reverend Vivaldi has caused me to see the error of my ways, and rightly so. I offer you my sincerest apology for the unjust accusations I made against you, and I pray you will find it in your heart to forgive me. If you ever find yourself in need of a recommendation, I would consider it an honor to assist you in any way I can.

Yours Sincerely,

Cardinal Ruffo

She raised her astonished eyes to his. "You did it, didn't you? You took on the Church—for me—" She pressed the back of her hand to her mouth to stifle a sob.

He pulled her into a hug. "I told you I'd set him straight, didn't I?"

She nodded against his shoulder, spurts of nervous laughter mingling with her sniffles.

He kissed her forehead. "I have to go. An opera company in Bergamo wants to do *Orlando furioso*, and I need to track down Pietro to help me prepare a copy to send them."

"Be sure to let your sisters know you're back," she said as he was leaving. "They've been frantic with worry about you too."

"I will. And don't lose that," he said, pointing to the letter she still held in her hand. "You never know when Ruffo's offer might prove beneficial."

She smiled and waved the letter at him as he headed for the stairs.

Chapter Twenty-two

It was early March, and the fog rose thick off the Grand Canal. The short gondola ride to Antonio's house on the Riva del Carbon seemed longer than usual. Annina clenched her cloak about her with one gloved hand while clutching her portfolio of scores with the other. He'd asked for her arias from *Siroe rè di Persia*, one of the operas he had originally planned to produce in Ferrara. Now a company in Ancona had ordered the opera, and he was pressed to get all the parts to the copiers.

"The *reverendo* is in his studio, miss," his housekeeper said when she arrived. "Allow me to take your cloak."

She rapped on his studio door, then stepped inside to find him slumped over his desk, his head in his hands. She hurried to him and placed her hand on his shoulder.

"Antonio, are you all right? Are you ill?"

He raised his head slowly and looked at her with bleary eyes, his face a mask of exhaustion. "Mauro has defrauded the entire Ferrara enterprise."

Her jaw dropped, and she stepped back. "*What?*"

"He's absconded with 300 *scudi*. This means the singers,

musicians and dancers will not be paid. And my investment is lost."

She stared at him, incredulous. "How did he get his hands on all that money?"

"He convinced the witless impresario that I'd authorized him to collect the money from ticket sales, and to manage the finances. This is what he's begged me to allow him to do for years, what I knew could never end well."

"But he's your sister's husband," she said as she placed the scores on his desk and pulled off her gloves. "You know where to find him. Isn't there some way to make him give back the money?"

"He's already spent the money. I should have known when I saw the new staircase go into their house, the expensive furniture, Cecilia's new jewelry . . ."

"Oh Antonio, what are you going to do?"

"Swear out a warrant, I suppose, but I don't know what can be proved. He's been too clever about filtering the money through his own accounts."

"And you only just found out about this?"

"The writing was on the wall, as they say, but I didn't want to see it. But a series of reports from others involved in the enterprise has left no doubt."

"This is unbelievable."

"And to think of all the thousands of ducats I paid him during the years he was in my service in the theater, how I gave him work out of compassion when he was in financial straits, took his son as an apprentice—" He broke into a rasping cough.

She rushed to the credenza to pour him a glass of wine. "You don't think Cecilia and the boys knew anything about this, do you?" she said, as she handed him the wine.

He took a long draft. "Cecilia may be greedy, but she's no

thief." He paused to take a labored breath. "And Pietro is the most honest young man I've ever known. No, this is all Mauro and his shifty mind. I just never thought he'd stoop so low."

ANTONIO'S LAWSUIT CAME to nothing, and the Ferrara contracts remained unpaid. She'd never seen him in such an extended state of melancholia and felt desperate to help him. She simply had to find a way to get him out of it. Then, while browsing through a bookshop, she came upon a libretto, and a wonderful plan began to form in her head.

"*Salve*, Antonio," she said, smiling cheerfully as she stepped into his parlor that afternoon.

"Hello, dear," he said, removing his reading glasses and looking up from his breviary with a half-hearted smile.

"You must see this."

"What is it?"

"A libretto I just came across." She handed it to him.

He put his glasses back on and squinted at the title page. "*Rosmira fedele*? What's it about?"

"It's about a young woman, Rosmira, whose fiancé, Arsace, has abandoned her to court an eligible queen. So Rosmira disguises herself as a shipwrecked Albanian prince and seeks shelter at the queen's palace to try to win him back. Why don't you read it?"

"Now?"

"Yes, now. I'll wait." She sat in a nearby chair.

He sighed. "Very well." Frowning, he opened the little booklet and began to read. After a few moments he looked up at her. "I suppose you're envisioning yourself in the role of Rosmira?"

"Of course. Go on, keep reading."

He continued perusing the play. Then, "I can see it would

require you to dress as a man."

"But I wouldn't *be* a man, I'd only be posing as one."

"Hmm." He was beginning to look doubtful.

She sighed with impatience. "Will you please finish? I think you'll like the story."

He furrowed his brow and continued reading. After a while he raised his eyebrows and looked up at her. "Are you trying to ensure that the censors will serve up my head on a platter?"

She grinned. "Whatever do you mean?"

He glanced down at the libretto again. The script requires Rosmira to appear bare-chested."

She burst into giggles. "No it doesn't. Not exactly. It only suggests that she *might* do that."

He gave her a wry look and returned his attention to the libretto. "It says very clearly that the queen, thinking Rosmira is a man, falls in love with her and then orders her to engage in a swordfight, bare-chested, with Arsace."

"And that's how Rosmira gets out of the swordfight, by revealing herself as a woman *before* she has to remove her shirt."

"Isn't that a bit anticlimactic?"

"Not the way I've envisioned the scene."

He put the booklet down. "I'm almost afraid to ask what you have in mind."

"Since Rosmira is impersonating a prince from the Near East, I'll be wearing some sort of turban, right? To hide my hair?"

"Most likely."

"At the moment I'm supposed to rip my top off, just before the swordfight, the audience will be on the edge of their seats wondering if I'm actually going to do it."

His eyes were fixed on hers. "Go on."

"But instead, I'll tear off my turban, my hair will come spilling out, and everyone will know I'm a woman. At that moment I'll burst into a brilliant vengeance aria, exposing Arsace for the two-timing traitor that he is."

His eyes brightened.

"Well?" she asked anxiously. "What do you think?"

"Annina," he said, as his face broke into a smile, "I think you're a genius."

She grinned with delight.

He jumped up with the libretto in hand and headed down the hall to his studio. She followed. He rushed to his desk, grabbed a pen and music paper, and started writing furiously. She watched as the staves on the paper filled with hundreds of notes. It was the happiest she'd seen him in a long time. He was composing again.

ON OPENING NIGHT, at the climactic scene near the end of the final act, the spectators were indeed on the edges of their seats, agape with anticipation. At the crucial moment she whisked off her turban with her left hand, while her right hand flourished a sword. Wearing nothing but knee breeches, boots, and a white shirt that gaped open at the neck, she shook out her hair as a furious ritornello announced her stirring rage aria:

> *I will revenge myself on the wicked traitor*
> *for my unjust and cruel suffering!*

The words gushed from her mouth like a biting wind, as the traitorous Arsace, hopping and cowering, tried to dodge the thrusts and sweeping swings of her sword. At the end of the aria the audience sprang to their feet, clapping vigorously amid hoots of laughter at the irony of the scene.

Later that night she and Antonio were making their way through the nearly empty *atrio*. He was eager to get some fresh air, but a small group of elderly aristocrats were waiting to talk to him.

"I'll wait for you at the door," she said, smiling sympathetically.

He raised his eyes heavenward, sighed, and nodded.

Gazing across the spacious lobby, she was astonished to see Count Landi, looking more mature and worldly than she remembered him. A shameful thrill coursed through her, which she struggled to suppress. He spotted her and smiled his boyish smile, waving as he hurried over to her.

"Signorina Girò, I've been waiting to congratulate you. What a stunning performance."

Before she could respond, an elegantly dressed lady, wearing a glittery half-mask, was at his side. She took his arm. He reached over and put his hand over hers. "My dear, may I present to you this evening's prima donna, La Signorina Anna Girò. Signorina Girò, this is my wife, the Countess Landi."

A little wave of disappointment, tinged by mild envy, swept through her.

The lady removed her mask and smiled mildly. "Lovely to meet you."

She smiled politely and bowed her head. "*Piacere*, My Lady."

The count gave her an avid look as his wife continued to hold his arm lightly. "I can't tell you how captivated I was by your bold performance," he said. "Such a welcome change from the foolishness one sees and hears these days on Venetian stages. You and your maestro have again enthralled Venice with your incomparable artistries." He looked at his wife. "Don't you agree, my dear?"

She smiled blandly. "Indeed."

Annina gazed for a moment into the young countess's pale,

placid face. She was pretty enough, perhaps even kind, but dull. A curious match for the vivacious young count. She smiled her thanks. "How kind of you. So nice to see you both," she said. "I must be going now."

Count Landi bowed, and his wife replaced her mask. "A delight, as always, Signorina Girò," he said, smiling his irresistible smile.

Her heart skipped a beat.

As she walked away from them she sighed. The handsome boy with his understated elegance and easy charm had grown up. She thought of the docile young countess. No doubt the perfect wife, not the type to question things. Is that how it must be when one finally grows up and marries? The thought of the tedium made her insides shudder dully. Yet how little about marriage she knew. Her parents were no example, certainly not one she'd want to emulate. No, she had everything she could want with Antonio—challenge, excitement, freedom. But that vague, persistent longing still plagued her. *So silly. The count means nothing to me. He's amusing at parties, or at least he used to be. But now that he's married* . . . Her thoughts trailed off as Antonio caught her eye and summoned her to join him.

ARMED WITH *ROSMIRA*, and two other new operas he managed to write with his customary speed, Antonio was able to regain control of the San Angelo theater during Carnival, and to pay off most of the Ferrara contracts. The season was a success, and things looked promising again. Nevertheless, a few months later he shocked her with astonishing news.

"I've made a decision."

"What's that?"

"I'm leaving Venice."

"What do you mean, you're leaving Venice? We just had a very successful season here. This could be the beginning of a big comeback."

He smiled gravely and shook his head. "No, we just had one last stroke of good luck. But my time is up here. I can't compete with this new wave of young composers, nor do I wish to. Everything has changed in Venice. The god of vice is celebrated here above all things. The finer things are no longer valued or appreciated. It's time for me to move on."

For a moment she was speechless. She stared at him, blinking. "Then . . . where will you go?"

"Vienna. My operas are still performed all over Austria, and I'm confident the emperor will secure a position for me."

She gazed at him uncertainly.

"Annina . . ." he said a bit hesitantly, with a half smile. "It's a lot to ask, but—would you consider coming with me?"

She didn't even have to think about her answer. She took a deep breath and smiled. "Of course I'll come with you."

He smiled too. Suddenly his face was lit with animation. "It'll be a chance to build a whole new opera company—a fresh start. We'll do it together."

She caught his enthusiasm and started to sizzle with excitement. "When will we go?"

"As soon as possible. I'll go to the customs office tomorrow and have the necessary papers drawn up."

The next morning there was an urgent knocking at her door. Could Antonio be done at the customs office already? He was probably anxious to plan their departure. She smiled happily to herself as she hurried to answer.

But it wasn't Antonio. She opened the door to find a young girl with disheveled red hair, frightened-looking blue eyes, and a tear-stained face. She stared at her in bewilderment.

"Nina?" the girl whimpered.

She gasped. "*Gigi!*" She pulled the trembling girl through the door and into her arms. "Gigi, what are you doing here? Where's your father?"

She sobbed into Annina's neck. "He's very angry with me. We had a big fight, and I ran away from him."

She drew the weeping girl to the sofa and grasped both her hands. "Tell me what happened."

Her story came out in spurts, amid chokes and sobs. "He's— trying—to—make me—get married!"

She took a deep breath and looked Gigi straight in the eye. "What do you mean? Who does he want you to marry?"

"A gross old man he met at a tavern. He brought him home, and the way the man looked at me made my skin crawl. Then he gave *Babbo* some money. They were both very drunk. Oh, Nina, the man has leering eyes, rotting teeth, and he smells bad. I'd die before I'd let him touch me."

She stared at her, incredulous. This was not to be believed, even of Iseppo. Could he possibly have sunk so low that he'd sell his own daughter? She kept these thoughts to herself. "Surely there was some misunderstanding."

"No there wasn't. After the man left, my father told me I was going to marry him. I said, 'No I won't! You can't make me marry that disgusting old coot!' Then he started shouting and said he'd put me in a convent if I didn't obey him." A fresh flood of tears came pouring out. "What am I going to do, Nina?"

She sighed and gently brushed the tears from Gigi's cheeks with her fingertips. "The first thing we're going to do is get you something to eat, then into a hot bath and clean clothes. After that, we'll talk more about this."

An hour later, fed, bathed, and clothed in Annina's cotton morning dress, Gigi curled up on the sofa beside her. A thousand questions had formed in Annina's mind, but she started with the simplest and most obvious. "How did you know where to find me, Gigi?"

She sniffed and drew in a shaky breath. "I went to Uncle Antonio's house first, because I know his address. But he wasn't home. His housekeeper told me where you live."

She nodded. "Oh, I see."

"Nina, can't I please, *please* stay here with you?"

"Of course you can. But I think you should discuss all this with your uncle before anything's decided."

Her eyes filled again. "But what if he makes me go back to my father?"

"He won't. Not after you tell him what you've just told me."

"But I *can't* tell him. It's too embarrassing."

"Then I'll tell him. He needs to know, Gigi. I promise this will all be worked out."

They walked the short distance to Antonio's house later that morning. He was even more shocked to see Gigi than she had been, and they had a joyful reunion. She'd persuaded Gigi to tell him herself what happened, and she tearfully repeated her story. He took her hand, and Annina saw his jaw tighten. He looked over at her, then back at Gigi. Finally, he said, "Where is your father now, Giovanna? Every letter I've received from him has come from a different place."

She sniffled. "We move around a lot, but most recently we've been staying near here, on the mainland. I'm not even sure what the town's called."

"How did you get here?"

"I sneaked a little money from my father's pouch, after he'd gone to sleep. Then I took an early morning boat into Venice. I know it was wrong to take money without asking, but I was so scared. I didn't know what else to do."

"It's all right," he said, smiling sypathetically. "You did the right thing. I'm just thankful you got here safely."

She smiled too, through her tears, and seemed to relax a bit. It was decided that Gigi would stay with Annina for the time being, and Antonio accompanied them back to her apartment. They had a light supper, then an exhausted Gigi fell asleep in Annina's bed.

She poured more wine for Antonio and herself. "How old is she now?" she asked him.

"Fifteen, I think."

She sighed and shook her head. "What are you going to do?"

"I suppose the first thing I should do is track down my fool brother and find out what in the name of God he was thinking."

She mused a moment. "I can't understand it. Why on earth would Iseppo sell his child into marriage—especially to such a dreadful creature as Gigi described?"

His lips tightened. "He must be mighty desperate."

"Financially, you mean?"

He nodded and downed a generous gulp of wine.

"How has he been supporting himself and Gigi?"

"He hasn't. I've been sending him a monthly stipend. That's the only reason he's made sure I always have his address." He sighed wearily. "I thought I was doing the right thing, arranging things so he and Giovanna could stay together. Obviously I was wrong."

"You mustn't blame yourself, Antonio. There's no way you or anyone could have imagined things would come to this."

He nodded again, then looked down, as if he were deep in thought. They sat in silence for a bit and sipped their wine.

Finally she said, "I have an idea."

He looked up.

"Why don't we take her with us to Austria?"

He gazed at her. "You must have been reading my mind."

She felt her face break into a smile.

IT HAD BEEN ten years since their last trip across the Alps, and Annina had no idea what to expect this time. Fortunately they were traveling in early autumn, so the weather was much more pleasant. Their first stop was Graz. A traveling opera troupe led by the Mingotti brothers, two former opera singers who'd sung in several of Antonio's early productions, had requested her for a revival of *Rosmira*. After that, she was asked to stay on for several more performances of Antonio's operas the troupe planned to do, and so she was engaged to remain with the Mingotti troupe until June. She was grateful for the work, and also for the change of scenery. Graz's balmy weather and tranquil majesty were a welcome respite from the musty dampness and constant bustle of Venice. The ideal environment for both Gigi and Antonio to restore their spirits.

Chapter Twenty-three

Antonio was restive. He was grateful the Mingottis had decided to stage two more of his operas, and that they'd engaged Annina as prima donna. But his lack of managerial control of the productions was frustrating. He felt superfluous, impatient to move on to Vienna and start laying the foundation for a new opera company. He had no doubt his royal friend and benefactor Charles VI would welcome his proposal. But if he left now, he and Annina would be apart for nearly six months. He didn't know if he could do without her for that long. She was the one person in his life who had always been there for him, and he'd grown to depend on her in so many ways. The truth was, he'd gone beyond wanting her, to needing her. It was selfish of him, really. As much as he hated to admit it, she was old enough to live her own life, and his dependence was holding her back. He knew he had to put some distance between them, at least for a while.

ANNINA WAS BOTH surprised and pleased when Antonio invited her to walk with him along the nearby Mur River. As they strolled, she noticed him studying her thoughtfully. She smiled with curiosity. "What are you thinking?"

He continued to gaze at her silently for a moment, then finally he said, "You've given up a lot for me."

This unexpected statement perplexed her and roused her curiosity. "What on earth are you talking about?"

"You're thirty years old. You should be married, with a family of your own."

"Must you remind me of my age?" she asked, feigning annoyance. He smiled, and she went on. "You know perfectly well I've never had marriage on my mind. All I've ever wanted was to sing in your operas. I even told you that when I was a little girl, during our very first conversation."

The corners of his eyes crinkled as his smile took on a warm glow. "Yes, you did."

"So there you have it. I have everything I've ever wanted."

His smile faded a bit, and he looked thoughtful again. "I worry what would become of you if anything happened to me. Who'd look out for you?"

Uneasiness began to stir in her, but she forced herself to put on an armor of confidence. "I'm a grown woman, Antonio. I don't need anyone to look out for me. Besides, nothing's going to happen to you."

"I'm not getting any younger, my dear. You need a husband to take care of you when I'm gone."

She didn't like the direction the conversation was taking, so she tried to make light of it. "Nonsense. Anyway, who'd want an old spinster like me?"

"A man would have to be blind not to want you, Annina. You're still as youthful and lovely as you ever were."

The old, familiar thrill gripped her. But she continued to be offhanded. "You've never been a very good liar, Antonio."

"I know. That's why I'm telling you the truth."

She sighed, and simpered. "You certainly know the quickest route to a woman's heart, don't you? But be serious. Who could I possibly marry? Who could ever measure up to you?" She raised her eyebrows and smiled brightly to mask the significance of what she'd just said.

His smile softened. "You must stop thinking that way."

She started to feel an uncomfortable tightness in her throat. "What do you mean?"

"I mean you have to stop putting me on a pedestal. I'm not going to be around forever. Someday you'll have to find your own path in life."

The tone of the discussion was becoming much too disturbing. She folded her arms and looked away, blinking back tears. He reached over and pulled her to him. She clutched his arm and leaned her head against his shoulder. "Why are you talking this way? Things are going so well now," she murmured softly.

He patted her hand gently. "I've decided to go on to Vienna."

She broke away and looked at him anxiously. "But . . . you can't. I have to be here until June."

"I know, but it'll be fine. You and Giovanna can join me there this summer."

She grasped his arm. "We need you here. Why can't you wait so we can all go together?"

"I'm useless here. The whole purpose of this venture was to launch a new company in Vienna. The sooner I can get things underway there the better off we'll be."

"I don't want you to go."

He put his hand over hers. "Annina," he said firmly, but not unkindly. "I've made my decision. I'm leaving for Vienna day after tomorrow."

ON THE DAY of his departure, after he'd said his goodbyes to Gigi, Annina walked with him to the waiting coach and made one last attempt to talk him out of making the trip.

"I still don't think this is a good idea, Antonio."

"You worry too much, my dear. I'll be fine."

"But you never travel alone. What if you get sick? Who'll be there to help you?"

"My health is fine. I've never felt better in my life. This crisp Austrian air must have curative powers."

She thought desperately. "Perhaps I should break my contract with the Mingottis and come with you."

"That wouldn't be wise. You know how unprofessional it is to walk out of performance commitments. Besides, while you're completing your contract I'll have time to meet with the emperor and begin negotiations for the autumn opera season."

She sighed and looked at the ground. "Very well, I suppose you're right."

"Now you're being sensible." She could hear the smile in his voice.

The coach had arrived, and the drivers were loading his baggage. She glanced up at him. "Will you write to me?"

"Of course."

She noticed his collar was awry. She flicked a tear from the corner of her eye and started fussing with it as she scolded, "You always say you're going to write, but you never do."

He was watching her, and his look was a combination of fondness and amusement. Then he gently clasped her wrist. "Annina, I promise I'll write."

Much to her chagrin, she felt a flood of tears well up. She locked her arms around his neck, and he held her very tightly. She felt his heartbeat, and his warmth enveloped her. For a single glorious moment she was at peace.

The horses stamped their hoofs, and the drivers grew impatient. "Sir," one of them said in clipped Italian, "we are ready to depart."

With his arm still around her, he turned to them. "One more moment, please."

She pressed her face against his shoulder. Her eyes were melting.

He kissed her forehead and handed her his handkerchief. "Goodbye, my Annina."

She sniffed and dabbed her eyes. "Goodbye."

From the coach window, he smiled down at her. "See you in Vienna!"

The coach pulled away from the curb, and smiling through her tears, she nodded and waved his handkerchief. A bittersweet pain rose and curled in her stomach as she watched the carriage make its way down the narrow cobblestone street and disappear around a corner.

A familiar voice, smooth and chilling, startled her from behind. "Such a tender scene, I think I shall cry."

She whirled around. And there she was, looking for all the world like a painted strumpet. True, she had aged, yet she would have known those eyes anywhere. They gleamed like emeralds, beautiful, yet cold. A shiver of aversion stung her like frost. "What in the name of God are you doing here, Chiara?"

"Why, I'm here to join the Mingotti troupe, of course."

"I don't believe it. Why didn't I know about this?"

"My, aren't we full of ourselves. If you must know, the Mingottis are old friends of mine. I helped them get this little troupe started several years ago. So you see, darling, I have quite a bit more clout with them than you do."

She felt suddenly ill. But she was determined not to let Chiara intimidate her. "I'm going to put a stop to this before you have a chance to stir up trouble."

She raised her eyebrows and batted her lashes. "And just how do you think you're going to do that, dear?"

"I'll make sure the Mingottis understand what kind of woman you really are."

She reclined her silvery blond head and laughed fiendishly. Then she returned her cold eyes to Annina's, and her smile hardened. She brought her face uncomfortably close, and her whisper was chilling. "There are two sides to every story. And I assure you, mine will be more convincing than yours."

The next day, Chiara approached her with a smug smile. "I see our dear Antonio has at last entrusted you with everything—even his pretty little niece. Perhaps that was unwise."

She felt herself go rigid as she glared at her. "If you do anything, *anything* to harm or frighten that girl, I'll make sure it's the last thing you ever do."

Chiara burst into her familiar laugh, only she noticed it had lost its old sparkle. Now it sounded more like a cackle. Then she snorted. "Spare me your empty bravado. Let me remind you that the coast is now clear. I can do anything I want, and there's nothing you can do about it."

The only thing she could think to do was keep Gigi with her at all times, to never let the girl out of her site. They slept together, ate together, even bathed and dressed together. Gigi was at her side during all her vocal and dramatic practice, often singing along and improvising her own dramatic gestures. At every rehearsal she was at the foot of the stage, watching and applauding. Gigi eagerly joined in her singing exercises, and she was astonished at what a beautiful voice the girl had. All the breathing and vocal techniques Antonio had so patiently and arduously taught her so many years ago seemed to come easily and naturally to his niece. For her, singing was effortless, and the energy and joy Annina heard in her voice warmed her heart.

She found herself thinking a lot about Antonio. She worried about him, with no close friends or family around him in Vienna. She wrote to him frequently, keeping him informed of all the Mingotti troupe's activity. For the time being she decided it would be better not to tell him Chiara had joined the troupe. There was no point giving him more bad news. The only letter she'd received from him was short and discouraging:

It grieves me to have to tell you that the emperor died quite suddenly, before I had a chance to meet with him, apparently from eating poisonous mushrooms. Nevertheless, I've arrived safely in Vienna and have taken a room at the house of a saddler's widow, Frau Waller. The address is Satlerisch Haus, on the Kärntnerstrassse. The house is across the street from the Kärntnertortheater, Vienna's most prestigious opera house. I'm trying to get an audience with the theater's leading patron, one Anton Urlich of Saxony-Meiningen, but without the emperor's endorsement that's proving to be difficult.

Things were not faring much better in Graz. As the winter dragged on, ticket sales dropped off considerably. Since the Mingottis were operating on such a small budget, the troupe members had agreed to wait until the end of the tour to be paid, settling in the meantime for room, board, and other living expenses. Antonio had invested the remainder of his profits from their last season at San Angelo in the Mingotti troupe, hoping it would yield enough revenue to launch the new company in Vienna. With the emperor's death, it was now more crucial than ever that this tour generate a profit. If not, the troupe would have to disband and everyone involved, including Antonio, would lose their investment.

Most recently she'd been able to send him exciting news. The Mingottis had persuaded her to stay on for one more performance. They were planning to perform his *Orlando furioso* that July and wanted her to sing Alcina. They thought the fact that she'd originated the role would be a draw for audiences. So she agreed to extend her contract for one more month.

Two weeks later she was thrilled to find another letter from Antonio waiting for her. As soon as she was settled in her room, she frantically tore it open.

Annina Carissima,

I'm so happy to hear that the Mingotti troupe will do Orlando in Graz! Nothing could please me more. Such a triumph there will help compensate for the disastrous injustices we had to endure in Ferrara. As for how things are going here in Vienna, despite some initial setbacks I have high hopes of putting together an opera company and launching productions in the fall. In fact, the owners of the Kärntertortheater are very interested in my Oracolo in Messenia, so things are looking quite encouraging. For now, I've taken on a few violin students at the choir school down the street. Not terribly rewarding, although one boy shows quite a bit of promise.

I trust you and Giovanna are planning to join me here by late July. As you well know, there are so many details to take care of which I can't begin to manage without your help. In the meantime I anxiously await word of the Orlando production. Alcina was one of your finest roles, and I know you'll sing it brilliantly.

Please let me know when you expect to arrive in Vienna, my Annina. I miss you.

Your Devoted Friend,
Antonio
15 June 1741

At once she felt such a violent longing that tears came to her eyes. How she missed him too. More than she ever would have imagined. And how anxious she was to be with him in Vienna, planning and rehearsing for a new opera season. The months since his departure had been stressful, thanks to Chiara, and she yearned for the comfort and easy familiarity of his presence. Now she was more determined than ever to make sure *Orlando* was a huge success. What better news to be able to give him on her arrival in Vienna. In his recent letter he sounded more optimistic than he'd seemed for months. How wonderful to be able to make him all the happier by ensuring that his *Orlando furioso* was a rousing triumph in Graz.

Later that afternoon she noticed Chiara whispering with some of the other singers. She was telling a story in a low voice, like a conspirator. The others were listening intently, clearly fascinated by what she was saying. They all looked Annina's way as she passed by, then covered their mouths and snickered.

For the love of God, will she ever learn to keep her wicked, meddlesome mouth shut? Does she have no other purpose in life than to destroy mine?

Smiling archly, Chiara broke away from the giggling little group and approached her. "So it seems your adored Antonio has thrown you over at last."

Her jaw tensed, and she lifted her chin. "You have no idea what you're talking about."

"Don't I? It doesn't take a genius to see that he's had his fill of you." She glanced back at the little crowd of singers. "Ask anyone here."

"I'm sure you've wasted no time feeding them so many lies they don't know what to believe."

"Well believe this. If he cared for you as much as you think, he wouldn't have left you alone here in Graz while he goes on to Vienna to cultivate new interests. The fact is he's tired of you. That's always what his liaisons with singers come to. He cares only about himself."

She felt the blood rise in her face. "I'm not going to stand here and listen to you—"

"Don't even bother defending him. You forget that my father is a nobleman. Yours was a common wigmaker."

"I really don't see—"

"Surely you've noted Antonio's fondness for friends in high places. Why do you think he rushed to Vienna without you? To hobnob with the emperor, of course, and you would have been a hindrance. He knows full well you're only a peasant with no knowledge of courtly decorum. I, on the other hand, being of noble birth, would be a priceless asset to him at the imperial court."

Her anger caused her last shred of dignity to collapse. "Yes, your father is a nobleman who won't even give you the time of day, because you're the bastard of a whore."

Chiara's nostrils flared and her eyes blazed with a fury Annina had never seen in her before. A vague fear pricked her insides, but she forced herself to shrug. "When will you give up, Chiara? Your empty threats sound like the rant of a crazed old woman. I used to despise you, but now I only pity you. You no longer have any power over me."

Her face hardened into a mask of smug hostility. "Oh no? Have you forgotten what happened in Ferrara?"

She stiffened and crossed her arms. "What does that have to do with anything?"

"It was the beginning of the end of your charmed relationship with your beloved maestro, was it not? Correct me if I'm wrong, dear."

Her jaw tightened painfully. "If there's a point to this, then please say it."

"Very well. Did you ever stop to wonder who brought your shameful manipulation of Antonio to Cardinal Ruffo's attention?"

"Surely not you."

A malicious smile crossed her lips. "None other, Annina dear. Of course, I was aided in my mission by an influential friend—your former benefactor."

"You can't mean the Duke of Massa Carrara was behind that whole scandalous fiasco."

"It wasn't difficult to persuade him. He hasn't forgotten how you made a fool of him, flaunting your intimacy with Antonio while spending the duke's money."

She wanted to kill her. Oh, how she wanted Chiara to suffer for the pain she'd caused. She was so filled with rage she could barely speak, but she managed to force a low, trembling voice. "Do you have any idea of the ramifications of your evil meddling, of your vicious lies? If your intent was to punish me, then you failed. Instead, you nearly destroyed Antonio. Severely damaged his reputation and left him with a mountain of debt. Worst of all, you've forced us apart at a time when he needs me the most."

"Then I haven't failed," she hissed, her face aglow with mocking triumph.

Annina glared at her, filled with more hatred than she ever thought herself capable of. "You're a fiend, Chiara." She could think of nothing more to say.

The *Orlando* rehearsals did not start out well. The castrato the Mingottis had hired to sing Orlando hadn't arrived, so Chiara stood in for him at the rehearsals. Then they received word that the castrato had been delayed and would not be able to get to Graz in time for the first performance. The Mingottis had no choice but to give the role to Chiara. She certainly had the build to carry the part, but Annina had misgivings about her ability to pull it off vocally. Her voice had been sounding more and more strained over the past few weeks, and Orlando was an extremely difficult and demanding role, consisting of several bravura arias and two extended "mad scenes." But since there was no one else available who was remotely capable of singing the part the situation could not be avoided, as uneasy as it made her feel. The best she could do was pour every ounce of herself into her Alcina role. And Gigi was there for every private practice session and every rehearsal. By the day before the performance, the show was completely sold out. And at the final dress rehearsal that afternoon Chiara opened her mouth to sing her first bit of recitative in Act 1, and nothing came out.

Annina had never seen her in such a frenzy. She strained until her eyes bulged, and the only sound she could manage was a strangled sputter. A doctor was sent for. He examined Chiara's throat, listened to her labored rasps, and pronounced that she had seriously damaged her vocal chords and would not be able to sing, or even to speak, for a very long time.

"I recommend immediate relocation to a warmer climate, preferably by the sea," the doctor told the anxious Mingotti brothers.

Arrangements were made for her to board a public coach for her transalpine journey. Annina would never forget the pathetic spectacle of Chiara's mute hysteria as she was dispatched to the depot. There was no more hatred in her heart for her old enemy. Only pity.

THE ENTIRE COMPANY sank into despair. The show would have to be cancelled. All the hoped-for profit would disappear, and the troupe would dissolve. Annina was frantic. Not only would she have to break the news to Antonio that his entire investment had been lost, but she didn't know how she'd scrape the money together to get Gigi and herself to Vienna. When the emperor died, Antonio's only hope of patronage in Vienna had died with him. Charles's successor, his daughter Maria Theresa, had no interest in music and was now preoccupied with the war with Spain. Things couldn't possibly be more bleak. Antonio was already having a hard enough time making ends meet in Vienna. She couldn't burden him with two impoverished females.

Then a crazy, reckless idea occurred to her. It was madness, but it was the only possible way out of this dilemma. "I'll sing the Orlando role myself," she announced to Angelo Mingotti, putting on a show of confidence, while inside she quaked with terror.

He stared at her, stunned. "But you've always sung female roles, Annina. I can't imagine you in a heroic male role."

She couldn't imagine herself in such a role either, but she was determined to forge ahead with her bold plan. "I know Orlando like the back of my hand. I was at Antonio's side practically every minute while he was composing the opera. I'm sure I can do it."

He sighed. "Well, I suppose it's our only chance of salvaging this show." Then he gave her a desperate look. "No, this can't work. If you sing Orlando there'll be no one to sing Alcina. You can't possibly sing both roles."

In her zeal to think of a way to fill the Orlando role she hadn't considered that. How could she have been so stupid? Angelo was right, there simply wasn't anyone else who could manage it. Then another crazy thought came to her. "Gigi! I think Gigi could sing Alcina."

She knew she was taking the biggest risk of her life. She only had a little over twenty-four hours to completely change character, and to coach Gigi to do something she'd never done before. She'd committed to the impossible, but there was no time to panic. Seamstresses went to work altering Chiara's costume to fit her. She had to practice walking with a determined, masculine stride, and not allow her hips to sway. Before a mirror, she trained her face to express everything from courageous heroism to male desire, rage, and finally debilitating madness. With score in hand she read through all her recitatives and arias and planned every movement and gesture she would use onstage. She sang through the entire part, very softly, so as not to strain her voice.

Then she went to work on Gigi. She'd brought the dress she wore in the original production which, miraculously, still fit her. Amazingly it fit Gigi as well and looked absolutely stunning on her. As Annina took her through her recitatives and arias she was astonished how well the girl already knew the part. She had completely absorbed the role simply from watching Annina practice and rehearse for the past several weeks. Perhaps most surprising of all, Gigi wasn't the least bit nervous. She exuded a calmness and confidence, yet an intensity that was astonishing. As for herself, she was terrified. As soon as her costume was ready she tried it on and wondered how on earth she'd manage moving and gesturing like a man and singing this devilishly difficult role with a plumed helmet balanced on her head, a shield of armor in her hand, and a sword dangling at her side.

There was another dress rehearsal the morning of the performance, and everyone sang at half voice, avoiding extreme high notes. The Mingottis decided to cut the first half of Act I.

Alcina's opening aria was beyond Gigi's ability to sing at such short notice. So the first act was to open with Orlando's bravura aria "*Nel profundo*" and end with his equally dazzling "*Sorge l'irato nembo.*" That meant two technically difficult arias for her in one act. A big risk.

Just before the show, the question passed through her mind of what Antonio might have to say if he could see her and Gigi now. The thought made her shiver. But there was no time to dwell on that worry. The curtain was about to go up. To swirling violin music she strode to center stage and lifted her chin proudly. For once she was grateful for her lean, less-than-voluptuous figure. Her Roman warrior-style costume was a short tunic bound at her waist and over her breasts with leather straps, to which was attached a sheathed sword. Knee-high leather boots covered her calves, and the tunic reached to just below her knees.

Taking a heroic stance, she plunged into her opening aria:

> *Into the deep dark world,*
> *let the fate once merciless to my heart tumble down.*
> *Aided by courage, the power of love will conquer!*

Her voice soared from extremely low to dazzlingly high notes, and in between danced with so much vibrancy it took on a life of its own. All the while she felt her eyes shine with courage and confidence. Everything Antonio had ever taught her seemed to come together and infuse her with an empowering sense of male energy.

At the conclusion of the aria, moist with sweat, she made a grand exit. She barely had time to acknowledge Gigi's ecstatic smile before it was time for Alcina's entrance. She looked on tensely from the wing. Soon her tension melted into awe and admiration as she watched her sweet little Gigi seduce Orlando's fellow knight Ruggiero with all the charm and cunning of a seasoned temptress. Gigi was a different type of Alcina than she had been. Gigi's Alcina was less angry, less desperate. Instead she exuded self-confidence, warmth, and humor. Now she could see that Antonio had built both possibilities into the role. How she wished he could have been here to see his niece perform it.

The opera was such a tremendous success, the Mingotti's offered both Annina and Gigi extended contracts. As grateful as she was for the opportunity, she declined. Antonio needed her. She couldn't delay her journey to Vienna any longer.

The next day she and Gigi took a walk along the Mur River. "I'm envisioning great things for you in Vienna, Gigi," she said. "You astounded everyone with your performance, me most of all. I never imagined you had that in you."

Gigi lowered her eyes. "I've decided to accept the Mingottis' offer."

She blinked at the unexpected remark. "But . . . I was thinking that when we got to Vienna your Uncle Antonio would give you singing lessons."

"You could teach me, Nina, if you stayed awhile."

"I can't stay, Gigi, you know that. And I'd be no teacher for you. Antonio's a much better teacher than I am. I don't have his patience." She became pensive for a moment. "In fact, sometimes I wonder how he put up with me in my early years of singing study."

Gigi smiled, but the brightness in her eyes turned serious. "He loves you."

The unexpected wisdom and directness of the girl's reply left her speechless. She blinked back a tear and smiled at her as she realized something. She was so much like him. She knew then that

Gigi would be all right.

ON THE LONG coach ride north to Vienna she could barely contain her excitement at the thought of seeing Antonio again. This was the most time they'd been apart in nearly twenty years. Long ago she'd given up her girlish fantasies about him—or nearly so. Yet the comforting anticipation of his arms enfolding her once again filled her with an almost excruciating longing. Even more, she longed for the admiring gaze and approving smile he always gave her when she dazzled him with her dramatic performances.

She remembered the "fatherly" lecture he'd given her shortly before he left Graz, but she quickly dismissed it from her mind. There would be plenty of time to think about that sort of thing later. Right now all she could think about was how optimistic he'd sounded in his last letter. He was on the verge of finalizing negotiations with the Kärntertortheater for the following season, and he was anxiously awaiting her arrival so they could proceed with plans. What could be more wonderful?

Chapter Twenty-four

Antonio's mind was a hazy whirl. He gasped miserably until he had no more strength to gasp. The painful heaviness in his chest made him feel helpless and desperate. Fear and loneliness swept over him as he drifted in and out of consciousness. He didn't know what was real and what was a dream. Music and memories floated through his head like clouds that couldn't be grasped or brought into focus. His soul struggled to cling to something genuine, something comforting. *Lamb of God, have mercy on me.*

The scent of lavender. Soft fingers touching his cheek and smoothing a strand of hair from his forehead. A familiar-feeling little hand clutching his. His eyelids fluttered open, and he squinted in the morning sunlight. He managed a crooked smile. "Annina," he said faintly.

Dark eyes, filled with worry, and a brave smile. "It's all right, I'm here. Everything will be all right now," she said, as her fingers lightly stroked his forehead.

This was not a dream. He felt her touch and the warmth of her presence. And her love. A flood of happiness blotted out his pain.

Gently the morning sun rays turned a brilliant white and caused everything else in his field of vision to fade and seem far away. It was the brightest, most pure white light he'd ever seen, yet it was in no way blinding. He squeezed the warm little hand that held his so steadfastly and heard a voice, the most beautiful voice he'd ever known, softly pleading, "Antonio . . ."

But he had to go. The light beckoned him, and the music. Annina singing. Or was it an angel? Peace enveloped him. He drifted toward the music, and became one with the light.

SHE STILL HELD his hand. The characteristic firmness of his grasp had gone limp, its familiar warmth already fading to coldness. *"Er ist tot,* He is dead," the doctor pronounced dryly, as he passed his long, pale fingers over Antonio's face to close his eyes. The blue eyes that had looked so luminous and filled with wonder barely a moment before. *Er ist tot.* Hideous words. She marveled at the porcelain smoothness of his cheek, the gentle smile that lingered on his lips, the golden flecks that still sparkled in his faintly graying hair. *He doesn't look old,* was the only thought her mind would allow. Not old at all, but young, and at peace. And for the first time since that first horrid night at Signora Malvolia's boarding house nearly twenty years before, she felt a terrible loneliness. An unbearable emptiness.

The hideous, unbelievable words reverberated in her head. *My God. How can he be dead?* It wasn't possible. He who was always so filled with life. The room reeled about her as she stood. Her knees buckled. She felt Frau Waller's strong arms supporting her and pressing her to her ample bosom, while she made tender maternal sounds—the kind her own mother never had—and called her *Liebchen.* The rest of the day was a terrifying blur. A priest appeared and gave last rites. The doctor half-heartedly jotted notes. Antonio was taken away, and she was ushered down the street to a massive cathedral, where solemn chants, incense, and prayers for the dead swirled about her like a ghastly nightmare. Nothing seemed real. The ache of loss overcame her.

She didn't sleep that night. Instead, she was kept awake to be tortured by ruthless agony. The demons that tormented her mind and heart so viciously and relentlessly through the dreadful darkness were far more cruel and insidious than even Chiara ever was or could have been. They told her what she already knew: This was her fault. She had failed him. It all started six years ago, with the stolen kiss. The one romantic encounter of her life, however brief, fleeting, and forbidden. She had violated the unspoken code of honor that had always existed between them. He'd forgiven her, of course, but the demons of her own mind were much less forgiving. That was why things had gone steadily wrong and grown progressively worse ever since. Losing him forever was her final punishment.

Suddenly she was overwhelmed by a tidal wave of grief. It was as if she were drowning. She clung to his violin and pressed it to her breast as if it were a life raft. He had given her nothing but love, respect, and kindness—and this was how she'd repaid him. She used to think Chiara was the heartless one, turning her back on him when his luck was down. What she had done to him was much worse. She was responsible for the destruction not only of his reputation, but of his very life. She longed to open the floodgates of her grief. But she couldn't. The crushing guilt she felt was so suffocating she could hardly breathe, much less cry. There could be no relief from her anguish. She was completely alone.

THE CATHEDRAL WAS serene, other-worldly, and immense with quiet. The boy gazed at her, speechless, his eyes filled with magic and wonder. Finally, he said, "That's the most amazing story I've ever heard."

She had no idea how much she'd actually told him, or how long they had been in the vestibule together. It was as if time had stopped, her reverie encapsulated in a frozen moment. She looked at the boy. "Yes, it *is* amazing, isn't it? I don't think I've ever realized how amazing until now."

His smile faded, and he looked down sadly. "I only studied with him for a few months. But Herr Maestro Vivaldi was so kind to me. Much nicer than my other teachers."

She smiled with sympathy and blinked against the stinging in her eyes. How familiar this sounded. "You must have felt very sad when he died," she said gently, putting a comforting hand on his shoulder.

"Oh, yes. I could hardly believe it, his death was so sudden." He looked up at her and squared his shoulders bravely. "I sang at his funeral yesterday, you know. I almost thought I wouldn't be able to, but somehow I think I sang better than I ever have."

She hadn't noticed, but she responded with as much interest as she could muster. "So you sing as well?"

"Ah, *sì* signora. That's why I'm here. They recruited me for the choir school because of my singing voice."

"Well then, you're obviously quite talented."

He smiled proudly. "Yes, that's what I'm told."

The stinging in her eyes was excruciating, but she forced herself to smile. "You're very lucky, you know, to have had even a few lessons with Maestro Vivaldi. He was considered to be the greatest violinist in Europe."

"Yes, I know. I hope someday I can play like him."

"Is it your ambition to be a professional musician?"

"Actually," he said almost shyly, "I wish to be a great composer."

"Really? What do you want to compose?"

"Everything. Symphonies, operas, church music—everything!" His eyes brightened, and his face became animated with joy. His exuberance was strangely contagious, and she felt her own sadness dissipate a bit.

"Did you tell Maestro Vivaldi about your desire to compose?"

"Yes, and he encouraged me. All my other teachers just laugh or scold me when I try to tell them about my ambitions, but Herr Maestro Vivaldi took me seriously."

The boy was fascinating and delightful, and she began to feel a real fondness for him. It was easy to see why Antonio had taken such an interest in him. It occurred to her that this must be the boy he spoke of in his last letter, the one he thought showed so much promise. She decided to put in her own word of encouragement.

"Then you have every reason to feel confident that you will succeed. You must never give up your dream, no matter how much anyone tries to discourage you or stand in your way."

At that moment she was startled by a stern voice. "Josef!" She turned to see a man in an academic robe, glaring severely at her young friend.

The boy snapped to attention, then looked at her apologetically. "I'm afraid it's time for my singing lesson."

"Of course," she said, rising. "Josef, so that's your name?"

"Yes, signora. Josef Haydn."

"Well, it was very nice to meet you, Josef," she said, taking his hand. "I'm Annina. Annina Girò."

"Very nice to meet you too, Frau Girò," he said respectfully, as he gazed up at her and pressed her hand.

The teacher cleared his throat impatiently and took young Josef firmly by the arm.

BACK AT FRAU WALLER'S house she shakily packed Antonio's scores and his few other belongings. She couldn't bear the blank horror of losing him, this unendurable flatness of grief. Burning tears, tears that refused to fall, threatened to flood her eyes as she doubled over, helpless as a frightened little girl, aching to be picked up and cuddled. Quivering, she pressed one of his shirts to her face. It had been freshly laundered, but a faint wisp of his fiery, briny scent lingered. At once her heart melted, and she felt comforted—an inexplicable lifting of her spirits. She remembered that magical night, so many years ago, when he told her she brought his music to life as no one else could. It was the most wonderful thing he'd ever said to her. Now she knew what he meant. If she could bring his music to life, she could bring it *back* to life—not just for herself, but for Gigi, Josef, and the world. At that instant, she became aware that there was something much bigger at stake than her personal fears or desires—even bigger than her relationship with Antonio: *His music*. The music he'd been moved to compose so furiously and prodigiously all his life would outlive its creator. It would outlive them all. She smiled as she realized she'd known that all along.

SHE DIDN'T HAVE the heart to tell Gigi of Antonio's death by letter. That sweet innocent girl had known almost nothing but instability and loss all her young life. Annina wanted to be with her when she heard the sad news. So she would return to Venice via Graz. From there Gigi could decide if she would stay on with the Mingottis or return to Italy.

As her coach began to wind around St. Stephen's square, toward the gates of Vienna, the boys from the choir school were processing to the church, led by a stern looking music master. She leaned out the carriage window and spotted little Josef. At that instant he looked her way and smiled with joy. With misty eyes, she smiled back and waved farewell.

Epilogue

Venice seemed different without him. The charm and excitement of the city that had so captured her heart nearly twenty years before had gone flat. All the sparkle and delight had sunk beneath an oppressive gray mist, as had her heart. She felt no bitterness, only a massive sense of loss.

Gigi's decision to stay with the Mingottis had deprived her of a devoted protégée and friend, someone whose talent she could have nurtured as Antonio had nurtured hers. But Gigi's absence also freed her to pursue her new mission, to rescue his manuscripts from oblivion. But where to begin? Having settled back in her old apartment at San Angelo with Paolina and their mother, she sat at her desk and glared through her newly acquired reading spectacles at a list she'd started to compile from memory. The list was clearly incomplete. She'd brought back to Venice the few scores he'd had with him there, and a search of his house had turned up a handful more. But she had no means to track down the multitude of missing manuscripts. Her spirits began to disintegrate into frustration and despair.

Paolina peeked in the door. "A gentleman wishes to see you."

"Who is it?"

Before she could answer, he appeared at the doorway and stepped into the room. She stiffened and put down her pen. "What can I do for you, Count Landi?"

His tri-cornered hat was in his hands. He smiled and bowed. "Please pardon the intrusion, signora. I've come to offer my condolences."

She removed her glasses. "Thank you. You are very kind," she said warily.

He stood in awkward silence for a moment and fingered his hat nervously. Finally he cleared his throat and said, "As you know, I've long been an admirer of yours, Signora Girò."

She frowned and felt the corners of her mouth tense. "Is your wife an admirer of mine as well, Excellency?"

He gazed at her and blinked. "My wife passed away last year."

A wave of shame passed over her. She gave a trembling sigh. "Forgive me, sir, I had no idea. Please accept my deepest sympathy."

He managed a faint smile. "I fear I've given you the wrong impression, signora. I assure you I mean no disrespect. The other reason for my visit is that I've heard about your project and I find it admirable. I'd like to offer my assistance, to support your efforts in any way I can."

"That's a most gracious offer, Excellency. But what could you do?"

He sighed. "If there are financial concerns, I could be of help in that regard. But perhaps more importantly, I have influential contacts who I believe would share your interest in gathering and safeguarding the maestro's original scores. I'd be happy to speak to them on your behalf."

The man was a godsend. She gazed up at him and felt the faintest stirring in her middle, noticing again how handsome he was. His eyes sparkled, and his mouth was gentle and kind. Suddenly she remembered her manners. "You must pardon my rudeness. Please make yourself comfortable," she said, gesturing toward the nearby settee.

He smiled at her as he seated himself.

"I hardly know what to say, Excellency. How can I possibly thank you for your generosity?"

He grinned. "The first thing you can do is stop calling me Excellency. It makes me feel like a pompous old relic."

She couldn't help smiling. "Very well then, what shall I call you?"

"My name is Antonio."

Her heart lurched and she felt the blood drain from her face.

His look of concern was immediate. He leaned toward her and rested his elbows on his knees. "I'm so sorry, I didn't think. That was *his* name, wasn't it?"

She nodded slowly. "Yes." Her voice was pinched.

His gaze was tender, and he gave her a boyish half-smile. "You can call me Tonio if you like. That's what my mother used to call me."

The moment of tension burst, and she broke into a nervous laugh. "All right, Tonio it is. And please call me Anna, or Annina if you prefer."

The count's unexpected visit was both thrilling and disturbing. Thrilling, because of his offer to help her with the monumental task of gathering Antonio's manuscripts. But the memory of their lively conversations the few times they'd met, and the feelings his easy charm had stirred in her, was disturbing. Most of her past experiences with noblemen had taught her not to trust them. And Antonio's admonitions still rang in her heart. There was no one to advise her now. Graziana and Fortunato had moved to Padua to care for Graziana's aging mother, and Antonio's friend Piero had passed away the year before. She got along pleasantly enough with his sisters but had never felt close enough to them to bring them into her confidence. Paolina was not one to talk to about matters of the heart. And her mother's mind was fading, her former impetuosity replaced by sullen resignation.

Thank heaven for Pietro, who stopped by from time to time. She had no idea if he knew about his father's role in the collapse of the Ferrara enterprise, and she never asked. She only knew Antonio was right. He was as genuine a young man as one could hope for. His visits were like a breath of fresh air.

"WHAT ON EARTH will I do with the rest of my life?" she asked Pietro at his next visit.

"You have your work cut out for you organizing Uncle Antonio's manuscripts."

"But that won't last forever. What will I do when that work is finished?"

"Have you thought about resuming your opera career?"

She sighed. "I don't have the heart for it anymore. Without Antonio it wouldn't be the same."

"You could marry."

"Heavens, Pietro, no. At my age. And besides, who would I marry?"

"Well—Count Landi seems to have taken quite an interest in you."

She scoffed. "There's only one thing these amorous noblemen want, and it's not marriage."

"That may be true of most noblemen, but I think this one might be different." He looked serious.

She smiled indulgently. "Pietro, you're a hopeless romantic, and very naïve."

"I'll admit I have a bit of a romantic bent, but I'm not naïve. I'm pretty good at knowing what's in a man's heart."

She folded her arms. "So tell me, what great secret have you discerned in Count Landi's heart?"

"He loves you."

She caught her breath. "Even if that were true," she said slowly, "which I doubt, it doesn't mean he'd want to marry me. Noblemen don't marry show girls."

"No one would describe you as a show girl, Annina. You're a respectable, intelligent lady, and very attractive besides. A man would have to be crazy not to want you."

She gazed into his eyes for a moment and blinked. "Do you know who you reminded me of just now?"

"I can't imagine."

"Your Uncle Antonio."

He grinned. "I'll take that as a compliment."

"As well you should. So tell me, how do you know so much about the count?"

"He's come by my copy shop several times."

"To talk about me?"

He smiled. "You and Uncle Antonio's manuscripts are all he talks about."

"And what has he said?"

"That your mission to preserve Uncle's music is the most commendable thing he's ever known a woman to do. That if he'd had a choice he would have married someone like you."

"If he had a choice?"

"His marriage was arranged."

"Oh . . . I see. What else has he told you?"

"Let's just say he has a heartfelt interest in you, and in Uncle's music."

The unexpected conversation left her mind whirling. She didn't know what to believe.

THE FOLLOWING WEEK, several large crates were delivered to her apartment. "On the orders of His Excellency, Count Landi," one of the delivery men told her.

Perplexed, she asked the man to pry open the crates before he left. After handing him a coin, she rushed over to examine the contents. One crate seemed to be filled with old opera manuscripts, all in Antonio's hand as far as she could see. Another contained countless concertos, and still another vast amounts of sacred music. With trembling hands she picked up one of the concerto scores. Her eyes misted as they scanned his familiar, brisk notations. The liveliness, the spontaneity that so characterized his music seemed to jump off the page. Further down the score she could see his increasingly agitated and energetic strokes, his racing pen barely able to keep up with the strenuous speed of his tirelessly creative mind. A teardrop fell on the page and she gingerly brushed it away, careful not to smear the ink. She sighed deeply and smiled. In his music, he was still so very much alive.

"I HOPE YOU don't think we're going to store all this here, Annina," Paolina said, staring at the crates in dismay.

"I'll talk to Tonio when I see him. I'm sure this is only temporary."

"It had better be. There's no room for the three of us and that hodgepodge in this small apartment."

"It's not a hodgepodge. These are Antonio's manuscripts."

Paolina smiled patiently, and her voice grew gentler. "I know how important his music is to you, Annina, but I had no idea there was so much of it. We just can't keep all this here."

"Don't you realize how valuable these scores are?"

Her sister's smile looked doubtful. "I'm sure they are to you," she said kindly.

She sighed. "I'll work something out, I promise."

Paolina started to untie her apron. "Fine. Mamma and I will be out for awhile. As soon as she's dressed I'm taking her on some errands with me. She's hardly left her room for days, and I think some fresh air will do her good."

Soon after they'd left, Tonio arrived. "Oh good, they're here," he said as he walked in the door. He stepped over and examined the contents of the crates. "And I see the delivery company packed them very nicely."

"How on earth were you able to get these? I've been trying for months to track all this down."

"There isn't much money can't buy. A survey of the theaters turned up dozens of his opera manuscripts. And the Pietà was in possession of hundreds of scores he'd written for them over the years."

"But what shall we do with it all? The scores can't sit here in my apartment forever, as much as I'd love to keep them for myself."

"The first thing we need to do is catalogue his works. Fortunately he made that task an easy one. If you'll notice," he said, picking up a concerto score, "he numbered his compositions in chronological order."

She took the score from him and examined it closely. Sure enough, there was a small number inscribed at the top left-hand corner. She smiled and slowly shook her head. "I had no idea he was so meticulous about his work." There was so much about him she didn't know.

"I've also engaged a bookbinder to hard-bind the scores into volumes, to help ensure their preservation."

"I'm in awe, Tonio. I don't know how to thank you."

"This isn't all of it, I'm sure you realize. Pietro tells me his scores could number upwards of a thousand."

"It doesn't surprise me. He was always composing." She sighed. "We still have so much work to do, don't we? I'm glad. Every time I look at another of his scores I feel he's with me again."

In the foyer, as he was about to leave, he turned and looked at her uncomfortably. "I fear this is an impertinent question, but I feel I must ask it."

"Ask then."

He hesitated, but only for a moment. "There were rumors—about you and the maestro." He ran his hand through his light-brown hair. "The talk was just that, I trust, idle gossip surely. Yet still . . . however absurd—"

"Yes, it was absurd. Nothing could have been further from the truth. He was a priest, and I respected that, always."

"You loved him, though?"

"How could I not? He was my mentor and helper, and the very dearest of friends. He made it possible for me to have the kind of life I'd always dreamed of." Her voice broke and she could say no more.

He pulled her into his arms. "I can't imagine how you must have felt when you arrived in Vienna."

She pressed her face to his shoulder. "I felt as if the world had ceased to turn," she said, choking.

"And has the world begun to go round again?" he asked gently.

"It has," she said in a muffled voice. "Thanks to his music, and to you." And the tears she'd held back for so long flooded her eyes and fell hot on his shoulder.

He lifted her chin and pressed his gentle mouth to hers, and the taste of him was so warm. She felt like the world was whirling around them.

"Do you know how long I've waited for this moment?" he said softly.

The hardness of his body made her quiver with desire, and she clung to him as her insides melted. Was this true love?—what she'd craved for so long? It seemed too perfect to be real.

THE FOLLOWING EVENING there was an unexpected knock at her door. Still holding the score to *L'Atenaide* she'd been about to add to the catalog, she walked into the hall. "Who is it?" she asked through the closed door.

"It's Tonio."

A wild thrill coursed through her as she quickly unlocked and opened the door with her free hand.

He stepped inside, his arms laden with fresh flowers, champagne, and an intriguing looking package. He gave her an affectionate peck on the cheek, then glanced around as he entered the parlor. "It's so quiet here. Where are your mother and sister?"

"They left for Mantua this morning, for a short visit." She laughed lightly. "As much as my mother always complained about *la vita provinciale*, she misses the spring season there. And Paolina was in despair over the clutter and disorder my project has brought about. I'm sure she was more than happy to get away."

He grinned. "I'm sorry to have missed them, but I'd be lying if I denied that I prefer having you to myself."

She smiled. "What's all this?" she asked, as he set his gifts on the table.

"I feel like celebrating tonight."

"Celebrating?"

"Yes. Why don't you get a vase for the flowers and some glasses, while I open the champagne."

She set the opera manuscript on the table and did as he asked, anxious to know what they were celebrating. Maybe he'd found more of Antonio's manuscripts.

The flowers arranged and the champagne poured, he held up his glass. "To you, Annina, the most enchanting lady I've ever known. *Salute.*"

"*Salute.*" She took a sip. "Oh," she said, setting her glass down. "Let me put this score away before something gets spilled on it." As she lifted the manuscript from the table a sheet of paper fell out. She bent to pick it up. "*Dio mio*, I'd almost forgotten about this."

"What?" He came over to see what she was holding.

"It's the sonnet that was distributed at the Pergola, while Antonio and I were in Florence performing *L'Atenaide.* Holy heavens, that was over twelve years ago. I was so young." She read the poem softly:

> "*Neither the wind that blows among the leaves*
> *Nor the nightingale that sings its love*
> *Touches my heart like your sweet tones*
> *With their countless charms and loveable caresses.*"

She looked up at him. "Antonio wondered at the time who wrote this. I had no idea he'd saved a copy all these years."

He set his glass down. "I have a confession to make."

"Tell me."

He grinned and threw up his hands. "What can I say? I was a foolish young bachelor, completely smitten by your charms."

Her heart lurched. "You can't mean *you* wrote this, Tonio."

"I've never considered myself much of a poet. But your performance that opening night was so spectacular I was moved to pen those words that very evening. The next day I had hundreds of copies printed to hand out at the next performance. I wanted the world to know how you stirred my heart, even if I was too much of a coward to let my identity be known."

She stared at him, stunned. "Why did you never speak to me while you were there?"

He chuckled. "You were so swamped by admirers I couldn't get close to you. And your maestro, of course, never left your side."

She lowered her eyes, smiling at the memory.

"I'd say the resurrection of my brilliant little ditty calls for another glass of champagne." He turned to the table and poured two more glasses. "Oh, and I almost forgot." He picked up the package and handed it to her. "This is for you."

Eagerly she pulled off the string, and the brown paper wrapping fell to the floor. A black velvet face and empty eyes stared back at her. She gasped. "*La moretta.*"

"Yes, it's an old *moretta* mask. It was my mother's."

She turned the mask over and gazed in bewilderment at the familiar crack and *CZL* inscription.

"My mother wore this mask often when I was growing up. But it mysteriously disappeared when she died, about twenty years ago. And then I found it, floating in the canal the opening night of your maestro's *Orlando furioso*. At first I thought of it only as a souvenir of my Venetian sojourn. But when I saw the inscription I knew it was my mother's. It was like a miracle."

Still holding the mask, she looked up at him. "Your mother gave it to a Gypsy woman, as payment for telling her fortune."

His eyes widened. "How can you know this?"

"I bought the mask from the Gypsy when I first arrived in Venice. She told me how she got it, and that it would shield and protect me. Five years later I threw it into the canal. I didn't think I needed it anymore. It was the same night you found it, the opening night of *Orlando.*"

He looked at her in astonishment. "And to think the *moretta* has always reminded me of you, because I found it the night I first saw you. If I'd known it had been in your possession I would have treasured it all the more."

"I don't know what to say, Tonio. I'm completely overwhelmed. The sonnet, the mask, flowers and champagne. What other surprises do you have in store for me?"

He put down his glass and came to her. "Only one." Taking her glass from her hand and placing it on the table, he drew her into his arms. "I'm in love with you, and I'd like you to be my wife."

Tears sprang to her eyes. "Tonio—"

His mouth was on hers, and the shivers of delight that coursed through her were almost unbearable. When she thought she'd drown in his kisses, he pulled back slightly and smiled down at her. "Well? What's your answer? Will you marry me?"

Tears came once again. Tears of happiness. She nodded. "Yes."

Gazing down at the mask, her mind filled with memories of the man who for most of her life had been the center of her world, her safe harbor, her other Antonio. His was a different kind of love, but love all the same. She would never forget him. He would live in her heart forever.

Blinking back fresh tears, she picked up *la moretta* and ran a finger over the mysterious *CZL*. "Tonio, what does the inscription mean?"

"Zanardi Landi is our family name. I usually drop the Zanardi, except for official occasions." He gently took the mask from her. "That's what you'll be called when we marry, Countess Zanardi Landi."

She threw her arms around his neck, and he tossed *la moretta* onto the table before clasping her in a passionate embrace.

Afterward

Cardinal Ruffo's promise to Annina did indeed prove beneficial. Venetian law prohibited noblemen from marrying beneath their station, so Annina and Count Landi had to be married secretly by the Church. The Venetian Church required extensive interrogation, due to Annina's long association with Vivaldi. The marriage was finally sanctioned when a letter arrived from Rome:

With unbiased prudence and conscience I remit to this Sacred Congregation the attached request of Anna Maddalena Tessieri, who wishes to get married. When she meets with you, you won't find any legitimate obstacle to this, nor need you impose the usual difficulties to rule out polygamy; and I wish her happiness.

Cardinal Ruffo

I found this letter among the records associated with Annina's petition to marry Count Landi. I translated the letter myself and was astounded when I realized this was the same Cardinal who had prohibited Vivaldi from coming to Ferrara, partly because of his association with Annina. I was amazed at the flip-flop, and concluded that Vivaldi must have "set him straight" at some point after the Ferrara fiasco.

It remains a mystery how Vivaldi's scores were salvaged. After his death he was all but forgotten, and his music virtually disappeared for nearly two centuries. Then, miraculously, half his original manuscripts were rediscovered in 1927, at the Monastery of Monferrato, in Turin, Italy. Three years later, the other half were found in the private library of Marquis Giuseppe Maria Durazzo, in Genoa.

The entire collection had been purchased around 1765 by the marquis's ancestor, Count Giacomo Durazzo, who at that time was Ambassador to Venice. Previously, he had been Ambassador to the Imperial Court in Vienna, where he was in close touch with Josef Haydn.

Count Durazzo bought the manuscripts from a Venetian book collector, Jacopo Soranzo, who had purchased the collection no later than 1745. Prior to that, following Vivaldi's death in 1741, someone had gathered all the manuscripts, organized them, and had them bound and prepared to be archived.

The unlikely "resurrection" of Vivaldi's long lost autograph scores is one of the marvels of music history.

A Message to the Reader

This is a work of historical fiction, and although the story is based for the most part on documented events, I've altered and/or embellished some of the "facts" for dramatic purposes. Most of the characters are based on historical persons. However, Gigi is a fictional character, symbolizing the younger generation of Antonio Vivaldi's family, some of whom aided him in his work and thus helped disseminate his music.

After many years of research and piecing together all the scattered bits of evidence, I've tried to depict Anna Girò's relationship with Vivaldi as accurately and realistically as possible, within the context of a good story. Above all I hope that, like Vivaldi's music, this story will stir your heart.